PAST PRAISE FOR

T0014013

For *The Aloha Spirit*

❦ 2020 Grand Prize winner for CIBA Goethe award
❦ 2021 Independent Publisher Book Awards
(IPPY Awards): Bronze Winner in
West-Pacific—Best Regional Fiction
❦ Included in *Parade*'s list of "Poolside Reads You'll
Want to Pick Up Before the End of Summer!"

"The poignant and atmospheric tale captures the pre–World War II diversity of Hawaiian culture, a melting pot of religions and ethos . . . Evocative and engaging, with a protagonist determined to keep the aloha spirit in her heart."
—*KIRKUS REVIEWS*

"Ulleseit writes with a strong grasp of local color to send the Hawaiian spirit flowing through your veins . . . an exceptional story of a woman whose unwavering spirit has been tested at a very young age and continues throughout her years."
—**READERS FAVORITE**, FIVE STARS

"Linda Ulleseit has written a heroic tale of family, friendship, loss, and redemption. With undeniable beauty, she captures the courage of a young woman and community stunned by unforgettable tragedy. She writes with humility, grace, and a quiet brilliance as she portrays young Dolores's search for family and the generous, hardworking heart at the center of *The Aloha Spirit*."
—**MILANA MARSENICH**, author of
Copper Sky and *The Swan Keeper*

THE RIVER REMEMBERS

THE RIVER
REMEMBERS

A NOVEL

LINDA ULLESEIT

SHE WRITES PRESS

Published 2023
Printed in the United States of America
Print ISBN: TK
E-ISBN: TK
Library of Congress Control Number: 2022919522

For information, address:
She Writes Press
1569 Solano Ave #546
Berkeley, CA 94707

Interior Design by Tabitha Lahr

She Writes Press is a division of SparkPoint Studio, LLC.

Dedicated to Franklin Levi Ulleseit,
who will carry on the story

Upper Mississippi River c. 1836

*St. Anthony Falls

*Coldwater Spring

Fort Snelling

*Nicollet Island

*Lake Calhoun

*Cloud Man's Village

Mendota

MICHIGAN TERRITORY

*Lake Harriet

St. Peter's Agency

Ojibwe

Dakota

*Minnesota River

Dubuque

WISCONSIN TERRITORY

Sauk

Galena

Fox

ILLINOIS

Iowa   MISSOURI

Mississippi River

From Fort Snelling to:
St. Anthony Falls   7 miles
Cloud Man's Village   6.5 miles
Lake Harriet Mission   7 miles
Coldwater Spring   2 miles
St. Peter's Agency   ¼ mile

St. Louis

*see glossary for Native American/English/French name

said. "Your neighbors will be French fur traders and their Indian wives. Quite a change from the family farm in New York."

"That it is." Samantha couldn't muster enthusiasm, but she didn't want to disappoint him. Relief that her journey neared its end warred with dismay at the rough log houses and mud roads of the tiny village.

The sound of the boat's engine changed, thrumming through the deck as the big sidewheel stopped, then edged backward. The river churned as the boat approached the dock. Vast expanses of grass stretched into the distance beyond the bluff that dominated the tiny dot of human habitation.

"It's not an easy life," James Henry said in a smug tone, "but the land is full of opportunity, especially for men connected to the Indian trade."

"No doubt they will all rush to marry me," Samantha said. She winced at the sharp sarcasm that laced her words when she'd tried for a light tone. Then again, maybe it was time to let her true feelings be known.

Her brother's gold-rimmed spectacles hid his eyes, but the tight set of his mouth betrayed his disapproval. "Is that why Father sent you to live under my watch? Did you refuse another suitor?" He glared at Samantha. "It's bad enough I had to lock my store and sacrifice income to fetch you. And now I'll have to spend every waking moment watching over you."

"Stuff and nonsense. I can assist you in your home and your store. And I will have a voice in the matter of suitors." She was good at offended outrage.

"We'll see." He turned his back and strode down the steps to the main deck.

Samantha followed. She watched as other passengers greeted James Henry and bantered with him. They treated him as if he owned the territory. Little did they know how insufferable he

CHAPTER 1:

May, 1834
Prairie du Chien, Michigan Territory

SAMANTHA

Samantha's older brother had told fabulous tales of the frontier's wild beauty and the danger of the natives, but in all his stories he neglected to speak of the mud. She knew James Henry loved the wildness of this raw territory on the edge of the country. He'd told her over and over that someday this land would be homes and farms, and there would be new states in the United States of America. But everywhere there was mud. With one hand, she grasped the railing of the passenger barge as the steamboat *Warrior* towed it past the remains of old Fort Crawford, rotting on St. Feriole Island. With the other hand, she fidgeted with the letter in her reticule. The envelope had grown soft with constant rubbing and folding over the last six weeks. It was a miracle it had stayed sealed. It was a miracle she hadn't tossed it into the river.

As the boat approached a cluster of buildings nestled under a tall bluff, her brother waved his arm toward the eastern bank of the Mississippi River. "Your new home, Prairie du Chien," he

PART ONE
1834

Each mother's tear that falls, of joy or despair, becomes part of the river's love for her children. The river that flows today contains the last of all mothers' tears and the first of all daughters'. The tears of nations run in the river, and the river remembers.

PROLOGUE

The Mississippi River brings life and death, creation and destruction, nourishment and deprivation. It connects all animals, plants, mountains, and humanity. Anywhere you step into the water, you touch the very last drops of what has passed and greet the flow of what is to come. You could walk in the great river every day, and every day it would be a different river.

Born before memory, the river is the mother of all living things. The river never doubts its path, drawing strength from its headwaters and flowing with the confidence and strength of maternity, watering fields, supporting dugouts, and providing a serene beauty. A riparian community thrives as the river waters the trees where the songbirds nest, swirls around rocks where fish hide, and pools in the shallows where animals drink and bathe. A powerful and tranquil force exists in all the moods and textures of the river.

Sometimes the river sweeps you along, but sometimes rapids appear from nowhere. Floods scour the riverbanks, destroying homes, fields, and lives. Turbulence on the river smashes watercraft, upends trees, and muddies the water with debris. Winter ice prevents river travel even when the heart of the river flows beneath.

could be. Samantha trailed behind him because she didn't know where she was going, not by choice.

Papa had arranged for a neighboring family to chaperone her as far as St. Louis, and for James Henry to meet her there. Her father had given her a sealed letter for her brother, a letter that no doubt explained her transgressions with the amount of detail befitting a scandal reporter. It probably also instructed him how to marry her off with her father's blessing.

Samantha hadn't given her brother the letter in St. Louis, or while they were on the river. Not yet. Maybe never. Let him wonder. She planned to enjoy her independence, not transfer her yoke from father to brother.

On shore, men tied the boat to the dock. They unloaded kegs of salt, tea, and gunpowder, as well as boxes of fabric and blankets, and crates of guns. Black and white men rushed to fetch the passengers' trunks from the barge. People disembarked amid excited chatter, but James Henry said nothing to his sister, nor did she speak to him.

A young woman and two men stood on the dock. The older man, dressed in rough civilian clothes, inspected new arrivals with a look that both welcomed and warned. The younger man stood ramrod straight and wore the uniform of an officer. James Henry strode up to the older man and shook his hand. Without looking at his sister, he said, "Colonel Taylor, may I present my sister, Miss Lockwood."

Colonel Zachary Taylor nodded his head and said, "Your servant, ma'am."

"Pleased to meet you, Colonel Taylor," Samantha said. She gave him a gentle smile.

Colonel Taylor said, "Miss Lockwood, may I introduce Lieutenant Davis, and my daughter Miss Taylor. I hope your trip aboard the *Warrior* was pleasant. Captain Throckmorton acquitted himself well during the war last year. His boat played an important role in stopping Black Hawk's escape." He was friendly but formal, as an officer should be.

James Henry responded with hearty reassurances about their trip before Samantha could acknowledge the introductions.

Colonel Taylor said to Samantha, "The local tribes think well of your brother for his fair treatment."

James Henry beamed at the compliment. "Lieutenant Davis treats them fairly, too. He made quite a name for himself with his courteous treatment of that old blackguard, the chief, as he was transported downriver to Jefferson Barracks in St. Louis. People say they were fast friends by the time they arrived in port."

Lieutenant Jefferson Davis embodied an officer from his erect bearing to his steely blue eyes. "I treated him with respect is all," he said.

Sarah Taylor, a handful of years younger than Samantha, couldn't look away from the young lieutenant. Her expression reminded Samantha of her little sisters drooling over Mama's cherry pie. Sarah wore her long brown hair in ringlets, and her hazel eyes sparkled as she laughed at the lieutenant's words. Petite and vivacious, Sarah was the type of woman that always made Samantha feel heavy. Her mother described the short, thick women in the family as being from strong pioneer stock. Samantha was one of those.

"It takes a great man to treat an enemy well," Samantha said. "It's nice to have arrived." And it was, she realized. She already liked Sarah Taylor, who might even make living in the territory bearable. Samantha looked around her with more interest.

Black and white servants scurried between their masters, loading trunks into wagons. Passengers she'd had a nodding acquaintance with reunited with family and walked toward the town. A small group of new recruits proceeded toward the half-constructed Fort Crawford and the village of Prairie du Chien. Colonel Taylor and Lieutenant Davis followed.

"I must see to my goods," James Henry said. "Would you prefer to wait for me or walk into town now?" He pursed his lips, and his eyes darted to the cargo being unloaded. Stuffing his hands in his pockets, he rocked on his feet.

Samantha bristled at his obvious eagerness to get away from her. He might tell people he had gone to meet her in St. Louis, but Samantha knew he'd been more interested in fetching the items he'd ordered for his store than about fetching his sister. "I can find my own way," she said. She turned away from her brother and walked toward the town.

Sarah Taylor fell in beside her. "Let me accompany you," Sarah said.

Samantha gave her a grateful smile. They walked up a small hill toward the town and fort with the other arriving passengers. The women held their hems up to avoid the mud as best they could, but the men disregarded their muddy trousers. Samantha could see a couple dozen buildings. Houses nestled under the tall bluff covered in green prairie grass and had fields running down the slope to the river.

"It's a pretty place to live," Samantha said. She wondered if the mud would dry up before it froze with the onset of winter.

Sarah shrugged. "I make the best of it. We've lived in many places where my father has been stationed, and this certainly isn't the worst." She smiled at Samantha. "At least life here is never boring."

That sounded promising to Samantha.

James Henry's home, which would now also be hers, was one of the nicest houses in the village, with two stories and an attached single-story wing for James Henry's store. The doors of the house and store both faced the road that led to the new fort.

Samantha and Sarah wiped the mud off their boots on the iron scraper near the door and entered the house. A large brick fireplace filled most of the wall opposite the door. Windows on either side of the front door allowed natural light to ease the dark heaviness of the overhead beams, and a colorful painted floor cloth covered the floor. Samantha liked the room. It still had a feeling of her brother's wife, deceased now for several years. Her death from influenza had been a blow to the entire family.

Sarah called, "Sally!"

An older Black woman came from the other part of the house. "There you are, Miss Sarah," she said.

"The house looks wonderful, Sally. Thank you for getting it ready for Miss Lockwood," Sarah said. She turned to Samantha. "Sally is a treasure. My mother sent her over to make sure the place was ready for you."

"I'll run along to your parents' house then," Sally said. "Miss Lockwood, there's a stew simmering for your dinner." She returned downstairs to the semi-basement kitchen, no doubt to leave through a back door.

"Is she a servant or a slave?" Samantha asked. Her brow furrowed in confusion as she recalled the Black servants at the dock. Had they been enslaved? "I thought Michigan was a free territory."

"My father's regiment comes from the south. Soldiers are allowed a stipend for servants, so they brought their slaves with them."

Samantha didn't know what to say. Mother did have paid domestic help, but took personal charge of the household chores of cooking and cleaning. She had taught Samantha and her six sisters to do so, too. "Well," she said. "I appreciate that Sally has started dinner."

Sarah said, "I'll leave you to settle in, but I'll come for tea tomorrow to have a good chat." She grinned to soften the audacity of inviting herself to tea.

"I look forward to it," Samantha said. She beamed at her new friend.

Sarah took her leave, and Samantha explored the house. The scrumptious odor of fresh baked bread drew her downstairs to the kitchen. High narrow windows along the kitchen ceiling, at ground level from outside the house, let in a bit of light. At the top of another set of steps, a door led to the yard behind the house.

Wanting to step into her responsibilities right away, Samantha peered into the stew pot and gave it a stir. She tasted it, then took an onion from the dried bunch hanging above barrels of stored staples, chopped it, and added it to the simmering stew of meat and root vegetables.

Returning to the parlor, Samantha considered putting Papa's letter on the mantle, as if it had appeared independent of her. She wasn't foolish enough to believe Papa's instructions to James Henry would vanish if her brother never read the letter, but it would be so nice to begin anew here. It would be a month at most before another letter could arrive, a month to establish herself, to show her brother and father she could think for herself. She took the letter out of her reticule and unfolded it. Her brother's name glared at her in her father's handwriting.

Papa would have met with James Churchman by now and broken the marriage agreement she'd never agreed to. Mama most likely had made tea and consoled the poor man, the latest in a string of suitors rejected by Miss Samantha Lockwood. Papa had roared when she refused this one. But Mr. Churchman bored her to tears, and she couldn't bear a lifetime of boredom. She'd blurted out that she'd rather go live with James Henry in

Michigan Territory than marry James Churchman. She hadn't expected Papa to immediately agree and arrange her trip.

Samantha took the letter out of her reticule and tapped it against the fireplace bricks. Papa's fury had overshadowed everything else in the days before she was banished. Mama had seemed empathetic, but maybe it was Samantha's own longing. Surely Mama could understand that Samantha wanted to marry someone she chose, a man she could love and work alongside to build a life?

The frontier offered opportunities for a woman. She could make her own choices here, far from her father's rigid control. She refolded the envelope along familiar creases, then crumpled it in her hand and threw it into the fire.

THE NEXT MORNING, SAMANTHA went to help James Henry in the store. Opposite the outside door, a counter ran along the wall. Shelves behind the counter were crowded with all manner of small goods—jars of candy, small boxes of beads and bangles, combs and ribbons, and small canvas bags of bullets and flints. At the far end of the store, several chairs gathered around an iron box stove. A checkerboard sat atop a barrel marked "nails." She pictured her brother sitting there pontificating about territorial politics with like-minded men. James Henry had been appointed judge, and he had further political ambitions. At least territorial politics would be more interesting than the incessant legal details James Churchman had wanted to discuss.

Her brother stood next to a jumbled pile of goods near the door, his spectacles on the tip of his nose. He flipped through a stack of papers, double-checking the delivery that had arrived on the *Warrior* with them.

"Good morning," she said. He was her brother and her host. She intended to be pleasant.

"Good morning," he said, without looking up at her. Last night at supper, James Henry had complained about his loss of income from the store being closed for the two weeks it had taken to go to St. Louis and return with her. He still looked angry.

Samantha walked through the store, admiring the organized shelves of blankets, calico, cotton, and broadcloth, and the barrels of flour on the floor. One corner held guns, lead, flint, powder, and a few tools. Looking back toward the connecting door to the house, Samantha spotted a sign announcing the store was a designated U.S. post office, and she remembered how proud James Henry had been to tell their father he'd been appointed the first postmaster in Prairie du Chien.

The back of her neck prickled and she looked up to see her brother glaring at her over the top of his spectacles. "Are you ever going to tell me why Father banished you to the territory?"

A vision of the burning letter came to mind. She tensed with trepidation and tried to keep her voice from trembling. "He sent me for a visit, that's all." She reached into a box of glass beads, and picked out a string of purple ones. She held it up to her bodice next to the amethyst brooch she always wore and looked for a mirror. Not seeing one, she put the beads back and looked for another way to occupy her hands and ignore her brother.

He narrowed his eyes and examined her face. "That doesn't sound like him."

Samantha waited, trying not to hold her breath as she hoped he would drop the subject.

James Henry stared at her as if deciding what to say. He said, "So I was thinking . . ."

She'd never heard this speculative tone from her brother, just from her father. And that meant matchmaking.

"Lieutenant Davis seemed taken with you yesterday. I think I'll invite him to tea."

She was already shaking her head. "Stuff and nonsense. Or you'll entertain him without me."

"Samantha," he warned, "you'll need a husband on the frontier."

Why was she surprised that her father and her brother thought alike? James Henry didn't need a letter to discern Papa's intentions. She said, "I don't mind a husband, truly I don't, but I will not take someone else's!"

James Henry frowned and said, "Lieutenant Davis isn't married."

"Can't you see the evidence before your own eyes? He and Miss Taylor are so much in love it's amazing she could tear herself away to walk me here yesterday!" Samantha took a deep breath.

"I don't think it's that certain," James Henry said. "Colonel Taylor disapproves."

"So you do know about them. Sarah greeted me as a friend. I will not entertain a man she loves."

"We'll see about that." He went back to checking items off his order list with his lips pressed together.

Samantha clasped her hands to keep them from shaking. It was going to take effort to establish herself independent of the men in her family.

LATER THAT AFTERNOON, SARAH arrived with a cheery smile. "Time for tea, Samantha. We can get to know each other and you can tell my mother I was a big help at settling you in."

Samantha laughed. Sarah was a fresh breeze on a stuffy day. "Wonderful idea! Let me get the tray."

She returned, balancing a plate of buttermilk biscuits with a jar of raspberry jam and a pot of tea. Samantha set it all on the table, and Sarah fetched porcelain cups from the hutch.

Samantha poured tea for herself and her guest. She remembered helping James Henry pick out the china set and wondered if his late wife had appreciated its pattern of delicate lavender flowers. "Mmmm, Young Hyson," Sarah said. "James Henry always has the best tea." She looked over the top of her teacup. "That's a pretty brooch you have. It's cheerful."

Samantha's hand went to the small flower brooch on her bodice. It contained a bright amethyst in the center surrounded by lighter purple paste stones. She loved it. "I've always had it." She laughed. "I'm not even sure where I got it!" Her smile slipped a little at the lie. She'd always admired her mother's brooch, and before she left home, she'd taken it off her mother's bureau. Samantha regretted the theft almost immediately, but when she touched the brooch it reminded her of her mother, of comfort and support in spite of Samantha's rash actions.

Sarah laughed and began talking, telling her all about the personalities in the territory and the increasing tensions between Indians, fur traders, and soldiers. It seemed the world centered around Lieutenant Jefferson Davis. "Fort Crawford was in terrible disrepair. Our family had to live at Fort Snelling while it was rebuilt. Jeff supervised cutting the timber for the fort, on the Red Cedar River."

"Your father must respect him," Samantha said, amused by the younger girl's obsession.

"My father thinks Jeff's a good soldier but not a potential husband. It doesn't make sense. My sister Ann married a soldier. My mother, too!"

"Fathers don't need to make sense," Samantha said with authority. This was something she knew well. "They're fathers, after all. What they say goes. My father paraded every single man that wandered through Clinton County, New York, in front of me. James Henry has already said he will introduce me to local men. Some days I just want to run away into the woods with the first man I can find."

"Oh, Samantha! Don't say that. The frontier is full of wonderful men who are too busy to send back East for a wife. They want a woman who can thrive in the wilderness." She hefted her porcelain cup full of imported tea. "And enjoy such niceties as are available, of course."

"I do enjoy my niceties," Samantha admitted. "Adjusting to life here would be much harder without you, Sarah."

"When Jeff and I are married," Sarah said, "we will work together to make a home and a family, and have all the niceties we can." She cupped both hands around her teacup, and stared out the window.

It was a beautiful day for daydreams.

CHAPTER 2:

Moon for Planting, 1834
Sugar Camp

DAY SETS

With one hand, Day Sets gathered her long dark hair and pulled it over one shoulder to keep it out of her way as she picked up a stack of blankets. She hated the braids her sisters wore, preferring her hair loose even when it sometimes got in the way. The mother river ran swiftly past the island to tumble over *Owamni Yomni*, the turbulent water that the white man called St. Anthony Falls. She'd been born on *Wita Waste*, Beautiful Island, as had her mother and her daughter. The noise of the nearby falls covered the sounds of childbirth, and the ancestors' spirits protected both mother and baby. Being in this sacred place gave Day Sets courage and a sense of belonging. The women of her tribe came here every year as soon as the sap began to flow. Although oak trees dominated the island, a grove of maple trees provided an important source of food for her people. They gathered sap and made maple syrup, which they used to sweeten bread, stew, tea, and vegetables.

Day Sets walked across the grassy clearing, leaving the large oval birchbark lodge that housed the women of her village during sugaring. She threaded her way through the trees to the riverbank and placed her blankets into one of several beached birchbark dugouts. Other women loaded their dugouts, too, their silence and efficiency a result of long years of practice.

Another dugout approached through the glare of sun on the river. Two Dakota hunters paddled toward her, upriver away from the falls. They brought the dugout into the shallows next to Day Sets. She didn't know either of the young men as they were from the Wahpeton band of Dakota rather than her own Mdewakanton. Several packs in the dugout indicated they'd been to the trading post or even to Fort Snelling. They stayed in the dugout, using their paddles to hold it in place, and one called to Day Sets, "Message for Cloud Man's daughter."

Day Sets wondered which of the four sisters he wanted but was too curious to ask. "Speak," she said.

The hunter nodded. "Word from Fort Snelling says Seth Eastman has renounced his marriage and is going east." Having delivered the message, the two men paddled away as if they hadn't just shattered her sister's life.

Day Sets frowned. She'd received the message; now it was her duty to tell her sister, Stands Sacred, that her husband, the man she loved, the father of her daughter, had left.

A thin woman sat with her back against an oak tree. She pulled her dirty blue woolen petticoat down over her leggings. She raised a bottle of alcohol toward Day Sets. "So the mighty family of Cloud Man suffers," she jeered.

Day Sets gritted her teeth and said nothing. Star Dancing's troubles had more to do with the drink than with Day Set's family. She was so unpleasant, though, that it was as difficult to befriend her as it was to ignore the power of the thunder spirit who lived above the falls.

Stands Sacred came down the path, carrying a large kettle of maple syrup. Star Dancing leaped to her feet, staggered a bit, and called out, "Your darling Seth Eastman has left you!" Her eyes gleamed with a delight bordering on madness.

Stands Sacred stepped up beside her sister, chin held high. Her chin was always in the air, though, because she was the shortest of Cloud Man's daughters. She looked to Day Sets for confirmation, and Day Sets nodded. Stands Sacred said, "He was a good father." Her lips trembled and she pressed them together.

Day Sets nodded again, acknowledging the unspoken pain. She knew her sister dreamed of a *wasichu* marriage where her wasichu husband stayed near her and their daughter. Seth Eastman had made many paintings of Dakota life, and he'd learned a great deal of the language for a white man, which gave Stands Sacred hope. False hope, as it turned out. Day Sets hated to see her sister's dreams dashed, but a Mdewakanton woman didn't need to be bound to one man. She said, "All Nancy needs is a good mother."

Day Sets and Stands Sacred stood beside each other, drawing peace from the trees and sun and each other. Near the lodge, a small girl had seated herself in one of the wooden troughs used to gather the sap. She mimicked paddling a dugout. Day Sets smiled, remembering when she and her sisters had done the same thing. Across the clearing, other Mdewakanton women loaded dugouts for the short trip off Wita Waste to the shore. Two were in charge of loading the huge brass kettles of precious maple syrup. Day Sets spotted another young girl swipe a fingerful of the syrup when her mother wasn't looking. Day Sets could imagine past generations of Mdewakanton women tapping the trees and boiling the sap, their spiritual forms layered behind today's women, passing on their strength and knowledge with love.

"I don't understand why our father insists all his daughters marry wasichu," Stands Sacred said.

Day Sets knew the answer as well as her sister did. Cloud Man believed that in order for his tribe to survive they must learn the ways of the wasichu, the white man. He'd arranged for Day Sets to marry the wasichu Indian agent when she was fifteen. Her three sisters married a soldier, a trader, and a slave. Day Sets knew her father's highest hopes lay in her association with the Indian agent, the United States government official most directly involved with the tribe.

Stands Sacred continued, "Even Iron Cutter went East and married a white woman." She shrugged. "How long before he moves East for good like Seth?"

In her head, Day Sets heard the words her mother had said since she was a small girl. *Never forget you are Mdewakanton, the daughter of Cloud Man.* She drew in her breath and straightened her shoulders. Her marriage to Iron Cutter served the future of the tribe as her father wished. She didn't need her husband to live in her tipi with her. As an Indian agent for the government, he lived at St. Peter's, close enough to provide for Day Sets and their daughter. "Mary and I are fine."

Their mother came out of the lodge with another armload of blankets. Her graying hair and thickening waist did nothing to weaken the glare she focused on her daughters. Day Sets jumped to help, her sister right behind her. With the onset of the Moon for Planting, the Mdewakanton women would leave the sugaring camp and return to their summer camp on the shores of *Mde Make Ska*, White Earth Lake. The island's bark lodge would be left and used again next year, and the year after that, as it had since before anyone there could remember. The men of the village, currently away hunting muskrat, would also return to *Heyate Otunwe*, the Village at the Side. Reunited, the villagers would plant fields as the wasichu, the white man, had taught them. Day Sets shook her head. At least that's what her husband, Iron Cutter the Indian agent, would believe. In reality, the women did all the work as they always had.

When the dugouts were loaded, the women of Heyate Otunwe paddled across the current from the island to the shore. Day Sets sat in front of the dugout, with Stands Sacred seated behind her. Her other two sisters paddled the next dugout. Their mother steered a dugout that carried her three small granddaughters, paddling alone in a fierce declaration of her strength and her care for the children. The river pushed against the laden dugout, but Day Sets held firm. She noticed one of the strong younger women had taken charge of Star Dancing's young daughter, who was *iyeska*, half wasichu, like the daughters of Day Sets and her sisters. Star Dancing herself lounged in a dugout paddled by two grim-faced women. They all beached the dugouts on the shore near the place their horses were tied. They redistributed the load among the horses, then tied the dugouts to trees overhanging the river.

Day Set's big black horse pulled the largest travois with the syrup kettles. The rest of the women also led horses with loaded travois and packs of blankets on their backs. Muted conversations accompanied the scrape of travois poles along the forest floor, the creak of leather harness, and the calls of wild birds. Day Sets led her horse on a short rein. Her sisters and mother walked nearby, watching the three small cousins as they capered beside Day Sets.

Nearing the marshy banks of Mde Make Ska, Day Sets could see their village of fourteen summer lodges. Each lodge held two or three families. Awnings made of bark shaded the door to the elmwood bark lodges and provided a place for the Mdewakanton, the Spirit Lake People, to watch the village as they sewed, repaired fishing lines, sang and chatted. Bare cornfields surrounded the village. By the end of summer, the tall green corn would almost hide the lodges. Women and children would stand on raised platforms to scare away the blackbirds, but only a small lane between the cornstalks would give access to their home.

Shading her eyes, Day Sets watched a group of boys, including her young brothers, playing with long willow javelins. They'd stripped off bark in long spirals, then smoked the bare places to leave black and white stripes on the tapered javelin itself. Now shouts came across the bare cornfield as the boys jeered at the more feeble throws or cheered the best ones.

For seven years Heyate Otunwe had been their summer home. Day Set's husband had created this village and named it Eatonville, after a wasichu far away. The wasichu who lived nearby, though, called it Cloud Man's Village. As a child in Black Dog's village, Day Sets didn't remember any talk of white men, certainly no plans to learn about their culture. Stories were told of Cloud Man, her father, joining Black Dog to fight with the British in 1812, after her parents married. The British showered both men with medals, and they returned to their village. When the Americans arrived in 1819 and built Fort Snelling, Iron Cutter came with them. As an Indian agent, he convinced Black Dog and Cloud Man to give up their British medals to show their loyalty to the Americans. Day Sets had been a young girl at the time, but she had giggled when her father showed her one medal he'd kept and hidden away. For years, she'd seen that medal as her father's way of clinging to his past pride, part of his success as a warrior.

Then in the fall of 1828, Cloud Man led a hunting party in search of game. A sudden blizzard overtook them, and they could do nothing but huddle on the ground and wait for it to pass. Day Sets shuddered, remembering her father's bleak story of the three days he'd spent trapped under the snow. That was when his mind and heart changed, when he decided it was better for the Mdewakanton to learn to farm the wasichu's way. The buffalo and other game had grown scarce as more wasichu arrived. Cloud Man's people did grow some corn, but growing it the wasichu way would be a more stable source of food, and safer to produce.

When the blizzard ended, Cloud Man and his hunters poked their way out of the snow and made their way home. Cloud Man went right to Iron Cutter and accepted the offer of help to start a farming village. In a show of good faith, Cloud Man gave up his last British medal.

Iron Cutter provided tools and training, and doted on the inhabitants like they were his children. He had designated her father, Cloud Man, the head man of the village because her father was widely regarded as brave in battle and wise in counsel. In return, Cloud Man gave fifteen-year-old Day Sets to Iron Cutter in marriage. In the seven years since, the village had grown to over one hundred people who had struggled to hunt game or gather wild rice, people who saw the necessity of learning to grow food like the wasichu. Day Sets knew that Iron Cutter expected her people to live in the village all year, but the Mdewakanton needed to move to hunting and sugaring camps as they always had. It was tradition as well as sustenance.

Day Sets saw a group of boys running through the village, which meant that the men had already arrived back at the village from their hunting camp. Most of the women hurried to their lodges to be reunited with husbands they hadn't seen for a couple of months. Day Sets's husband didn't live in the village. Neither did any of her sister's husbands. Star Dancing staggered and fell against Day Sets's horse. Day Sets's mother took the hand of Star Dancing's daughter, and Day Sets took Star Dancing's arm. She smoothed the other woman's braid, which hung down her back and had started to come apart. Star Dancing's stained print cotton bedgown smelled of too long without washing, and her breath reeked of alcohol. As Cloud Man's daughter, Day Sets felt a particular responsibility to embrace the tradition of compassion, even if she was relieved during those times when someone else assisted Star Dancing.

Star Dancing's husband hadn't built them a proper summer lodge. Day Sets led the woman to her tipi made of worn buffalo skin. She lunged past Day Sets and threw aside the flap. Her husband must have been inside. Star Dancing's strident voice harangued him, and his own anger erupted in return. "Get away from me!"

Pale Crow stormed from the tipi and gritted his teeth as he brushed past Day Sets and Stands Sacred. His fury swirled behind him, leaving an aura of disturbance that only a wasichu could create.

Star Dancing appeared in the doorway and lamented, "Pale Crow is going to go live at the fort! I am alone now to raise my child without a father!"

Day Sets said, "Can I bring food for you? For your daughter?"

Star Dancing's daughter broke away from Day Set's mother and ran to her own mother. Her thin arms and legs made her dark eyes appear larger. She was no cleaner than her mother. Star Dancing's eyes flashed and her chin jutted forward, challenging Day Sets to say more.

Stands Sacred looked miserable, but she didn't say anything.

Day Sets wanted to like Star Dancing. She was near Day Set's own age, a Mdewakanton girl married to a wasichu, with an iyeska daughter. Star Dancing had been beautiful once, before she married Pale Crow. His divided loyalties, between the village and the fort, had broken Star Dancing in ways Day Sets would never understand. But Star Dancing never looked to the ancestors for guidance, nor to her daughter's future.

Day Sets realized there was nothing she or her sister could say to comfort Star Dancing, who was not ready to hear that three of Cloud Man's daughters were in the same situation, that Mdewakanton mothers raised their children, not fathers.

Of the wasichu fathers, Iron Cutter seemed the one most interested in building a school for the iyeska children. So far, though, his promises had been empty. Day Sets did what she could. She made sure her daughter anticipated her father's visits and appreciated his gifts, and that she addressed him in English. But Day Sets only knew a few words of her husband's language. Her father had settled on the idea that his granddaughters and the other iyeska children were the future of the tribe, the link that smoothed the Mdewakanton way with the wasichu. They would need a school. She wondered if the ancestors would be able to follow the children into a wasichu school, into the wasichu world. What a tragedy if they could not.

CHAPTER 3:

May, 1834
Prairie du Chien, Michigan Territory

SAMANTHA

Every day, Samantha held her mother's amethyst brooch for a moment before pinning it to her bodice. Having a piece of her mother over her heart gave her confidence, even though she balked at her mother's advice. When she said she just wanted to be happy in her marriage, Mama had said, "A really good wife is almost always unhappy. While she does so much for the comfort of others, she nearly ruins her own health and life. It is because she cannot be easy and comfortable when there is the least disorder or dirt to be seen." Samantha didn't believe her happiness rested on the amount of dirt in her house. That was just as well, given the amount of mud in Prairie du Chien.

She helped James Henry in the store, and they came to a level of companionship that worked. It mostly involved not talking about anything personal. The street door opened, and a man entered. A large black Newfoundland followed him, panting and wagging its tail.

James Henry's face lit up. "Samantha, this is Major Lawrence Taliaferro."

Major Taliaferro bowed his head to Samantha. "Your servant, ma'am."

"Pleased to meet you," Samantha said. She curtsied to the major. It seemed the right thing to do since he was clearly a prominent person in the community. He dressed well and carried himself like a gentleman. Major Taliaferro appeared to be around the same age as her brother, thirty-five. The dog lurched forward to lick her hand.

"Enchanted, Miss Lockwood," the major said. "Nero, come here!" The dog ignored him.

Nero was big enough that Samantha could pat his head without bending over, a fine specimen of a Newfoundland. She ruffled his ears. "I love big dogs." He licked her hands, his tail already wagging. Samantha stood, brushed her skirt with her hands and looked up in time to see stern disapproval on her brother's face. It seemed she'd see that expression often.

"Major Taliaferro is the government agent for the Sioux Indians," James Henry said. "The Sioux call him Iron Cutter, a translation of his last name." He laughed.

"What exactly does a government agent do?" Samantha asked.

"I prevent hostilities between the Dakota and the Ojibwe." The agent's chest puffed out a bit. He was a proud man.

"It's no easy task," James Henry said.

If Lawrence Taliaferro had been a woman, Samantha would accuse her brother of being in love. As it was, the Indian agent was someone her brother respected and admired. The feeling seemed to be mutual.

Major Taliaferro turned to James Henry. "I stopped in to tell you that Mr. Culbertson, the sutler at Fort Snelling, has retired.

They've appointed a new postmaster that will also fill in as sutler for now. Do you know Mr. Miree?"

"Miree?" James Henry said. He frowned. "No, I haven't met him. Make sure he knows I'm available to assist, should he need it. He's not a creature of Rolette's, I take it?"

"There is no indication he knows King Rolette," Major Taliaferro said. "I'm not sure where he comes from."

"Sit for a bit, Lawrence," James Henry said, waving a hand to indicate the chairs around the stove.

"I'm on my way downriver to St. Louis. When we came East for the summer, I left my wife there to visit her relatives. I'm only here as long as it takes Captain Throckmorton to see the *Warrior* loaded, then I'm off to fetch her."

"If I'd only known! We could have combined the duties of fetching the women and saved one of us the trip," James Henry said as they walked to the chairs around the potbelly stove. Nero flopped down happily at his master's feet. Samantha followed, but didn't sit down.

The major said, "Eliza insisted on accompanying me when I told her I planned to winter here this year."

"She'll winter over with you?" James Henry's surprise caused his friend to wince.

Samantha took a few steps closer. "So who is King Rolette?" she asked, finding the notion of territorial royalty much more interesting than an absent wife.

Lawrence snorted in derision. "He's no king but he's certainly a monarch."

James Henry removed his spectacles and put one end of them in his mouth. It was his pontification look. He was about to regale her with facts. He said, "Joseph Rolette was one of the last independent traders. Recently, he joined with Mr. Astor of American Fur to crush Columbia Fur. Now Rolette represents

American Fur. To make matters worse, he's been appointed Chief Justice of Crawford County."

Samantha knew that her brother was a prominent man in this little community. In addition to the store and the post office, James Henry was a judge. Samantha said, "He must be a constant thorn in your side."

James Henry frowned.

Lawrence said, "Anything James Henry wants to pass—any law, any improvement—Rolette opposes. A few years back, Mrs. Lockwood started a school to teach all the children. Rolette spread the word that her goal was to turn all the children into Protestants. Attendance dropped off."

James Henry flinched at the mention of his deceased wife, but recovered in time to respond. "I figured a way to get around him, though. If I support an issue, I have someone else suggest it. If Rolette doesn't know it's my idea, he won't automatically oppose it."

"So clever, dear brother." Samantha laughed with the men. "So it's Lockwood and Taliaferro against the world?"

Her brother didn't look at her but acknowledged her words with a grim smile.

"Not against the world, just against traders like Rolette," Lawrence said. "Sometimes it seems they *are* the world, but we have right on our side. I won't let people like him mistreat the Dakota and Ojibwe."

The men discussed details of various treaties, tribes, and traders Samantha didn't know and couldn't yet sort out. She returned to dusting the shelves. Her head spun with alliances and feuds—traders against traders, traders against Indians. Where did the soldiers fit in? What about the settlers that were arriving in greater numbers every day? She wondered how many women lived in town, and how many actively supported their husbands.

Back home, her older sisters supported their husbands in everything. Her oldest brother's wife, though, fought him on every decision. Samantha never agreed all the time with any of them. In her parents' marriage, Mama obviously deferred to Papa, her own opinions kept to herself. Could a married woman agree sometimes with her husband and sometimes speak her own mind? If such a thing were possible, she vowed to find it here on the frontier. On her own terms.

Samantha felt a cold nose on her thigh and looked down into Nero's beautiful dark eyes. "Hello, handsome," she said. "Would you like a cookie?" The dog's tail wagged, threatening to clear the lower shelves. Samantha took a molasses cookie from the jar on the counter and led the dog out from behind it. He sat, every muscle perked, head tilted as if to point out what a good dog he was. Samantha laughed and gave him the cookie.

"Now you're his best friend," Major Taliaferro said. "I'd better go before Nero eats your entire cookie inventory and he's too fat to board the boat." He tipped his hat to Samantha. "Welcome to the territory, Miss Lockwood." Nero followed him out the door.

TWO DAYS LATER, ANOTHER man came into the store to see James Henry. The stranger wasn't a soldier—no uniform. He wore the clothing of a civilian, his blond hair tousled by wind or neglect. He was nothing like any man her father would ever approve. Curious, Samantha walked behind the counter and busied herself straightening merchandise as close to the two men as she could get.

"Mr. Lockwood, I'm Alexander Miree, the new postmaster at Fort Snelling. Heading back upriver to the fort tomorrow. I was told to contact you while I was in Prairie du Chien." His face twisted into an endearing grimace, and he rubbed the back of his neck. "I don't want to appear unprofessional, but the previous sutler rather mismanaged the place, and the living quarters aren't very livable." He looked up and smiled. His green eyes sparkled, and Samantha took a deep breath. "So I need a few supplies and some advice."

James Henry nodded, his customer-pleasing smile on his face as he held out his hand for a handshake. "Well met, sir. I'm happy to assist you with whatever you need."

"Would you care for a bag of taffy to sweeten the journey?" Samantha asked. "Or a ribbon for your lady's hair?"

"My sister, Miss Lockwood," James Henry said with a dismissive wave of his hand in her direction.

Alexander Miree smiled, and Samantha's stomach flipped over. "Thank you, Miss Lockwood. Taffy would be fine, but I've no need for female fripperies." He gathered a few more things to put on the counter.

Samantha bagged the taffy and moved aside as James Henry rang up Alexander's coffee and coffeepot. The way he stood and moved and smiled, with casual confidence but not arrogance, entranced her. She struggled against her instinct to giggle and bat her eyelashes, things she had never done for a man and refused to do now. Nonetheless, she hovered close enough to hear the men's conversation. Her heart thumped so loudly she thought they'd hear it.

The men chatted a bit about postal matters, then James Henry wrapped everything in paper and said, "Just the basics, huh? Life goes on if you have coffee."

"Too many tea drinkers in this area. Must have my coffee in the morning." Alexander took his package and chuckled with James Henry as if they shared a secret, even though Samantha knew James Henry was a tea drinker.

"Have a safe trip upriver, Mr. Miree," Samantha said. "James Henry will be happy to help you with any more postmaster questions, I'm sure."

He rewarded her with another smile that made her fluttery, then he left the store with a confident stride.

As soon as the door closed behind him, James Henry turned to Samantha. "Don't throw yourself at my male customers. If you can't behave properly, you will not work in the store."

"Nonsense. I am being friendly, not forward." The notion of throwing herself at Alexander Miree made Samantha smile, and that took the steel out of her words. She didn't understand why this man affected her so much. She'd met handsome men before, but he didn't have the polish that made a man handsome. Her heart couldn't explain it to her head.

James Henry ran a hand through his dark hair and let out an exasperated breath. "I still think Lieutenant Davis . . ."

"Stop right there." Samantha held up her hand, palm flat. "I will not discuss the lieutenant with you. He and Sarah Taylor will get married despite her father's objections." Over the past few weeks, she'd gotten to know Sarah and her mother, both strong, opinionated women.

James Henry took off his spectacles and rubbed his eyes before glaring at her. "You're twenty-three years old. Time to stop being picky and settle down with a good man."

"I'm already that much of an imposition to you, James Henry?" She tried for a teasing tone but failed, even to her own ears. She didn't have a place in James Henry's life. He had managed the store without her for years. Some of his dealings were more political than financial, and her mind whirled with the twisting alliances of tribes, traders, soldiers, and settlers. She felt her throat tighten and tears tickle her eyes. "I'll just start supper, then," she said, heading for the adjoining door.

Closing the door behind her, she leaned against it and took a deep breath, then another, until her chest eased. Despite what she'd said to her brother about starting dinner, Samantha continued to the upper floor with its two bedrooms. Her room wasn't anything special, lacking the comfort and familiarity of her bedroom at the farm in New York. This room had a rough wooden bedstead and a mattress covered with a pretty quilt made by her late sister-in-law. A small, battered dresser stood by the bed. Samantha's trunk sat in the far corner. It was the only seating she had besides the bed. A window looked out over the street toward the Mississippi River. It was a stunning view, but Samantha wasn't in the mood to appreciate it.

She flung herself on her bed and let the tears fall as she thought of her family back in New York. Her amethyst brooch caught on the quilt. Samantha untangled it and covered the brooch with her hand. She missed her mother most. She missed the big family gatherings with her siblings and their families, and she missed the familiar farm. The frontier felt new and strange. Here James Henry was a powerful figure, manipulating the players in local politics to his benefit. She missed the brother who alternately hid her dolls and brought her apples from the neighbor's orchard.

Maybe when she was finally married, life could return to normal. She and her husband could go East for a visit, and Mama would welcome them. A husband would please Papa, even a man he hadn't chosen. James Henry could be her brother again instead of a father substitute. It was true that she was welcome to go home if she agreed to marry someone her father chose, but her father chose men like James Churchman, and she wanted something more than stuffy and proper.

She must distract James Henry from the idea of Lieutenant Davis as a suitor, but so many other men she'd seen so far were grizzled and old, or soldiers whose loyalties lay in faraway homes. She needed someone that was close to her age, with a job that kept him close to home. Green eyes and tousled blond hair popped into her head, and her breath caught. Alexander Miree might be perfect. She would have to figure out how to visit Fort Snelling and use Mr. Miree to distract James Henry from Lieutenant Davis.

OVER THE NEXT FEW weeks, it became usual for Samantha to invite Sarah to tea, including Lieutenant Davis, too. Sometimes Jeff would bring a friend to talk to Samantha while he and Sarah continued their courtship. Samantha liked seeing her new friend so happy.

On one of these afternoons, Samantha, Sarah, and Jeff sat at the table in the front room. They each had a cup of tea in the good cups, and Samantha's fresh honey cookies on a plate. Sarah was discussing her favorite subject—her father's refusal to consider an army man to be her husband.

"He says he's seen how my sister, Ann, struggles to raise a family on the frontier," she said. "He never remarks about how happy she is."

Jeff said, "Sarah's mother is an army wife, too. The Colonel says Mrs. Taylor's a better soldier than he is." Jeff chuckled and took a bite of his cookie. "These are delicious, Samantha."

"Thank you, Jeff," she said. "Sarah, your father wants you to be happy, doesn't he?"

Sarah said, "Oh, I'm sure he does. He respects Jeff, too, as a soldier and a person. Just not a son-in-law." She wrinkled her nose in distaste. "Fathers know what makes a daughter happy, right? I know you have the same situation, Samantha."

Samantha thought of James Churchman and shuddered. "Maybe you two should run off and get married," she said.

The door to the adjoining store opened, forestalling any response, and her brother came in, smelling of whiskey and cigars. The men had a very different afternoon gathering than the women. If he wasn't so smitten with Sarah, Jeff would probably prefer to be with the men.

James Henry nodded at the women and gave Jeff a hearty handshake. "So, Mr. Davis, when are you going to make an honest woman of my sister?"

Samantha groaned and focused on her tea, too embarrassed to look at Jeff and too angry to look at James Henry.

Jeff grimaced, then forced a smile. "Sir, I believe we've had this discussion. Your sister's honesty is not mine to ensure."

Sarah said, "Jeff, you need to be more direct. James Henry, your sister isn't going to marry Jeff."

James Henry looked at each of them with a phony smile on his face, the one Samantha called his campaign smile. "Well, he certainly isn't going to marry you, Sarah, if your father has his say."

Jeff stood. "I need to be going. While I feel welcomed here, it's not the sort of welcome that makes me comfortable." He nodded curtly to James Henry, then turned to the ladies. "Thank you for a lovely repast and conversation, ladies." He walked to the door and settled his hat on his head. Then he was gone.

James Henry pointed his finger at Samantha. "You have work to do there, sister." He took what remained of the cookie on Jeff's plate and went back into the store.

Sarah and Samantha looked at each other in silence for a moment. Samantha said, "He is stubborn like my father. If I ever have sons, I pray they lack the Lockwood stubbornness." She thought for a moment. "I have an idea." She told Sarah about the unmarried sutler who lived at Fort Snelling. Sarah hadn't met him, but she started smiling when Samantha's description waxed poetic.

"Oh," Sarah teased, "you've settled on him for his eyes and the toss of his head?"

"I haven't settled on anyone," Samantha said. "He has a good job. It might be enough to distract James Henry. At least he'd be pestering me to marry someone whose affections aren't already taken, someone I might be interested in." She paused. "Maybe I can encourage my brother to go upriver to see how Mr. Miree is doing. After all, he did offer his help. Then I can accompany him, saying I wish to visit the fort."

"I'll write to my sister, Ann, to tell her you might be coming."

Sarah and Samantha made it a point to meet every boat after that, waiting for Ann's reply. One day, as they stood on the dock watching a newly arrived boat unload, Samantha gasped as the disembarking passengers passed them. Her hand went to her heart, covering the brooch pinned there.

"Samantha?" Sarah asked. "Are you all right?"

Samantha stared, frozen in shock, as a tall, neatly dressed man smiled and waved. "Oh, sweet heaven, it's James Churchman."

"James? Your father's James?" Sarah burst into laughter. "I can hardly wait to meet him."

The man approaching them wore a tightly belted coat that made his shoulders look wider and slim trousers that accentuated his long legs. Sandy brown side whiskers showed beneath his top hat, and he sported a trimmed mustache. Samantha had thought her past washed away with the river current. Instead, it had come upriver to bedevil her. Samantha forced herself to focus on the expression of delight on James's face.

"Samantha, my darling!" he said. "I had hoped to surprise you with my visit, and here you are surprising me by greeting my boat." He took her hand in his and kissed it with a dramatic flair.

"It was a complete coincidence. I didn't even know you were coming. Whatever made you come west?"

"Oh come, dear," he said. "Introduce me to your friend, why don't you?"

Sarah extended her hand as Samantha said, "James Churchman, allow me to introduce you to Miss Taylor. Sarah, this is Mr. Churchman."

"Your servant, Miss Taylor," James said. "Always a pleasure to meet a friend of my intended."

"Pleasure is mine, Mr. Churchman," Sarah said.

"Your intended?" Samantha said. "Papa must have talked with you."

James regarded her with cold eyes. "Are you so weak that you would run away without taking your leave of me? I always believed you to be a strong woman, therefore I am here to discuss the matter with you in person."

Samantha, stung by his accusation yet flattered by his compliment, said, "You must come to tea. Sarah, would you join us? James, where are you staying while in town?"

James surveyed the dried mud that encrusted the fort and village. Samantha remembered her first impression of Prairie du Chien and smiled. The frontier would be too different for James. He wouldn't stay long.

"I haven't yet made arrangements," James said.

"You will be able to find a spare bed," Sarah assured him. "First, though, some tea after your journey."

James Henry came up the road. He had a satchel of incoming mail over his shoulder, intended for the post office. "James? Is that you?"

"James Henry! Well met, sir," James said. The two men shook hands and laughed with the delight of renewed acquaintance.

Samantha wondered if James knew about her father's letter, the letter that had never reached James Henry. It didn't matter. James Henry would now learn why Papa had banished her from the family farm. He would now try harder to marry her off. At least she'd had several weeks to settle in.

"Well, I can guess why you're here in the territory," James Henry said with a sidelong glance at his sister. "Has she invited you to tea?"

"We're on our way," Samantha said. "Sarah will join us." She turned and walked up the road toward the store. Sarah fell into step beside her. The two men followed, chatting like long lost friends.

"Today suddenly got interesting," Sarah said in a low voice.

"I'm beyond words," Samantha whispered back. "I never thought he'd pursue me this far. It's out of character. What could Papa have told him?"

"It doesn't matter what your father said. It matters that he had the nerve to come after you. That's impressive."

"You know what I've told you about this man. He's a lawyer. He lives and breathes laws and treaties and legal technicalities. If James Churchman were a plant, he'd be late summer prairie grass, dry and brown as far as the eye can see in all directions."

Sarah laughed. "All right, I understand. What are you going to do?"

"Leave for Fort Snelling, alone if necessary, even if we don't get an answer from your sister soon."

"He followed you here from New York. You don't think he'll continue a couple of days upriver?"

Samantha's shoulders slumped in defeat. They arrived at the house, and Samantha hesitated at the door. "I suppose I'll make do," she murmured to Sarah. Louder, she said, "Welcome to James Henry's humble home, James." Then she entered the house, leaving the door wide open for the others.

"Not so humble," James Henry protested. He led James to a chair by the fireplace. "Are you content with tea or can I offer you something stronger?"

James demurred. "Tea is fine, thank you."

Sarah went to the hutch to fetch teacups. Samantha went straight to the kitchen, where she prepared a tray of bread and jam as well as a pot of tea. She muttered to herself as she worked. "Why would he follow me here? Papa must have given him hope. I guess I can't be angry with Papa. He probably thinks I'll come crawling home in defeat before midsummer. He's always thought I was weak! But how could he send me here and then send James?" She touched her brooch. "What did Mama say?" Samantha longed to have a private conversation with her mother, away from Papa, where true feelings could be discussed. She didn't want to believe Mama supported Papa's decision to send her here in the first place, much less to send James after her.

With a deep breath, Samantha put a smile back on her face, picked up the tea tray, and went up to the parlor. She poured tea for the men and gave them the cups where they sat by the fireplace. There were only two chairs by the fire. Sarah sat at the table, already nibbling a biscuit topped with berry jam that Samantha's late sister-in-law had preserved. Samantha didn't know whether to feel excluded by the men or relieved she didn't have to talk to them about the latest in a series of Indian treaties the government signed then ignored. Samantha sighed. It would be a long afternoon. She sat with Sarah and poured herself a cup of tea.

"The treaty of 1804 was the impetus of the Black Hawk war," James was saying. "Black Hawk never believed we could sell away his lands. The government made an incredible deal. All the land east of the Mississippi River from St. Louis to the Wisconsin River for a thousand dollars paid to the Sauk and Fox."

"The amount of money wasn't the problem," James Henry said. "The Indians simply don't understand the concept of land ownership. They live on the land and it provides for them."

"In this most recent treaty, the United States acquired something like half a million acres. What does that mean? The Indians still live there. Life continues." James sipped his tea.

Sarah whispered to Samantha. "So far he's been very pleasant. And he's an attractive enough man with a dashing air."

"Yes, he makes a good impression," Samantha said. She picked up a biscuit and spread it with jam. If she stuffed her mouth, she wouldn't be able to make the stinging retorts James usually inspired. She never liked the person she became when she was with him.

But Sarah was right. James was being pleasant, no doubt because he was ignoring her. After all, he'd been caustic at the dock. As if she should be blamed for whatever nonsense her father had used as an excuse for her journey to Prairie du Chien. Whatever he'd said, Papa hadn't made it clear that he'd banished her for refusing to marry James.

The afternoon stretched to another pot of tea, with the men discussing treaties, and the women discussing their trip to Fort Snelling in hushed tones at the table. When Sarah rose to take her leave, the men also stood.

"I'd best be finding myself a bed for the night," James said as Sarah left.

"Don't be ridiculous. You'll stay here with us tonight and tomorrow we'll find proper lodging in the village for you," James Henry said. "Samantha can add one more for supper."

Samantha noticed the trunk that had been delivered to the house and left by the door. It looked like James meant to stay.

"I'll fix a pallet for James in your room," Samantha said to her brother.

After supper that night, James suggested he and Samantha take a walk. The spring evening turned chilly, so she collected her shawl as they left the house, pinning it around her shoulders with the amethyst brooch. Her hand lingered there to gather strength.

Samantha led him to a path along the river. The bluff behind them towered over the town and would make the sun set sooner than on the prairie beyond, its tall grass spiked with black-eyed Susans and purple bergamot. There wouldn't be an opportunity for a long stroll. She stopped and stood watching the river instead. The Mississippi flowed around the sand bars and islands with their abundant foliage.

"It's a beautiful setting," James said.

"True, except for the mud," Samantha said.

"Your father came to me the day after you left. He said you didn't want to marry me, but he was hazy on the details of why you ran away." James waited. She said nothing. "He was unclear as to your reason for refusing me, so I came to find out for myself."

Samantha watched as the sky grew dimmer over the bluff and washed the river with orange and gold. "I told Papa I wouldn't marry you, and he sent me here. It was not my choice."

James nodded. "All right. I understand that. But not marrying me? That was your choice, was it not?"

She couldn't tell him he was boring. "I didn't feel we knew each other well, I guess."

"Many brides are frightened at first."

She bristled. "Stuff and nonsense. I wasn't frightened. I just don't want to marry a man I hardly know. There must be more to a marriage than an agreement on paper with my father."

James smiled. "There's the spunky girl I thought I would marry."

He liked her spunkiness? Samantha had never known that.

"Maybe it was your father that was in your way," James said, "and your decision was more about defying him than refusing me."

Samantha tried to hide her shock at his perception. "There is some truth to that, I suppose," she admitted.

"That's why I came west. I'll find a little place to live and make a living offering legal services. It will give me an opportunity to court you properly."

Samantha nodded. "That would be fine. I'm sure James Henry will help you get started."

They walked back to the store in the gathering darkness. Before entering the house, Samantha said, "How do you know? I mean, our relationship has been teacups and drawing rooms. How do you know there's any more?"

"Discovering that is part of the process, isn't it?" he said.

James kissed her hand and retired upstairs. To her surprise, Samantha realized she'd enjoyed their conversation.

CHAPTER 4:

Moon When Strawberries Turn Red, 1834
Cloud Man's Village

DAY SETS

Day Set's five-year-old daughter, Mary, pushed her way into her grandmother's lap. "Tell me a story?"

Red Cherry Woman gathered Mary into her arms with a loving smile Day Sets rarely saw on her mother any more. "Would you like to hear the prairie rose story again?" Red Cherry Woman asked.

Day Sets smiled at her sisters as Mary's younger cousins snuggled in for the story, too. All three little girls loved the prairie rose story as much as their mothers did. Red Cherry Woman sat in her usual place outside the chief's lodge. Day Sets sewed and Stands Sacred continued weaving a basket as her mother began. A third sister, Hushes Still the Night, listened as she worked on an intricately beaded bag.

"Can you believe there was a time when no flowers bloomed on the prairie?" Red Cherry Woman began.

Day Sets swept her hair over one shoulder and closed her eyes. Her mother's story gave her an excuse to focus on listening rather than mangling the sewing in her lap. Sewing was a chore. The tale's cadence flowed over Day Sets as it had since her mother first told her the story when she was Mary's age.

"*Maka Ina*, the Earth Mother, was sad because her robe, the prairie we love, was dull and brown. In her heart, she held many flowers of unparalleled beauty. There were flowers as blue as the summer sky, white as the winter's snow, pink as a spring dawn, yellow as the midday sun. How she wished her robe was as beautiful!"

"The pink one," whispered Mary. Hushes Still the Night's daughter, three-year-old Jane, shushed her.

"Yes, it was the pink one who volunteered to leave Maka Ina's heart and go forth to beautify her robe. But the Wind Demon saw her . . ."

Stands Sacred's two-year-old daughter, Nancy, made the whooshing sound that mimicked the Wind Demon. Her mother laughed, and Red Cherry Woman smiled.

"The Wind Demon shouted and roared, angry that the pretty flower dared to venture onto his prairie. With his mighty breath, he blew out her life. The spirit of the pink flower returned to the heart of Maka Ina. Other flowers gathered their courage and went forth, one after the other, and the Wind Demon sent their spirits back to Maka Ina's heart.

"Finally, the delicate Prairie Rose offered to go. Maka Ina loved Prairie Rose's beauty and sweet scent. She said that the fragile flower would charm the Wind Demon. When Prairie Rose appeared, born from the womb of the Earth Mother, the Wind Demon drew in great breaths to blow powerful tornadoes. He caught the fragrance of the flower and paused. He didn't have the heart to blow out such sweetness. Instead, he made his voice gentle and sang sweet songs so as not to frighten her away. Gentle breezes stirred the prairie grasses. The other flowers came up through the dark ground from the heart of Maka Ina. They made her robe so bright and joyous that even the Wind came to love them.

"Sometimes the Wind forgets his gentle songs and becomes loud again, but it doesn't last long. And he never harms a person whose robe is the color of Prairie Rose."

Day Sets opened her eyes. The story calmed her, as it always had. Her mother looked content to have three granddaughters listening so intently to her story. Learning the wasichu's way of farming and storing food, as well as their language and customs, consumed most of the tribe's energy these days. Day Sets appreciated the traditional story. She was proud her daughter did, too.

Laughing Bird, Day Set's recently married sister, walked up to the lodge. "Jim Thompson says the *Warrior* is on its way. A hunting band saw it down the river."

"I must go," Day Sets said. She stood up, preparing to meet the boat. Laughing Bird slipped into her place.

Day Sets picked up Mary and walked toward the lodge she shared with her sisters. Jim Thompson was the only one of the sisters' husbands who lived in the lodge. The others lived elsewhere and visited their wives in the village. As much as she enjoyed her sisters, Day Sets appreciated the peace of the lodge when no one was there. Inside the bark lodge, a bench ran around the walls a couple feet off the ground. Buffalo robes covered the top of the benches, which doubled as beds. A banked fire smoldered in the center of the lodge, sending tendrils of smoke toward a hole cut in the roof, five feet above. Day Sets pulled a child's dress from a basket under the bench. She fingered her sister's beadwork on the soft cotton. Day Sets didn't have any patience with her own beadwork. Mary wiggled and fussed as her mother changed her dress. "Hush, sweetheart, your papa is coming. You must look nice." Day Sets tucked loose strands of hair back into her daughter's braid.

Mary said, "Papa always comes with Nero."

"Yes, darling." Day Sets sat on a folded trader blanket and pulled her daughter onto her lap. Her daughter loved all dogs, but Nero would always be her favorite.

Iron Cutter spent winters back east with the white woman he'd married there about a year after he wed Day Sets. A wasichu husband almost always had a white wife in addition to his Dakota wife. Dakota custom recognized both wives, but wasichu law only recognized wasichu wives. Iron Cutter had brought his wasichu wife to the agency for the summer a few times, but she'd received word that this year they both would stay through the winter. Day Sets didn't know what that would mean for her or for her daughter. It would be different.

Iron Cutter's other wife, his *teya*, didn't have any children. Iron Cutter would come to see Mary in the village, and he wouldn't bring his teya, whom Day Sets had never met. By United States law, iyeska children like Mary were white. If the teya stayed all year, would she expect Mary to live at the agency?

It was Day Set's duty to be here in the village. At least that's what Iron Cutter always told her. But she'd never known a Dakota woman to sit around waiting for her man to arrive. And Dakota women raised their own children. Day Sets understood her father's desire to assimilate his granddaughters into the wasichu world. She could let her daughter learn English words and wear wasichu dresses. She could do what Iron Cutter told her was proper for the mother of his daughter. But that didn't mean she had to like it. And her curiosity about Iron Cutter's other wife wouldn't go away.

Day Sets wrapped Mary in her arms, easing her hold only when the girl wiggled in protest. Her father said Iron Cutter and his kind were the future. The Mdewakanton could keep their way of life if they held tightly to the wasichu as he blazed through their land. In the Mdewakanton culture, though, a woman made decisions about her home and her children. As important as it was for her father to have grandchildren rooted in the wasichu's world, it was important to Day Sets that her daughter keep her Mdewakanton heart. That meant not waiting around in the village for her husband to come to her.

"We'll go meet Papa at the fort, shall we? Remember the pretty beads he brought you last time?" Day Sets took out the necklace of blue glass beads and put it on Mary's neck. If she looked grown up enough, maybe Iron Cutter would work harder for a school for the Dakota children, or at least the iyeska children like Mary, Jane, and Nancy. If the cousins were going to be adults in a wasichu world, they needed to go to a wasichu school.

She led Mary outside to her black horse, tethered nearby. Day Sets gathered the reins, mounted, and drew Mary up in front of her. For once Mary didn't start off by asking for her own pony, promised by her grandfather, Cloud Man.

Day Sets reminded her husband of his daughter as often as she could. It was especially important now that everyone knew he was bringing his other wife, his teya. Iron Cutter must remember his promises to little Mary.

She felt someone watching her and turned to see Star Dancing sitting in front of her tipi, her daughter rolling in the dirt with two of the mangiest tribal dogs. Star Dancing's eyes were hooded and vacant. An empty bottle sat next to her. Day Sets tried to find some trace in Star Dancing's face of the pretty girl she'd grown up with, the girl who laughed all day.

Star Dancing stood up. "You're no better than me. Your father is better than mine, that's all," she said, dissolving into laughter as if she'd told a funny joke. Day Sets said nothing while Star Dancing composed herself. "After all, you have a daughter like mine, with a father whose entire white life is more important than his child." She narrowed her eyes and glared at Day Sets.

Day Sets couldn't answer without showing an emotion she'd regret. She turned her horse away, preparing to leave the village. It was true she had a daughter with a wasichu who didn't live in the village, but Iron Cutter was a better man than Pale Crow. Day Sets knew Cloud Man was more important than Star Dancing's father to the wasichu. Here in the village, though, the men shared responsibilities for leadership in council. If they listened more to Cloud Man, it was because of his wisdom and experience, not because the wasichu called him chief.

Horses approached on either side of her. Stands Sacred and Hushes Still the Night were coming with her to the agency, their daughters mounted before them as Mary was. Day Sets smiled and shook her head. She knew they must be as curious as she was about Iron Cutter's teya, and she was glad for their company.

The sisters rode to *Wakpa Tanka*, the big river, then headed downriver toward the *mdote*, where the mighty rivers, called Mississippi and St. Peters by the wasichu, met below the fort. The bluffs above the river were as close to *Ate Makpiya*, Father Sky, as a Mdewakanton living on Maka Ina could get. Riding here always gave Day Sets courage in herself and pride in the lineage of her people.

"The river touches everyone it passes," Day Sets said, repeating something their mother had said since they all were small.

Hushes Still the Night nodded. "It waters our fields and supports our dugouts. It also gets angry and destroys. But the sky is the same. It contains all the beauty of the stars and the violence of storms."

Stands Sacred also echoed her mother's words to them as she said, "Every mother guides her daughters and cries for them in both joy and despair."

As usual, Hushes Still the Night pointed out the negative and Stands Sacred the emotional. Day Sets rode in silence for a few minutes. Below them, the river tumbled over the boulders along its banks. Above, a red-tailed hawk soared in a blue sky studded with clouds. Day Sets said, "As the daughters of Cloud Man, how do we help our people who have lost their way?"

"Are you thinking of Star Dancing?" Hushes Still the Night asked.

Day Sets nodded.

"So full of anger," Hushes Still the Night said.

Stands Sacred said, "Our mother says you have to experience hatred to feel love, and sorrow to feel joy."

Hushes Still the Night said, "Does that mean we are happier for Star Dancing's pain? That doesn't seem right."

Day Sets appreciated her sisters' support even more considering how alone Star Dancing was.

"The tears of our nation run in the river, and the river remembers," Stands Sacred said.

The sisters rode in sober silence, lost in their own thoughts. They'd always make her strong, Day Sets knew. Together, they would work to make each other's lives joyous. Even on this visit to the agency, which would include an unpredictable meeting with her husband's teya, her sisters would support her.

Day Sets felt lucky to have a husband who loved their daughter and stayed nearby, but what she'd really enjoy was a traditional warrior husband who brought food he'd hunted to the home, and honor he'd earned to the tribe. What she'd really enjoy was to live the way the tribe used to, following the game as the seasons progress. It was a life she learned from her ancestors.

Staying in one place watching plants grow did not fulfill the heart of a Mdewakanton woman.

Day Sets sat tall on her black horse and let the breeze waft through her hair as she rode toward St. Peter's. Hushes Still the Night and Stands Sacred rode beside her. All three sisters held their daughters in front of them.

"We'll support you," Hushes Still the Night said, echoing Day Set's thoughts. Her eyes narrowed and lips tightened. "Especially if he rejects you."

Day Sets grimaced. Hushes Still the Night expected rejection as she expected all manner of tragedy.

Stands Sacred said, "We want to see Iron Cutter's teya, too. I want to know if she's pretty." She giggled like a small girl.

As usual, Stands Sacred made Day Sets smile. Her younger sister was the dreamer, the romantic in the family. Stands Sacred and Hushes Still the Night both had the rounded, comforting shape of their mother. Hushes Still the Night, though, was taller and had the angular face of their father that caused her expression most often to appear negative. In contrast, Day Sets was a tall, lean amalgamation of her parents. Her mother said Day Sets stood straight as a tree so she could hear what her ancestors whispered in the breeze.

The buildings that comprised St. Peter's Agency stood on military ground about a quarter mile from the fort. Iron Cutter, Indian agent and Mary's father, lived in the agency house. A handful of tipis dotted the large fenced enclosure around the agency. The number of tipis grew and shrank throughout the year but never seemed to completely disband. With Iron Cutter set to arrive for the summer, the temporary village had grown. The winter had been hard. The government owed the tribes iron tools, tobacco, and government money, and they were there to collect from Iron Cutter. Day Sets, Stands Sacred, and Hushes Still the Night rode past the tipis to the bluff overlooking the river.

Day Sets felt no need to challenge her husband's wife. After all, the white woman had yet to give him a child after several years of marriage. Now that he had brought her west and would live with her, that might change. Day Sets wanted her own daughter to remain present in Iron Cutter's life. After all, Mary was the future of the Mdewakanton people. She and her iyeska cousins blended the traditional ways of their tribe with the new ways of the wasichu. When Iron Cutter arrived, she would learn more about his plan for little Mary's education.

Stands Sacred and Hushes Still the Night dismounted. Day Sets lifted Mary down to them, but stayed watchful on horseback. The three little cousins could be sisters. All had dark hair in braids, although the youngest's was barely long enough. All three wore identical print cotton petticoats.

Mary bossed her smaller cousins like a mother. "I am the mommy," she said. "You and Nancy are the babies. I get to make your food and take care of you when you're sick."

"I make food," Jane said, her lip trembling. Jane was only a year younger than Mary, but Mary was in charge.

"You're crying? See, you *are* the baby!" Mary's delight would have caused Jane's tears to flow if two-year-old Nancy hadn't started crying first.

Stands Sacred scooped Nancy into her arms and comforted her.

Hushes Still the Night said, "You are still the mother of Iron Cutter's daughter. Why confront his teya?"

"Curious, maybe," Day Sets admitted.

"I'd want to know if my husband loved her more than me," Stands Sacred said.

"Status and comfort are more important. As daughters of the chief, we have that already," Hushes Still the Night said.

Day Sets said, "Be quiet, Hushes. Let Stands Sacred dream."

The two older sisters laughed when Stands Sacred wrinkled her nose. "Better to dream than see nothing but ill will," she said to Hushes Still the Night. Turning to Day Sets, she said, "Or be someone who is far too practical to enjoy the beauty of love."

Her younger sister's daydreaming wasn't new, so Day Sets couldn't take offense. What was left other than to be practical? Mary would be important someday, both to the Mdewakanton and to the wasichu. "Mary will have a choice in the life she will lead."

Hushes Still the Night waved an arm in a circle over her head, indicating the temporary gathering of tipis. "Look at the people here. So far, the wasichu have done us no favors. Why is it so important to you that Mary be successful in that world?"

It was true that all around her Day Sets saw broken pieces of bands, starving families, and desperate individuals who all needed food. Her father had foreseen this and embraced Iron Cutter's vision of a farming village for the Dakota that produced enough surplus to keep its people fed. "It's important to our father and to her father."

Hushes Still the Night looked dubious. "He's not the Great White Chief our father thinks he is."

Day Sets didn't respond. For the Mdewakanton to thrive, they must deal with the wasichu. She knew they were too numerous, too powerful, to defeat. There must be a way for her people to exist alongside the wasichu. So far, no one but Cloud Man had any ideas. Day Set's marriage, and her daughter, were for the future of the tribe, not personal romantic fulfillment. Sacrificing romance for the tribe was what a head man's daughter did.

Movement among the Dakota gathered on the bluff had alerted Day Sets to a cloud of steam downriver. She pulled her daughter back up on the big black horse, and Mary nestled against her mother. Day Sets held the reins in one hand and her daughter in the other. Her sisters stayed behind with their daughters while Day Sets galloped toward the fort along the bluff high above the confluence of the big rivers. Hair and mane and tail streamed like dark rivers. Little Mary squealed with delight, twining her little hands into the horse's mane.

Puffs of steam, like a signal fire in the middle of the river, revealed the *Warrior*'s progress as it came up the Mississippi River from Fort Crawford at Prairie du Chien.

Along with word of Iron Cutter's return had come stories of devastation by cholera along the Mississippi River from St. Louis to Prairie du Chien. Last September the *Warrior* had stopped at Galena when cholera broke out on the boat. The captain refused to continue to Prairie du Chien. It hadn't helped. The illness still raged all around Fort Crawford. The white people may fear the Dakota, or the Sauk and Fox, but the cholera had killed more wasichu in the past year than even Black Hawk's war. More of the tribespeople, too. So as much as Day Sets anticipated the boat's arrival, she felt a frisson of fear, too.

The cholera had not yet touched their village at all. The women planted squash, potatoes, cabbage, and corn in quantities greater than they ever had. They also continued the traditional duties of making clothes, gathering wood, and maintaining the home. Hunting was hard as game grew more and more scarce, so the wasichu had taught the Dakota men to farm. Iron Cutter provided seeds, metal tools, and draft animals to help with cultivation, but the men weren't interested in farming. Growing food was women's work, and each year the village produced more food than the year before. When there was a surplus, the men gave it away to hungry families in other villages, much to Iron Cutter's dismay. He desperately wanted Cloud Man's village to succeed, and to feed itself as it grew. That meant storing more food for the winter. Iron Cutter would have them turn away hungry outsiders, but to the Mdewakanton, the other villagers were *mitakuye oyasin*, all part of the family of living beings.

But the harvest was months away. Day Sets needed to put out of her head her sisters' ideas, her fear of illness, and her own ideas of marriage. Mary's immediate future was paramount. She was due to start school, but as yet school existed only in promises. Day Sets must do what she could to fix that.

CHAPTER 5:

May, 1834
Fort Snelling, Michigan Territory

SAMANTHA

The imposing majesty of the fort high on its bluff impressed Samantha as she approached Fort Snelling by river. The whitewashed limestone fort glowed against the sky, and the American flag swelled her heart with patriotic pride. A semicircular artillery battery arced out from the wall to ward against attacks. Below the fort, the Mississippi and St. Peter's Rivers converged in a celebration of power that took her breath away. For the first time she felt the promise of the territory, the future this beautiful land held for Americans.

The trip to the fort had come about after a month of mentioning it to her brother. James Churchman had found a room in Prairie du Chien to lease where he could live and work, and he called on Samantha almost every day. It was becoming more difficult to remember why she'd been so determined to refuse him, so it was even more important to get away.

Major Lawrence Taliaferro had returned, this time accompanied by his wife, Eliza, who was older than her husband. She wore her glossy black hair in sausage curls that framed her face, and she was one of those women who wasn't aware of the beauty in her fair skin and dark eyes. She would be in the territory all summer, then winter over. Eliza appeared more resigned than eager. James Henry decided to accompany the Taliaferro household upriver and invited Samantha. She agreed even though she hadn't warmed to Eliza. Even Nero ignored Eliza. The big dog knew who was important.

Once they arrived at the fort's dock, Samantha pushed Nero aside to climb into the Taliaferro's wagon with James Henry, and they rode up the steep road on the south side of the fort under the protection of a three-story hexagonal tower with cannon on top. Wagons and passengers streamed up the road like a forgotten tributary of the great river.

Lawrence, of course, had been to Fort Snelling many times. "St. Peter's Agency is where the Dakota come to talk to me," Lawrence told Samantha.

"The house will need a stiff cleaning," Eliza had said. "I hope the Negro girl can handle it."

Samantha grimaced and darted a glance at the enslaved woman who stood nearby. She maintained an impassive face, more than Samantha could do.

On the trip upriver, Samantha had seen her brother and the major talking. The major's agitation showed in the way he waved his hands as he talked. Later, James Henry told her that Eliza's extended visit with relatives in St. Louis hadn't been Lawrence's idea. The major wanted to focus on this summer's business of trade and treaty without worrying about getting his wife settled. So he'd continued upriver to the agency then had to go back and fetch her just a few weeks later. Now the major's entire household arrived with bustling fanfare at Fort Snelling.

The Taliaferros and Lockwoods climbed aboard a wagon that also held their personal trunks, and Nero took his place at the major's feet. Other wagons filled with cargo rumbled up the road to the fort, but the six slaves walked up the hill. Samantha noticed an older Black woman struggling with the steep hill. From her brief experience with Eliza Taliaferro on the trip upriver, she knew it would be worse for the woman if Samantha brought her to Eliza's attention. She turned away, flushed with guilt.

At the top, Nero almost knocked Samantha out of the wagon as he jumped down and raced for a young Indian girl. Nearby, a magnificent Indian woman stood next to a black horse. She wore a cotton dress with leggings and moccasins. "Who is she?" Samantha asked.

"That's Lawrence's daughter," her brother said, pointing to the little girl, "and that's her mother." He shook his head and distanced himself from the encounter, climbing out of the wagon and busying himself unloading their trunks from the back. A wagon stood ready to take his trunk and Samantha's on into the fort while the major's wagon continued to the agency building.

"Oh," Samantha said. Her eyes darted to Eliza, whose eyes narrowed and lips tightened.

CHAPTER 6:

May 1834
Fort Snelling, Michigan Territory

HARRIET

In the spring of 1834, Harriet Robinson took her first steps, at age fourteen, into free territory. Drawing a deep breath, she concentrated on how the air smelled as she walked with Major Taliaferro's other enslaved women up the steep wagon path from the dock to Fort Snelling. She searched for the feel of freedom she expected and raised her head a little higher.

Beside her, Ellie said, "I know what you thinking. You still a slave."

The older slave, Hannah, shook her head. "She just a girl, Ellie."

Chastened, Harriet hung her head and peered from lowered eyes at the sheer stone walls of the fort, at the gardens they passed, and at the stables. Ahead, she could see a small cluster of buildings that must be her new home, St. Peter's. A smattering of Indian tipis were just outside the agency fence. Curious, she squinted to see the details. She'd never had a good look at an Indian.

Two wagons, filled with household items and supplies, creaked and groaned as they rolled up the gravel road to the fort. Luckily the three enslaved women had moved to the side of the road as the first wagon carrying their master, Major Taliaferro, rumbled uphill. Mrs. Taliaferro sat tall, facing forward, a pristine statue with not a single hair out of place despite the long journey. The huge brim of her hat framed her face like a halo and carried more flowers than the surrounding prairie. She was elegant and beautiful, but cold. Harriet figured her mistress would either give up completely like a fragile flower or use that frigid demeanor to control the entire territory. The judge and his sister, Mr. and Miss Lockwood, had joined them in Prairie du Chien. They rode in the wagon, too, as did the enormous black dog, Nero. So far, Nero was the best part of this move to the territory.

"How fancy to ride in a wagon up a steep hill," said Hannah as she stopped to catch her breath at the top of the bluff. Of the three enslaved women, Hannah was the oldest, a large woman who gasped at the exertion of the walk. Her headscarf covered iron gray hair, and she often complained of pain in her knees and back and hand.

Ellie stopped, too. Tall and thin, she towered over the round Hannah like a mop over a bucket. Harriet realized Ellie was trying to hide Hannah's exhaustion.

"We wait and walk with you," Ellie said. She gave Hannah a warm smile.

Two enslaved men walked past. William nodded at the women, but Thomas gave Harriet a saucy wink. She turned away, unsure how to respond. Thomas had been forward the entire trip, which both intrigued and scared Harriet. He was a little older than she was, nice looking, she supposed, but prideful.

"You stay clear of the men," Hannah warned Harriet.

"And the mistress's temper," said Ellie.

"I will," Harriet promised, again. Hannah and Ellie had been giving her advice and over-explaining things for the entire journey from Pennsylvania. She wasn't stupid just because she was young and this was her first trip to the territory. Ellie was five years older, but that didn't make her Harriet's mother, and Harriet was well aware of their mistress's temper. She had worked for Eliza Taliaferro's family since she was Eliza Dillon, daughter of a Bedford hotel owner. Mr. Dillon had owned Harriet for half her life.

"I won't be in the way if I'm doing laundry in the yard," she said.

"This household is much smaller than the Dillon family's hotel," Ellie said. "Less chance to hide behind your work. And not as much time for visiting as at the plantation."

Stung, Harriet pursed her lips. How dare Ellie presume to judge a plantation she'd never seen? Some of Harriet's favorite memories were of doing laundry with her mother at the Virginia plantation where she'd been born. Harriet remembered her mother's exhaustion after a long day of laundry, but she remembered laughter, too. At eight years old, Harriet was sold away from the Virginia plantation to the Dillons in Pennsylvania. She'd put in the day's work of a full-grown woman without her mother beside her, working long days doing laundry for the family's inn. When the daughter of the household married Lawrence Taliaferro, Harriet had been given to the bride. "There weren't no time for visiting at the hotel," she said.

Ellie shrugged.

Harriet changed the subject. "The mistress's papa was shocked when Major Taliaferro say she staying all winter this year."

Ellie laughed. "That's the plan, but he'd no nerve to try it before now. Too tough here in winter." She gave Harriet a long look.

"I know cold weather," Harriet said. She straightened her shoulders and lifted her chin. Even so, she barely reached Ellie's shoulder.

Ellie shook her head. "Territory's cold enough to freeze bones and blood. None of that ice skating on the pond or sledding you seen before." Her tone dismissed the East. Ellie was proud of the territory.

"Not for the weak," Harriet said, agreeing with Ellie's words to keep the peace. Inside, she knew she was strong enough to thrive through the winter and excited for the adventure of living in the territory. She knew better than to share her enthusiasm. Ellie didn't approve of enthusiasm, and Hannah was too old for it.

Several Indians on horses milled around the wagons. Harriet swung her head left and right, trying to take it all in without looking like that was what she was doing. She jumped as Nero barked and leaped from the wagon. He ran to a young Indian girl who slid off a black horse and ran toward the dog, her braids flying. An Indian woman dismounted, unbound dark hair tumbling past her shoulders. As their master and mistress got out of the wagon to speak with the Indian woman, Harriet looked toward St. Peter's Agency and the tipis surrounding it. She stayed close to Ellie and peered at the tipis with a mixture of curiosity and apprehension. Constructed of well-used hides, the walls of the tipi were covered in simple line drawings and dirt. A small cluster of beads and feathers hung over the doorway. Dogs ran through the village, naked children chased each other, women cooked over open fires, and men walked toward the agency or the fort. Barking, laughing, and yelling filled the air.

"Some of them're dark as us," Harriet said. The village seemed busy and full of life.

"Maybe so," Ellie said, "but they live in the land of their mothers and choose their own path."

"Nothing like that in Virginia," Harriet said. "Not for Black folk."

CHAPTER 7:

Moon When Strawberries Turn Red
Fort Snelling

DAY SETS

Mary squealed as she ran toward Nero, and the two collided like reunited lovers. The wagon stopped, and James Henry Lockwood, the judge from Prairie du Chien, jumped out of the wagon, followed by Iron Cutter, who reached a hand up and helped two women down. One of the women wore every shade of beige known to the natural world. Her dark hair was fixed in rigid curls under her large hat, and her face was pretty enough, but she dressed as if her intent was to blend into her surroundings. Day Set's eyes raked over her and focused on the other woman, the one with purple ribbons on her hat. That woman's eyes sparkled with interest as she surveyed the fort and St. Peter's Agency, bustling with Dakota and soldiers and carts of supplies. Day Sets sat motionless on her horse until Iron Cutter smiled at her. Then in one fluid motion she was on the ground, standing tall before her husband, his friend, and the two women. She wasn't sure which one was the teya.

Iron Cutter stood tall in his light colored linen trousers, silk vest, and frock coat. His printed cravat was neatly tied, and his short hair covered by a tall straw hat with a wide brim. She was proud of his confidence and of the way he took charge of those around him. She was not, however, in love with him. Iron Cutter was more of a father figure, to be respected rather than loved.

Mary and Nero tumbled on the ground as if they were both puppies. For the moment, the adults ignored them. Day Sets turned to the sparkling woman and said in Dakota, "I bid you welcome."

The woman curtsied and smiled. Iron Cutter translated her words. "Hello. I am glad to arrive safely. Is this your little girl? Nero certainly loves her!"

The beige woman said something. Iron Cutter didn't translate. He didn't need to. The woman's expression of disdain and Iron Cutter's embarrassment spoke volumes.

Day Sets narrowed her eyes and glared. She said, "Yes, this is Mary. She loves dogs." Iron Cutter translated.

"As do I," the other woman said. "He's a good boy, isn't he, Mary?" she said to the girl. To Day Sets, she said, "Do you live near here?" Again, Iron Cutter translated.

Day Sets said, "This is a temporary village for visiting the Indian agent." She nodded toward Iron Cutter. "Our home is Eatonville at Lake Calhoun." Day Sets hoped her use of the English names for places would show her intelligence. She did not need to impress anyone, but she didn't want to come across as a dumb Indian either.

Iron Cutter translated, then said, "Samantha, let me introduce Day Sets." He put a hand on the vivacious woman's elbow. "Day Sets, Samantha Lockwood. She is Judge Lockwood's sister."

"Pleased to meet you, Miss Lockwood." Day Sets noticed that Samantha Lockwood waited for translation but never looked away. It always irritated her when wasichu began conversing with the translator instead of with her.

Day Sets turned her attention to the beige woman at Iron Cutter's side. She didn't sparkle like the judge's sister. Day Sets waited to be introduced, her head held high and eyes respectfully looking down.

Iron Cutter cleared his throat. "Day Sets, this is my wife, Eliza," he said in both languages. He didn't smile at either woman.

Eliza barely glanced at her husband's Dakota wife. Day Sets straightened to her fullest height, mentally urging every bit of ancestral pride to show in her demeanor. Iron Cutter looked from her to Eliza. Mary disentangled herself from Nero and turned to her father. She seemed to sense the coolness between the adults and shrank back next to her mother instead of throwing herself at her father. Day Sets said, "Mary is Iron Cutter's daughter."

Eliza frowned and shook her head. She said something that made Samantha Lockwood gasp. No translation needed. Day Sets took a step forward.

Iron Cutter put his hand out, as if to touch Day Sets, as if to stop her. He spoke first to Eliza, then repeated to Day Sets. "Mary is an intelligent girl. She'll be no trouble." He patted Mary on the head. "We're off to the agency. Will you be there?" Iron Cutter said to Day Sets in her language.

"I am needed elsewhere." She beckoned to Mary. The little girl flung her arms around the dog and assured him she'd see him soon.

Day Sets leaped on the horse and pulled Mary up after her. She turned the horse and set off at a walk toward the tipis at the agency, knowing Iron Cutter and his teya would have to get back in their wagon and follow her. Only one road led to the agency.

Mary turned back, leaning around her mother's body to wave at her father. Day Sets didn't turn, so she didn't see how he reacted, if at all. She didn't expect to be friends with Iron Cutter's teya, but she hadn't expected the woman to ignore her, either. As long as Iron Cutter kept to his agreement to see Mary educated, though, she would make it work for Mary's sake.

Day Sets turned her horse toward the cluster of tipis around the agency. She could hear Iron Cutter's wagon continue on to the house. She didn't turn around. Mary called out to Nero, who barked back at her.

CHAPTER 8:

May 1834
Fort Snelling, Michigan Territory

◦⟋⟍◦

SAMANTHA

Samantha watched Day Sets ride off on her black horse, long dark hair flowing in mimicry of the horse's mane, and wondered what emotions swirled behind that ramrod-straight back and impassive face.

"Why did you attempt to speak to her?" Eliza asked. "If Indians can't speak English, you shouldn't bother."

Samantha frowned. "She's not stupid just because she doesn't speak English."

"She'll be difficult to civilize," Eliza said.

"Let's go," James Henry said. "Major Bliss will expect us."

The Taliaferros got back into the wagon, which followed Day Sets down the road to the agency. Samantha and James Henry walked toward the fort, which was as formidable from the ground as it was from the river below. Wagons rumbled up the road and through a warehouse door about halfway to the gates. Soldiers, Indians, and slaves scurried to and fro. Everyone had a task and hurried to complete it.

When James Henry had said he needed to come to Fort Snelling on business, Samantha begged to come along. An extra room for Samantha was available in the officer's quarters next to him, so he agreed. Now they approached the sally port on the western wall, where a boy, maybe eight or nine, raced past the Officer of the Day who waited for them.

"Welcome to Fort Snelling," the boy said. His voice rang with authority. "I am John Bliss. My father is the commandant. I have an Indian pony, a double-barreled gun, my own dugout and fishing pole, and two squirrels."

"All that and squirrels, too? I'm impressed," Samantha said. She smiled. John Bliss clearly had the curiosity of a small boy but the responsibility of a young man.

"My father says you're to come to the house," John Bliss announced and ran off.

The Officer of the Day headed in the same direction at a more reasonable speed, and they followed him past the barracks and offices. The store was just to Samantha's left as they walked to the right of the diamond-shaped parade ground to the commandant's house. She couldn't see anyone near the store, and turned her attention to the house, which occupied the point of the diamond farthest from the fort's gate. The commandant's house, built of yellow dressed stone, gave off an imposing air with its tall facade. Young John Bliss had disappeared.

Samantha tried to put her mind to the near future, to meeting Major Bliss and his wife, to living at the fort while James Henry completed his business, but her thoughts kept returning of their own volition to Alexander Miree's laughing smile. It was impossible to fall in love at first sight! He would only be someone to distract her brother's matrimonial intentions away from James Churchman or Jefferson Davis, someone to buy her the time to make her own choice.

Major Bliss stood outside the commandant's house, and his wife greeted them in the hall. They all went into the parlor.

"Thank you for inviting us to stay with you, Mrs. Bliss," Samantha said.

"Please, call me Olive. It's a pleasure to have another lady to talk to," Mrs. Bliss said. She resumed her seat and patted the spot next to her. "What a lovely brooch that is."

Samantha touched the amethyst flower as she sat down. "Thank you. It was my mother's."

"How was your journey upriver?"

Samantha said, "The surrounding country is beautiful, and we had a smooth trip. I'm sure it's much faster and easier than traveling overland."

"I'm curious why you wanted to come to Fort Snelling with your brother, Miss Lockwood," Olive said. "His business here doesn't involve you, surely?"

"Please call me Samantha. No, I'm not part of his business," Samantha said. "I haven't been to Fort Snelling yet and want to see everything I can in the territory. I plan to visit the Falls of St. Anthony while I'm here, and maybe Major Taliaferro will take me to see Cloud Man's village. I'd love to see it since he's spoken of teaching the Indians to farm with such pride."

"Oh, the falls are just lovely. We will have to arrange a day trip." Olive sipped her tea, holding the cup in both hands. The remainder of the conversation centered on discussion of the Falls of St. Anthony and other scenic places in the area. No mention was made of visiting Cloud Man's village.

The men came inside, and the entire party surrounded the supper table. Olive Bliss instructed Hannibal to bring in the meal. The Black man served them prairie chicken, fish, and vegetables from the fort's garden. Afterwards, he brought a lovely chess pie. Samantha ate silently, letting the men talk of treaties and traders, and of how best to interact with the Dakota, Fox, and other tribes.

At nine o'clock sharp, the fort's band played several popular tunes, after which the inhabitants of Fort Snelling took to their beds. Samantha, tired after her journey and the excitement of arrival, fell asleep despite the unfamiliar noises in the unfamiliar house.

Just as the first rays of sunlight peeked over the walls, the drums and fifes began marching the circuit of the parade ground and awakening the entire fort. Samantha stretched as she sat up in bed, then dressed while the fort came alive with men's conversations, shouts, and footsteps. She ate a breakfast of bread and dinner leftovers with Olive Bliss and her son as the soldiers ate in their barracks. The men had already breakfasted and were off to conduct business. Not long after Hannibal cleared the meal, he announced a visit from Ann Taylor Wood to see Samantha.

Sarah's sister waited outside with her two small sons. After exchanging introductory greetings, Ann said, "I need a few things from the sutler this morning. Samantha, would you like to join us?"

Samantha stared at her. She knew Ann had responded to Sarah's original letter, and Sarah had written to tell Ann of this trip. "That would be lovely." Samantha tied her bonnet with its purple ribbons, took her leave of Mrs. Bliss, and followed Ann out the door. Ann's boys cavorted around them.

"I thought if I went with you, a visit to the sutler wouldn't be awkward," Ann said. "I do need some things, too. My husband has learned that he will be transferred to Fort Crawford as soon as a replacement surgeon arrives. I'm excited to join my parents, Sarah, and the little ones, but the cholera is bad there. Is it not?"

Samantha said, "It is terrible around Prairie du Chien, but no one I know has succumbed. The residents will welcome

Dr. Wood." She was excited for her friend, who would welcome Ann and her family with open arms.

They crossed the road and entered the store. The one-story stone building had windows on either side of the door, but inside the light was dim. Shelves, drawers, and bins lined the walls, much like her brother's store in Prairie du Chien. Long counters ran the length of the store. Pickles, dried apples, raisins, butter, cheese, eggs, coffee, and tea lined the walls. The sutler also carried alcohol and tobacco products as well as home goods like pins and needles, thread and scissors.

"Good morning, Mr. Miree!" Ann said with robust cheer. "This is a visitor from Prairie du Chien . . ."

"Good morning, Mrs. Wood. Ah, Miss Lockwood," he said. "So nice to see you again. May I inquire after your brother, James Henry?"

Samantha's breathing quickened as his smile captured her, even as her mind said to stop being silly. "He is fine, Mr. Miree. Thank you for inquiring. I believe he will come by to see you soon."

"How long will you be visiting?" he asked.

"I'm uncertain how long my brother's business will require his presence here," Samantha said.

"I can only hope he runs into complications that prolong your visit," the sutler said with a smile before he left her side to assist Ann.

Ann perused the household items and sewing notions on the shelves, making careful selections to avoid packing too many new purchases for her move. Samantha put a coin on the counter and helped herself to two hard candies that she handed to the boys. They popped them in their mouths and went to sit near the iron stove.

"Look, Samantha," Ann called. "Mr. Miree has lovely fabric." She held up a length of cotton fabric in a light shade of lavender. "And matching ribbon," Ann added, holding up the ribbon.

"I won't be here long enough to sew, Ann," Samantha said. "Thank you, Mr. Miree, but no." She tugged the purple ribbons on her bonnet.

"You like the color, I take it?" He grinned as she hastily clasped her hands, but an awkward silence followed. He said, "So you've been in the territory a month or so now. How do you like it?" His interest seemed genuine.

"It's lovely," she said. "I enjoy helping James Henry in the store and knitting in front of the fire on cool nights." Her mouth widened into a grin that appeared too eager, but she was powerless to change it.

"Summer nights are still cold here in the north," he said. He walked to the end of the counter and put something in a bag. "Here's a bit of tea, a new kind from England. Try it and let me know how you like it."

"Thank you, Mr. Miree." Samantha took the little bag and smiled. "You're too kind."

"Despite what they all say, you mean?"

Samantha's grin faded and she stared. It was just a phrase people said. But there was a shadow in his eyes. She shook off a shiver of concern and forced a laugh.

They continued to make pleasant but awkward small talk while Ann shopped. When the words ran out, Ann had Mr. Miree wrap her purchases in paper and tie them with a string. Then the women collected the boys and left the store.

Samantha said, "What have you heard about Mr. Miree?"

Ann looked at her sharply. "What do you mean?"

"Oh, nothing, I suppose. He made a comment that implied he had a reputation of sorts."

Ann waved her hand. "No man is an angel. I'm sure it's nothing." But her eyes darted toward Samantha once more, and Samantha worried.

Activity at the fort's gate showed that a boat had arrived while they'd been shopping. Outside the commandant's house, Samantha said goodbye to Ann and the boys. Inside, she discovered the boat had brought a surprise for her, too. James Churchman and Sarah Taylor sat with Mrs. Bliss in her parlor, having tea and a pleasant conversation. Samantha's heart jumped to see James, and she smiled. Confused by her body's reaction, she turned to Sarah with a delighted exclamation of welcome. "What a wonderful surprise! You just missed Ann. She has news for you," Samantha said.

Sarah's eyes sparkled. "Mr. Churchman insisted on coming upriver to see the fort. I tagged along because I had important mail to deliver." She handed two envelopes to Samantha.

One was a letter from her mother. Samantha's first word from home. Heart pounding, she tucked the letter into her reticule to read later when she was alone. The other was for James Henry. The sender had written on the envelope with a feminine script.

"I'll take that." Her brother had come into the room while she greeted Sarah, and now held out his hand for the letter. He peered at it over the rim of his spectacles, then stuffed it in his pocket. "Just business," he said.

"Stuff and nonsense," Samantha muttered to herself. It didn't look like business to her. Curiosity piqued her. It wasn't Mother's handwriting. She knew of no women in his business world. Did her brother have a secret lady friend? Samantha smiled. Maybe she should push him to remarry and see what he said.

Her brother took James to see Major Bliss in his office. Mrs. Bliss said, "I've a few things to see to, and I'm sure you ladies would like to visit." She left the room, leaving Samantha and Sarah alone in the parlor.

"He couldn't catch a boat fast enough," Sarah said about James. "I had to come along." She laughed. "I may have said something about him needing a guide." Sarah turned to a topic of more personal interest. "Jeff's being considered for the First Dragoons." Her pride in the man she loved was clear.

"You deserve to be proud of Jeff," Samantha said. She drummed her fingers on her leg, her hand close to where Mama's letter burned a hole in her reticule. "So your father likes him more now?"

"Papa just doesn't want me to live at army posts like Ann or Mama. He wants better for me. How does he know what that is? I despair of convincing him I must marry Jeff."

"I know how you feel," Samantha said. "My father was so furious when I said no to James that he sent me to Prairie du Chien. Where can your father send you?" Her tone teased her friend.

"Ann's my only older sibling," Sarah said, "and she's close by."

"We must look out for each other," Samantha said. She reached for Sarah's hand.

"Yes, we must," Sarah agreed, squeezing her hand.

Hannibal entered and placed a tea tray on the table. He poured tea for both women, who smiled their thanks. James Henry and James returned with Major Bliss. James smiled at Samantha, and she smiled in response. Hannibal poured tea for the men and left the room. James Henry and James joined Samantha and Sarah.

"Is anyone else sick with cholera?" Samantha asked. "I know Ann worries about that and I can't reassure her. It was bad when we left to come up here."

Sarah's smile faded. "Four citizens and two soldiers died this week. Last month recruits arrived at Fort Crawford and were quarantined even though they weren't sick. The tribes in the area are hard hit, too. Ann and the boys will need to stay apart from all but family. Her husband will treat the sick, of course, but he doesn't want to risk any of his family."

"That makes perfect sense. I hope it runs its course soon. There's no cholera here at Fort Snelling, but I plan to stay close to home once we return to Prairie du Chien," Samantha said.

James said, "The Indians at Fort Crawford are just beggars now. They're wearing cast-off clothes and clutching loose blankets. The cholera has taken so many it's left a motley group of survivors."

James Henry winced.

"I'm sorry, James Henry. I know you try to help them," Samantha said. She sipped her tea after giving her brother a sympathetic smile.

James Henry said, "I've been advising the Indians, trying to prepare them for the treaty talks at Fort Dearborn this September. It will be a big gathering, with thousands of Indians attending."

"What's the gathering about?" Samantha asked.

"Land. It's always about land," James Henry said. "The government will want every inch of land the Dakota value, and give them next to nothing for it. Or worse, the government will promise money they'll never deliver. I know Lawrence has trouble with the dichotomy of serving a government that doesn't look out for the Sioux, while doing a job that supports the Sioux. It's not easy."

Major Bliss had been sitting apart from the others, and a quiet word from him now drew James Henry and James over to him.

"So tell me about your sutler," Sarah said in a low voice. She settled back into her chair with her own teacup, as if preparing for a long tale.

Samantha smiled. "He's very nice. Your sister had me accompany her to the store today."

They laughed together at Ann's obvious matchmaking.

"What do you know about him?" Sarah asked.

Samantha hesitated, remembering his odd remark about what people said. "Not much. I know he used to trap with the

Indians before he was appointed postmaster at the fort, and now he's sutler, too."

"The Indians believe that by being at the fort they will earn the favor of the government," Sarah said. "You know, the sutler position is a good one. He's protected by the fort, pays no rent, and has none of the expenses of a storekeeper like James Henry. It's a great advantage. I think Mr. Miree should try to hold on to the position, but many powerful men are angling for the appointment. James Henry says American Fur Company traders have their eye on it. I'll say my prayers for Mr. Miree, though." She winked at Samantha, who blushed again and looked at the ground.

The men looked up from their conversation across the room and James said, "We've persuaded Major Bliss to lead a trip to the Falls of St. Anthony for all of us."

"That sounds nice," Samantha said. She gave James such a delighted smile that his face glowed with pleasure, causing Sarah to hide her grin with her hand.

Mrs. Bliss returned with Hannibal and announced that she'd readied rooms near James Henry and Samantha for James and Sarah.

It wasn't until after supper that Samantha could retire. She leaned close to the tallow candles on her bedside table and took out Mama's letter.

My dear daughter,

I do hope you are getting on well, my dear. I miss you dreadfully and I know your father does, too, even though he won't say so. He's just told me that Mr. Churchman has undertaken the journey to Prairie du Chien intending to pursue you. He's a lovely man, Samantha. I hope you are able to see him with fresh eyes so you may assess him for yourself apart from your father's regard. You may not believe it, but your father

wants you happily married to a man with the means to make
you comfortable. He is poor at expressing his love, I know, and
is prone to ranting and making hasty decisions. Please know
that you have our love always.

As if that was enough said, Mama went on in a chatty tone
to talk of Samantha's siblings, the neighbors, and even the farm.
Before she finished reading, Samantha's cheeks were tear-damp-
ened. "Oh, Mama," she said out loud, "I do miss you."

But Mama had said nothing when Samantha stood up to
her father and refused to marry James Churchman. She'd said
nothing when Papa flew into a rage and declared Samantha was
unwelcome in her own home and she must go to James Henry.
Mama had no words of consolation as she helped Samantha pack
her things in silence. Samantha clutched her amethyst brooch
as if it was the only tie to a past that loved her, a past she may
never see again.

CHAPTER 9:

May, 1834
St. Peter's Agency, Michigan Territory

❦

HARRIET

Harriet, Ellie, and Hannah approached the stone agency house, passing the two-story council house with scars of a fire covered by the beginnings of repairs.

Ellie said. "The master meets with the Indians at the council house. Last year one tried to burn it down. Master prob'ly have the Indians in the house now." She shrugged.

Harriet looked at the burned part of the building and shivered at the idea of Indians in the house.

"This where the major told me to go," Hannah said. "Mr. Campbell and his family still living here while the house's being repaired. I'll cook."

"We'll see you sometimes," Ellie promised.

Hannah nodded and walked toward the back of the building, lumbering from one tired foot to another.

"Will we?" Harriet asked.

Ellie furrowed her brow.

"Will we see her?"

"The major rents his slaves to others." She shrugged. "Makes more money that way than selling us. Hannah be around. You'll see."

Harriet followed as Ellie resumed walking. She was no stranger to white people wanting to make money more than anything else. She knew about them selling people, but she'd never heard of renting people.

A fence enclosed the agency house and grounds, including the council house. It would keep the livestock in, but Harriet hoped it would also keep trouble out. The stone house had four rooms and a basement kitchen. Four pairs of windows flanked the door, and a chimney rose on either end. It should have been an impressive place, but it needed a lot of work. It certainly wasn't the most impressive home Harriet had seen.

Thomas and William unloaded the wagon in the yard. They unhitched the horse and led it on toward the stables. Disappointment flooded Harriet when Thomas didn't look back at her. Then she was angry with herself for being disappointed. She had no intention of encouraging him.

"They sleep with the livestock," Ellie said. "We sleep on pallets in the kitchen."

Harriet nodded in approval. "Where it's warm."

Mrs. Taliaferro appeared in the doorway. "Ellie, please make up the bed before you show the new girl how to beat the rug." She went back inside.

"I know how to beat a rug," Harriet said. It was true that she had been a laundress, not a house slave. That didn't mean she was ignorant of household tasks.

"Of course you do," Ellie said.

On the trip up from St. Louis, Mrs. Taliaferro made it clear that her husband had been living as a frontier bachelor and that would now change. Now she bustled through the house, telling the enslaved what to do with the furniture. Nero ran between rooms, wagging his tail and enjoying the flurry.

Usually working with the laundry, Harriet was new to being a house slave. She would take her cues from Ellie, who had been part of Major Taliaferro's household a long time, through winters in the territory and summers in the east. Ellie and Harriet went upstairs to the master's bedroom. Their first task was to stretch new hemp rope across the wooden bedstead. Then they laid the mattress on it and spread the blankets they'd retrieved from the wagon.

Nero barked at Ellie. She turned to the big black dog and scolded him. "No food for you if you going to order me around like a master."

The dog wagged his tail and looked hopefully at Harriet.

She loved dogs and reached out to pat his big head. "As soon as I can, handsome boy," Harriet promised him.

While they worked, Ellie instructed Harriet. "Mrs. Taliaferro demands tidiness. We'll take messages to the fort for Mrs. Bliss, the commandant's wife, or go to the store there for something or other." Ellie paused and leaned toward Harriet. "Don't get too friendly with the soldiers. Major Bliss's high yellow girl, Fanny, had so many admirers hanging around the kitchen her master sold her downriver to St. Louis."

Downriver. Back into slave territory. Harriet nodded. Do your work and nothing more. This, she already knew. She thought of the Indians in the nearby tipis, working for themselves and laughing while they did it. Harriet tugged the coverlet over her side of the bed. Ellie gave her an approving nod.

When they finished the bed, Ellie led Harriet to the basement kitchen. A large brick hearth, blackened from years of use, dominated the room. A wrought iron crane held an empty pot over the cold fireplace. Ellie set about making a fire with the pieces of oak logs stacked in a nook near the hearth. Harriet knew it would take days to build up a decent layer of coals for baking. It would be her job to bank the fire each evening and tend it in the morning. A scarred wooden work table sat along one wall, below shelves filled with crocks and jars. A rack held dried herbs and pots hung on hooks near the fireplace. Harriet saw rolled up pallets that she'd spread on the uneven brick floor near the fire at bedtime.

Nero padded behind them, light on his feet for a dog that weighed over a hundred pounds. He whimpered and sat up straight, staring at a crock on the shelf. Ellie laughed. "Some pieces of dried horse meat in there for the dog."

Harriet laughed and lifted the lid. Nero drooled and wagged his tail. She gave him one of the pieces of meat, and he bounded up the stairs to eat it in the yard.

Ellie said, "The master and mistress stay at the fort tonight but they'll want tea before they go. The house need to be ready tomorrow."

The ceiling of the kitchen, which was the floor of the parlor, consisted of wooden planks spaced to allow for easing and expanding according to the weather. A rug covered the floor upstairs. Harriet could hear Major Taliaferro's deep voice as he conversed with his wife. He walked across the floor, and dust rained down upon Harriet.

"No matter how much you beat that rug, it still finds dust," Ellie said. "At least we can always hear interesting conversations through the floor." She smiled at Harriet and her eyes twinkled. She pointed to the storage room. "We can hear the dining room conversation from there."

Harriet smiled. "Important to know what's going on."

Ellie had Harriet take the tea tray upstairs. First, though, she used her hand to brush down Harriet's thin cotton dress, its tattered hem barely reaching the girl's ankles. Self-conscious, Harriet tugged the dress down. "You'll need a warmer dress before winter," Ellie said.

Harriet, carrying the tray carefully with both hands, nodded and walked up the kitchen stairs, out the door, and into the yard. Along the outside wall, she saw a bench stacked with large laundry tubs. That, at least, was familiar. Harriet carried the tray to the house's back door, suspecting by the time winter fell in earnest, she would wish for a convenient door from the kitchen to the main floor. Ellie followed her and opened the door. Nero slipped past Harriet into the house. Harriet walked in, put the tray on the table, and curtsied. "Will there be anything else, Missus?"

Mrs. Taliaferro sat in a large chair by the fireplace. A painting of an ancestor of his hung on the wall. Mrs. Taliaferro's piano sat against one wall. The mistress looked up, but her gaze cut straight through Harriet as if she wasn't there. "Ellie, serve the tea. And in the mornings I'd like you to attend me."

Ellie looked only at their mistress. "Yes, ma'am." She poured the tea for the major and his wife, who resumed their conversation. Harriet returned to the kitchen, exhaling with a bit of relief. Not used to waiting on the mistress of the house, she preferred the kitchen and doing the laundry.

After tea, the Taliaferros left in the wagon for the fort. Harriet and Ellie moved the furniture, rolled up the rug, and took it outside to beat as clean as they could. After laying it on the floor and returning the furniture to its place, they cleaned and straightened the rest of the house and made a dinner of stale cornbread and bacon. Harriet worked alongside Ellie without complaint. By the time they sat down to dinner, she felt she'd earned Ellie's smile of acceptance.

Thomas and William joined Ellie and Harriet at the kitchen work table for the meal. They talked about working in the stable and in the fort's corn and wheat fields, and caught up on news from people they knew who'd passed by.

"You know Hannibal at the fort?" Thomas said.

"Hannibal? Major Bliss's boy?" Ellie said.

Thomas nodded. "Yes. He brewed a vat of spruce beer this past winter and sold it to the soldiers. The sutler returned this morning and went to Major Bliss in a rage."

"What happened?" Ellie asked. She explained to Harriet, "Only the store can sell alcohol."

"Major Bliss put him in the Black Hole for two days."

Harriet raised her eyebrows at Ellie, who said, "Not in the ground. A dark cell in the guardhouse Major Bliss likes to use to punish the soldiers."

"And for us," Thomas said. He winked at Harriet and gave her a small smile.

Harriet felt a thrill at the attention, but it made her nervous, too. "Why is the sutler the only one who can sell alcohol to the soldiers?" Harriet asked Ellie, keeping her eyes off Thomas.

"The soldiers walk on eggshells around the tribes. Fur traders soothe ruffled feathers then stir them all up again," Ellie said. "Alcohol makes troubles worse. That's why the sutler controls the sale."

"What about slaves?"

"We do what we are told and hope our masters make the right decisions."

"But I thought when a slave crossed into free territory they were free," Harriet said. She ducked her head in embarrassment when the others laughed.

"Honey, there's no magic in a territorial line," Thomas said. "The regiment comes from the South. All the officers have slaves."

Harriet warmed at the endearment. She had hoped life would be different in a free territory. What folly to think she'd be free when she stepped off the boat in Michigan territory.

Over the next few weeks, it became clear that Mrs. Taliaferro preferred Ellie and kept her busy with tasks. As a result, Harriet spent most of her time doing laundry and serving the major's guests, which suited her just fine. Part of her responsibility included taking Nero out of the room when the master was meeting with dignitaries, so she and the dog became great friends.

In the evening, the Taliaferros sat in the parlor beside the fire. The major told his wife of the day's events while she knitted. His words traveled through the floorboards into the kitchen below. As a result, Harriet soon became knowledgeable about the local squabbles between soldiers, Indians, and traders.

One evening, she worked in the kitchen kneading dough to rise overnight for tomorrow's bread. Her ears perked up when she heard her master mention the chief, Hole in the Day, to his wife.

"Yes," Mrs. Taliaferro said, "I saw the Ojibwe delegation in their birchbark dugouts."

Mr. Taliaferro nodded. "Hole in the Day told me his tribe hunted with the Dakota near Lac qui Parle and shared meat. When most of the Ojibwe had left to return home, the Dakota killed the remainder. The Ojibwe demanded to kill an equal number of the Dakota tribe to make fair restitution."

"That's a normal reaction. He must have expected you to do something different or he wouldn't have brought it to you."

"Very astute, my dear. The chief said Joe Renville was there."

In the kitchen, Harriet shrugged her shoulders at Ellie.

"An important trader," Ellie said. "He a *métis* half breed, French and Indian. Has a big family at the trading post near

Laq qui Parle." She shushed Harriet's response so they could hear more.

"Hole in the Day suggested the Ojibwe land be officially marked off to avoid war. To avenge this incident, he wanted a Dakota man killed for every Ojibwe man that died. Well, I couldn't do that. I agreed to have the surveyor mark off Ojibwe borders, and I plied Hole in the Day with blankets and tobacco. That seemed to pacify him for the moment."

"You said nothing about Mr. Renville?"

The master laughed, shifting position in his chair and causing dust to rain down in the kitchen. Harriet leaned forward to cover the bread with her apron.

"I told Hole in the Day that this was a serious incident for Renville to witness."

Ellie told Harriet, "Indians count on traders for goods they can't get nowhere else, guns, gunpowder, cooking pots, and such. You know, it's too bad the original treaty, with the Dakota and Fox, has never been completed."

"What do you mean?" Harriet asked.

"Major Taliaferro says the government will survey Indian lands, but the government's sent no one to do it like the treaty says, and it's going on ten years."

Harriet nodded, her mind whirling. Treating the Indians fairly must be difficult if the government made promises they didn't keep. It was like being enslaved, only on a larger scale. When Mr. Dillon had been her master, he'd made empty promises. And the government made empty promises to the Indians. Maybe they weren't so different, Indians and slaves.

CHAPTER 10:

June, 1834
St. Peter's Agency, Michigan Territory

HARRIET

Harriet opened the agency's door to receive Major Bliss. She led him to the front room that her master used as an office. The captain brushed past her to enter the room. Nero's tail thumped the floor as he lay by the fireplace.

"Major Bliss." The major leapt to his feet and held out his hand to shake. "Harriet, bring the decanter," he said. She scurried to get the master's whiskey and two glasses from the sideboard.

Major Taliaferro led his guest to the chairs before the fireplace. "What can I do for you today?"

Harriet had noted the urgency of the captain's entrance, and the way he now held his hat in one hand and smoothed his hair with the other. She hurried downstairs where she and Ellie could listen. Harriet could've stayed in the room, invisible as always, and heard the conversation, but she preferred to listen from downstairs where Ellie could answer her questions.

"They say they want to devote their lives to the Indians," Major Bliss was saying. "I demanded they come to the fort and show me passports or any other authority for entering Indian country. They had nothing but a letter from an Illinois preacher."

"The law requires missionaries to obtain permission from Washington to preach to the Indians," Major Taliaferro said.

"They're brothers. Samuel and Gideon Pond. Unordained, but righteous. Very sincere. What am I to do with them?"

Harriet could hear the captain's heavy boots pace the room. Dirt rained down through the floor, but she and Ellie were ready, holding pot lids over their heads.

"Are they hard workers, do you think?"

"They sure want to be."

Major Taliaferro hesitated, then said, "I may have a solution for you. Little Crow has asked several times to be given farming equipment like Cloud Man. I gave him a plow and a team of oxen. The stubborn Sioux is too proud to admit he doesn't know how to use it."

Both men chuckled.

"Why does he call them Sioux when others say Dakota?" Harriet asked Ellie.

Ellie frowned. "Because he don't know better. Sioux means 'little snakes' in Ojibwe. It's not a nice term. The Dakota never call themselves Sioux. Or Indians, for that matter. Around here, they are Mdewakanton."

Harriet nodded. She repeated the word to herself so she wouldn't forget it.

"Little Crow is a very proud man," Major Bliss said.

"So what if you sent the Pond brothers to Little Crow's village at Kaposia? If you treat them as help sent from the government, then Little Crow's pride is intact, and they still begin farming."

"Excellent idea." Major Bliss stopped pacing. "That means the trip is off. Judge Lockwood is here with some guests. They want to visit the Falls of St. Anthony. I agreed to escort them, but I have to get these brothers settled."

"Hmmmm. I can take a day for the trip. My wife and I would be happy to escort the Lockwood party to the falls."

"That would be wonderful, Major. Thank you."

"And Captain? If the Pond brothers don't work out at Kaposia, I can take them to Cloud Man."

Amid the captain's noises of affirmation, the two men made their way to the front door.

Harriet and Ellie turned back to the day's baking. Harriet took two bake kettles with loaves of bread off the coals while Ellie rolled out the biscuits.

"Wouldn't it be nice to take a day off to visit the falls?" Harriet asked. She imagined the boat trip upriver, the beauty of nature, the sound of the falls. Thinking about the relaxed attitude of taking her own time to enjoy the day as she chose made her sigh.

"No taking days off around here. You know that." Ellie's words were firm but kind.

Harriet nodded, but her imagination conjured dresses she would wear on a holiday trip and happy relaxed people who would accompany her. She hummed as she worked. Ellie shook her head, but smiled.

When six loaves of bread and two dozen biscuits were cooling on the table, Ellie poured them each a cup of tea. By Harriet's reckoning, they had a scant ten minutes before they needed to fix dinner as well as a tea tray for the mistress. As if summoned, the mistress's voice came through the floorboards.

"What? A trip to the falls?"

It was clear from the strident tone that Mrs. Taliaferro did not approve of the planned trip.

"Now, Eliza, it's not a backwoods adventure. Miss Lockwood would appreciate another woman along, I'm sure."

"And the trip is tomorrow? Rather short notice."

"Her friend, Miss Taylor, is visiting, as well as Miss Lockwood's young man. Major Bliss wanted to escort them, but he's been called away."

"Oh, Lawrence, Judge Lockwood is capable of taking his group to the falls. It's not as if one needs a guide," Mrs. Taliaferro said.

"Miss Taylor is the daughter of the regimental commanding officer. I'm sure you'd like to meet her. There aren't many ladies in the territory, after all." The major's voice cajoled his wife with expertise.

Ellie snorted and said to Harriet, "Plenty women in the territory. Just not white women."

"Shhh," Harriet said. The major's attempt to convince his wife to go on the trip fascinated her.

"Very well," the mistress said. "I will accompany you."

Harriet turned to Ellie in surprise. Ellie shrugged and said, "He knows what makes her tick."

THE NEXT MORNING WAS full of flurry as the master and mistress prepared to depart for the fort where they would meet the rest of their party and board the boat taking them upriver. Nero knew a trip was coming, and he ran around the yard barking until Major Taliaferro ordered him to get in the wagon.

"So much fuss for a day trip," Harriet marveled. "They don't need to stay overnight or cook anything." She shook her head and tsked.

Ellie just smiled.

The house was quiet. It wasn't often that both the master and mistress were absent, so Ellie and Harriet took advantage of the time to deep clean and finish the laundry. Harriet was in the yard behind the house, boiling the sheets from her master's bed, when a large Black man appeared. He was dressed in clothes that were part Indian and part trader. When he spoke, his accented English surprised Harriet, and she wondered what language he had learned at his mother's knee.

"Good morning," he said. "Is the major at home?"

With no idea who he was, Harriet didn't know whether to curtsy and invite him into the parlor or just take him to Ellie in the kitchen. "No, sir, he is away."

He smiled. "I'm Stephen Bonga. Used to work for American Fur Company, but now I interpret Ojibwe and Dakota for the soldiers and whoever else needs me. I hear there are some new white men in the area?"

"Oh, yes! You must mean the Pond brothers." She smiled. "I'm Harriet."

Ellie came out of the kitchen with several shirts of the master's to launder. Her face lit up when she saw the man talking to Harriet. "Stephen! Nice to see you! How's that beautiful wife of yours? Those gorgeous children?"

He laughed. "Just fine, Ellie. Happy to see you're still around. I wondered, when I saw Harriet here."

Harriet knew he meant sold downriver. It was the worst thing that could happen to a Black person at Fort Snelling.

Ellie turned to Harriet. "Stephen was born near here. His father's a freed slave and his mother Indian. He and his brothers work for American Fur." She turned back to Stephen. "How are George and Jack?"

"We're all fine, Ellie. We're the first white men born in the territory, Harriet." He laughed.

"Oh stop," Ellie chided. She explained to Harriet, "The Indians call anyone who isn't one of them white."

"Can you ladies tell me about these new men bringing the Word of God to our tribes?"

Ellie filled the visitor in on what little they knew of the Pond brothers. "They prob'ly need you," she said. "A new white man at the fort, too, the sutler. You know Mr. Miree?"

"Miree? Isn't he the one the Dakota call Pale Crow? He's decided to be a white man again?" He laughed and shook his head. "Wonder how long that will last. Well, nice meeting you, Harriet. I'll be off to Kaposia to see if I can help the Pond brothers. Next time, Ellie." He tipped his hat to both women and walked toward the fort.

Across the yard, Thomas stood near the stable, staring at Harriet. Was he jealous? A shiver of delight tickled her spine. She waved, but Thomas turned away and walked into the stable.

"What did Mr. Bonga mean about Mr. Miree deciding to be a white man?" Harriet asked, her eyes on the empty stableyard.

"Mr. Miree has, um, close ties with the Indians. I don't spread rumors, and I don't know the facts." Ellie pursed her lips.

Harriet pulled the bedding out of the big iron pot and beat it with a big paddle to remove some of the soap. Ellie helped her roll the laundry into a pot of clear water to boil it again. Harriet couldn't stop thinking about the big Black freed man.

"Ellie," she said, "why do masters free slaves? I mean, if they need them, they need them, right?"

"Major Taliaferro says he'll free us," Ellie said.

"I haven't heard that. Why don't he just do it?" Harriet still struggled with the idea of being a slave in a free territory.

"The master born in Virginia. Slavery been a big part of his life. Now he rents slaves to make some money. A white man don't give up money even for what's right."

They wrung out the boiled sheets and hung them to dry, flapping in the breeze like tethered wings.

"This territory's an odd place to be a slave," Harriet said.

"Don't get me wrong, it's better than where I was, but it teases me with freedom."

Ellie shrugged. "It's one thing to see freedom on the horizon and another thing to reach it. Many men in the territory own slaves. Others, like Judge Lockwood, come from northern states, where slavery is illegal. They know how to get along without a slave."

Harriet nodded. "I was born in Virginia as a slave, but at the Dillon home in Pennsylvania, children born to slaves was free. I didn't really see any difference between me and the other slaves' children until I was older."

They worked a while longer in silence.

"We'll make a simple supper tonight," Ellie said. "If you make cornbread, I'll be back to help with a stew in just a bit." Ellie untied her apron and patted her hair into place. "Get Thomas or William to help you with those big tubs."

"Where are you going?" Harriet asked, her mind already on fetching Thomas from the stable.

"I have an errand at the fort." Ellie gave her a nervous smile and walked off in the direction Stephen Bonga had taken a few hours ago.

An errand? Ellie's words puzzled Harriet. Maybe Ellie was meeting Stephen for a secret rendezvous. She smiled to herself and let her imagination run away as she pictured Ellie and the Black man in a torrid affair.

Ellie returned an hour later with a small brown bottle. Harriet asked if she'd been to the sutler's.

"Just picked up a tonic from the doc." Ellie didn't meet Harriet's eyes. Her hands trembled as she stirred the stew. "The sutler wasn't there and the store was closed. Hannibal say Mr. Miree joined the party going to the falls at the last minute. He also say Mr. Miree's sweet on Miss Lockwood."

"Mr. Miree with his close ties to Indians?" Harriet frowned. She was less interested in the sutler, though, than she was in his freedom of movement. Imagine being able to shut your business and take off for the day to do whatever you desired.

CHAPTER 11:

July 1834
Falls of St. Anthony, Michigan Territory

❦

SAMANTHA

Since Major Bliss was unable to accompany the party to the falls on the chosen day, his wife stayed behind with him. Lawrence and Eliza Taliaferro agreed at a moment's notice to join the group's adventure. The group gathered early in the morning on the dock, where a small steamboat waited to take them upriver. Nero bounded along beside them, ready for any adventure. To Samantha's surprise, Alexander Miree also waited on the dock.

What was it about the cocky tilt of that man's head, and his slow smile, that made her heart skip a beat? He held a battered hat in his outdoor-roughened hands. His shaggy blond hair curled a bit over his ears, but his side whiskers were well trimmed. He wore rumpled clothes, but he smiled at her with true affection that drew her own smile and put a flutter in her stomach.

"Good morning," he called to Lawrence. "Mind if I join you? I could use an excursion, and it promises to be a slow day at the store."

Lawrence said, "The more the merrier. Come along, Mr. Miree."

Samantha caught Sarah smirking at her. "A day with both your suitors? This should be fun," Sarah teased in a low voice. Samantha wrinkled her nose at her friend.

The party got underway with the rumbling growl of the steam engine and answering puffs of smoke from the stacks. The Mississippi River wound around sparsely wooded islands and glinted silver in the sun. Massive bluffs reached for the sky. Indians paddled dugouts in the shallows, and their villages dotted the shore.

James Churchman came to stand next to Samantha at the railing. "Beautiful view," he said.

Samantha turned to face him, words of agreement dying on her lips as she realized he was looking at her, not the river valley. She turned back to the river. "James Henry told stories of the wild beauty of this land long before I came out to join him. He wasn't wrong. I've even gotten used to the mud."

"I remember being at a Lockwood family dinner when James Henry was visiting. No one could get a word in edgewise as he extolled the virtues of these panoramic views."

"My father . . ." Samantha began. She intended to say he'd be happy they were being friendly, but James cut her off.

He raised his hand between them, index finger out, and shook his head. "We won't discuss your father today," he said.

Samantha paused. She said, "All right then, tell me about your plans for the future." She said, pretending to interrogate him as a potential suitor.

James laughed. "I'm a lawyer. As civilization grows out here, the territory will need lawyers. Surely, your brother has told you that?"

His laugh made her feel warm inside, but not tingly like Alexander's. "Yes," she said, "he is a firm believer in the growth and success of this area. He talks about statehood." She shook her head. "That's pretty far off, though."

"Michigan Territory is huge. When the government makes states, the land will be broken up into smaller territories, providing an opportunity for justices."

"You want to become a judge?"

"It's a long-term goal." He grinned at her. "Your brother advises me to become a circuit judge for the name exposure that traveling around the region will give me. When it comes time to appoint a new chief justice, my name will come up. That's the goal."

Impressed with his vision, Samantha said, "I wish you the best."

"I could do worse than follow James Henry Lockwood into a career. His own mentor, James Doty, was just elected to the territorial legislative council. Meanwhile, Joe Rolette was elected pound master." He laughed. "King Rolette in charge of stray animals!"

Samantha smiled. "He's long been my brother's nemesis."

"Enough about politics. Tell me all about your time at Fort Snelling."

She told him about the Taliaferros and the agency house, about Ann Wood and her family, about Major Bliss and his family, and even about wanting to visit Day Sets at the Indian village. His smile may not set her heart aflutter, but it felt natural to talk to him like this. She did not mention Alexander Miree.

The boat docked on the west side of the river at the government sawmill, a small operation that had been in place and protected by Fort Snelling for over a decade. The party disembarked and walked to the falls. In the distance, Samantha could see a group of Indian women gathering something from dugouts in the shallows of the river. She could feel the pounding of the falls through the ground beneath her feet before she could see more than mist over the treetops. Then they rounded the headland, and the majesty of the falls spread before them. More water than Samantha had ever seen in one place plunged over the cliff to the river below.

It was a place that took her breath away. The roar of the falls overtook the beat of her heart and mesmerized her. This may not be the source of the mighty river, but this was its heart. The magnitude of its splendor continued as it had since the dawn of time, rushing with purpose past whatever paltry efforts humans made on its banks, intent on its journey downriver. A millennia of women echoed in the mist, women who had gathered food or washed in the river, women who had cried in passion, pain, or pleasure and added their tears to the river.

Her brother touched her elbow and broke Samantha's reverie. He led her away from the water's edge. "We have picnic lunch laid out," he said once she could hear his voice. "We'll have time to look more later."

The party came together as they walked back toward the sawmill. Eliza detached herself from the group. Lawrence followed her. Sarah, James Henry, and James were already walking toward the sawmill and lunch. Alexander Miree took advantage of the opportunity to drop back and speak to Samantha alone.

"When you return to Prairie du Chien, I'll miss our talks," he said. "Some days we talk of the weather, some days about your family. I remember conversations about nothing and conversations of import. I enjoy that."

Samantha had grown comfortable talking to him and liked their daily chats, too. Now she realized how much she would miss them. She'd been so caught up in James and relating the events of her visit that she hadn't taken a moment to listen to her heart. She'd gone to Fort Snelling with ideas of a fairy tale romance dancing in her head. Reality had surprised her. It may have lacked the dashing nature of a fairy tale, but there was no denying the attraction she felt. "To be honest, I will miss our talks, too, Mr. Miree."

"We've spoken together enough that you can call me Alex," he said.

"I will, Alex." Samantha smiled. "Please call me Samantha."

In her mind, he bowed and kissed her hand. That's how romantic the day suddenly became. They walked in companionable silence for a few steps. The sun glinted off the falls and highlighted the sawmill's rough buildings. Samantha imagined a life in this beautiful, wild land, a life with Alex. He was as unpredictable as the territory itself. He would never be boring.

"Samantha, I haven't planned this well. As you may have discovered, I'm rather impulsive. The truth is, I will miss more than our chats. I will miss you." He paused. "I'll just say it. I want you to be part of my life, to live with me and be my partner. Will you marry me, Samantha?"

She gasped at the suddenness of his proposal, but at the same time, a warmth spread from her heart. She placed her hand over that warmth, covering her brooch. "Aren't you supposed to get down on one knee?" she teased.

He took her hand and turned her to face him. Then he dropped to one knee. "Samantha Lockwood, will you do me the honor of becoming my wife? Is that better?"

She laughed and squeezed his hand. "That's better." She looked at his beaming face and smiled. He made her feel good. More importantly, her father had never met him. Alex would be her own choice. But in reality, the choice wasn't hers alone. "You must convince my brother, who will feel the need to stand in for my father. James Henry will say it's too soon. I barely know you."

He stood, but didn't release her hand. "That's not a no. I can speak with James Henry."

And James Henry already knew James wanted to marry her. If her brother asked, she'd say with Alex she could see a future filled with romance and adventure, which appealed to her.

Away from the family in New York, James had proven to be a solid man. He was practical and planned for everything. Coming into the territory after her had probably been the most impulsive action of his life. There was something to say about the stability of a husband like James. She admitted to herself that she enjoyed his company when she relaxed and let herself do so. Then again, he was Papa's choice. Imagining her father's smug I-told-you-so face raised Samantha's ire. She couldn't bear it for the rest of her life.

Did she truly know either man well? She knew their occupations. She knew a bit about James's background and goals, but nothing about Alex. She didn't know what drove either man's heart.

CHAPTER 12:

Moon When Chokecherries Are Ripe, 1834
Owamni Yomni

DAY SETS

"*Taku Wakan*, grant that the Dakota may pass here without incident, that we may kill buffalo in abundance, conquer our enemies, and avenge the deaths of our kindred." Day Sets stood tall, facing the roaring Owamni Yomni as it spilled over tremendous rocks and plummeted to the frothing pool beneath. This was the place of all beginnings, of inspiration and rebirth, one of many places she felt the presence of Taku Wakan, the life force that suffused everything—the river, the trees, the boulders, and the people.

Mary tugged at her dress. "Mama, tell me the story."

As she did every time they visited the falls, Day Sets sat cross-legged on the ground and pulled the girl into her lap. Mary was getting almost too big to sit there, but she didn't squirm. Once again Day Sets was glad her daughter loved the traditional legends. The five-year-old fingered the beads of her mother's necklace as she listened to the familiar story.

"Long ago, a Dakota woman named Clouded Day was the devoted wife of a fierce warrior. In time, the warrior brought a second wife into their tipi."

"Like Papa has done?" Mary asked.

"Rather like that, yes," Day Sets answered. Her thoughts began to drift to Iron Cutter's teya, but she shook her head to clear it and continued the story. "One day Clouded Day's band camped near Owamni Yomni."

"The Falls of St. Anthony!" Mary exclaimed in English, pointing toward the rushing water with its roaring mist.

"Hush now, stop interrupting," Day Sets scolded. "Listen to the story." She wrapped her arms around Mary, anticipating the next part of the tale. "Clouded Day was heartbroken at her husband taking a second wife. One day she stepped into a dugout, bringing her little son with her. She paddled into the swift current, chanting her death song, and was lost. If you listen, you can hear echoes of her song in the water's thunder. They say sometimes, in the early morning, you can see the spirit of mother and son in the mist." Day Sets placed her cheek on Mary's head.

"She was sad," Mary said.

"Very sad. The falls have always been a sacred place." She pointed to a majestic eagle soaring over the tumultuous spray at the foot of the falls. "*Wakinyan*, the Thunderbird, reveres this place for its abundant fish and its beauty. At the foot of the falls, though, waits *Unktehi*, the spirit in all the lakes and streams. He demands many gifts and sacrifices to appease him." She pointed again at the swirl of mist. "See the spirits fighting? Wakinyan and Unktehi crash together at the foot of Owamni Yomni in constant conflict." Like men always do, she wanted to add. The epic battles never happened between women.

Mary snuggled into her lap, and Day Sets stole a moment of peace. She was glad to be married to a man she didn't love.

That way, the time he spent with another woman hurt only her pride, not her heart.

"Come on, Mary," she said when she could no longer justify sitting there. "We need to help." She stood, setting Mary on her feet and holding her by the hand.

They walked beside the river to where her sisters and several other Mdewakanton women in birchbark dugouts gathered wild rice in a quiet pool by the riverbank.

"Look! It's Papa!" Mary pointed upriver to where the water-wheel of the American lumber mill dominated a tiny settlement.

Day Sets could see a small group of people walking away from the falls toward the sawmill. "I think you're right, Mary." She recognized Samantha Lockwood but not the man with her. Pale Crow was there, as was Iron Cutter. And his teya.

"Come on, Mama!" Mary scampered through the hemlock and spruce trees to where the five visitors stood. Day Sets wasn't sure if Mary hurried toward her father or his dog, but she followed, head up and shoulders back.

Nero bounded into sight. He bounced around Mary. Iron Cutter caught his daughter's arm, preventing the rough and tumble greeting the child and dog usually enjoyed. He said, "No, Nero. Be a good dog! Mary is a little lady now, too old to roll on the ground with you." He repeated it in Dakota, knowing Mary wouldn't understand all the English.

Day Sets thought Mary looked disappointed. The teya, on the other hand, didn't hide her satisfied smirk. Pale Crow and Samantha joined them. Iron Cutter translated for Day Sets, and Pale Crow for Samantha.

"It's so nice to see you again, Day Sets," Samantha said with a warm smile. "Mary's grown so much this summer!"

Day Sets said, "School starts soon."

Iron Cutter looked uncomfortable. "About that. There's been a lot of discussion about how to teach Dakota children. Traders know the language, but they aren't teachers. Missionaries want to teach, but they don't know the language. We do have several people trying to learn."

Day Sets heard only that Mary would have no school that year.

He must have read it on her face, because Iron Cutter said, "It would help if the Dakota would try harder to learn English."

It was true. Very few of Cloud Man's people could speak more than a few words of English, and they spent more time with white men than almost anyone else. But the wasichu didn't bother to learn the Dakota language, either.

"Does it have to be a missionary who teaches them English?" Samantha asked.

Iron Cutter stopped translating, and the conversation washed over Day Sets as she watched Pale Crow and Samantha Lockwood. Pale Crow's eyes wouldn't leave her, reminding Day Sets of how Nero looked at Iron Cutter when he had food. The other three members of the wasichu party came to see what was holding up their friends. Iron Cutter introduced Sarah Taylor and James Churchman. Day Sets remembered James Henry Lockwood from his previous trips to the fort. She nodded at him in recognition.

James Churchman moved to Samantha Lockwood's side. His hand reached out as if to take her arm, then dropped to his side. He leaned toward Samantha as she talked to Pale Crow. When she laughed at something Pale Crow said, her eyes lit with stars and James Churchman's eyes dimmed.

Both men loved her, Day Sets concluded. She wondered if Samantha preferred one over the other. She wondered if Star Dancing knew why her husband was living at the fort now. Maybe that explained the number of empty alcohol bottles near her tipi.

"We teach the Dakota to raise cattle and plow at Eatonville," Iron Cutter said. "Next we teach them how Christianity can save them. Missionaries need to do that. The missionaries will come to common ground on the language."

"Quite a task you have in front of you," James Churchman said, his eyes still on Samantha.

"Most traders in the area can get along in Dakota, English, and French," Pale Crow said. He, too, talked to the men while his focus stayed on Samantha.

The teya had walked away from the group to gaze at the falls, still visible above the trees. She appeared to be in deep contemplation of the water or of something internal. Day Sets beckoned Mary to her. She whispered in the girl's ear, "Why don't you go tell Papa's teya the story of the falls?"

Mary's face lit up, and she walked over to her father's teya. She took the woman's hand and began telling her Clouded Day's story in the Dakota language, with the cadence of a born storyteller. The teya's face glazed over with shock as she pulled her hand away from the little girl's. She leaned away from Mary as if to get as far away as possible. The little girl kept telling the story. Day Sets enjoyed watching the teya's discomfort.

"This is a beautiful place," Samantha Lockwood said. "Your tribe gathers food here?" She spoke to Day Sets and indicated the Dakota women still harvesting rice from their dugouts.

Iron Cutter translated the words so the two women could converse.

Mni Sota Makoce was a place created for the Dakota people to be a source of life both physical and spiritual. Generations of women in her family had been born here, gathered the gift of food left for them, and returned to the mother when they died. How could she explain this to a wasichu?

Samantha Lockwood said, "This spot must be the very heart of your people."

Day Sets wanted to tell her that in the Dakota language, a baby's first cry was called *mdote*. It was the same word used for the sacred place where rivers come together. Each mother's tear that fell, of joy or despair, became part of the river's love for her children. She said, "The river that flows today contains the last of all mothers' tears and the first of all daughters'." Day Sets could feel her ancestors who revered this place touch these newcomers.

Iron Cutter fidgeted as he translated her words. Samantha looked suitably pensive, so Day Sets was satisfied he'd conveyed her words properly.

James Churchman walked over to Iron Cutter's teya just as Mary finished her story. Mary smiled and ran back to Day Sets. James Churchman talked with the teya. Pale Crow took advantage of the opportunity to pull Samantha aside into their own private conversation. She leaned toward him as he spoke to her. Day Sets recognized the sign of a woman's body wanting to be close.

Mary found a stick for Nero to fetch. That left Iron Cutter and Day Sets to speak privately.

"I'm sorry about the school," he said. His brow furrowed, so she knew he was being honest.

"She can learn." Day Sets wouldn't let him give up.

"Mary is a fine girl. I'm proud of her. The area around Fort Snelling sees more visitors every year, and many stay. I'm sure the right person for our school will come along soon."

Day Sets bristled. Come along? Did that mean he wasn't trying to start a school? That's not what he'd promised. "Why is it easier for the Winnebago agent than for you?"

"It's true a school has been approved for the Winnebago at Prairie du Chien." Iron Cutter shook his head. "But Rolette opposes it. He doesn't want the Indians to become farmers instead of hunters and fur trappers because he says he loses five hundred dollars every time an Indian learns to read and write. Rolette favors American Fur Company all the way, even since John Jacob Astor sold the company. In fact, American Fur has accused the Winnebago agent of misconduct. Rolette's behind it. It's all a fabrication."

Day Sets considered this. Rolette had friends among the wasichu who still called him King. The Dakota called him Five More because he always tried to barter for five more furs. He gave the Winnebago easy access to the wasichu's drink, and the wasichu's disease decimated their tribe. She shook her head. "Neither you nor I can fix the Winnebago. We need a school here for the Mdewakanton." She tried to keep desperation out of her voice. Mary must learn English to ensure her place in the future of the tribe.

Iron Cutter looked away from her. He faced the falls that roared as they had for centuries, ignoring the plight of humans, be they American, British, French, Dakota, Ojibwe, or Fox. "They released Black Hawk from jail. I was told he said that his home at Rock River was beautiful country, that he loved it, and had fought for it. He hopes everyone takes care of it." He turned back to Day Sets. "This place will draw visitors. I hope it remains pure, but that will only happen if your tribe remains in control of the land."

"What do you mean?" Day Sets asked. Black Hawk had been imprisoned by the wasichu after he led his Sauk warriors into battle against them.

"Tribes sign away land every day. The government promises food, money, schools, all kinds of goods, but they don't always get what the government promises. The Indians lose their land and get nothing for it."

"I don't understand." Day Sets furrowed her brow. She knew about the weakness of government promises, but how could land be lost?

Iron Cutter blew air through his lips in a show of exasperation that caused Day Sets to bristle. He said, "The government is moving Indians off their land, forbidding them access to places where they've always lived and hunted. They say they need the land for their own people, for forts and settlements. They don't understand how to live together and share."

Day Sets didn't know what to say. Leave their land? Cloud Man's village had been a new idea. Instead of moving camps with the season, Cloud Man's band had built in the wasichu way, a permanent year-round settlement. The women still moved to sugaring camps in spring while the men hunted, but most of the year was spent at the village growing and harvesting food. The Mdewakanton revered the land where their people had been born for centuries, where the spirit they honored dwelt in the rocks and rivers and caves. No one had the authority to send them away from this place.

She was still puzzling over the idea when her sisters called to her from their spot further downstream. They were ready to return to the village. With a flash of guilt that she hadn't done her part to help them, Day Sets gathered Mary and took her leave of Iron Cutter, Samantha Lockwood, Pale Crow, and James Churchman. She ignored Iron Cutter's teya, who also ignored her.

A MONTH LATER, DAY SETS and Mary joined Hushes Still the Night and Stands Sacred where they sat on blankets near their lodge. Jane and Nancy slept behind them. Stands Sacred's hands flashed as she wove a basket from light and dark reeds. Hushes Still the Night beaded a deerskin pouch. Both women created a common pattern of light and dark triangles, inverted to fit next to each other. The triangle represented spirits of the earth, its people, and other life forces. The inverted triangle represented the heavens, the stars their people came from and where they would someday return. Both sisters looked up when Day Sets and Mary arrived.

"Mary, your little cousins are sleeping," Day Sets said. "Can you play with the dolly quietly?"

Mary nodded and fetched the doll from Stands Sacred's bag.

Day Sets sat with her sisters, who waited for her to speak. "The teya's spirit is damaged. She couldn't even look at me." Her sisters nodded. They'd heard her say this before, but even though the meeting with Iron Cutter's teya had happened weeks ago, it still bothered Day Sets. She wasn't jealous of the teya's time with Iron Cutter himself. It was more the idea that if the teya were to have a baby, that child would benefit from the education Mary needed.

Stands Sacred nodded. "She's one of those white women who sees us as lower than the Black Frenchmen."

Day Sets frowned. "Slaves aren't French."

Hushes Still the Night said, "Maybe not French, but wasichu look down on them."

The sisters fell silent as they focused on their work. Day Sets looked at Mary and for the first time wondered whether her father's path was the right one. Cloud Man took pride in his iyeska granddaughters and saw them as the future of the tribe. But would the white world ever accept Mary and her cousins, or would the iyeska always be lower? Day Sets took pride in her position as daughter of a leader. She wanted Mary to take pride in her life, too. The more she thought about it, the more Day Sets vowed to make sure Mary kept part of her spirit in the Mdewakanton world.

In the Moon When Leaves Turn Brown, Day Sets overheard Cloud Man and Red Cherry Woman talking. The despondency in her father's voice caught her attention as he said, "The Ojibwe, Ottawa, and Potawatomi tribes signed a treaty with the American government giving away five million acres of land for money and goods."

Her mother murmured reassurances.

Cloud Man said, "The tribes must move west of the Mississippi River where the government promises them five million acres of their own."

"But the Mdewakanton already live west of the river," Red Cherry Woman said.

Day Sets turned away. It had come to pass just as Iron Cutter had predicted. What would her father do now? She wondered exactly how his iyeska granddaughters could benefit the tribe in a world where the wasichu blundered through sacred land and thought it theirs. Anger flooded her. She'd supported her father as she'd been trained to do, wasting her life raising a daughter whose future was disappearing as fast as the tribe's.

CHAPTER 13:

July 1834
Falls of St. Anthony, Michigan Territory

SAMANTHA

Late in the afternoon, the weary party boarded the steamboat to return downriver from the Falls of St. Anthony. Once underway, Samantha stood alone at the port-side railing. She watched the trees on the riverbank cast long afternoon shadows while she thought about Alex Miree and James Churchman. James was safe. He was her father's protection and a solid future all wrapped up together. Alex was the spirit of the frontier. He was unpredictable, wild, and beautiful. Both had merit. Both were attractive.

From the bow of the boat, she could hear her brother's voice.

"She seems to be responding well to you," James Henry said.

He was out of sight around a bulkhead. Samantha suspected he was discussing her and wondered if Alex had approached James Henry already. She smiled as she imagined the impulsive, tousled Alex approaching her brother, who could be quite formidable when he chose. But it was James, not Alex, who spoke.

"Your father said it wouldn't be easy. I've tried to do everything he suggested," James said.

It was lucky James Henry laughed just then because it covered Samantha's gasp. James and her father had planned her seduction? Her hand covered her brooch in the reflexive motion she used to comfort herself.

"Samantha has long been a mystery to our father. Mama must have given him a piece of her mind so he could pass it on to you," James Henry said. "In the meantime, you live in limbo here in the wilderness."

"It's not so bad," James said. "I see opportunity here." When James Henry laughed, James said, "I mean other than your sister, of course."

"You're persistent at least," James Henry said. "I suspected Papa had grown tired of Samantha's churlishness. I thought he'd just insist on her marriage. You say he banished her here to me? I had no say in that matter."

Now James laughed. "Sometimes I feel I had no say in the matter either. He came to me and told me his daughter was being willful, that I should follow her and woo her. Then she'd agree he was right and marry me."

"Well, at the rate you're going, you'd better settle in for the long haul," James Henry said. Their voices faded as they moved away.

"Well, stuff and nonsense," Samantha muttered to herself. She gripped the railing. Her parents had encouraged James, knowing she didn't want him. That colored every pleasant conversation with him. What did James feel for her, and how much had been scripted in advance? She stared into the dark river that rushed alongside the boat.

James Henry had been thirteen years old when Samantha was born. By the time she was old enough to have memories of him, he was in law school. His entire life was outside her world, outside the farm, outside the family. The one thing she remembered was his laugh. It had always been hearty, full of joy. When he laughed with James, though, it had been sardonic. Not a quality she admired. Not one that endeared her to a brother who seemed more of a stranger every day.

Samantha stared into the river that flowed just as it had five minutes ago, before her heart shattered. The Mississippi didn't care about family betrayal. Her family was only a speck in the river's history. Both her mother and the river mother caressed until an opportunity arose to destroy. Samantha's mother had let her father banish her own daughter from the family. The river mother watched for her chance to do the same. Maybe the boat would sink. Samantha gripped the railing.

"There you are!" Alex said, as he came toward her from the stern of the boat. He smiled, but looked uncomfortable. "I'm sorry about earlier. I am rather impetuous. Anyone can tell you that." He grinned at her.

Her heart beat faster, but her brain stopped short. Was he taking away his proposal? The sick feeling in her stomach made tears even more likely.

"Samantha, you are a ray of sunshine in my life." He scanned the riverbank. "All this natural beauty is only the background for your own beauty. I'm bowled over, struck dumb by your presence."

Samantha smiled. He was silly. "Nonsense, Alex."

He turned to look into her eyes. "I love you, Samantha. I know it makes no sense. We haven't known each other long. One thing the frontier teaches you, though, is that you must take advantage of every opportunity that comes your way. You are the best opportunity I've seen in a while, and I don't intend to let you go without saying so."

"You're planning to let me go?" Her stomach churned and her heart ached.

"Never." He leaned close, and for a moment Samantha thought he would actually kiss her right here in public. He stopped himself, though, and took her hand instead.

Her anxiety dissipated. Alex moved to take advantage of his opportunities while James waited for his.

"Oh, Alex."

He pulled her into a quick hug. When he pulled away, a loose thread on his shirt button caught on her amethyst brooch. The thread broke and his button sailed into the river. Alex didn't notice, but Samantha smiled.

When they arrived home at Prairie du Chien, James Henry had three letters waiting from his mysterious female correspondent. Samantha had seen letters from her before, but not all at once like these. This woman must spend half her life writing to James Henry. He settled himself in his chair with the letters. Samantha asked who she was. James Henry ignored the question. He opened the letters in front of his sister and smiled at the contents, but didn't share. He must have written back, but Samantha never saw him post a letter.

She didn't know if Alex had talked with James Henry about a future together. Her feelings for Alex were sweet but fragile. He was all she could think about, but deep inside she still wondered what others weren't telling her about him.

Over the next few weeks, James Churchman must have sensed Samantha's withdrawal as well as the chill between her and her brother. James left Prairie du Chien, headed downriver. A letter from him, for Samantha, arrived with almost every boat after he left. He wrote that he was an attorney downriver in Galena, representing Indians in their ongoing lead mine controversy with the American government. Nothing in his letters hinted at a romantic relationship. Samantha wondered if he was waiting for instructions from her father on how to proceed. She opened his letters because she was curious about what he was doing. Gradually, she let herself enjoy James's stories about his life in Galena. She never answered any of the letters, but they kept coming.

In late June, Samantha sat in the front room of her brother's house with her sewing on her lap. She hoped that adding an embroidered row of purple roses to the bodice of her gown would distract her from the complexities of her life.

James Henry came in from the store. Samantha looked up to greet him, but he was holding a letter from *her*. Samantha tightened her lips and focused on tying the best French knot she could manage.

James Henry dropped into his chair with a sharp exhalation of air. "Samantha, I need to talk to you." He peered at her over the top of his spectacles.

She wove the needle into the fabric and set her embroidery on her lap. In a sweet tone dripping with venom, she said, "Of course, dear brother."

He hesitated. "Look, I know it's been difficult. I haven't been honest with you."

"Stuff and nonsense, James Henry. It's hard to be honest when you say nothing at all. At least, you haven't lied."

He held up the letter. "I met Catherine Wright in St. Louis early last year."

Samantha remained silent. He was going to have to tell the story without help from her.

"We've corresponded." He hesitated at her unladylike snort. "She's a good woman."

Samantha waited.

"Catherine's accepted my proposal. I'm going to marry her in St. Louis this fall."

Oh, to be a man! How wonderful to decide upon marriage without permission from anyone! Samantha said nothing.

"You'll like her, I think." James Henry's face lit up as he told her of his intended's glowing personality.

He must plan to bring Catherine Wright to Prairie du Chien. What would that mean for Samantha? She said nothing.

James Henry looked at the ground between his boots. He ran a hand through his hair and shifted in his chair. "I'm sorry, Samantha."

Sorry for not telling her? Or sorry for something she didn't know yet? Had he refused Alex? Is that why she'd received no letters? Her brother had better not be planning to send her home to New York, or to Galena to marry James. But James Henry's new wife wouldn't want another woman in the house, surely? Samantha said nothing.

"This reminds me of the story of the falls," James Henry said to Samantha. "You know, where the brave brings home a second wife and the first one kills herself?"

The demon rage unfurled itself in Samantha's belly as she struggled to find words. "You defile an ancient legend about a place the Indians hold sacred. I am not your wife. I am your sister, who has asked nothing of you but support in her choice of mate." She drew herself up to her full height with dignity and pride. "We need to discuss this now, without lies or omissions."

"I'll need something stronger than tea." James Henry walked to the sideboard and poured himself a whiskey. At Samantha's nod, he poured her a glass of wine.

Unspoken thoughts swirled through the room on currents of anger, betrayal, loss, and love. Samantha wondered which direction the conversation would take. Samantha and James

Henry faced each other with honest faces for the first time in months.

"Did you speak with Alex?" she said first.

"He wants to marry you. The idea's absurd. I told him Father promised you to James Churchman, and he laughed. Miree is unreliable and impulsive, Samantha, and stories have been told about him . . ." His voice trailed off, as if he couldn't decide what he should tell her.

"What if I want to marry him?" She wouldn't give James Henry the satisfaction of asking about the stories. Still, she put a hand on her brooch, feeling the familiar amethyst cabochon in the center of the flower shape. She took a deep breath. "What about James? He seems to write often."

"He's a nice man, something I didn't know before he came out West, but I won't marry him. James's roots are in the East. His letters are chatty and impersonal, not romantic. Who knows how long he'll play at being a frontier attorney before he returns to civilization?"

"You could return East with him."

Samantha thought about entering her father's home on James's arm. Her lips tightened. She never wanted to see that knowing smirk directed at her, never wanted to admit to him that she'd been wrong. "James hasn't asked me to marry him. Alex has."

"But Miree hasn't written at all."

"At least he hasn't gotten letters from Papa telling him how to woo me." Samantha tried to keep from snapping at her brother, but he raised an eyebrow. He did not deny it. "Alex is fun to talk to. He has a good job and is making his mark here, just as you did."

"You want to marry him?" James Henry's brow furrowed. "Why am I only now hearing this?"

"Why are you only now asking?"

James Henry hesitated. "Samantha, James Churchman is a good man. He has a solid future and he loves you. Why must you be so stubborn?"

Samantha wanted to insist in a cold voice that he should include her in the plans for her own future. She wanted to snarl that he and James had betrayed her. She wanted to cry, but she gritted her teeth and said nothing.

James Henry must have seen the fire in her eyes. He changed the subject. "Let me tell you about Catherine Wright. Her family has lived in St. Louis for generations. She's sweet and nice with a tough enough spine to tackle frontier life."

"Is she someone you love or someone you want to sell at auction?"

"Samantha! That's unnecessary. It's difficult to find words to express my heart. I will marry her in St. Louis next summer and we will return to Prairie du Chien before fall."

"Where do you see me in this vision of married bliss? She could be the most wonderful woman on the planet, but your house is too small for two women."

"I give you permission to marry Alex Miree, if he will still have you."

Hardly a ringing endorsement, but it allowed her to move forward.

James Henry said, "I hope you will be at my wedding."

"Will Papa be there?" Her stomach squirmed at the thought of facing her father, but she could attend on Alex's arm. Maybe Papa would be proud of her.

"Does it matter? You'll be there for me, not for him."

A great weight of depression, anger, and frustration slipped from her. He was her brother, and family always came first. Even if she'd resisted her father's choice for husband, she did want Papa to know Alex. "Alex and I will be there." It may be too early for her to be committing Alex to family events, but it felt right.

James Henry held his glass out for a toast, and Samantha lifted her wine glass. "To family," he said.

"To family."

THE NEXT DAY, SAMANTHA hummed as she sat at the table writing a letter to Alex. James Henry would write an official letter to him, but Samantha knew it would be a cold approval. She wanted Alex to know how much she cared for him and was looking forward to their wedding. She sipped a cup of tea and considered the best words to use.

Someone knocked on the door, and Samantha opened it to see Sarah Taylor. Eager to share her news, Samantha said, "James Henry has given his approval for me to marry Alex." Samantha felt her cheeks flush. "Would you be my maid of honor, Sarah?"

"I'd be delighted! How wonderful." Sarah grabbed Samantha and danced around her.

After a moment, though, Sarah's delight faded.

"Sarah?" Samantha asked. "Are you all right?"

Sarah looked at Samantha with tears in her eyes. "Papa's done it now. He transferred Jeff to Fort Gibson in Oklahoma. He's already gone."

"Oh, Sarah, I'm so sorry." Samantha could not be happy when her friend was so distraught.

"I hope you won't mind, Samantha. I told Jeff he could write to me and send the letters to you."

"Of course."

Sarah paced the room. "I miss him so much already! I know we are meant to be together. Maybe I'll run away to Oklahoma!"

"Sarah, stop. Sit a minute." Samantha left her unfinished letter on the table, took her friend's arm, and led her to a chair near the fire. "Maybe some tea?" She fetched a cup from the cabinet and poured tea for Sarah from the pot on the table. Topping off her own cup, she joined Sarah by the fire. "That's better, isn't it? You have friends here. We will support you."

Sarah sipped the tea and took a deep, shaky breath. "Thank you, Samantha. I'm so sorry to dampen your excitement with my problems."

"I understand about a father not respecting your choice. Maybe this territory will give women the strength to live the lives they choose."

Sarah sipped her tea and nodded.

Samantha wanted Sarah to be happy, but she also saw every day how attached she was to her parents and sister. All the more reason for Sarah to preserve her connection to her family. "I will pass on Jeff's letters to you, Sarah. Your father will come around. He loves you."

Jeff's first letter arrived at the end of the week. Samantha waited until Sarah visited to give it to her. Sarah opened it and her face blanched as she read it. Samantha watched her friend's eyes scan the page again, as if she didn't believe what it said. Sarah looked up, stunned. "He resigned his commission. He's no longer part of the army."

"Oh, Sarah, that's a big decision! Your father respects him so he'll approve the wedding now?"

Sarah's eyes went back to the letter, one of her ringlets falling forward to shield her face. "He's on his way to Mississippi. His brother has given him a plantation. It's called Brierfield, and it's next to his brother's Hurricane Plantation. Jeff's going to develop the plantation and make the house comfortable for us. Then he will come for me." She looked up, her eyes shining.

"See, Sarah? Have faith in Jeff. He loves you and he'll make this happen."

Sarah hid the letter in her reticule and left, humming the same tune Samantha had earlier that week.

CHAPTER 14:

July, 1834
St. Peter's Agency, Michigan Territory

HARRIET

"I never baked nothing as fancy as a wedding cake," Ellie said, shaking her head. "Mistress say there'll be two dozen guests."

"Two dozen guests isn't hard," Harriet said. "I'm here, and the master's bringing Hannah over to help, too." She shrugged. "A wedding cake's just bigger and decorated prettier. We can do this."

Ellie laughed and relaxed. "We've not had many weddings of white women at Fort Snelling, but it's just a big party. We'll do it up right."

Harriet nodded. "We'd better get our order to the sutler." It still amazed Harriet that they could take off their aprons and just walk out of the kitchen all the way to the fort without telling anyone where they were going. For weeks, she'd looked over her shoulder, expecting to be caught escaping. Now she enjoyed the sensation of freedom.

Inside the gate at the fort, Ellie stopped and frowned at a gathering of men outside the hospital. She lingered until she saw Dr. Jarvis emerge, then she turned away, fluttering her hands. Ellie looked back at Dr. Jarvis three times before they got to the store, and her nervousness increased. Harriet wondered what exactly was the relationship between the doctor and Ellie.

A very young Indian girl sat on the porch step of the store. Her dirty hair hung over her face. Harriet looked around, not seeing the child's mother. "Where's your mama, sweetheart?" she asked. The girl looked up with wide dark eyes but said nothing.

The door opened, and an Indian woman appeared in the doorway. She was looking back over her shoulder, spitting words in Dakota at someone inside.

Harriet cringed at the venom in the woman's voice. The little girl scrambled to her feet and took the woman's hand as she dashed down the step toward the gate.

"Star Dancing and her daughter, Winona," Ellie said. "They're here a lot." Her tone implied Harriet should know them. Before Harriet could ask, they were inside the store. Only Mr. Miree was there.

"Hello, Mr. Miree," Ellie said. She nodded at him and walked over to the shelf of spices.

Harriet thought the sutler looked a bit rattled. His blond hair was mussed more than usual, and he didn't answer Ellie with the slick smooth words he used with Harriet when she came to the store. He ran a hand over his hair, which didn't smooth it at all, and walked behind the counter. He stood staring through the door in the direction Star Dancing had gone. It reminded Harriet of how Nero looked through the closed door to try to see what was outside. It made her smile when the dog did it.

Most of what they'd need to feed the wedding guests was already in the kitchen storeroom at the agency. Ellie chose a large sack of flour and one of sugar as well as a small bag of spices. She tucked the bag into her apron and told Mr. Miree one of the men would collect the sacks later that afternoon. Harriet followed her out of the store, feeling like a grand mistress. Imagine always ordering goods and having someone else pay for them and collect them. How grand!

As they left the fort, Ellie paused and gazed for a long minute at the hospital, her face pale. The crowd of men outside had gone. Harriet frowned at the look on Ellie's face.

Back at the agency, as they approached the kitchen, Harriet turned toward the stable. "I'll ask Thomas to fetch the store items." She didn't wait for Ellie's response.

William came out of the stable as Harriet approached. Tall and lean, he walked with confidence as long as the master wasn't around. She looked behind him for Thomas.

"Thomas ain't here," William said.

Embarrassed, Harriet stammered, "Sutler has a couple things for us."

William nodded. "I'll send Thomas when he gets back. Best to get his head straight now."

"What do you mean?" Harriet said.

William hesitated, then leaned toward her with a cautionary finger raised. "Thomas ain't a good man, Harriet. You stay away from him. He chasing every female slave and Indian he runs across. Don't think you special."

Harriet felt her breath whoosh from her body. How embarrassing that her infatuation with Thomas was so obvious that William felt it was his place to caution her. She mumbled something and fled to the kitchen.

The following morning, with the wedding scheduled for the next day, Ellie and Harriet assembled the ingredients for the cake according to a recipe Ellie remembered from her life before St. Peter's Agency.

"I need three pounds of butter," she told Harriet, "four pounds of flour, and three pounds of sugar."

Harriet fetched the butter crock from the coolest part of the cellar. She'd churned more butter this week than she had in years, so they'd have enough for regular use as well as the wedding cake and feast. While she was there, she called to Ellie, "How many eggs?"

"Twenty-four!"

Harriet brought the butter, then returned with a basket for the eggs. Together, they collected four pounds of currants, two pounds of raisins, mace, and three kinds of nutmeg. Ellie fetched half a pint of the master's brandy, and Harriet pulled out the molasses. They took turns stirring the batter in the biggest bowl they had. The cake had to be baked in several layers, in Dutch ovens placed over coals in the hearth. Ellie used a shovel to put coals on top of the Dutch ovens' lids to ensure even baking.

"How long will it bake?" Harriet asked.

"Three hours." Ellie wiped her hands on her apron and turned to Harriet. "Wash up these dishes and we'll fix the smoked meat."

Harriet and Ellie spent the rest of the day fixing everything they could do before the next day's feast. Ellie beat egg whites into a froth and added ground loaf-sugar to make icing for the cake.

"It's beautiful, Ellie!" Harriet said. "It'll be the best part of the feast." She drew a deep breath of the aroma that permeated the kitchen. "It smells so good!"

Miss Lockwood arrived on the *Warrior* later that day. Her brother, as well as Miss Taylor and her family, accompanied her. The Taylors would stay at the fort except for Miss Sarah Taylor, who would share the guest bedroom upstairs with Miss Lockwood. After the wedding, of course, Miss Lockwood would move into the fort as Mrs. Miree.

Harriet brought a tray of tea and tiny apple cakes upstairs in the late afternoon, after the two women unpacked. They sat next to each other on the bed, laughing and talking. Miss Lockwood glowed with happiness. Harriet could only smile back. "Tea," she said, putting the tray on the bedside table.

"Have a cake, Harriet," Miss Lockwood said.

"Thank you, ma'am, but I gotta go." She grinned. "Someone's getting married tomorrow and there's a lot to be done."

Miss Taylor laughed. "Off with you, then! Make sure it's all perfect!" Both women laughed, and Harriet returned to the kitchen with a smile on her face. She liked Miss Lockwood.

The next day, Miss Taylor and Miss Lockwood helped Mrs. Taliaferro rearrange vases of prairie roses around the front room. "That negro girl has no sense of style," Mrs. Taliaferro said. "I should never have allowed her to handle the flowers."

In the kitchen below, Ellie and Harriet heard the mistress and shook their heads. At least Mrs. Taliaferro didn't have time to berate them.

Thomas and William set up tables in the yard between the house and the stable. Mr. Campbell, the interpreter, sent Hannah to help. Harriet and Ellie sent platter after platter of food out to the tables. Guests arrived, and the mistress called Hannah upstairs to help Miss Lockwood dress for her wedding.

When it was time, Ellie and Harriet left the kitchen to go upstairs and peek into the front room. Miss Lockwood wore a pale lavender gown with a fitted bodice, her purple brooch pinned in its usual place. She'd sewn satin ribbons in a deep purple along the hem and sleeves, and fashioned small decorative bows out of the same ribbon. Delicate purple embroidery covered the bodice. The bride carried a small bouquet of purple bergamot and violets. Harriet smiled. Miss Lockwood made no secret of her preference for purple! The Taliaferros and Miss

Lockwood prepared to leave for the chapel at Fort Snelling, where the wedding would take place.

"Come on, Harriet," Ellie whispered. "We've seen the gown. There's work to do!"

They returned to the kitchen, where Hannah was already slicing loaves of bread.

"Imagine marrying a man for love," Harriet said.

Hannah said, "I was married once."

Ellie and Harriet looked at the old woman, waiting to hear the story, but Hannah just kept working. Ellie shrugged. She said, "No slave has time to meet the man of her dreams. If she does, she ain't working hard enough!" All three of them laughed.

After the Taliaferros and Miss Lockwood left, Thomas and William came to help them carry the big wedding cake into the yard. Harriet had saved a handful of violets from the baskets of flowers that she and Hannah had picked for the wedding. She arranged them on top of the cake. "Beautiful," she said. She turned toward Thomas, expecting him to flirt with her, wanting him to, but he had already begun to walk back to the stable with William. Harriet shook off her disappointment. He wasn't the man of her dreams, not at all, but she enjoyed his attention. She wondered if William had said something to Thomas about leaving her alone.

She shook off her personal feelings and looked at the tables groaning with sliced pork and beef, biscuits and bread, and root vegetables. Harriet nodded in satisfaction. However, it was the table of sweets that made her eyes glow. The cake was the focus, but plates of cookies and tiny cakes, and bowls of maple candy made the table a treasure trove of delicacies.

When the newlyweds and their guests spilled out of the house into the yard, Harriet, Ellie, and Hannah put on clean, starched aprons and hung back, waiting to be of service. The bridal party and guests converged on the food.

Mrs. Taliaferro approached them and snapped her fingers. "Girls, get out there with the beverages."

Ellie and Hannah served lemonade, wine, and whiskey. Harriet ran back and forth to the kitchen to replenish platters of food as needed.

On one trip, she heard Major Taliaferro's voice coming from the side of the building. His tone caught her attention. "Do you think this is the best thing for her?"

Harriet held her breath, wondering who her master was talking to. Who was he talking about? Why was he angry?

"It was her choice. I hope she hasn't made a mistake in her insistence on being independent." Judge Lockwood sounded as if he didn't care. "She could have stayed in New York, married Churchman, and had a good life. But no, she had to throw caution to the winds and marry a backwoods man."

He was talking about his sister, the bride.

The major said, "I don't think she knows about his other life."

"She hasn't had time to learn anything about him," the judge said. "But it's her life to deal with now. She has to lie in the bed she's made."

Harriet had lingered as long as she could. She delivered the plate of sliced apple bread to the table in a daze. Miss Lockwood's, no, Mrs. Miree's, own brother didn't approve of her new husband.

After a long afternoon of well wishes, food, music, conversation, and cake, Harriet was exhausted but happy. She knew they had done their best for the new Mrs. Miree. Thomas drove the bridal couple off to the fort in Major Taliaferro's wagon, and the guests dispersed to wherever they were sleeping. Harriet, Ellie, and Hannah still had hours of cleaning up to do.

On the morning after the wedding, subdued guests gathered once more in the yard. Harriet prepared coffee and tea while Ellie kept the biscuits baking. Hannah put out plates of biscuits with jam and trays of fruit. The bride and groom, of course, were not in attendance. When the *Warrior* left for its downriver journey, the guests from Prairie du Chien departed, too. The agency returned to normal.

Later in the afternoon, the newlywed Mirees arrived from the fort. Harriet admitted them to the house and ran downstairs to position herself to listen. Ellie and Hannah were cutting up the leftover meat for a stew. All three paused to listen.

"Sir, we've come on a particular errand," Mr. Miree said.

"Go on," Major Taliaferro said.

"We are in need of a household servant to assist Samantha."

"I won't own a slave," Mrs. Miree said. It sounded as though she'd said this before.

"We need a slave but can't buy one," her husband said in a tight voice.

"I can help with that," Major Taliaferro said. "Why don't you rent Hannah from me? You need her more than Campbell."

Harriet looked at Ellie.

"That would be fine, wouldn't it, Samantha?" His bride must have nodded agreement since Harriet heard nothing but the men haggling a price.

Hannah kept chopping vegetables to add to the pot. Harriet held in her anger that an older woman could be sold away like a horse. It reminded her once again that the freedom of the territory was an illusion. Her whole life was a lie, a pleasant lie that could vanish on her master's whim. Somehow that basic truth seemed harder to accept here than it had in Pennsylvania.

PART TWO
1834-1835

CHAPTER 15:

Moon When Corn is Hoed, 1834
Cloud Man's Village

DAY SETS

Day Sets and her sisters hoed the weeds among the potatoes and squash. The dirt was hard. The crops could use rain, but the spring had been dry. Day Sets stretched to the sky, releasing the kinks from her back.

She had been watching for new arrivals since Iron Cutter's return a month ago, still hoping this would be the year for the children's school. Now Iron Cutter had brought two unknown men to see her father, along with a handful of translators. She wondered why each man needed his own translator. Day Sets walked closer so she could hear their conversation.

The rest of the women went back to work on the weeds, and the little girls played. They didn't understand the potential significance of these strangers.

Her father stood motionless while Iron Cutter and the two men approached. Next to Cloud Man stood the shaman, Blue Medicine, his face painted mostly blue. Blue Medicine carried his deer hoof rattle and wore a mirror on a cord around his neck. He would use the rattle to scare off unwelcome spirits and the mirror to peer at the truth of the strangers' spoken words.

Cloud Man wore the dark army coat given to him by a British soldier during the 1812 war. His buckskin leggings and feathers in his hair reflected his Mdewakanton heritage. He wore more necklaces of bones, shells, and beads than usual. Impassive, he waited for Iron Cutter to speak.

Iron Cutter said, "Cloud Man is chief of the Sioux here at Eatonville where they are learning to farm. Before they can be taught to seek eternal happiness through God, they must be taught the temporal benefits of this life through agriculture. Chief, I have brought these brothers to help you. I am sure they will be trustworthy assistants."

Day Sets still winced when Iron Cutter spoke directly to her father. He had always done so, but tradition taught that a Mdewakanton husband never talked to his wife's father, nor did he even look at the father or speak his name. Sometimes, of course, it was necessary. At that time, the husband should speak with respect and refer to himself in plural third person. For example, Iron Cutter might have looked at the ground and said, "We have brought you men to teach your grand-daughters." It had taken her many years to discover all that Iron Cutter didn't know about how the Mdewakanton did things. He expected the Dakota to work hard learning his way of farming but made little effort to understand their ways. He should at least know that *Sioux* was the Ojibwe word for their enemy, the Dakota. It was an offensive word, meaning *little snakes* in the Ojibwe language. Iron Cutter was on Dakota land, tasked with helping the Dakota. He should at the very least use their own name for themselves—Mdewakanton band of the Dakota tribe.

The taller, skinnier wasichu showed many teeth as he smiled and held out his hand to her father. Cloud Man shook it, and the tall man spoke. "Greetings, Cloud Man," he said in passable Dakota. He looked very proud to be speaking their language. Or maybe he was just a proud man.

The other man was quieter, shorter but still tall, stocky but not fat, with well-muscled arms. He waited for Iron Cutter to introduce them.

Iron Cutter pointed to the tall one. "This is Gideon Pond. He is a farmer and a carpenter." He turned to the other. "Samuel Pond is a teacher."

Day Set's heart beat faster. *A teacher.*

Cloud Man welcomed the men as he would anyone Iron Cutter brought—with cautious but polite words. Blue Medicine said nothing. He peered at them with narrowed eyes, then lifted his mirror to reflect the truth of their words.

Iron Cutter said, "Gideon will build a cabin nearby. They will help you in the fields, teach you to get the most out of your plowing and planting so you won't run short of food in the winter."

Day Sets grew impatient waiting for the men to discuss the most important part. They needed to choose a site for a school and decide how to go about teaching the children.

"Welcome, Red Eagle," Cloud Man said to Samuel, bestowing him with a Dakota name. He turned to Gideon. "Welcome, Grizzly Bear."

Day Sets smiled. The younger brother did indeed resemble a burly bear.

Grizzly Bear walked toward the lake. He scooped up a handful of water and, in the Dakota language, asked a nearby warrior, "What do you call this?"

The warrior looked at Cloud Man, who nodded. "*Mini.*" He then picked up a handful of sand and said, "*Wiyaka.*"

Grizzly Bear repeated the words and returned to the group, smiling. So he knew some of the Dakota language. Hadn't Iron Cutter said that was the first thing a teacher needed to know?

While he and his brother continued to speak with her father, through interpreters when necessary, Day Sets pulled Iron Cutter aside. "Will they build a school?" she asked.

"They wanted to be missionaries," Iron Cutter said, "to bring the white man's God to the Dakota. Major Bliss at Fort Snelling must approve such a venture, but these brothers are not ordained ministers. They have no experience and no permission. Major Bliss was going to send them away, but I stepped in and offered them a place here. They can improve the farm, learn the language, and then teach the children."

Day Sets didn't understand his explanation of God and missionaries. "They will teach English?"

"My little colony of Sioux will learn all the arts of civilized life, how to read, write, and do arithmetic. The boys will learn gardening and agriculture, and the girls will learn spinning, carding, weaving, and sewing. All will learn how to worship God. Only then can the tribe fully assimilate American life, prepared to take their place next to the powerful chiefs in the East." He glanced toward the Pond brothers, who talked with Cloud Man and Blue Medicine. "You know the United States government believes the Sioux, and all the Indians, must adopt American culture or they will become extinct as a people. It is my duty to help you survive."

Day Sets stared at him. He spoke their language but seemed unable to fathom what was in their hearts. Day Sets knew Iron Cutter wanted the village to adopt the wasichu's religion. Red Eagle's school would teach that first. She didn't care. Mary must learn English, and she must learn how a white woman behaved. If that meant learning about the wasichu's God, that was acceptable. For now.

That night, as Red Cherry Woman served Cloud Man his dinner of fresh berries, rabbit stew, and corn, Day Sets asked her father about Iron Cutter's plans. Hushes Still the Night and Stands Sacred kept their heads bowed, feeding their daughters but listening.

"Father, we've learned the wasichu's way to farm. What is next?" she asked.

Cloud Man looked at her with the deep gaze that meant he was considering how to respond. She waited. He said, "We will always be Mdewakanton, but times are changing. Fur traders compete with us for game. The buffalo are declining. As a result, it is harder to feed the village. The people go hungry."

Day Sets nodded. There had been many lean months.

"White Buffalo Calf Woman teaches us to follow the Seven Sacred Rites to be good neighbors with all the children of the stars, the mitakuye oyasin, all life. The blood of Maka Ina flows in rivers that nourish us. In accordance with the teachings of White Buffalo Calf Woman, we share food with those in need and show compassion for everyone."

Impatient with her father's lecturing tone, Day Sets sighed. Iron Cutter had told her that the American Fur Company was already trying to take back the guns, kettles, and knives given to the tribe on credit. They showed no respect for persons or property. "The people trust in you, Father, for the survival of the village," she said. Day Sets trusted and respected her father, but her impatience with her husband's promises of food, tools, and a school sharpened her tone.

Her father's lips tightened. "Iron Cutter will intervene for us until the harvest. This village will feed itself so that its warriors can defend it from a position of strength."

Day Sets knew the people of Heyate Otunwe would harvest almost a thousand bushels of corn this year. "And the children?" she asked.

"We teach the little ones how to take the tribe forward. If we don't know what that means, we cannot teach them. For now, they learn our past. Only then can they appreciate the future. We will remain Mdewakanton at heart, even if that means adopting the wasichu's ways."

Red Cherry Woman said, "Enough talk. Eat the meal you have in front of you before worrying about tomorrow."

Day Set's brothers and sisters ate in uncomfortable silence. Day Sets put a couple of berries in her mouth. The legendary White Buffalo Calf Woman may have taught the people how to balance the interconnectedness of all things, but she had not anticipated the wasichu's religion that consumed all others, or the wasichu's land ownership that was for them alone.

OVER THE NEXT FEW weeks, Cloud Man's village assisted Red Eagle and Grizzly Bear to find a site for a cabin and build it. The village consisted of over two hundred people now, scattered between White Earth Lake and *Bde Unma*, the other lake, called Lake Harriet by the wasichu. The brothers placed their cabin on the east side of White Earth Lake, which the wasichu still called Lake Calhoun.

Day Sets felt pangs of regret as the white men slashed the prairie grass, cut down trees and moved boulders with no respect for Taku Wakan, the spirits within. The men couldn't move one large boulder, so they had to adjust their plans and work around it. Before anything else was born, Inyan, the stone spirit, was soft and shapeless. He gave his red blood to form Maka Ina, the Earth Mother, and his blue blood to form Wakpa Tanka, the river the wasichu called Mississippi. Day Sets laid a hand on the cool stone and said a prayer to Inyan, cheered that at least one of the spirits resisted destruction.

They built the cabin with split oak logs. Poles from tamarack trees held up a roof of tree bark fastened by strings made from the inner bark of the basswood tree. Wooden planks from the old government mill at the Falls of Saint Anthony formed the interior ceiling. It had two rooms and a cellar. Iron Cutter had provided a gift of glass for one window. Day Sets couldn't imagine living inside such a small, dark place. To her, the best part about the cabin was its unimpeded view of the loons on the lake.

Grizzly Bear said, "This house is a testimony to the faith, zeal, and courage of its builders." He then said a prayer and read from his Bible to officially open the house, and he invited all the helpers to a feast of mussels from the lake served with flour and water.

Day Sets found as many excuses as she could to walk with Mary past Red Eagle and Grizzly Bear. When Day Sets and her sisters hoed the cornfield, Red Eagle worked alongside them.

"Bring the water skin," Day Sets said to her daughter.

The little girl ran to where the skin hung on a nail and lugged it to Red Eagle without spilling very much at all. "For you, Red Eagle," she said in English.

"Thank you," he said, speaking slowly so she could process the words. They both smiled at the successful communication.

Grizzly Bear spent time repairing a plow Iron Cutter had brought from a nearby settlement. Day Sets sent Mary to him with a pouch of buffalo jerky. She beamed with pride as her daughter concentrated on using English words to describe what it was.

The little girl taught the brothers Dakota words, and she picked up English words quickly. It wasn't long before she regaled her mother with stories of the Christian God.

"Mama, the Christians believe in Taku Wakan like we do but call him God. They tell of the time Taku Wakan brought the rain to destroy the earth people that displeased him. The Christians don't know about the turtle bringing mud up from the bottom of the deep water, but they tell of Taku Wakan creating land and people and animals."

Day Sets said, "Your grandfather believes the wasichu to be smart and powerful. Why wouldn't they know about the creation of the Earth?" Her heart swelled with pride at Mary's ability to grasp the language and the concepts.

"Red Eagle writes down all the Dakota words I tell him," Mary said. "And words the people tell him, too. He says he's going to make a book of Dakota words translated to English words so more people can learn our language."

"And we can learn theirs," Day Sets said, encouraged by what Mary said. Her daughter was learning. She'd be ready when the brothers opened their school.

Day Sets watched Mary with the pride of a mother and the hope of a chief's daughter. It wasn't much different, planning for the future of a child and planning for the future of the tribe. What was to come remained hidden. All her father could do as a leader of the tribe was to follow the teachings of White Buffalo Calf Woman, to keep the Mdewakanton close to the spirits of their ancestors. It was all she could do as a mother, too. Follow what she knew in her heart to be true and hope it would be enough for her daughter to navigate the world to come.

After a dry spring, the rain fell constantly in *Wazustecasa Wi*, the Moon When Strawberries are Red. Day Sets fumed when she heard about the Winnebago school in Prairie du Chien being completed in *Wasuton Wi*, the Moon When Corn Is Gathered. Five More, still called King Rolette by some, opposed the school. Rolette had the Winnebago agent, General Street, recalled to

Washington for misconduct. The government shuffled Indian agents around Prairie du Chien and Fort Snelling, putting General Street in charge of the Fox and Sauk, transferring him away from Prairie du Chien. And Five More became the Indian agent for the Winnebago from Prairie du Chien all the way to the Falls of Saint Anthony. He would now directly confront Iron Cutter, agent for the Dakota, in everything having to do with the government and the tribes. Five More and Iron Cutter at odds in the wasichu world, echoing the Fox and Sauk at odds with the Mdewakanton in the Dakota world. It didn't promise good things for anyone involved.

CHAPTER 16:

September 1834
Fort Snelling, Michigan Territory

❧

SAMANTHA

"So is married life what you expected?" Eliza Taliaferro asked. She held a cup of coffee in both hands and eyed the plate of honey cookies Samantha set in front of her.

Samantha sipped bitter coffee from a pottery mug with a cracked handle and tried not to make a face. She missed James Henry's pretty porcelain teacups and his imported tea. Alex was a coffee drinker and kept only basic tea in the shop. She was still trying to decide which was acceptable. Neither was good.

The newly married couple had been living at the fort all summer. Eliza was Samantha's most frequent visitor, invited in for coffee. Samantha kept the door open between the store and the living quarters so she could visit and still watch the store. Alex was gone again, so she was in charge. "What single woman ever knows what to expect of marriage?" she said. "When a girl plans, she dreams of romance. Reality is a surprise."

"So the blush is off the rose?" Eliza said, taking one of Samantha's honey cookies off the chipped plate.

Samantha smiled, thinking of how her heart still reacted to her husband's smile. "Oh no, there's still plenty of blush. Fort Snelling's store is a bit more work than the store in Prairie du Chien, though. I can handle it, but I didn't expect it."

"Where is Mr. Miree, anyway? Your Hannah tells Ellie he is hardly ever home."

Samantha sighed. Every slave at the fort knew everyone's business. Alex had insisted that she needed help running the house and store, but she'd flatly refused to own a person. Renting one wasn't much better. Samantha tried to treat Hannah like a friend, but the older woman still distrusted her. "Alex enjoys a trip now and then to trap with a Dakota man he's known for years."

Eliza nodded, a thoughtful expression on her face. "You know by now he has another reason to visit the Sioux?"

Samantha didn't know. Torn between humbling herself to ask outright and ignoring the busybody, she poured more coffee into her guest's cup from a battered tin coffee pot. She decided she didn't want to hear the gossip. "Of course. But what about you? How is Harriet coming along?"

Eliza sipped her coffee and nibbled her cookie. "She'll never be Ellie, but she's biddable and competent."

How awful to be described as biddable and competent. Not for the first time, Samantha empathized with the enslaved women in Eliza's household. It would never do to say that, as it would never do to entertain gossip about her husband. "James Henry and his new wife should be established at Prairie du Chien by now," Samantha said.

"Are you upset to have missed the wedding?"

James Henry was her brother, but Alex was her husband. "Alex regretted he couldn't leave the store for the time it would take to get to St. Louis and back. It's a busy time for trade. He needed to be here." Samantha winced. Would Eliza ask why he wasn't here now if the store was so important? She changed the subject. "Sarah Taylor writes that Fort Crawford has finally been completed."

"Mr. Davis hasn't returned for her yet."

"That's true. It's been hard on her."

"Her father was determined to break off their relationship," Eliza said. "It seems he succeeded." She set her half-empty mug on the table.

Samantha resented Eliza's smug tone. "Fathers get strange ideas. I applaud Sarah for holding out for what she wants. It turned out well for me, after all. It may yet do so for her, especially since Jeff is no longer a soldier."

After Eliza left, a sense of disquiet settled over Samantha. Despite her previous resolve, she wondered what Eliza knew about Alex.

Hannah came in from the kitchen. "I'll get the dishes, ma'am." She shuffled across the floor in her heavy shoes, back stooped from age and hard work.

"Let me help, Hannah." Samantha stood up, but the Black woman gathered the teapot, cups, and cookie plate into her arms.

"I got it, ma'am."

Hannah returned to the kitchen, and Samantha could hear her washing the dishes. Samantha went into the store. Taking a feather duster to the already clean store shelves, she swiped over cans of fruit and meat, bags of coffee and tea, and crocks full of cooking implements.

Samantha hated being alone in the store, hated wondering when Alex would return. To keep busy, she moved a crate of watered-down whiskey further back in the store. She didn't approve of selling so much of it to the Indians. Hiding it in the back wouldn't curtail demand, but she'd have a nicer display up front. She put a small round table in the space and laid out several bags of her honey cookies, each tied with a lavender ribbon. She'd had to insist to Hannah that it was all right for the mistress to make cookies in her own kitchen. The men at the fort liked her baked goods, so Hannah would have to get used to it. Samantha stacked preserved jam made from local raspberries next to the cookies. She and Alex had picked the berries shortly after their arrival at the fort, before she learned he had no intention of going to St. Louis for her brother's wedding. Now she was here without her brother, never having met his new wife, and without her friend Sarah, who grieved the departure of her love. That left Eliza Taliaferro, who was pleasant company as long as you didn't bring up slaves or Indians, and Olive Bliss, the commandant's wife, who couldn't seem to just relax and laugh at anything, and with Hannah, who had never learned to be a friend to a lonely white woman.

The outer door opened and shut softly. Eliza's young Black enslaved girl stood there, just inside, with her hands clasped Samantha said, "Hello, Harriet. Did Mrs. Taliaferro forget something?"

"Hello, Mrs. Miree. My mistress wants her usual tea, please." Anxiety flared in her dark eyes.

Samantha assumed Eliza was testing Harriet, who probably had no idea what kind of tea was her usual. "I have a small bag here. It's Bohea tea, from China. Did you know patriots destroyed over two hundred cases of it during the Boston Tea Party?" She handed the bag to Harriet, who smiled. "Better take some honey cookies, too, just in case."

"Thank you, Mrs. Miree," Harriet said. She gave Samantha a shy smile.

Samantha looked at Harriet, a young woman trying hard to please her mistress, not so different from servants Samantha had known. "I know your mistress can be difficult, Harriet. I'll help

THE RIVER REMEMBERS

where I can, all right?" Samantha did not know how she could help, but it felt like it needed to be said.

Harriet's smile dimmed and she shuffled her feet.

Samantha said, "Tell Mrs. Taliaferro I'll put it on account for her. And here are some cookies for you and Ellie. No charge." She handed Harriet a second bag.

"Thank you, missus." Harriet took the extra bag of cookies and scurried from the store with her mistress's purchases.

Harriet left Samantha's thoughts as soon as she left the store.

Samantha wiped the counter and wondered if it would be better to know how long Alex would be gone. He'd left with nothing more for her than a cheery wave, striding out the sally port to meet his Indian friend at St. Peter's. During the summer, he'd gone hunting for a day or two with Hawk, but this time the packs on his horse had been bigger. How long would he be gone? Or was he taking the food to someone else? When she allowed herself to doubt, she wondered if Alex had married her to watch the store so he would be free to leave for longer periods.

Forcing her mind elsewhere, Samantha considered a response to her mother's recent letter, in which Mama had congratulated her on her marriage and demanded to know everything about Alexander Miree and her life at Fort Snelling. That night, Samantha wrote the letter.

Dearest Mama,

I know my marriage must seem sudden to you, but Alex just swept me off my feet. He's kind and loving, very romantic. Every morning he has tea waiting for me when I awake, and a flower by my place at the table.

Samantha paused. Mama would not understand that Alex never drank tea, only coffee. Would she know the wildflowers near Fort Snelling had long gone to seed? It seemed closer to the truth to imagine the prickly dried stalk of a purple cornflower, rather than its beautiful bloom, as a symbol of her husband's romance. She started over and left out the flowers.

Dearest Mama,

I know my marriage must seem sudden to you, but Alex just swept me off my feet. He's kind and loving, very romantic. Every morning he has tea waiting for me when I awake. I keep the house clean and cook hearty meals like you taught me, and we are content. Alex works hard in the store so that he will be named the permanent sutler, which would be a boon to his confidence. I try to assure him that I would love him no less if he were just the postmaster, but his ambitions are higher for us.

She went on with news of the Indian agency and fort, tidbits from James Henry's last letter, and comments on the Indians she'd met. She set the finished letter aside with only a small flash of guilt. It would be sent with the next batch of outgoing mail.

ON THE DAY ALEX returned, Samantha shuttered the store windows and lit the candles in the front room as usual. The fire in the fireplace sent dancing light across the walls as it banished the chill of the coming winter. She had just settled into her chair and picked up her sewing when she heard his boots on the wooden planks of the porch. Her heart leaped, and she jumped up, reaching the door just as he opened it.

"Hello, wife," he said. His eyes danced with delight and she melted. "It's good to be home!" His clothes were dusty from a long ride, and it looked as though he hadn't bathed since he'd left home two weeks ago. He smelled of dirt and sweat and trees.

Samantha smiled, her heart full. "I missed you, Alex." She went right into his arms, face raised for his kiss. She snuggled for a moment before pulling away. "Have you eaten?"

"My horse is lucky I didn't eat him on that last mile. I didn't stop because I was eager to get home." Alex took off his hat and slapped it against his leg. Dust floated over the floor.

"Wash up and I'll be right back." She went into the kitchen. Hannah was wiping the counter before disappearing into her alcove off the kitchen for the night. "Hannah? Some dinner for Mr. Miree, please?" Samantha tried hard to make her requests sound like something she'd say to a servant rather than orders given to an enslaved woman.

Hannah bobbed her head in acknowledgement and gathered a plate of bread and cheese with salt pork that she sliced and fried.

He came into the room with shirtsleeves rolled up, wiping his face with a towel, just as Hannah set down the plate of dinner. "It feels good to wipe off the dirt of the trail."

Samantha wanted to ask Alex about his absence, but it still stung that she hadn't known beforehand how long he'd be gone. "So did you get a lot of beaver pelts?" Samantha didn't know if he'd even been trapping, but she didn't want to sound like a nag by asking outright.

The light in his eyes dimmed. "Fall is for hunting muskrats. It's much too early in the season for beaver. It's their thick winter coats that are desirable. Hawk will spend the winter following the streams from trap to trap, collecting pelts to sell next summer." He couldn't hide the wistfulness in his voice.

"You've done that, too, haven't you? Before you became sutler?" Samantha said. "Do you intend to take it up again?" She refused to ask aloud if she would spend winters alone.

"No, I can't." He didn't look at her, and he didn't sound convinced.

A sense of unease gripped her and didn't go away as she readied herself for bed. She unpinned her brooch and laid it on her dresser in its usual nighttime place, her hand lingering over it. There was something her husband wasn't telling her. She should ask him what it was, desiring no secrets between husband and wife. The feeling of unease settled into dread in her stomach. If she didn't ask him what he was keeping from her, then it didn't exist and couldn't hurt her.

CHAPTER 17:

Moon When the Corn is Gathered, 1834
Cloud Man's Village

DAY SETS

After a wet summer, harvest began in the mud. The Mdewakanton cut down the straight stalks that had grown taller than the lodges. Once again, Day Sets could see the lake and forest from where she sat in front of the lodge pounding berries that would be mixed with dried deer meat to make *wasna*, an energy food. When harvest was complete, school would start for Mary.

Iron Cutter rode into the village alone. He dismounted and stood before her, his usual tree-trunk straight bearing slumped. Day Sets frowned and stood up. Before she could say anything, Iron Cutter burst into what seemed to be a well-rehearsed speech. "I have come for my daughter. It's time she lived in the company of white women. Her school starts in two weeks. That will give us time to outfit her properly, and for her to settle in."

In the company of white women? That meant Iron Cutter intended to take her daughter to the agency, for his teya to raise, or to the fort. Day Set's eyes narrowed.

"I know the Sioux expect their women to raise the children. A white man, however, has charge of his family. Mary is white according to the law of the nation, and I will have my daughter raised properly."

Day Sets drew herself up to her full height and squared her shoulders. "No," she said.

"No?" Iron Cutter looked confused. "Who are you to tell me . . ."

Cloud Man approached from the area where corn was being put into bark containers to be stored for winter. "Iron Cutter!" he called, his voice anxious.

Day Sets turned to her father, suspicion dawning. Cloud Man wouldn't meet her eyes.

"I haven't yet prepared her," he told Iron Cutter.

It was unclear if he referred to Day Sets or to Mary. Day Sets glowered at both men and crossed her arms over her chest. Her words could not be trusted, so she scowled.

Iron Cutter rubbed the back of his neck. "Day Sets, I . . ."

Cloud Man squared off before his daughter. "Daughter, you have always fulfilled your duty to your people. The future of our tribe lies in your daughter. My wish is for her to get the education she needs to help our people survive."

What about Jane? What about Nancy? Day Sets wanted to scream, but she refused to lose any dignity in front of the two men she used to respect. She turned away from her father to her husband. "She will attend school?"

Iron Cutter nodded.

"You may be her father, but I am her mother. When school is over, she returns to me." Day Set's expression prevented argument.

Cloud Man hurried, in a very undignified way for a head man, into the tipi to fetch his granddaughter. Day Sets stared at Iron Cutter until her father reappeared with Mary.

"Mama?" Mary asked, clearly confused. She smiled at her father and looked for Nero. "Papa?"

"Mary, you will go with your father now. He will take you to school like we planned." Day Set's soft tone was for her daughter, her iron-hard expression for the men. She stood like stone, unforgiving and unmovable, until Iron Cutter had mounted his horse, settled Mary in front of him, and ridden off. Only then did she allow a tear to fall down her cheek.

It was the best decision for Mary, she told herself. Mary would get the education she needed to take her place with the wasichu in their ever-more-powerful presence in the territory. Day Sets knew she'd given Mary the heart of a Mdewakanton woman, and that heart was stronger than the teya's influence could ever be. She'd miss her daughter being in the village, but she'd find a way to make sure Mary remembered. And someday Mary would appreciate the strength it took for her mother to let her go, to let the men take her to a wasichu woman.

IT WASN'T THE POND brothers, after all, who opened the school. Earlier that year, Reverend Jedediah Stevens had arrived at Fort Snelling with his wife, Julia, and two sons. Cornelia, his sixteen-year-old niece, came with them. Cloud Man disliked Reverend Stevens, saying he was overbearing. Day Sets had heard that Reverend Stevens referred to her people as ragged, half-starved, and indolent. No one liked him.

It didn't matter. Reverend Stevens's school at Bde Unma, no, she must say Lake Harriet, was a government school for Mde-wakanton children, as well as the iyeska children that Reverend Stevens called half-breeds. Mrs. Stevens would teach household duties to Mary and the other Mdewakanton girls. They would also sew pieces of colored calico into quilts or counterpanes for a bed. Nancy was too young yet to attend school, but Mary and Jane would learn a lot from Mrs. Stevens. In Reverend Stevens' own words, the school would "create educated Christian women who will be good wives." Even though his tone was demeaning, the skills her daughter would learn were important.

Iron Cutter could be offensive, too, when he treated the Mdewakanton like children, but his position was always nurturing rather than controlling, more of a father than a war chief. For example, during a rare sunny day that summer, Iron Cutter had ridden past the village fields. Several Mdewakanton women were working in the field as usual. Iron Cutter challenged them to a friendly competition, offering a new blanket to the woman with the cleanest field. The other women would each receive a present, depending on their level of effort. Day Sets had heard him tell this story afterward with fatherly pride in the winner. She wanted to tell him that the women would have worked the fields exactly as they had without the promise of presents, but that would have hurt his feelings. Iron Cutter meant well. As he'd meant well when he took Mary away. After all, Mary would get an education. That's what Day Sets had wanted all along. So why did she resent his teya so much?

Last month, Cloud Man had asked Iron Cutter for help with building stables. Day Sets had been nearby when Iron Cutter praised her father for such a progressive move toward assimilation into European customs.

"New stables will give your band independence by allowing you to store food for the winter," Iron Cutter had said. Day Sets waited for him to pat the chief on the shoulder, but he wisely refrained. "I know white settlers are encroaching on your lands. It makes sense to learn from them."

Cloud Man said, "I am a Mdewakanton chief. The people of my village may learn to farm like the wasichu, but we will continue to share our corn with other villages. I cannot keep a stable full of corn when my brother is starving."

Day Sets knew if someone was hungry, and you had food, it was your obligation to feed them. Storing food for yourself only was a wasichu custom the Mdewakanton would never adopt.

Day Sets hadn't heard anything about Mary since Iron Cutter had taken her, so she accompanied Hushes Still the Night when her sister walked Jane to the school. Six children, including Mary, waited in the schoolyard. With her heart in her throat, Day Sets watched Jane run to join her cousin. When Mary saw her mother, she ran to her as if running to greet Nero. Day Sets folded her daughter into her arms.

"Mama, I miss you," Mary said. "Papa's teya hates me. I want to come home."

Day Set's lips tightened. "Do your best in school. Make me proud." She forced herself to encourage Mary to join the other children.

Iron Cutter had never had any children with the teya, and Day Sets knew how much the woman despised Indians. Her stomach churned. Jane would live at the school with the Stevens family. Maybe there was room for Mary, too. She'd convince Iron Cutter to let Mary live there. It would be easier for his teya, she'd tell him. It would also be easier for Mary to be with her cousin Jane, and for Day Sets to visit.

Red Eagle and Grizzly Bear temporarily gave up their cabin to make room for Reverend Stevens' school. Day Sets peered at the wall and shook her head. Snow would blow through those cracks this winter. She'd better bring a warm blanket for Mary. Nearby, the men had stacked logs for a larger school building. The walls were yet only a couple of feet high, but it would have two spacious rooms.

Red Eagle came forward to greet the children. He was the

only wasichu Day Sets knew who had the spirit of the Mde-wakanton within him. He valued the welfare of his entire tribe over his individual wealth. If Red Eagle's tribe was hungry, so was he. In the short time he'd been at the lake he'd accumulated cattle, horses, and sheep. He shared it all and welcomed visitors to his cabin. In the process, he'd learned a lot more of the Dakota language than most white men in the area. Red Eagle had wanted to teach reading and writing of the Dakota language to the entire tribe, but the men weren't interested unless someone served a feast.

Mary and Jane smiled at their new teacher. Day Set's heart warmed to see how eager her daughter was. The girls would do well here. Day Sets and Hushes Still the Night turned toward home.

AT CLOUD MAN'S VILLAGE in winter, her people moved into buffalo hide tipis, which were warmer than the summer lodges. Straw on the ground, covered with bear skins, made the interior cozy. Cloud Man's entire family shared a large tipi, eighty feet around and fifteen feet tall. Day Sets and her sisters had painted scenes on the outside of the tipi of the snakes and horses on the earth, and the buffalo constellation above it.

Day Sets walked past tipis tied closed against the world. Others were open, and women sat watching her go by with eyes sunk into starving faces, skin hanging from gaunt limbs. The only food in sight was yet another corn cake fried on a fire and shared by an entire family. Day Sets saw a small group of hunters gnawing on pieces of pemmican. Hunting grew worse every day. The game had all been hunted or driven away, the summer berries all gathered and eaten. Cloud Man's people shared the corn harvest among the tribe members, but it didn't go far. In her mind, Day Sets heard Iron Cutter admonishing them to put away part of the harvest until the dead of winter. But they were hungry now. If they didn't eat now, they wouldn't need food at all in a few months when *Iya*, the storm spirit of the north, came.

Star Dancing lifted the bearskin hide covering the opening of her small tipi and came out just as Day Sets passed. Her breath reeked less of alcohol than usual, and she'd made an effort to clean herself. She tied back the flap as she greeted Day Sets, who could see a large blanket-wrapped lump topped with a blond tousled head inside the tipi.

"Pale Crow sleeps like a baby." Her smile meant their daughter, Winona, slept, too.

"Alex," Day Sets said. "Alex Miree is his wasichu name." Her tone was flat. She liked Samantha, and she'd also learned more about the culture that tied a man to a woman exclusive of anyone else. Day Sets knew it was common for a wasichu to have both a white wife, what he'd call a legal wife, and an Indian wife, what he'd call a mistress. Usually, though, the wasichu husband didn't stay long with his Mdewakanton wife in the village. It didn't bother Mdewakanton women if their husbands had more than one family, but since she'd gotten to know Samantha Miree, Day Sets understood how deeply a white woman relied on her husband to love and support only her.

"I call him Pale Crow," Star Dancing said. "Winona calls him Papa." Her tone was smug.

Day Sets just stared as Star Dancing reentered her tipi. Had she just come out to make a point that Pale Crow was there? And why hadn't she sent Winona to the school? Surely Pale Crow wanted his daughter educated.

Two mornings later, Day Sets joined Hushes Still the Night in front of her tipi. Before the day's conversation could begin, Stands Sacred joined them. Near the center of the village, their sister Laughing Bird came out of the tipi she shared with her husband, Jim Thompson.

Jim Thompson had come west a few years earlier as a slave with George Monroe, the nephew of President James Henry Monroe. George Monroe had run up a debt at the fort store, and given Jim to the sutler, John Culbertson, as payment for those debts. When Culbertson left, he sold Jim to Captain George Day. The captain allowed Jim Thompson to live at Cloud Man's village as long as he came to the fort every day.

Laughing Bird met Jim Thompson at the Indian agency when she was there with Iron Cutter. While Jim's mother had been an enslaved Black woman, his father was wasichu. From the first time she saw him, Laughing Bird had loved Jim. She was entranced by his coffee-colored skin, even darker than her own. She fell in love with his intelligence and willingness to learn the Dakota language. Laughing Bird taught him more of her language, and he interpreted for his master. Day Sets sighed. She'd never loved Iron Cutter like that. Laughing Bird could be smug that hers was the closest any of the sisters had to a traditional marriage as the *wasichu* saw it. Jim was a Black man, not white, but the Mdewakanton still thought of him as wasichu, since he was not part of the tribes.

Laughing Bird joined her sisters, and the four of them enjoyed a moment's peace before their mother, Red Cherry Woman, brought Stands Sacred's daughter, Nancy Eastman, to the gathering. Tears streaked Nancy's face.

"What's wrong, daughter?" Stands Sacred asked. She glared at Red Cherry Woman, since Nancy had been fine a few minutes ago.

"Mary and Jane are gone," Nancy said, her chin trembling.

Stands Sacred reached into her pouch for a maple sugar candy to soothe the girl.

"I'm sorry," Day Sets said. She knew Nancy missed her cousins while they were at school. She could join them next year, but Day Sets wasn't sure now was the time to tell little Nancy that.

Stands Sacred changed the subject. She asked Day Sets, "How is the school doing?"

Hushes Still the Night said, "They have no supplies to teach. How can it succeed?"

"It's a beginning," Day Sets said. They had no books or materials, but the children couldn't read English anyway. Red Eagle spoke Dakota well enough to teach them, though.

"Daniel said the missionaries were more shocked by how the boys were dressed," Hushes Still the Night said. Her husband, Daniel Lamont, had spent some time with the missionaries that afternoon, settling the children who would stay with the missionaries rather than return home each evening.

"Were they dressed at all?" Stands Sacred said. She laughed. "Maybe that was the problem?"

The sisters laughed again at the idea of the modest missionaries dealing with the near-nudity of young Mdewakanton children.

When the laughter subsided, Red Cherry Woman again changed the subject. "A band of refugees came to Cloud Man yesterday. More tribes are being forced west."

"What of the Mdewakanton?" Stands Sacred asked the question they all wondered about.

"Iron Cutter will fight for us," Day Sets insisted.

Red Cherry Woman said, "Relying on the wasichu has not served us well. We must make the best of our farming village and hope it is enough to appease the government."

Laughing Bird said, "If we act too much like wasichu, we lose our Mdewakanton heart. If we act too Mdewakanton, we lose our land."

Her words echoed in Day Set's mind as they all grew quiet. Would Cloud Man's insistence that they adopt the wasichu's ways be enough? At first, it was farming. Now her father talked as though they all needed to become Christians. What would that mean for the Taku Wakan that surrounded and protected them? What would it mean for Mary, who lived in a wasichu household and went to a wasichu school?

As autumn grew colder and winter reared its ugly head, the little school at Bde Unma suffered. Boys left school when hunting parties went out for food. The tribe needed every hunter so the tribe wouldn't starve. Boys also skipped school to go fishing, claiming they needed the food for their families. Day Sets suspected it was just a boyish lark. Julia Stevens tried to teach the girls to weave wool from Joseph Renville's fleeces, but they couldn't quite master it.

Day Sets visited the school to see how Mary was doing. She arrived just as a group of government inspectors left, so the school was clean and orderly. The teacher allowed Mary time to sit outside with her mother. The six-year-old wiggled as she sat, and looked back toward the classroom door. Day Sets hid a smile, glad Mary was enjoying the lessons.

"What is your favorite part of the day?"

"I enjoy learning English, Mama. They have wonderful stories in books. Miss Julia promises we will get to read them all when more books arrive. Right now we are reading stories from the Bible." She wrinkled her nose. "Some are fun, but most are confusing."

Day Sets smiled. "What's the hardest part?"

"Arithmetic!" Mary didn't hesitate. "English letters are bad enough, but arithmetic is full of strange marks."

"Is it something you need to learn?" Day Sets had explained to Mary over and over that she must be a successful white woman as well as a chief's granddaughter.

Mary thought for a moment. "I can count the people in the tribe, and count animals in a herd if necessary. I've never seen a wasichu woman besides Miss Julia do arithmetic. Maybe I don't need it."

Day Sets nodded. "Try to master it, anyway, if your teacher says you must." She patted her daughter's leg and stood. Mary walked back to the classroom like a little lady. Day Sets pride faded as she thought of Mary's life with Iron Cutter and his teya.

CHAPTER 18:

October, 1834
Fort Snelling, Michigan Territory

SAMANTHA

Winter arrived at the end of September when half an inch of ice formed overnight. The weather had been cold and wet, but with the advent of October, it turned frigid and so dry that smoke from a prairie fire blanketed the fort. On the day Henry Sibley arrived, blustery winds whipped at the fort's flag. Snow squalls plummeted the temperature to below freezing. Samantha alternated between wearing fur gloves for warmth and taking off her gloves so she could use her hands. She'd never mastered the art of needlework with gloves, but then she'd never lived in a place where even the hearth by a blazing fire was cold.

The man rode into the fort as if he owned the place. His bushy mustache belied the receding hairline he'd tried to cover by combing a longer hank of hair across the top of his head. Samantha, sweeping the porch of the store, thought it just made him look vain. He dismounted and walked past her into the store with such a straight bearing he could have been a general.

Samantha kept sweeping. He'd come out again when he realized Alex wasn't there. Her husband had gone to deliver guns, ammunition, and other supplies to Hawk at Cloud Man's village. He planned to give them to the Indians on credit. They would pay with beaver pelts when they returned in the spring. So Samantha was once again in charge. Heavy bootsteps announced the man's return.

"Where's the sutler?"

Samantha swept twice more before turning to address him. "My husband isn't here at the moment. I am Mrs. Miree. May I help you?"

"Henry Sibley, ma'am." His tone was polite, but his eyes glittered, cold as the air. "When will he return?"

"May I give him a message, sir?" Samantha leaned the broom against the store's wall and rubbed her hands together.

Sibley gave her an appraising glance, in which it seemed he saw nothing of value. "Tell him the American Fur Company has a new partner in Mendota, across the river."

"I know where Mendota is. This new partner is you?"

"It is."

"I shall give my husband the message." Samantha retrieved the broom, then hesitated. "And what was your name again?"

"Sibley." He snapped out his name and turned to go.

Samantha resumed sweeping and smiled at her ability to rile this odious man.

Over the next few days, the fort buzzed about Henry Sibley. The American Fur Company had controlled trade in the region since John Jacob Astor ran the company. The company's presence in Mendota was not new. Sibley, though, brought a new arrogance. He began construction of an enormous stone building. Rumor said it would be the finest trading post in the territory.

Samantha worried what that meant for Alex. After all, his position as sutler was still temporary. As Fort Snelling's postmaster, however, he had no permanent place to conduct business other than the store. During winter, when the river froze, the U. S. Post Office paid traders and scouts to carry the mail overland between Fort Snelling and Fort Crawford. Letters and packages arrived sporadically during that time. The rest of the year, when the steamboats could make their way upriver, the mail arrived on schedule. In any case, Fort Snelling needed a place to receive and disburse mail, a place other than the store, which a permanent sutler would manage. Or they could continue to have the sutler handle the mail. Samantha shuddered. What would Alex do if he lost both positions? Colonel Bliss might choose Henry Sibley's American Fur Company to supply the fort.

The soldiers who frequented the store also passed along another rumor that the military planned to build another post somewhere on the upper Des Moines River. The new post required a sutler right in the heart of American Fur Company territory.

Late one afternoon, Hannah worked in the kitchen preparing a simple supper. Samantha sat by the fire sewing. The adjoining door to the store was open so she could hear customers if they arrived. A loud crash and prolific cussing caused her to set down her sewing and hurry into the store.

Alex stood at the counter, enraged. A broken crockery pot lay in pieces on the floor among the pickled onions it once contained. Samantha hesitated in the doorway, watching her husband pick up a crock of salted meat and hurl it to the floor. The resulting crash caused Samantha to wince. When he lifted the crock of butter, she stepped forward.

"Alex, stop! Whatever is the matter?"

"The damned American Fur Company, that's what!" He threw the crock.

Samantha ignored the mess of butter, pickled onions, and salted meat on the floor. "Let me make you a cup of tea. We can talk about this."

"I don't drink your goddamn tea! No drink other than whiskey can calm my fury at this moment!"

"Then let me pour you a stiff whiskey." Samantha forced her voice to remain calm. She'd never seen her light-hearted husband so angry. He took life as it came, pleasure first, and ignored anything negative.

She coaxed him into their home, settling him in his favorite chair with a large glass of whiskey. He huffed a bit longer from anger and exertion but regained control. Samantha waited.

"Thank you," he said, lifting his glass toward her. "I needed this, and home, and you." He looked at her with tortured eyes. "American Fur is coming."

Samantha nodded. "I met Henry Sibley. He came looking for you."

"No doubt to throw down the gauntlet. I fear my post here is in jeopardy. It's Joe Rolette's fault. He and Sibley were thick as thieves in Prairie du Chien. Rolette seeks to expand his personal control of American Fur territory while working within the company so he made Sibley a partner."

"What will you do?" Samantha knew how much her brother disliked Rolette. When James Henry spoke the man's self-styled title of King, he couldn't control his sneer. She wondered if she should encourage Alex to fight for his job. Is that what he wanted?

Alex rubbed the back of his neck and downed his whiskey. He poured another glass. "Major Bliss won't make the decision to hire sutlers. Too bad, because the major knows I have connections to the Dakota. He knows the job I've done."

Samantha wondered if Alex realized how much time she

spent covering for him when he was hunting with Hawk. The commandant saw that, too.

"No, Major Bliss will have no say in the decision. A dandy back East will bestow the favor of a position upon someone who can further his fortune or career. John Jacob Astor may no longer own American Fur, but the company has plenty of powerful political connections I don't have."

"Stuff and nonsense, Alex. Pull yourself together and assemble a plan to fight for your job."

"Fight what? So far it's speculation and rumor. The only solid evidence that anything is in the works is that monstrous stone building Sibley is putting up in Mendota. He's making a statement."

Saying any more to him was pointless. He was determined to wallow in defeat. Maybe in the morning he'd be in a different mood. Samantha sewed in silence as Alex poured himself another glass of whiskey.

She'd never seen this morose side of him. His attitude was always positive and light, like when he closed the store on a whim and went hunting. Now she understood what an imposition that had been for the fort before she was there to keep the store open.

James Churchman had done nothing on the spur of the moment in his life. Samantha had found his meticulous plans boring. She wondered about that. Looking back, he seemed stable and secure, not boring. Her hands shook as she set her sewing in her lap and looked at Alex, the husband she loved and had chosen. He stared into his whiskey glass and swirled the golden contents.

Hannah came in to say dinner was ready. Samantha and Alex moved to the table without talking. Pushing James out of her head, Samantha ate her meal while mulling over ways she could help Alex, who picked at his meal and said nothing.

The following morning, Alex rose at the usual time and went through the motions of starting a normal day. His sunny banter was missing, though. A restless night's sleep hadn't erased the strain in his face that had appeared yesterday after hearing about Henry Sibley.

Samantha pinned on her brooch and tiptoed into the kitchen to pour coffee for Alex. Hannah made a breakfast of toasted bread and jam, and even laid out leftover stew. A cloud of depression weighed Alex down. He muttered responses to his wife and offered nothing new. When he went to open the store, Samantha untied her bright purple apron. She hung it on a hook in the kitchen, remembering Alex's delight in acquiring the fabric in such a garish shade of her favorite color. She loved that he'd been so thoughtful.

Determined, she walked through the store. "I'll be back in a while, Alex. I'm off to visit Olive Bliss."

He nodded without looking at her.

At the commandant's house, Hannibal showed Samantha into the parlor. Mrs. Bliss appeared. If it was possible, her graying hair was pulled even tighter against her head. Hannibal returned with a tray of tea and scones.

"Mrs. Miree, what an unexpected pleasure." She took a seat near Samantha and directed Hannibal to pour tea.

"I am sorry to disturb you so early and without invitation," Samantha said. "My husband arrived home last night." She paused, uncertain how to approach the rumor.

"You must be glad to have him," Mrs. Bliss said, her tone neutral.

Samantha changed her tactic. "Mr. Sibley has made quite a stir on both sides of the river."

Olive nodded.

"I hear he hopes to take on a government position."

"Oh?" said Olive, still neutral.

Samantha wished she could just forego formality and ask about the major's plans for the sutler. With Eliza Taliaferro she could do that. Despite the woman's faults, Eliza was a friend. "Mr. Miree hears talk of a new government post in the area. Do you know of such plans?" Samantha winced at her own gall. But she had to help her husband.

"I am not privy to government plans," Olive said.

"Your husband may be."

"That is so."

Samantha changed her approach again. "It's unnecessary for me to know the plans. I just want you and the major to remember that my husband and I together are doing a good job running the store. Major Bliss will need a permanent sutler if the army builds a new post. My husband would like to retain the post."

Olive Bliss stood, ending the discussion. "I will pass on your preference to the major."

It was the best she could do. Samantha thanked her hostess for the tea and left the commandant's house.

CHAPTER 19:

October, 1834

St. Peter's Agency, Michigan Territory

HARRIET

Harriet ran downstairs to the kitchen where Ellie was baking the bread she'd started very early that morning. She looked up when Harriet rushed in. Harriet put a finger to her lips, then pointed to the ceiling. The rumble of men's voices reached them as the major and his visitor walked across the room and settled above the kitchen.

"Dr. Williamson," Harriet said to Ellie, who tilted her head, questioning. "Missionary," Harriet clarified.

"Another one?" Ellie said.

The visitor's voice carried to the kitchen. "Thank you for seeing me, major. I arrived a little later in the season than planned. I'm here to establish a Presbyterian mission at Lake Harriet. It will have to be in the spring, now."

"Isn't that where that dreadful Reverend Stevens is?" Harriet asked Ellie in a low voice.

Ellie nodded and shushed her.

Upstairs, Major Taliaferro said, "You're not the first to try religion on the Indians."

"I'm aware," Dr. Williamson said. "I'm not here alone. I will be the doctor and missionary, and I have colleagues with me. Our wives are with us, as well as two young ladies who will be teachers."

"The Dakota have a school at Lake Harriet already. It's new, but Gideon and Samuel Pond seem to have it well in hand." The major's tone questioned the doctor.

"It is my understanding that Lake Harriet is remote enough that the Indians have not yet been tempted by the white man's vices."

Major Taliaferro laughed. "Oh, they're aware of alcohol. They've also had help with farming at Eatonville. The Pond brothers have been out there all summer."

"We'll be at Fort Snelling all winter. It will give us time to learn the language. We've started a Presbyterian church there since Major Bliss allows us to preach to the Christian soldiers."

"You're welcome to talk to the Indians camped here at the agency," Major Taliaferro said. "A few of them know English. None of the soldiers know the Dakota language."

The new missionary went on to explain they'd actually been in the territory all summer, but had only recently decided to make Lake Harriet their mission.

Whining and scratching at the kitchen door distracted Harriet from the conversation upstairs. She let Nero in. "What's the matter, big boy? Did your papa throw you out instead of letting you drool all over the visitor?"

The dog panted and looked up at her with adoring eyes. Of course she had to give him a biscuit. Nero preferred Major Taliaferro, his master, but if the major shut him out, he ran to find Harriet.

The door still stood open, and Mary, the master's Indian daughter, poked her head into the kitchen. She'd been living there only a few weeks, and had learned to stay out of the mistress's way.

Harriet nodded at her. "Come on, then, little miss, I'll find some cookies."

Ellie laughed. "You spoilin' both of them."

"I never had a dog or a baby to spoil, so I'm enjoyin' it." Harriet patted Nero's head and he curled up at her feet, under the kitchen work table. She fetched two cookies for Mary and poured her a glass of milk to go with them. The girl smiled shyly and crawled under the table with Nero.

Ellie took two Dutch ovens off the fire and opened the lids to poke at the bread inside.

Harriet thought about the white people coming from the East to teach the Indians about God. The Indians considered Black people to be white. "Why ain't missionaries preachin' to slaves?" she asked.

"Maybe 'cause Presbyterians send missionaries but Baptists don't," Ellie said.

Harriet remembered the comfort of the Baptist church she'd attended in St. Louis, where she'd stayed several times when Mrs. Taliaferro visited her family there. Free Blacks and indentured servants attended Reverend Meacham's church in addition to slaves who'd been given permission, and the Taliaferros had allowed her to attend. "I suppose it's just as well," she said to Ellie. "We don't have a minute to spare for church service. I'm sure the Lord understands."

Ellie turned out the bread to cool and turned to chop a pile of potatoes.

Harriet had known free Blacks who'd attended Reverend Meacham's church in St. Louis. Missouri was a slave state. It seemed harder to be free there than to be enslaved here in Fort

Snelling. "Thomas says there are free Blacks besides Stephen Bonga 'round here. That true?" Harriet asked Ellie.

"It's a free territory," Ellie responded. "I s'pose we should all be free, but I'm sure the master wouldn't agree. Why you thinking about free Blacks?"

"I dunno," Harriet said. "It's just so different here."

Ellie covered the warm bread with a clean towel and untied her apron. "Come on, Harriet. We need to walk over to the fort for a few things. Mrs. Miree should have the order ready."

Harriet took off her own apron, picked up an empty basket, and waited by the outside door while Ellie wiped flour off her cheek. Nero bounded after them, but Harriet told him no. Mary held him by the collar and he sat by the back door to the house as they walked up the road to the fort.

At the gate to the fort, Ellie said, "You go on to the store. I'm to see Dr. Jarvis, the fort surgeon."

Harriet looked at her in surprise. "Are you ill?"

Ellie fidgeted with her hands and wouldn't meet Harriet's eye. "Something like that."

Harriet watched her with fresh eyes. As they entered the fort, Ellie's shoulders slumped. Her eyes darkened as she walked to the hospital just inside the fort's gate. She looked as though she was undertaking something dreadful.

Inside the store, Harriet collected the items her mistress had ordered, including her bag of Bohea tea. A brash man came to the counter, stomping like he owned the place, and ignored Harriet. He spoke loudly to Mrs. Miree. "Mr. Miree is gone again? Things will change around here once I'm appointed sutler."

A Black man slipped out of the shadows to follow the man from the store. He carried one big sack of sugar. Harriet's eyes followed him with interest.

Mrs. Miree gave a deep sigh, which brought Harriet's attention back to her. "Harriet, have you met the larger-than-life Mr. Sibley?" The wave of her hand indicated the brash man who'd just left.

"No, ma'am, haven't had the pleasure."

"He's out to conquer the world."

"Was that his slave?"

"Joe Robinson is Mr. Sibley's cook. They were here to buy sugar, much to Mr. Sibley's dismay. It seems the post in Mendota doesn't have sugar yet. I'm not sure if Joe is a slave or not. He acts like one, but Mr. Sibley can't be an easy man to work for."

Harriet puzzled over a Black man working for a difficult person by choice. She decided Joe must be enslaved. Why else would he stay with a man who mistreated him? If she were free, she wouldn't still work for Mrs. Taliaferro! "Why you say Sibley wants to conquer the world?" she asked Mrs. Miree.

"I'm sorry, I shouldn't have said that. Mr. Sibley makes no secret of the fact he flouts the law to bring whiskey upriver for the Indians. Major Taliaferro seizes these shipments. It won't be easy for the major to deal with Mr. Sibley should he be appointed to this position."

Harriet nodded and gathered her purchases into her basket. A frank discussion with a white woman made her uncomfortable. Once more outside the store, Harriet walked toward the gate, her eyes on the hospital door. She was just at the gate when Ellie hurried out of the building. Bits of hair escaped the tight braids on her head.

"Ellie, what's goin' on with you and the surgeon?" Harriet said as they left the fort. She was tired of Ellie's secrets. They were friends, and friends should be able to share everything.

"I'm pregnant, Harriet." Her lip quivered and tears dampened her eyes.

"Is Dr. Jarvis the father?" Harriet asked.

Ellie wiped her eyes and walked out of the fort, chin up and lips pressed together.

CHAPTER 20:

June, 1835
St. Peter's Agency, Michigan Territory

⟨≈∽≈⟩

HARRIET

The heavy rain in June pelted Indian, trader, soldier, and slave alike. It ruined the Indians' crops, and hunters had to range farther and farther from home to find the game they needed to feed themselves. Indians erected tipis along the river near the agency and ate the entire season's crop of potatoes by the end of June. Hunger persisted across the tribes. Promised supplies from the U.S. government didn't come. The Dakota lurked around the agency, wanting to be the first to hear of annuities being delivered. They made Harriet nervous, and she hid in the kitchen when they were close, keeping a sodden Nero nearby.

One day, Harriet heard her master and mistress talking as she and Ellie chopped vegetables in the kitchen.

"The *Warrior* turned back at Prairie du Chien," the major said.

"With our supplies?" the mistress asked.

He nodded. "It was full of items for the Indians, too, but they chose not to continue upriver."

Harriet thought he sounded defeated. Her own shoulders slumped. The supplies coming upriver were necessary for everyone near the fort.

"What will you do?" Eliza said. "More of them surround the agency every day."

"The Indians expected their annuity a month ago. It gives them hunting supplies as well as food. They can't hunt buffalo without those supplies, and they'll starve without the food. I will have to feed them from my own stored goods."

Ellie nodded to Harriet, who wiped her hands. They went upstairs just as their master called for them.

"Bring fifty-nine rations of pork and fifty-nine rations of flour to the yard at the back of the house," he told them.

"Yes, sir," Ellie said. Harriet nodded and followed Ellie back outside.

Ellie stretched and rubbed her back. Her pregnancy was not her first, but it was causing her difficulty. Harriet took over more of the tasks and urged her to rest. She knew of many slaves who'd become pregnant by white men, and she knew of the mothers' fear that the baby would someday be sold away from her. Again, Harriet wondered about Ellie's previous children. Again, she decided not to ask.

Ellie waved toward the stable, where the four men came running to help. They lugged the supplies up from the storage room off the kitchen, which was the only place they could be stored and stay safe from being looted. Thomas smiled at Harriet, but he rarely flirted with her any more. She missed the attention even though she didn't have time for such foolishness.

Major Taliaferro oversaw distribution of his largesse, logging each transaction and having the Indian receive the goods by making an X next to the entry. Nero sat tall, ears perked, monitoring all that food leaving his domain.

Several days later, Wah-pah-koota's tribe, eighty in all, danced the buffalo dance. They implored the Indian Great Spirit to send them food, but still the *Warrior* didn't come.

Major Taliaferro took to riding out from the agency every day in the morning, as soon as he'd delivered Mary to school. He spent the day checking on Eatonville, and on scattered tribes under his protection. Nero trotted along next to the horse. He always returned when Mary's school was finished for the day.

"His absence an excuse to get away from the starvin' beggars 'round here," Ellie said.

Harriet understood that her master had a limited ability to help, and that frustrated him. It wasn't fair that he was supposed to soothe the Indians with missed deliveries and broken promises. Besides, she approved of his presence at home when Mary was there. It provided a buffer between the little girl and the mistress's icy attitude toward the child.

At last, the *Warrior* arrived. Indians came out of tipis and walked trails to line the bluff and the road up from the dock. Major Taliaferro distributed the supplies and provisions to them. Iron for the forge at the agency arrived, too, as well as extensive supplies for Henry Sibley's trading post across the river at Mendota. Major Taliaferro told his wife about Sibley's delivery while Harriet served them dinner.

"Sibley's setting in basic supplies like bacon and hams, kegs of lard and tallow, bushels of corn, that sort of thing. He also has barrels of sugar from New Orleans, dried peaches and apples, molasses, and coffee. He received a large pile of trade goods for dealing with the tribes; woolen blankets, bright cloth, guns, traps, and tinware. The most ostentatious, though, are the luxury items he's stocking, the Cavendish tobacco, British soap, port wine, and sperm oil from Nantucket! He's determined to outdo every storekeeper in the territory."

Harriet told Ellie downstairs, "Master says competition a good thing."

Ellie smiled. "He probably believed that until this new man came."

In July, when a painter named George Catlin arrived, Harriet and Ellie watched from the agency house's back garden as tourists gawked at the Indians in their tipis.

"Like a trip to the zoo," Ellie murmured. She stretched her back, sore from weeding the vegetables.

Major Taliaferro came out to greet the painter. "George! Clara! Welcome!" Turning to the Indians nearby, he said, "This is Mister Catlin and his wife."

Nero stood next to his master, wagging his long black tail in support.

A small band of Ojibwe were visiting the agency, and Catlin set up his easel to paint them. Clara Catlin sat at his side.

Harriet watched an Ojibwe woman approach Mrs. Catlin. The Ojibwe woman had a baby strapped to her back in a bent-wood cradle, beads swinging from the crosspiece that protected the baby's head. The Indian mother offered a cone of maple sugar for sale, then spoke to Clara.

Harriet couldn't understand what the Indian said, but the hand motions that accompanied her words caused surprised delight on Clara's face. Her hand went to her belly. The Ojibwe woman must believe Clara to be pregnant with her first child.

"A child born in a safe world," Ellie said, a hand on her own belly, "safe and fed with its parents."

Harriet's heart wrenched at the words. She'd been sold away from her mother, but not as an infant. Harriet had memories of her mother singing as they did the household's laundry, memories of love surrounded by the scent of hot soapy water. If you had to be born to an enslaved woman, it was much better to be in a territory where the child would be free, not able to be sold away.

Ellie and Harriet watched as the painter bought an extra baby cradle from the Ojibwe mother. Part of the deal seemed to be a portrait of her, as she sat while Catlin painted her.

Later that night, Harriet was in the kitchen washing up the dinner dishes. Ellie sat at the work table. Upstairs, the Taliaferros were talking after finishing their meal.

"Why did Mr. Catlin paint only the Ojibwe women?" the mistress asked.

Major Taliaferro laughed. "He finds the Dakota women boring in their plain broadcloth skirts, and they cover themselves in shapeless, colorless blankets."

"The Dakota used to have trinkets and beaded clothing," the mistress said. "They traded them to Dr. Jarvis for food and medicine."

"Catlin was so impressed with the doctor's collection of authentic artifacts that he offered to buy it," Major Taliaferro said. Nero's tail thumped, causing dust to fall into the room below.

Harriet looked at her own plain gray dress. "I guess the painter wouldn't be interested in painting slaves, either." She smiled at Ellie. "Who's got time to pose for him, anyway?"

Independence Day dawned dry if not clear. The summer had been the coldest and wettest ever recorded at the fort, so momentary lack of rain was a cause for celebration. Cannons blasted the air as promised, and drums pounded the earth between the agency and the fort. For two hours, the Dakota and Ojibwe men played lacrosse. George Catlin exclaimed over the athleticism of He Who Stands on Both Sides. Later he painted the champion with his racquet in his hand. When the game was over, the tribes danced for three hours, traditional dances like the Beggars, the Buffalo, the Bear, the Eagle, and the Dance of the Braves.

After the games on Fourth of July, Major Taliaferro presented the winners with a barrel of flour, pork, and tobacco. The Dakota danced in appreciation of these trophies.

While George Catlin and his tourists remained at the fort, the Taliaferros had a grand party. Mrs. Taliaferro loved to entertain, and every visitor to Fort Snelling was an excuse to have company. For days, Harriet and Ellie washed the glassware and fine black and white china that had been transported from the East. They washed and ironed table linens, polished silver, and sharpened knives. Harriet dusted the high shelves in the parlor and scolded Nero for shedding upwards. They collected produce from the garden, baked buttermilk biscuits, made fruit sweets, and prepared a buffet of smoked game hens, prairie chickens, fish, ham, and geese. Harriet donned her best starched apron and watched from the sidelines, ready to serve lemonade and strawberries or refill glasses.

The evening began with toasts to Uncle Sam and the Constitution, and songs like "Yankee Doodle" and "The Star-Spangled Banner." The men shared war stories and Catlin related stories from his travels. He talked about the poorly clad, poorly fed Dakota. It was why he preferred to paint the Ojibwe.

The music died away late that night. Harriet stepped outside for a breath of fresh air and some quiet, Nero beside her. The horses and cattle seemed restless. Shouting came from the men near the stable. Thomas ran toward the house. "Master! Something's after the cattle!" Nero barked, and Major Taliaferro ran outside with his rifle.

Harriet stayed where she was, unwilling to jump into the melee. Dark shapes dodged and ducked. The master shot the rifle. Silence descended. Nero growled. Mrs. Taliaferro appeared in the doorway. The major came to reassure her. "It was a cougar, Eliza. I scared it off before it could attack Nero."

To Harriet, he sounded more shaken than reassuring. A cougar that close to the house was scary. She stepped back inside the kitchen and fastened the bent-nail clasp as firmly as she could.

Last year, the Taliaferros had wintered at the agency together for the first time. Now experienced, the mistress would stay through this winter, too. The household scurried to prepare for winter as the sumac turned bright red.

CHAPTER 21:

July, 1835
Fort Snelling, Michigan Territory

SAMANTHA

Samantha held Sarah's letter in one hand and clutched her amethyst brooch in the other. Sarah Taylor and Jefferson Davis had eloped during the rain that consumed the month of June. Unable to gain Colonel Taylor's permission to wed, the couple took matters into their own hands and married at her aunt's home in Louisville, Kentucky. Samantha remembered how the June rain had pounded the windows of the store as if trying to slap her in the face. After enduring her first brutally cold winter in the territory, she'd longed for summer sun but received June rain instead. It would not have been a romantic time to run away with your lover. Now that July had begun, the rain had lessened, and the sun appeared to be drying up the mud. Samantha smiled as she imagined Jeff and Sarah happily established at their plantation in Louisiana.

"Samantha! Are you ready?" Hurried thumping accompanied Alex's loud voice from the porch. The man made more noise the more he hurried.

"I'm coming," she said. Putting Sarah's letter in her dresser drawer, Samantha joined her husband outside the store, where a small crowd of people had gathered. The visiting painter, George Catlin, spoke of his favorite subject. His light eyes brightened with enthusiasm even as his hawk nose promised disdain.

"We shall create a Fashionable Tour, ladies and gentlemen! Visitors will see but a small part of the great Far West, but such magnificence! This tour will make unknown splendor accessible to the world, especially for the ladies."

Samantha smiled. The painter was moved by the splendor of the area. He nearly toppled himself, swinging his arms wide enough to encompass the entire vista. Despite a light rain, today his party would continue upriver to the Falls of St. Anthony, a trip Samantha remembered with fondness. Clara Catlin accompanied her husband, as did a group of school-aged girls chaperoned by respectable matrons with umbrellas. Tourists were new for Fort Snelling. Samantha was here only to see them off on their day trip, but Alex would accompany them. It had become usual for her to stay behind and mind the store.

She walked with the group to the top of the road down to the dock, but hung back as her husband joined the group around Mr. Catlin. Alex wouldn't miss her if she wasn't on the dock blowing kisses of farewell. To be honest, she was just too tired to walk down the hill and back up. She needed to conserve her energy.

As soon as the boat departed, Samantha returned to the wheat bread that she'd left to rise before rereading Sarah's letter. She began kneading as Hannah got out the cornmeal.

"I'm a bit tired today, Hannah." Samantha wasn't complaining as much as she was trying to start a conversation.

The older woman looked up from mixing cornbread. "You won't have much energy until after midwinter."

Samantha frowned. "Why would you say that?"

"You're with child."

Samantha stopped and stared. "With child?" She had only begun to hope for a child when her monthly bleeding hadn't come. "Are you sure?"

Hannah just smiled.

Euphoria brought a rush of energy to Samantha. A child! She would have a little person to keep her company and fill her days.

"Your husband'll be happy?" Hannah knew more about her marriage than Samantha had told her in words.

"I'm sure he will be." Samantha frowned. "We've never discussed children."

Hannah said nothing, but her lips tightened.

"What?" Samantha asked. When Hannah stirred her batter rather than reply, Samantha put a hand on her arm to stop her. She didn't want the other woman's friendliness to fade back into obscurity. "What, Hannah?"

Hannah sighed, put down the bowl of cornbread batter, and faced Samantha. "I din' wan' to be the one to tell you. I hoped you find out on your own."

All the innuendo surrounding Alex flooded Samantha's brain. She'd been stupid to ignore it. "Tell me." Her hand went to her brooch.

"That Hawk be a good friend of your husband, but he not the reason Mr. Miree visits the village so often." She hesitated, but continued when Samantha said nothing. "He go to see Star Dancing and her daughter."

"Star Dancing?" Samantha's gut clenched as her intuition filled in the story. She had to hear the words, though.

Hannah straightened. "The Indians say Mr. Miree, he marry Star Dancing in the Dakota way before you come to the fort. They got a daughter, Winona."

To her surprise, Samantha wasn't angry. She felt no jealousy, either. Even if she hadn't allowed herself to suspect, she'd known. Deep inside, she knew something else held most of her husband's affections. She tried to think of something sassy to say, something to lighten the tension that gathered between them. Nothing came to her. Both women resumed their work in silence.

Questions crowded Samantha's head. Married in the Dakota way, like Day Sets was married to Major Taliaferro? Did Star Dancing depend on Alex to introduce her daughter to the ways of the white man like Day Sets depended on Mary's father? Did Alex love Star Dancing? Did he love their daughter? What would Samantha's child mean to him? What did Samantha mean to him? The questions pushed all coherent words out of her head.

After setting the bread in the brick oven to bake, Samantha turned to Hannah. "Thank you for telling me. I didn't want to admit anything was wrong. How old is Winona?"

"She be four."

Samantha nodded.

"You know Hannibal? Belong to Cap'n Bliss? He friends with Jim Thompson. You know, Captain Day's slave?" Samantha nodded and Hannah continued, "Jim be married to Day Set's sister. Those Indian women raise their own children. When the father's a white man, he go back to his white wife, his white world, and leave his Indian family behind."

"Major Taliaferro hasn't done that."

"No," Hannah agreed. "No, he hasn't."

Alex was still part of Star Dancing's life, part of Winona's life, even though he was living at the fort with her. Samantha tried to tell herself she didn't care. She had more in common with Eliza Taliaferro than she'd ever dreamed, except that Eliza had no children and Samantha's child was on the way. "Hannah? Thank you. You've been a good friend today."

Hannah gave Samantha a small, tight smile and scraped her cornbread batter into the pan, her venture into friendliness finished.

At dinner that night, Alex waved his hands in the air as he spoke about the day trip with George Catlin's group of visitors. "You should have come along," he told his wife.

Samantha wanted to ask him about Star Dancing and Winona. She wanted to tell him about the baby. He seemed to sense something pensive in her mood because he kept narrowing his eyes when he looked at her. Instead of asking her, though, he kept talking.

"Catlin painted Blue Medicine, the Dakota shaman. Dr. Jarvis introduced them. Blue Medicine takes the potions that Jarvis gives him and presents them as magic to his tribe."

Samantha got up from the table to light the candles in the wall sconces.

Alex followed. "Are you all right?" he asked. "You've been quiet today."

Samantha considered. She could tell him she knew of his family. She could tell him she was pregnant. Both would lead to conversations she was too tired to have, so she forced a smile. "I'm just tired."

"Major Taliaferro heard they've hired a new sutler for the fort. It's not me." His tone was detached rather than angry.

"Do you think he knows what he's talking about?"

"Probably. Everyone talks to Taliaferro. He hears things from the tribes, the slaves, the soldiers, the traders . . ." His hand swept wide to encompass the entire world.

"I'm sorry, Alex. Has Major Bliss offered you a different location for the post office?"

"The man won't speak to me. More evidence Taliaferro is right." Alex poured himself a drink and sat before the fire.

Without even saying goodnight, she headed to bed, too tired to discuss his life.

THROUGH THE REST OF the summer, Samantha ignored her husband's other family. It became a relief when he left, because she didn't have to feign happiness in her daily life. She still hadn't told him she was pregnant. Part of her saw it as a punishment for his other wife and child even though she knew better. While he was gone, she didn't have to hide her nausea in the morning, or her fatigue over the simplest daily chores. While he was gone, it was possible to plan for the baby with joy and write to her mother about her state of happiness.

In late September, a letter arrived for Samantha from her brother. She held it like a treasure. Had it only been a year since he dominated her life? It seemed far in the past. He hadn't come to Fort Snelling since his wedding, so Samantha hadn't met her new sister-in-law. Even though he was only two days downriver, letters were infrequent. Samantha recognized that was partly her fault, but what would she write? How often her husband visited his Dakota family and left her alone in the store? She savored the opening of the envelope.

Dear Samantha,

Hoping all is well with you and Alexander. We are all fine here. I had a letter from James Churchman yesterday. I'd written to him about your marriage and he said to wish you well. How like him to be gracious.

Samantha gripped the letter tighter. She could hear her brother's disapproving tone in his written words. He must have been angrier about her marriage, and her absence at his own, than he'd let on in person.

Since I'm writing to inform you of a tragic incident, I will not waste more words. You've been close to Sarah Taylor Davis and know of her wedding to Jefferson Davis this past June. I'm sorry to inform you that she has passed away of malaria, contracted at the Davis plantation in Louisiana. Such a vibrant life to snuff so quickly. I know the news will devastate you as it has all of us in Prairie du Chien. Peggy Davis is a shadow of her former self, and the Colonel has become taciturn.

There was more, about how the extended Taylor family was coping, but Samantha barely skimmed it before letting the letter drop from her shaking hands. Sarah was dead. How could that be? Her chest tightened as she struggled to contain her grief. What good had it been, all their discussion of finding their own way despite their fathers? Samantha was stuck in a loveless marriage with a child on the way, and Sarah was dead. Her grief poured from her as she cried from the very bottom of her soul where all her dreams lay dashed.

Alex returned home that night from a long day with Hawk. Or with Star Dancing. She had never told him she knew about his Dakota family. Now it seemed a just punishment for Samantha's determination to have her own life. Alex went to the kitchen sink to wash his face and hands. He peered at Samantha's reddened eyes.

"Everything all right?" Alex asked her.

"I'm four months pregnant," Samantha said. She didn't know why she hadn't told him, or even if he'd care.

"Oh." Alex considered, then opened his mouth to say more.

Samantha interrupted him. "Sarah Davis is dead. Malaria."

"Sarah Davis?" Alex looked confused at the turn the conversation had taken. This time, he waited before trying to say anything.

"I know about Star Dancing and Winona," Samantha said. It was better to have it all out in the open, and she no longer had the emotional capacity to sugarcoat anything.

Alex nodded. "Everyone knows. It's not a secret or anything. I guess we've just never discussed it."

A wry smile twisted Samantha's lips. "That's convenient. If I cared, I'd ask what else you just never discussed."

"So you're pregnant." He paused. "Due after the new year? February maybe?"

"Thereabout."

"I'll try to return by then."

"What . . ." She couldn't even phrase it as a question.

"I'm going hunting with Hawk. The river will freeze and the mail delivery will stop. Henry Sibley will take over as sutler next week. I thought I'd just leave it all for him since none of it was ever mine, anyway."

"Were you planning to tell me? Or leave me for Sibley, too?"

Alex had the grace to look guilty. "I'm going to ask the Taliaferros to take you in until I can settle us somewhere."

"Mr. Sibley arrives next week. I assume you'll be gone by then. When were you planning to ask? What if the major says no?"

"You'll be fine, especially now that you're pregnant. Not that many babies have been born at the fort. Every woman for miles will fuss over you." He grinned as though he'd said something funny.

Even though she'd barely touched her plate, Samantha got up to clear the table. How ironic that she'd fought so hard to have control over her life only to have no one to help her now. She went to bed early, her chest tight with grief for Sarah, and for her own marriage. She pretended to be asleep when Alex joined her.

CHAPTER 22:

October, 1835

St. Peter's Agency, Michigan Territory

SAMANTHA

Samantha settled in with the Taliaferros at the Indian agency, where it pleased her to see Harriet holding her own with Eliza. Ellie seemed glad of Hannah's assistance in the kitchen, even though they teamed up to keep Samantha in her place—out of the kitchen.

Samantha knew that Mary had been living at St. Peter's, but she didn't see the girl for the first few days she was there. She asked Eliza about it one afternoon while they were having tea in the parlor.

In response, Eliza frowned. "I've told Lawrence I cannot abide that half-breed child in this house."

"You what?" Stunned, Samantha didn't know how to respond.

"She rolls on the floor like an animal. She's dirty and doesn't speak English. How can he expect me to clothe her and treat her like a child of my own?" Eliza pursed her lips, but not before Samantha spotted them trembling.

Mary must be a constant reminder to Eliza that she'd been unable to have her husband's child. Samantha tried to understand, but she knew that if Alex returned tomorrow with Winona in his arms, she'd welcome them both. Her husband's wayward behavior and other wife had nothing to do with the little girl. "So what have you done with her?"

Eliza waved a hand. "Lawrence has taken her away to live at the school with some of the other children. I'm sure she's fine." She turned to Harriet, who was standing against the wall. "A warm pot of tea, please, Harriet."

"Yes, ma'am." Harriet scurried to take away the teapot.

Samantha understood Eliza's aversion to Mary although she didn't like it. What would happen when Samantha's child was born? Would he or she remind Eliza anew of her inability to have children? Would Eliza turn them out?

THE WINTER OF 1835 saw weather as troubled as Samantha's emotions. Half of October was warm, and prairie fires filled the air with smoke. The other half of the month was freezing, with six inches of snow falling on October 22. Samantha hummed as she sewed baby clothes and planned for the birth, then she cried in despair thinking of her absent husband's other child. Nero lay at her feet and seemed to sense her mood. He whined, as if commiserating with Samantha.

One morning in November, Samantha awoke early to an unusual household flurry. It was so cold she hadn't undressed when she went to bed, and she was reluctant to leave her blankets. Curiosity got the best of her, however, and she went downstairs, wrapped in a blanket from her bed.

Harriet stood up after tending to the fire that warmed the parlor. Ellie stood nearby, hugging herself with both arms. Nero, stretched out on the hearth, perked his ears and looked ready to leap.

"Ellie? Is something wrong? Is it the baby?" Samantha's hand went to her own stomach, as if in sympathy with the Black woman.

"No, missus," Ellie said. She darted a glance at Harriet. "It's Hannah, missus. She passed in the night."

"Passed?" It was a reflexive question, one asked to gain time to process what she heard rather than get an answer.

"It's just too cold in the territory for some people," Harriet said, a stricken look on her young face.

"Poor Hannah," Samantha murmured. "She found it difficult here. Will arrangements be made?"

"Arrangements, ma'am?" Harriet asked.

"The master'll have the body removed," Ellie said.

Samantha twisted her hands together. She felt helpless, wanting to acknowledge the end of life. It was true Hannah was Major Taliaferro's slave, not hers, but she fancied herself close to the woman who'd helped her at the store. "I'll miss Hannah," she said. A thought struck her and she stared at Harriet and Ellie. "Oh, I'm sorry. You two will no doubt miss her more than I."

Harriet and Ellie exchanged a look before they nodded.

Samantha settled herself in her chair by the fire, feeling the light kiss of warmth as she stared into the flames. The territory was a harsh place. It was bitter cold in the winter. All year personal and physical danger surrounded them from starvation, political maneuvering, even drowning in the river. She wondered why everyone didn't just go back east, where life was manageable. Nero caught her mood. He moved to sit at her feet and whined.

On November 17, a spectacular display of the northern lights arced over the glow from prairie fires in an impressive display of God's wrath and benevolence. It eased Samantha to think that Hannah's passing had been celebrated celestially. Although it was wild, the prairie and the mountains and the river had a soul-restoring beauty.

The government appointed Colonel Samuel C. Stambaugh as sutler at the fort. It said a lot about the man that he always referred to himself with the middle initial. Samantha pictured the haughty man interacting with the soldiers and proud Indians she'd known at the fort.

December brought warmer, clear days. Spirits brightened as Christmas approached. Samantha was seven months pregnant, and Ellie about the same. It seemed Eliza tried to ignore the fact that Ellie tired more easily and sometimes felt ill. That left Harriet to do most of the Christmas preparation. Major Taliaferro distributed the traditional Christmas boxes to his slaves, full of clothing and lengths of cloth, and Eliza entertained the household by playing carols on her piano. The snow and cold prevented visitors, but on occasions when the weather cleared, one or more Indians appeared at the agency expecting a small gift of food or tobacco.

Samantha wanted to give the Indians more than the token small gift of food since they were clearly starving. But Samantha could only give a sympathetic smile. It was not her household, not her food. The circumstances of her life allowed her to enjoy the position of guest rather than beggar, but she was not that far above them in position or circumstance.

"Samantha," Eliza called, "come help me with these branches." She stood before the fireplace, fussing with the pine boughs on the mantel.

Samantha got up from her chair by the fire. Nero, who lay at her feet, looked up with perked ears. Samantha reached up to hold one end of the branch.

"If I wrap the pine in cotton batting, it will appear as if snow has fallen on it," Eliza said.

"Most people would like to see less of the snow," Samantha said. "Warm snow, though, that's a novelty." She laughed.

Eliza smiled. She pinned the batting and stepped back. "Very festive. Do we have a bowl of cranberries?" She turned to Harriet. "Fetch a bowl." Harriet nodded and went out the door to the yard, headed for the kitchen where a very pregnant Ellie prepared dinner.

"Are those the cranberries you bought from that Indian woman last fall?" Samantha asked.

"Yes. They'll make a wonderful sauce, but until then their red will look festive with the greenery. And some candles." She retrieved several brass candle holders and set them on the mantel among the pine boughs.

A loose bit of pine bough slipped away and dropped to the floor. With a laugh, Samantha picked it up and tucked it into Nero's collar. He looked up with an expression that showed clear displeasure. Samantha laughed again and walked to the side table to get the candles out of a drawer. "Here you are." She handed them to Eliza, who placed and lit them.

The two women stood back to admire the effect. Samantha patted her distended belly then slid her hand around to massage her aching back. The baby kicked, and Samantha's stomach rippled like pond water. With movements like that, not controlled by her, Samantha felt the wonder of the life within her. She sank into her chair, and Nero put his head on her foot. She was clearly forgiven for decorating him.

"Has there been any word from Mr. Miree?" Eliza asked.

It was uncanny how often the woman's pointed questions dashed Samantha's dreamy contentment. Eliza knew there had been no communication. It was her house, after all. Everything that came in went through her: letters, messages, deliveries, guests.

"No, Eliza. I don't know where he is." She didn't know where his Indian wife was, either.

Over the next few days before the holiday, Harriet, Ellie, and Samantha planned and prepared as much food as they could. Harriet brought potatoes from deep in the cellar to be mashed and served with rich gravy. A pig would be slaughtered and roasted on a spit, but they fixed venison sausage, onion soup, wild rice dressing, boiled turnips, and cabbage. Samantha baked her honey cookies and gingerbread. She enjoyed working in the kitchen with Harriet and Ellie, once they relaxed and talked to her as someone other than their mistress. In fact, Samantha preferred laughing with them to watching her words with Eliza and trying to avoid emotional undercurrents.

Harriet greeted visitors at the door and led them to the study. Lawrence spent most of his time closeted there with Joseph Nicollet, a visiting Frenchman who had just returned from an expedition to explore and map the source of the Mississippi River. Samantha heard Lawrence marvel at Nicollet's accuracy, correcting many errors made by the original explorer of the area, Zebulon Pike, in 1805. She was curious about Lawerence's interest in Nicollet, and his willingness to host him for the winter, given that the American Fur Company had funded the Frenchman's expedition, and an Ojibwe chief had guided them. Lawrence didn't oppose the fur company or the tribe, but neither was his area of interest, either.

Sometimes when Joseph Nicollet arrived from where he was staying in a room in the stable building, Samantha looked up from her position by the fire and smiled. The Frenchman had thick dark hair and long side whiskers. She thought maybe the sideburns were intended to emphasize his large dark eyes. Eliza seemed to think she had another reason for staring at the Frenchman.

"He is single, Samantha." Eliza's voice was neutral, but her eyes held speculation.

"And I am not," Samantha said, making her tone as firm as she could. She refused to let any wistfulness enter her voice. Besides, Nicollet's tapering chin was far too effeminate. She preferred a more rugged man. Samantha gasped as she realized the image that leapt to mind was James Churchman, not Alex Miree.

She wondered what James was doing now in Galena. It was improper of her to receive letters from a former suitor now that she was a married woman, and James Henry rarely thought to mention James in his infrequent letters that were often delayed by the weather conditions. Samantha wasn't sure if the two men were corresponding, or even if James was still in Galena. He could be back in New York for all she knew. Maybe he was married. Her heart ached and that made her angry. She refused to wallow in grief for her situation.

Samantha's second Christmas as a married woman dawned cold and gray. At least it wasn't snowing, and the temperature was above zero. She'd learned to be thankful for such things. Christmas was a joyous time, especially magical for children. Next year she'd have a baby of her own. Would Alex be there? When she thought of Alex, Samantha forced herself to imagine him hunting with Hawk, not spending time with his Indian family. Happy memories of family Christmases growing up in Champlain added to the day's sparkle. Visitors came to exchange gifts with the Taliaferros and share spiced wine and dried apples, gingerbread and honey cookies. Samantha liked the kitchen. It was warmer there, and she didn't have to be polite to people she didn't know, people who would know she was a charity case. They would stare at her large belly, and pity would cloud their eyes. Everyone would be uncomfortable.

Eliza gave Samantha a small box at Christmas breakfast. It contained a gold brooch that Samantha had seen Eliza wear. "It's pretty," she said.

Eliza said, "I thought you'd like to have something other than that old amethyst brooch to wear." She punctuated her words with a dismissive hand gesture.

Samantha left the gold brooch in its box. It meant nothing to Eliza since she'd given it away. Why should it mean anything to her? She smiled at Eliza, though, and thanked her while blinking away tears. Eliza's words stung. Samantha still felt a connection to her mother through the brooch, a connection that sometimes seemed tenuous.

Samantha had knitted scarves for Harriet and Ellie, who'd been shocked to receive such a personal gift. She'd embroidered handkerchiefs for Joseph Nicollet and the Taliaferros, making Eliza's quite fancy. She'd even baked a special dog treat for Nero. Samantha had no money of her own and refused to shop on credit at the sutler's store. She refused even to go inside the fort, where it seemed as if every eye turned toward her with pity for her circumstances or humor at her naive belief in the former sutler. Everyone but Samantha had known exactly who he was and wondered why on Earth she'd married him. Samantha didn't know if it was better to let them believe her stupid or insist she didn't know her own husband had an entire second life.

At home in New York her brothers and sisters would gather at her family's farm. There would be food, presents, music, and laughter. The children would have rosy cheeks and bright eyes, excited about being together and getting presents. If she'd married James Churchman instead of being banished to the territory, she would be there, too. She'd have at least one baby by now. She imagined what a baby with James would look like, then imagined James himself. Samantha realized she didn't know if James had much family in New York. Would he be alone in Galena for Christmas? For a minute, she wondered again if he'd married, but she believed James Henry would have written to her if that was the case.

James Henry would spend his second Christmas with his new wife, Catherine, in Prairie du Chien. From her brother's letters, Samantha knew he was disappointed that Catherine had not yet had a child. He'd not had time with his first wife to have children. Samantha had not yet met Catherine and never wrote her letters. She was afraid if she went to visit, her anguish over the state of her marriage would lead to her brother and his wife pitying her. Now that she was pregnant, she didn't want to make Catherine sad.

Restless, Samantha donned her coat, then pulled bison hide moccasins over her shoes. She went for a brief walk along the bluff above St. Peter's River. Below, the frozen river was a milky road to where it met the Mississippi below the fort. She knew that the Dakota revered the Mississippi River, which they called Big River. It was the mother of all rivers, flowing at the heart of Dakota land, fed by the tears of mothers and daughters. In her lifetime, Samantha had cried for love, for joy, for fear, for despair. She placed a hand on her belly. "I know you will cry, my darling," she said to the baby within, "but I will do my best to make sure that yours are tears of joy."

CHAPTER 23:

Severe Moon, 1835
Cloud Man's Village

DAY SETS

When her daughter had lived at the village with her, Day Sets had been busy. When Mary went to school, the days were as empty as the winter fields, as empty as the building where the food was stored, as empty as the stomachs of her people. The Mdewakanton had known hunger before, especially during long hard winters. In the spring, though, hope usually sprouted with the corn, and the men hunted for food. For the first time, though, Day Sets felt no promise in the faraway spring. The wasichu had pushed too many tribes west into Mdewakanton lands. More wasichu soldiers, traders, and settlers came, too. The land just could not support that many people, but what was the alternative? To push the Mdewakanton off their land, too?

Her sisters seemed oblivious to the future, maybe because they were so content in the present. Laughing Bird lived with her husband, Jim Thompson, in the village. Their entire focus was on each other, except when he had to serve his master at the fort during the day. Hushes Still the Night devoted her days to visits from her husband, Daniel Lamont, and to her beadwork. Her beaded bags were of substantial value in trade, especially to Henry Sibley at Mendota. Stands Sacred had given up missing Seth Eastman. Her romantic nature demanded a lover, and she had taken up with one of her father's braves. Her daughter Nancy would join her cousins at the wasichu school next year. Iron Cutter didn't dare show his face in the village. Day Sets would never forgive him for taking Mary away. Day Sets knew they were all hungry, but none of them admitted to lack of faith in the future. None of them had Day Set's long days alone to worry.

Cloud Man stated his support of the village, its farming, and its connection to the wasichu. Day Sets, though, could see the conviction in his eyes lessen as his people starved. Nearby tribes, especially the Fox and Sauk, assumed Cloud Man's village was prospering. When they asked for food, and Cloud Man told them the baskets were empty, it angered the other tribes. They raided and took everything that remained, scant as it was. Yet more people sought refuge in the village.

"You can't keep taking people in," Day Sets said. Her father looked tired. Not defeated, not yet, but tired. It was time someone helped him understand his ideas weren't working.

"They are mitakuye oyasin," he said over and over. "All are descended from the Dakota who came from the stars. Therefore, they are all family. We take care of family."

"Even when we have nothing ourselves?"

"If we have nothing, we share hope."

But to Day Sets, even hope was fading. On a bitter cold day, she rode to the agency. Iron Cutter would surely help the people of his daughter.

Harriet, Iron Cutter's young Black slave, opened the door. Her eyes widened. Day Sets didn't know if that was from fear or recognition.

"I am Day Sets. I am here to see Iron Cutter," Day Sets said in English. She pulled herself to her full height and looked down on the girl.

Harriet nodded and closed the door. A moment later, she opened it and gestured for Day Sets to enter. "The major will see you in his parlor."

Day Sets had not spent very much time inside Iron Cutter's home. He usually visited her, either at her father's village or in a temporary tipi at the agency. She certainly had not been here since his teya had arrived. There was no sign of Mary. Iron Cutter and his teya sat on either side of the fire. A very pregnant Samantha Miree sat directly in front of it. She twisted sideways to see who had arrived and smiled at Day Sets. A tray of cookies and biscuits sat on a table near the teya, and they were drinking tea. Day Set's stomach rumbled. Her last meal had been a handful of dried berries for dinner the night before.

Nero was at his master's feet and leaped up to greet Day Sets with his tail wagging. She patted his head, wondering why he wasn't with Mary. The big black dog always made her smile with his devotion to her daughter. She nodded acknowledgement to the women and faced Iron Cutter.

"What brings you here today, Day Sets?" Iron Cutter said. He spoke to her in Dakota.

For a moment, anger flared. He sat here in his warm house, enjoying food that most of the Mdewakanton would consider a full day's meal. Did he even know her people were starving? Did he care? "At the village, we are hungry." She refused to let her voice tremble with weakness or self-pity. It came out sounding like an accusation. She hoped Mary benefitted from this food and warmth. Without being obvious, Day Sets scanned the room for evidence of her daughter and found none.

Samantha Miree smiled and looked at her as if she was following the conversation. Day Sets knew Samantha understood about as much Dakota as Day Sets did English. It was hard to grasp concepts when you only understood about one in ten words. But at least Samantha made an effort. The teya ignored her. Day Set's stomach growled as the teya picked up a cookie.

"Cloud Man didn't set aside enough of this year's crops," Iron Cutter said.

Day Sets struggled to see his words as an observation rather than a condemnation. "Many of those in my village will not live to see the spring."

Samantha Miree leaned forward and said something to Iron Cutter. She sounded sympathetic. Maybe she'd understood more than Day Sets gave her credit for.

The teya made a disapproving noise, still not looking at Day Sets.

Iron Cutter spoke to Samantha in rapid English. She got slowly to her feet and spoke to Day Sets in English, indicating she should follow.

Day Sets followed Samantha Miree out the back door, then back in the kitchen door, searching for Mary as she did so. It was warm there and smelled of meat and fresh bread. Day Sets breathed deeply in appreciation.

"You are hungry," Samantha said slowly in English.

Day Sets nodded and said, "Yes."

Samantha spoke to the enslaved girls, Ellie and Harriet, and pointed. Day Sets understood Iron Cutter had told Samantha to give her food.

Day Sets noted Ellie was just as pregnant as Samantha. Harriet kept her distance from Day Sets, scurrying to the storeroom as soon as she could. Ellie smiled at Day Sets and continued stirring whatever she was making for the next meal. Samantha went up into the yard. Day Sets heard her call out, then the sound of running feet. Day Sets went into the yard in time to see one of the men from the stable bring her horse to the kitchen door. In a short time, Harriet had loaded sacks of flour, beans, and dried meat onto the horse. Day Sets took the reins and prepared to mount.

"I wish we could give you more," Samantha said in a mix of Dakota and English. "Next time bring a wagon or a bigger horse." She spread her arms wide to emphasize her words.

Day Sets smiled and responded in English. "Thank you."

Harriet came forward. "Here, Day Sets. For you." She handed Day Sets a small bag of Samantha's honey cookies.

She opened the bag, took one out, and bit into it. "Oh, very good."

Harriet's eyes sparkled. All three women laughed. For a moment all thoughts of status and language, cold and hunger disappeared.

"Is Mary here?" Day Sets asked.

Samantha shook her head. "No. She is at school." It looked like she wanted to say more, but her lack of Dakota words prevented further conversation.

Day Sets nodded and rode out of the yard.

It was a struggle, but Day Sets saved some cookies for her sisters. She slipped them to Hushes Still the Night, Stands Sacred, and Laughing Bird when no one was looking. Her sisters giggled and huddled in Day Set's tipi to eat them.

"Oh, these are wonderful," Stands Sacred said.

Hushes Still the Night nibbled hers. "Did Iron Cutter's teya welcome you?" She laughed. "Did you see Mary?"

Day Sets shook her head. "You know Iron Cutter's teya ignored me. Pale Crow's teya said Mary was at school. I like her."

Hushes Still the Night shook her head. "We're supposed to support our own people, but Star Dancing makes it hard. She insists her husband stay here in the village. She doesn't understand how to share him with his teya."

Day Sets nodded. "Our father chose wasichu husbands for us to ensure the future of our people."

"I chose mine," Laughing Bird protested.

Hushes Still the Night said, "You were lucky. Papa doesn't realize how poorly the soldiers and traders treat the Black Frenchmen. If he had, you'd be married to Henry Sibley."

Stands Sacred said, "Henry Sibley's spending a lot of time with Dakota tribes. You watch. He'll end up with a Dakota wife yet." They all laughed.

Day Sets knew her father believed that Iron Cutter and his wasichu ways would preserve the tribe. The wasichu, though, ate better than the Mdewakanton and lived in warm houses. The way he treated them like children offended her. It was worse now, though, because no parent would let their child starve. She said, "Life is difficult enough. Iron Cutter makes it worse."

"I don't pretend to be an elder," Hushes Still the Night said, "but the future is bleak for all the tribes. The wasichu tramples over them all. I don't see a clear path for the Mdewakanton."

Outside the tipi, loud voices and hurrying people drew their attention. Day Sets opened the flap and saw that the party of trappers had returned. Cloud Man's daughters came out to join the rest of the band. It was too early in the season for them to return. Usually, they trapped fox and beaver until the ice cracked and thawed. The tribe relied on a successful winter pelt hunt so that they could trade for food at the trading post, food that would keep them alive until they could harvest what they grew.

Hawk led the group. He rode slumped over his horse's mane. The other men were no better off. They dismounted stiffly, cold and discouraged. Pale Crow untied a small stack of pelts from the pack horse.

"The beaver are gone," Hawk said to Cloud Man.

Pale Crow approached the chief and put the pelts on the ground. Without speaking, he retreated.

Cloud Man looked at the pitiful stack. Day Sets had never seen him without words. A delighted exclamation rang out, out of character for the mood that had descended on the village.

"Welcome home!" Star Dancing called to Pale Crow as if he were the answer to all her prayers. He straightened his back and lightened his step. As he approached Star Dancing's tipi, little Winona came out and raised her arms to him, her eyes shining. Pale Crow enveloped her in a hug.

Day Sets missed her daughter at that moment. She missed the universal love and acceptance of a child. Winona loved her father despite his unsuccessful stint as a trapper, just as Mary loved her, no matter what happened in the world. A child's love made a mother strong enough to stand up against the disapproval of others. A child's love made a mother divine. Maka Ina the Earth Mother, Wakpa Tanka the Mother River, made divine by the love of the Dakota people.

The wasichu didn't seem to honor Maka Ina the way the Dakota did. Day Sets wondered if their God, portrayed as male, could give them the fierce love of a mother. Samantha Miree didn't seem to have the connection to her mother that Day Sets did. Neither did Iron Cutter's teya, as far as she knew. What did that mean for Mary? Day Sets turned and went back into her tipi. She wept.

CHAPTER 24:

January, 1836
St. Peter's Agency, Michigan Territory

❧ ～ ☙

HARRIET

Day Set's visit to the agency unsettled Harriet. Her brain told her there was nothing to fear from starving Indians, but her heart started beating faster and it was difficult to breathe whenever one came close. Mrs. Miree treated Day Sets with respect, so Harriet tried. She'd wrapped up cookies and offered them to Day Sets. The Indian woman's smile had rewarded her.

As January's cold continued, Major Taliaferro rode out to Coldwater Spring to play cards with the trader there. Often, Dr. Jarvis went with him. One day Dr. Jarvis came by the agency, intending to ride out with the major. He dismounted in the yard behind the kitchen, talking to Major Taliaferro while the latter's horse was being saddled. Nero ran around the yard, his panting breath creating clouds in the cold air.

Ellie and Harriet did laundry in the yard, too far to hear the men's conversation. Harriet lifted a pile of wet shirts from the wash water, but Ellie stiffened and wrung out the clothes in the rinse tub with unusual force. Clouds of steam appeared in the cold air over the warm wash tubs. Harriet's wet arms chilled. Before taking the clothes inside to hang before the fire, Harriet looked toward the men, now mounted and ready to ride out. Dr. Jarvis looked toward the house with arrogance. Harriet shivered.

Ellie glanced at him but turned away, her face grim. "Don't give him the satisfaction of seeing you looking," she told Harriet.

JUST A FEW WEEKS LATER, Ellie's water broke while she was in the kitchen storage room gathering vegetables to prepare for the evening's meal. Harriet noticed Ellie's damp skirt when she returned to the work table in front of the fire. She watched as Ellie gritted her teeth.

"Your labor's beginning, ain't it?" Harriet said, fluttering her hands. She'd never been the only one to help during a birth.

"I've done this before. It'll be a while," Ellie said. She doubled over and clutched her belly.

"You need to lie down. I'll get the mistress." Harriet swallowed hard to quell her rising panic.

Ellie smiled. "Harriet, honey, you're what? Sixteen now?" Harriet nodded. "On a plantation you'd have one or two babies by now. It's a natural process. And the mistress never helps."

Harriet hoped when she was twenty-one she'd be as calm as Ellie. "How many children have you had, Ellie?"

Ellie's smile faded. "I've birthed three and kept none." She grimaced as another pain wracked her.

"I'm sorry," Harriet said. Three children. Had they all been sold away? Or had some died? It didn't matter. Ellie would never see any of them again.

Ellie insisted on standing at the work table and chopping vegetables, even though Harriet's discomfort grew as Ellie's pains worsened.

Dirt rained down from above as foot stomps came from upstairs. Harriet set down her own chopping knife and wiped her hands. "Mrs. Taliaferro needs something. I'll go."

Harriet walked out of the kitchen and through the house door. Mrs. Taliaferro and Mrs. Miree sat near the fire, as usual, sewing and talking. Nero wasn't in his usual position at their feet. He must be out with the master. The women looked up as Harriet came in.

"Is there a reason tea is late, Harriet?" Mrs. Taliaferro's chilly tone made it clear that no reason was acceptable.

"It's Ellie," Harriet said. "It's her time." She waved her arms toward the kitchen.

Mrs. Miree stood, her hand on her own pregnant belly.

Mrs. Taliaferro's face was impassive. "She's done this before, hasn't she? Can't you manage tea on your own?"

Of course she could. But Ellie needed her. Harriet just nodded and hurried back to the kitchen.

Ellie sat in a chair, evidence of her increasing discomfort. Her face dripped with perspiration as her pains came faster. Harriet gathered a pot of tea and the biscuits already at hand and rushed them upstairs, managing not to drop the tray in her haste.

Returning to the kitchen, Harriet knelt beside Ellie, who did, indeed, know what she was doing. It seemed like days later when Harriet finally caught the baby boy. She bathed and swaddled him then put the baby on Ellie's chest. "What'll you call him?"

Ellie's face tightened. "His name's Jarvis," she said.

Ellie had been very secretive about the time she spent with the doctor. Now everyone would know. Harriet patted her arm. "It's a fine name."

Harriet finished preparing dinner while Ellie nursed baby Jarvis and sat by the fire.

The next day, though, Ellie was back at work. She wrapped a shawl around her body to hold the baby so that he would not interfere with her chores. Harriet watched Ellie to make sure she didn't need help. The new mother was too stubborn to ask for it. Harriet wondered about Mrs. Miree. Most mistresses took to their beds after childbirth, but slaves went right back to work. Mrs. Miree was different. She would have a doctor at her birth. What would Harriet have done had it been a difficult birth?

January continued to be cold. When the storms hit, the raging rain and wind made it impossible to think. It was all Harriet could do to focus on her tasks. She preferred the silence of snowfall without the wind. The snow deadened all sound and left her alone with her thoughts, thoughts that often brought babies to mind and left her feeling alone and depressed.

Harriet loved helping Ellie with little Jarvis. Bathing him, dressing him, rocking him, she marveled at his tiny fingers and toes. Longing for a baby of her own grew, and that led to thoughts of husband and family. She lost herself in momentary fantasy until Mrs. Taliaferro called. Then reality crashed around her. Where would she find a husband? Enslaved women could marry, but only with their master's approval. Even then, the marriage was not a legal one. In a free territory, children of a slave should be free. The law, though, said a child took the status of its mother. Any children of Harriet's would be slaves if they were born in Michigan territory. She daydreamed of traveling to Pennsylvania to birth a free child.

Mrs. Miree's baby would no doubt have a hard life, but it would be free. As it grew, she would encourage that child to be educated, to learn about the world, to go forth and be its own person. It was all that mothers through time had ever wanted, be they mistresses or slaves, rich or poor, Indians or settlers. The silent snowfall was dangerous. It encouraged fantasies that distracted Harriet from her work.

CHAPTER 25:

February 1836
St. Peter's Agency, Michigan Territory

SAMANTHA

The coldest, dreariest winter in Fort Snelling memory continued. On February 23, a cold spell dropped temperatures below zero. Samantha, her baby due any day, huddled in front of the fire covered in blankets and furs. She wore both of her dresses as well as her coat, gloves, and hat, two pairs of socks and her warmest boots. Her brain told her it was colder outside, but her heart could not believe such a thing was possible. Eliza, also bundled, stayed close to the fire and to Samantha. Nero snuggled as close to them as he could. Harriet kept warm by moving, running back and forth from the warm kitchen to the warm parlor through the icy yard. On February 26, Samantha's water broke, and she worried it would freeze before the baby arrived. When Eliza realized what had happened, she jumped into action.

"Harriet! Fetch Dr. Jarvis! The babe is coming!"

Harriet ran out the door and raced to the fort.

Eliza helped Samantha into her bedroom. The fire was lit, but the room was drafty. Wafts of cold air battled with spreading warmth, leaving Samantha chilled. Eliza helped her into bed. By then Ellie had arrived with hot water bottles, a well-swaddled Jarvis in a sling across her chest. Eliza turned to her in obvious relief. Of the four women in the household, Ellie was the only one who'd given birth. Samantha wasn't sure where Ellie's other children were, or even if they had lived. It was a subject that was not discussed, like the identity of baby Jarvis's father. As her pains progressed, Samantha was glad for Ellie's calm demeanor.

Harriet left to make sure Major Taliaferro got his dinner. She made Nero come with her to keep him out of the way.

"Not long now, missus," Ellie promised in the cooing tones of a mother talking to a child. She unwrapped the shawl tethering Jarvis to her chest and laid him on the floor, cushioned by a blanket.

"Ellie . . ." Samantha wanted to ask about Ellie's first child. She wanted to ask how Ellie could have another baby without a father to help her, but knew the Black woman's experience was not like her own. She wanted to share her fear of Alex never coming back, her fear of raising a child alone. All the fears that she'd buried came forth now with her pain.

Ellie seemed to understand. "Hush now."

Dr. Jarvis arrived and approached the bed without a glance at Ellie, or baby Jarvis. "All right, now, Mrs. Miree. The child's coming. Concentrate on pushing."

The world shrunk to pain and baby. The cold retreated, and Ellie's voice was naught but background as Samantha fought to bring her baby into the world.

"This is my own baby." Ellie's words floated through Samantha's head. She never heard the doctor respond to Ellie.

"Welcome, little Emily," she whispered many hours later to the scrawny baby girl.

"Well done for a first birth," Dr. Jarvis said.

Samantha could see Ellie standing behind the doctor, baby Jarvis in her arms, the whites of her eyes intensified as she glared at the doctor. The names clicked in Samantha's head for the first time, and she groaned. Dr. Jarvis was the father of Ellie's baby. How had she not put that together before now? "Thank you, Doctor," she said. "Now you can have a moment with your son."

Dr. Jarvis frowned. "I'm needed at the fort. Send Harriet if you have need of me, Mrs. Miree."

He gathered his things and strode out the door without a single glance at Ellie. Samantha shivered at Ellie's murderous glance.

Ellie whisked Emily away to bathe and swaddle. When Samantha saw the baby again, she was an angelic face amidst a thick cocoon of wool blankets. Nero sniffed her face then lay down, uninterested, at the foot of the bed. The world disappeared for Samantha as she basked in the joy of her baby. She pushed away thoughts of her husband and her circumstances, refusing to ruin this special time. Before long, however, she could no longer ignore reality.

COLD AND HUNGER CONTINUED. The Dakota men, no doubt with Alex included, were still hunting. The frozen river gave up no fish to the Dakota women, who huddled over holes in the ice. Starving Dakota came to the door saying, "*Hirharha nampetchiyuza*," which Samantha learned meant "I give you my hand with pleasure." It seemed a polite way to beg. It was so cold that the agency's cattle bled from their noses. Of the two hundred cattle Major Taliaferro kept, fifty died. The cold, blowing winds and drifting snow continued.

The frozen winter held on longer than usual, with the ice on the river not breaking apart until April. As the days warmed to more tolerable temperatures, Samantha dreamed of the meeting between Alex and their precious daughter. By the time spring wildflowers spread across the prairie, Emily was three months old and no word had come from her father. Anger replaced Samantha's dreams.

"He has to know she's been born," Samantha told Eliza. "Rivers are passable. Why hasn't he the decency to send word?" She held Emily on her lap. Eliza sat with her in front of the fire, darning socks.

Eliza said, "No one knows but him, my dear."

"When do the trappers return from the beaver hunts?"

Eliza hesitated. "They move as soon as the weather allows. Sometimes they have far to go to meet the fur traders."

"Alex won't do that, will he? I mean, he's traded before. He just likes to hunt with Hawk, right?"

Eliza nodded at Emily, sleeping in her mother's arms. "He has to provide for you and the little one, and he no longer has the income from the sutler position. Mail delivery will resume soon. I hope for the sake of his position as postmaster that he returns soon."

Both women looked up as Major Taliaferro entered the room. Nero's tail thumped the floor, but he didn't leave his place by the fire. The major rubbed the back of his neck, and he looked uncomfortable.

Eliza put down her sewing. "Say what you've come to say," she told her husband.

He took a deep breath and looked at Samantha.

Her heart dropped into her stomach. "Major Taliaferro," she said, "have you word of my husband's trapping party?"

His lips tightened into a line. "It is why I have come. Hawk returned from the wilderness four weeks ago." He hesitated. "Mr. Miree was with him."

Samantha felt like the air left the room with an audible whoosh just as something punched her in the stomach. She made a strangled noise, part shocked gasp, part scream of anger. Conscious of the baby in her arms, she didn't jump up and pace the room, even though she had to move or explode. How could Alex ignore her? Did he even know he had a beautiful, innocent daughter?

The major continued, "A Dakota man came to see me this morning, and when our business was done I asked about your husband. They call him Pale Crow. He's been bringing Star Dancing food from the store at the fort all winter. I guess he's been doing that since Winona was born. The store is no longer his, though, and last week he almost got caught. It seems he plans to stay in the village with Star Dancing."

"Stay in the village?" Samantha repeated. Her shock eased as anger flooded her.

Alex had no right to leave with no word, to leave her with a new baby, beholden to someone else. She'd lived all winter without him, birthed their daughter without him. She deserved to be told he was leaving her. Rage and hurt combined to twist her stomach. She refused to cry. He didn't deserve her tears.

Guilt stabbed Samantha as she realized this was how James Churchman must have felt when she left New York without telling him herself that she wouldn't marry him. Samantha felt a bond with the absent James and wondered why she'd ever pushed him away. If Emily were his baby, he would have treasured her as much as he would treasure Samantha as his wife. Tears of despair fell as she imagined the impossible. Then she looked down at the face of her sleeping angel, the daughter who would never know her father, and cold rage triumphed. "Major, will you take me to the village? I must speak with Alex myself," she said.

Major Taliaferro looked uncomfortable, but not surprised. He nodded.

Samantha stood up and handed the baby to Eliza. "Eliza, please take Emily." Her voice was calm and determined. "I have to go on an errand." She noted Eliza's face, full of disapproval, as she left the room. Upstairs, she gathered mittens, a hat, and a coat. She was already wearing her warmest clothing and boots.

Returning downstairs, she met Harriet in the hallway. "Will you be gone long, Mrs. Miree?"

"No, Harriet, this will not take any time at all."

In the parlor, Major Taliaferro stood before the fireplace. Someone had poured Eliza a cup of tea. She sat and held Emily. Samantha nodded to the major. "We'll be off then."

She walked out the front door, knowing he would be behind her. A slave brought two saddled horses. The major assisted Samantha aboard her horse, then mounted and turned toward Cloud Man's village. Samantha followed.

CHAPTER 26:

Moon for Planting, 1836
Cloud Man's Village

DAY SETS

Iron Cutter rode into the village as if he'd never stolen away her daughter. Day Sets straightened her shoulders and prepared to confront him. A Mdewakanton woman, a chief's daughter, did what she must. She'd been raised to honor mitakuye oyasin, to treat every person as family and every living thing with honor. If Iron Cutter's teya couldn't teach that to Mary, then she would find a way to do so herself.

To Day Set's surprise, Samantha Miree rode behind Iron Cutter. Day Sets followed as Iron Cutter rode to Star Dancing's tipi. Pale Crow sat out front, wearing buckskin pants, moccasins, and a red woolen flannel shirt. He looked up and nodded to Iron Cutter as he pulled up the big black horse and dismounted. "Pale Crow," Iron Cutter said, "you have a visitor." Pale Crow's face blanched when he saw Samantha dismount, and he leaped to his feet.

Samantha gave her horse's reins to Iron Cutter and strode forward, her head up and shoulders back. She didn't let her husband speak first. Day Sets hid a proud smile. Samantha spoke in English to her husband in a clear voice. He scratched his head and wrinkled his brow before responding.

Swallowing her pride, Day Sets moved near to Iron Cutter. "What are they saying?"

"She told him he has a daughter named Emily. He said another daughter is nice."

Star Dancing peeked out of the tipi to see who was there, then ducked back inside. Winona, however, was too curious. She stepped out, her long braids mussed and cheeks rosy from sleeping. Her feet were bare, and she wore a woolen petticoat softened from many years of wear. "Who's that?" she said.

Pale Crow ignored her. He stared at Samantha, who stared right back.

"You have a baby sister," Samantha said to the little girl. Iron Cutter translated for Day Sets.

Winona stepped forward, her face puzzled at the English words, but Pale Crow pulled her back. Day Sets watched Winona hide behind her father's leg, trying to entice one of the grownups into playing hide and seek. Growing bored after a few attempts, she went back into the tipi.

Samantha looked neither right nor left. "I will not continue to live like a charity case with the Taliaferros," she said. "I will know from your lips why you left." Again Iron Cutter translated.

Day Sets was proud of Samantha's confident tone even though she could see the tension in the other woman's straight back.

Pale Crow tried to speak, but Samantha continued, "I must hear in your own words if you intend to live here or with us. I will go anywhere you want if you find a job somewhere else, but I will not stay at St. Peter's alone."

Pale Crow seemed to settle into himself. His look of startlement eased into something more cunning that Day Sets didn't like. "I will stay here with Star Dancing where I am needed." He repeated himself in Dakota. Day Sets heard a satisfied snort come from inside the tipi. "You are a strong woman, Samantha, too strong for a man like me."

The whining tone of his voice disgusted Day Sets. Samantha remained silent.

"Star Dancing needs me. You don't need me. You push and push, wanting me to get a better job, be home more. I never feel needed."

Day Sets knew Samantha needed him, too, but she didn't beg. Samantha was strong. Her spirit was Mdewakanton.

"Emily and I will not stay at St. Peter's Agency any longer. Do not come to find us."

She turned and remounted her horse. Samantha didn't look back as she rode out of Cloud Man's village with her back straight and head high. Iron Cutter translated, and Day Sets fixed her eyes on his. Taking charge of a daughter?

Pale Crow shrugged his shoulders and ducked back inside the tipi saying nothing to Day Sets, who seethed when she heard Star Dancing's laughter. Day Sets turned on Iron Cutter. "I, too, will raise my daughter."

Iron Cutter had taken up his horse's reins, ready to mount and race after Samantha. He hesitated. "Day Sets," he began. He paused and swallowed. "Mary is living at the school with the Stevens family."

Day Sets felt her fury rise.

"She's with Jane, at least." Iron Cutter looked miserable. "Eliza wouldn't have her. I thought she'd like to have a child, but not Mary." His eyes grew troubled as he faced her.

"They can't care for her at that school like a mother can." Day Sets knew her daughter belonged with her. She knew it deep in her heart, in a place words couldn't find.

Iron Cutter's eyes held more pain than she'd ever seen. Day Sets didn't love this man, but he was Mary's father. She never wished him pain. Day Sets had scant experience with broken men. It was true her father had become a shadow of himself, questioning everything he stood for. Iron Cutter had the same hunted look. She bit back words that might have been consoling and froze him with a look as fierce as that of Iktomi, the shape-shifter god, the trickster, whose gaze must be avoided to prevent trouble coming to you.

Iron Cutter mounted in haste and galloped from the village.

CHAPTER 27:

April, 1836
St. Peter's Agency, Michigan Territory

SAMANTHA

Pride kept Samantha's head up as she rode back to the agency, and rage stiffened her back. "How dare that cowardly man sneak off to be with his Indian family without a word to his lawful wife!" Her anger startled a flock of swallows. The birds flapped and chittered as they erupted into the air, adding their outrage to Samantha's.

She wished it was the fort she was returning to, the home at the sutler's store she'd shared with Alex. She'd search for every remnant of Alexander Miree—a sock needing darning, a forgotten hat, an old shirt—and hurl everything into the fire.

But Major Taliaferro's house was her destination, the house where they'd taken her in out of pity for her husband's poor treatment. Heat filled her cheeks as she realized no one but her would be surprised at Alex's actions. Only she had believed him worthy of her love. She shouted to the sky, "You aren't worth loving! You don't deserve the beautiful daughter I bore you!" The birds had not yet returned to their tree, so the forest responded with silence.

Hoofbeats brought sound back into the world as Major Taliaferro caught up with Samantha. She kept her chin high and eyes on her horse's ears, but the major didn't say anything when he came up next to her. She snuck a glance at him. He seemed lost in thoughts of his own, his mouth etched into a frown. He urged his horse past Samantha and took the lead.

Samantha twisted the reins in her hands. She couldn't storm into the major's home yelling about the husband everyone but her had known was useless. Samantha's anger faded as she envisioned her life. Living with the Taliaferros was supposed to be temporary. She was supposed to be living with a husband and raising her daughter. Alex had made that impossible. It was his fault she was now an object to be pitied. No, she refused to be pitied.

Presumably she could stay with the Taliaferros, at least for the immediate future, or she could go back to her brother at Prairie du Chien and finally meet his wife. Samantha took a deep breath. Or she could go home to her parents in New York. Her parents would be disappointed in her, but not as disappointed as she was in herself. She'd been so determined to make her own choice that she'd hurried into marriage with a man fated to disappoint her. Samantha sighed.

She arrived at the agency without speaking a word to the major. He dismounted in front of his home and turned to Samantha. Eliza Taliaferro came out of the house and greeted her husband. Eliza's demeanor was stiff and formal. Any strong emotion she felt was tamped deep inside her. She'd never want to hear Samantha's heart.

Baby Emily must be sleeping inside the house where she was safe and warm. There was more to life than that, though. A woman needed to make her own decisions and take responsibility when she made the wrong ones. Samantha wouldn't allow herself to wallow in self-pity, accusing Alex of ruining her life. It was her life, and it was her duty to be strong for Emily. She had to leave St. Peter's Agency.

CHAPTER 28:

Moon for Planting, 1836
Cloud Man's Village

❧

DAY SETS

The day after Samantha Miree confronted Pale Crow, frantic activity around Laughing Bird's tipi drew Day Set's attention. Her sister and Jim clung to each other. Laughing Bird cried into his shoulder. Day Sets walked over.

"Are you all right?" Day Sets looked from Laughing Bird to Jim. Tragedy etched both faces. Day Sets took a deep breath.

Laughing Bird started to speak, but emotion clogged her throat.

Jim, one arm still around Laughing Bird's shoulders, said, "My master is being transferred to Fort Crawford. I must go with him." He looked down at his wife, who still had her arms around him. "Take care of your sister, Day Sets. She must stay here with the children."

Day Sets saw him swallow hard, trying to keep his own emotions in control so Laughing Bird could control hers.

"The soldiers won't allow Laughing Bird to stay at the fort, so she'd have to live on her own outside town. It's in Winnebago territory, so she won't be welcome there either." He squeezed his wife. "She's safer here."

Day Sets nodded. Her sister would be without her husband's support, just like Samantha Miree. At least Laughing Bird had the love of her tribe surrounding her. Samantha only had the petty jealousies and incomprehensible social constraints of the wasichu.

Jim's meager belongings were already gathered into a bundle. He held Laughing Bird tight once more, then set off on foot toward Fort Snelling to join his master.

Day Sets took her sister's hand.

"If he had another wife, I could accept that. If he had duties that took him away, I could accept that." Laughing Bird took a deep breath. "But how can someone own a man and take him away from his family?"

Day Sets knew that slave owners often separated families, but now was not the time to mention that to her sister. The men at the fort saw Jim as necessary, even with his dark skin. Mdewakanton skin was not acceptable. Even at Fort Snelling, soldiers tolerated Mdewakanton presence for visits to the store and other errands, but not for lingering or living there.

"Once again the wasichu stick together," Laughing Bird said.

Day Sets knew the white people did not respect the Black people. In fact, they looked down on them. White men respected the advice and knowledge of the Dakota more than they did the Black man, and that wasn't saying much. Jim was a possession to be taken with Captain Day, not a friend leaving his family.

Day Sets followed Laughing Bird into the tipi. Inside, Stands Sacred sat with their mother. Hushes Still the Night cried in her arms.

"Daniel Lamont's spirit has returned to the stars," Stands Sacred said.

"Hushes Still the Night and Laughing Bird have both lost husbands today," Red Cherry Woman said.

Day Sets didn't point out that Laughing Bird's husband hadn't died.

"Daniel's partners in the Upper Mississippi Outfit will bury him as a Christian. He will have no one to see his spirit to its resting place, no one to lead the Ghost Dance," Hushes Still the Night said.

"We will grieve him with you so that his God will take care of his spirit," Red Cherry Woman promised.

Day Sets settled next to the women of her family, their silent bond supporting each other. Her sisters' grief melted Day Set's fury over Eliza sending Mary away. Today her sisters needed her more than Mary. A day would come when that would change, when they would help her bring Mary home.

A SUBDUED ATMOSPHERE CLUNG to the village as the days grew longer. The Moon When the Corn is Hoed brought two steamboats, within days of each other, filled to the brim with cargo that was not intended for the Dakota. The American Fur Company was well stocked, as was Fort Snelling. Cloud Man's village population swelled as starving Dakota from surrounding bands sought food. Day Sets helped distribute their harvest to the hungry, which was everyone.

In the Moon When Geese Shed Their Feathers, Dakota from the western tribes gathered at St. Peter's Agency for their annual meeting. Some of the Mdewakanton, including Day Sets and her sisters, stayed over at the agency even though they lived close by. The Yankton, Sisseton, and Wahpeton bands camped in sight of the agency. Over the next few weeks, hundreds of Dakota dressed in their finery and met with Major Taliaferro, wanting their payment and supplies from the government. Then they danced. The Yankton had more horses than any other band, and it seemed they brought every one of them. Red Cherry Woman's Sisseton family brought quillwork pouches as gifts.

For Day Sets, witnessing the gathering gave her an opportunity to renew her resolve to raise her daughter with traditional Mdewakanton values. Living at the school might be better for Mary than living with Iron Cutter's teya, but the best place for Mary was home with her mother. Times were hard in the village, though. Mary had plenty of food where she was. It was hard to find solace in the legacy of the ancestors when your stomach rumbled.

CHAPTER 29:

April, 1836
St. Peter's Agency, Michigan Territory

HARRIET

By the spring of 1836, Harriet, now sixteen years old, had been at St. Peter's Agency for two full cycles of Fort Snelling weather. She had come through a bad winter, and experienced death, birth, and starvation in the people around her. Winter was a great equalizer. Hunger and cold affected everyone, whether they were slave, Indian, trader, or soldier. Roles Harriet thought she knew had been redefined. Baby Jarvis was even allowed to stay with his mother. Harriet had the freedom to walk by herself to the store at the fort, and even to decide when such an errand was necessary.

One day, after an Indian chief had left the agency, Major Taliaferro said, "The chief believes whites have killed all the Indians in the south."

Harriet looked around the empty room. Could he be talking to her? No one else was there besides Nero, snoozing in front of the fire. The major sat in his big chair, nursing a glass of whiskey he'd poured after the chief left. Harriet continued dusting the shelves of the bookcase, feeling self-conscious. Usually she dusted when the master wasn't in the room.

"He knew about the Great Fire in New York, and asked why the people didn't run away when they lost their fine houses," the major said.

Harriet focused harder on her dusting.

"He didn't seem to believe that friendly, powerful nations like the United States and France could ever go to war." Major Taliaferro said. Nero thumped his tail and the major ruffled the fur on the dog's head. "Yes, I must protect them like children," he said.

Harriet thought the Indians probably needed education more than protection, but it was not her place to say so.

In February, just about the time baby Emily had been born at the agency, the interpreter's daughter, Madeleine, got married. Her métis father, mixed European and Dakota, spoke both the English of his European ancestors and the language of his mother's Dakota heritage. Madeleine was the only other teenager nearby, so her marriage to a man employed by Mr. Sibley interested Harriet. Madeleine's marriage, and Ellie's new baby, fueled Harriet's dreams of her own husband and family.

Harriet knew of Marguerite, Stephen Bonga's older sister, the only free Black woman in the area. Descended from former slaves and the granddaughter of an Ojibwe chief, she and her Swedish husband lived at Coldwater Spring with their children. She'd never heard of an Indian man marrying out of his tribe. To be honest, while Harriet dreamed of the security of marriage, the reality of marrying an Indian held no allure. She couldn't imagine living in a tipi and fixing only muskrat, dog, or vermin for meals much of the year. Even though she was enslaved, she'd traveled on steamboats. She knew how to iron a shirt and set a table with linen and silver.

A generation earlier, it had not been uncommon for an enslaved woman to marry a Frenchman. They knew how to run a settlement household, which Indian women did not. Now the Frenchmen in the area that weren't already married were just passing through. Most lived and trapped in the wilderness. The remaining men were soldiers, but Major Bliss had sold his slave Fanny south when he discovered her liaisons with soldiers. So Harriet couldn't think of marrying a soldier.

And she still was enslaved. Major Taliaferro would have to approve any marriage Harriet might want to make, and she'd still be a slave after her marriage. Slave marriages weren't legal, so she wasn't sure he would even entertain the idea. Ellie claimed he'd promised to free them. If he did so, Harriet would be able to marry. If she could find a man to marry, of course. Thomas stayed close to the stable now. He never smiled at Harriet any more. She missed him even though she'd long ago decided he wasn't the man for her.

In April, the river ice broke up, bringing hope of contact with the outside world. The sun peeked out from its winter shroud, causing jubilation. Then it snowed four inches. The cold didn't deter the people in Harriet's life, however. They'd scented spring, and they spent more time outside as the hours of daylight grew.

Spring also brought skirmishes between tribes. Harriet heard Major Taliaferro rage against government plans to remove the Ojibwe from their land. They'd already cleared the land east of the Mississippi River of the Fox and Sauk tribes. Now they set their sights on the Ojibwe because the tribe occupied land covered in valuable timber forests. In part, this led to Michigan becoming a state. The rest of Michigan Territory, including the area around Fort Snelling, became Wisconsin Territory that summer. Territories created under the Northwest Ordinance still outlawed slavery, but since no one at Fort Snelling enforced the law, Harriet remained enslaved.

The United States government, as it repositioned state and territory boundaries, had to adjust its military presence. That meant they transferred Major Bliss away from Fort Snelling to replace him with a new commander. Dr. Nathan Jarvis would depart at the same time as Major Bliss and the regiment, as would Mrs. Miree. They would leave as soon as the new regiment arrived, probably in the same boat on its return voyage downriver.

Thomas rushed into the Taliaferro yard on May 8 with news of the arrival of the Fifth Infantry. Ellie and Harriet had been preparing the garden for planting. Ellie untied her apron, wiped her hands, and neatened her hair. She picked up baby Jarvis, who had been sleeping on a blanket, and turned to Harriet. "Come on, we've gotta go to the fort."

Thomas looked at Harriet. "Walk with me to the fort." He reached out his hand and took hers.

Harriet bristled. Thomas ignored her for weeks then had the audacity to take her hand? "I'll walk with Ellie." She pulled her hand away and turned her back to him, not even looking to see his reaction. She preferred to dream of romance instead of being faced with a real relationship that couldn't happen.

At the front of the house, Major Taliaferro settled Mrs. Miree and baby Emily into the wagon. William loaded a trunk that Mrs. Taliaferro had filled for the departing mother and babe. Harriet would miss Mrs. Miree and Emily, but she understood the need to get away from an uncontrollable situation. After all, Mrs. Miree was not enslaved or a beggar, so she didn't need to live like one.

Ellie walked briskly toward the fort. Harriet hurried after her. Ellie must want to say farewell to Dr. Jarvis, to let him see the son he'd shown no interest in. At the fort, though, the road bustled with troops arriving and departing. Harriet even lost sight of her master. She watched as Ellie scanned the deck of the boat as the men loaded it. Ellie must be looking for Dr. Jarvis.

Harriet's attention riveted on one of five Black men to get off the boat. He accompanied a man dressed in an official surgeon's uniform, who must be Dr. Emerson. The doctor was tall, over six feet, but limped. The Black man was shorter and neatly dressed. He had the loveliest dark skin Harriet had ever seen.

"Look!" Ellie said. "There's Jim Thompson getting on the boat." She shook her head and tsked. "So sad."

"His wife's a chief's daughter! She and their children should go with him," Harriet said.

Ellie shook her head. "You've lived in a free territory for two years and you've already forgotten? Jim Thompson's enslaved. His master's a captain being reassigned to Fort Crawford."

They watched as Jim boarded the boat behind his master. Harriet's heart ached for Jim's wife. How awful to be married and then be separated because you had no choice to stay. She shuddered. That was a good reason *not* to get married.

Ellie and Harriet walked back to the agency house, Harriet lost in thoughts of marriage, family, and freedom.

CHAPTER 30:

Moon When Strawberries Are Red, 1836
St. Peter's Agency, Michigan Territory

DAY SETS

In the middle of the Moon When Strawberries Are Red, Day Sets and her sisters shared a tipi at the agency, waiting for the steamboat *St. Peters*. It finally brought the promised payment and supplies that the Mdewakanton needed. Long lines of Dakota wove through the tall prairie grass as Iron Cutter distributed the bounty with a gleeful smile. Nero caught the excitement and ran back and forth, barking. Day Sets noticed, though, the downcast eyes of her tribesmen, the thin limbs and trudging feet. The Mdewakanton appeared defeated, and it broke her heart. Iron Cutter smiled too much and laughed too big. Couldn't he see the despair?

The *St. Peters* had also brought updates on a smallpox outbreak downriver. Day Sets sat inside the tipi, struggling with beading a dress and wishing her sisters had stayed to help instead of running off to gawk and visit. Nero burst into the tipi, licking her face before she realized he was there.

"Nero!" Iron Cutter's sharp tone brought the dog to a sit, whining, near Day Sets. Iron Cutter squatted beside her, petting the dog to calm him.

"Exciting day," Day Sets said, her tone flat.

Iron Cutter said, "The smallpox is coming north. It already devastated Wabasha's village. A few cases have been reported just south of here. We are vaccinating the Dakota to prevent illness."

Day Sets sighed. She remembered the defeat and slumped shoulders of her tribe. An illness would devastate them even further, if that were possible.

"Will you set an example?" Iron Cutter asked. "Get vaccinated? Many Dakota have agreed to do it, but many are reluctant. It's nothing more than a cut in your arm."

Day Sets bit her lip, not wanting to admit her own reluctance. "I will do this for my people." Day Sets set her rumpled beadwork aside and rose. Nero, eager to be going somewhere, leapt to her side. Day Sets ruffled his ears.

"Thank you," Iron Cutter said. They left the tipi. A strange man stood at a table with a Black man Day Sets had not seen before. "This is our new doctor," Iron Cutter said. The doctor was already cutting the arm of a Dakota man, assisted by the Black man. "Dr. Emerson, this is Day Sets, daughter of Chief Cloud Man."

The doctor looked up and smiled at her. Day Sets nodded to acknowledge him. "Thank you for doing this, Day Sets," he said in English. "Etheldred will assist." He indicated the Black man at his side. Iron Cutter translated, but Day Sets was proud she'd understood the doctor's English words.

Iron Cutter said, "Dr. Emerson will rub this ointment into the fresh cut. They mix the medicine with mashed smallpox scabs, giving it a bit of the disease that will make sure the person vaccinated will never get the disease."

Day Sets looked at the ointment with new respect. It had powerful magic. She scanned the group of Mdewakanton that stood nearby. Blue Medicine, the tribe's shaman, was absent. Day Sets knew her people's reluctance stemmed more from the missing shaman than a small cut in the arm. If the shaman didn't trust the wasichu medicine, why should they? Day Sets took a deep breath. "Will the students at the school get this magic?"

Iron Cutter nodded. "Yes." Day Sets nodded.

Dr. Emerson cut her arm while Etheldred gripped it to keep her still. Day Sets didn't mind because she'd participated in cutting rituals. She winced a bit when the doctor rubbed the magic into the cut.

Day Sets stood by as Iron Cutter and Dr. Emerson vaccinated hundreds of Dakota. At the edge of the crowd, Day Sets spotted Blue Medicine. He stood half hidden among the trees. Blue Medicine didn't have his usual drum, but Day Sets could hear the faint clicking of his deer hoof rattle. He wore his large round mirror on its red ribbon around his neck and held it to his eye with one hand. Day Sets smiled. The Mdewakanton would have the added protection of their own spirits in addition to the wasichu magic.

After vaccination, the Dakota bands left. The Yankton chief shook Iron Cutter's hand and gave him a peace pipe as a token of respect. The pipe was carved of red stone from the sacred quarry. Day Sets told the legend to the wasichu, so they'd understand.

"The sacred pipestone quarry was formed from the blood of our ancestors. When the world was freshly made, Unktehi the water spirit fought the people and created a great flood that engulfed the lands. Everything was under water except the hill next to the sacred red pipestone quarry. The people climbed to save themselves, but it was no use. The rising waters swept over the hill, and falling rocks smashed down upon the people. Their red blood turned to pipestone. Pipes made from the red rock are a great honor."

The head man standing before Iron Cutter nodded at her words. "The pipe brings harmony between men when they smoke it. You can't lie through the pipe."

Iron Cutter nodded his understanding and reacted with proper reverence. By the time the meadow was once again empty of Dakota, Iron Cutter had received twenty-two pipes.

Day Sets walked to the bluff overlooking the river. All day she'd watched faded examples of her people interacting with well-fed, confident wasichu. The Mdewakanton would never allow one tribe to eat well while another starved. It was clearer than ever that the wasichu would never see the Mdewakanton as part of mitakuye oyasin. Their notion of the family of all living things was odd. It included the white men in charge of the fort, in charge of the government, in charge of the towns. Everyone else, including women, slaves, and Dakota, were something less.

Although Cloud Man's resolve had clearly been shaken, he still supported the Mdewakanton adopting wasichu ways. Day Sets had come to question that. Her daughter was at school learning to be a good wasichu wife, but Day Sets no longer wanted that for her daughter. She never wanted Mary to depend on a husband totally as Samantha had. It was the wasichu men who had all the power, and no amount of education would make Mary a wasichu man. At best, education at the Lake Harriet school would teach Mary how to speak English and how to interact with the wasichu that now dominated their land. Day Sets vowed her daughter would never marry a wasichu man. Mary would remain Mdewakanton.

It was natural for a mother to protect her daughter, to want the best life for her. Cloud Man had convinced his daughters that meant marriage to wasichu. Stands Sacred had loved Seth

Eastman, and he had left her. He might as well have died. Hushes Still the Night had been luckier, having Daniel Lamont close by for years before he died. Laughing Bird still loved Jim Thompson and prayed he would return. Day Sets had no illusions of romantic love with Iron Cutter, but at least he had kept Mary fed and put her in school. For all that was worth. She wanted to bring Mary home from the school more than anything, but she wasn't sure she could keep Mary fed. And she couldn't face her father's disappointment.

CHAPTER 31:

April, 1836
St. Peter's Agency, Michigan Territory

HARRIET

A few days later, tranquility returned to the fort and the sun shone. Harriet, doing laundry in the yard, basked in the warmth on her back. Thomas sauntered in her direction from the stable. His gait made her uneasy, but she didn't know why.

"Hey, beautiful," he said.

Harriet frowned and ignored him.

"Cat got your tongue? You're usually not so quiet," Thomas said. He smirked at her.

She winced at his tone and forced herself to stay silent. Thomas reached past her into the laundry tub and pulled at one of the master's shirts. Harriet slapped his hand away. "I can do my job." She picked up the last shirt and hung it on the line.

"Oh, so you *can* speak!" He laughed. "We can have fun, you 'n me." He leered at her.

Harriet avoided his eyes and looked across the plateau toward the fort. She spotted the newly arrived Black man walking Dr. Emerson's horse. Now there was a man worth getting to know.

She dried her damp hands on her apron and hurried inside. "Ellie, I need to go to the fort. You need somethin' from the sutler?"

Ellie looked puzzled, but said, "We can always use coffee. The major gave away the last of ours to the Indians."

Harriet nodded, untied her apron, and headed out the door. Thomas still stood in the yard. "Sudden trip?" he said.

"Gotta run an errand," she said.

She walked toward the fort without looking back. The days had been growing longer and warmer, so it was a pleasant day. She fastened her eyes on the handsome Black man, who was now currying his master's horse outside the stable. As she approached, uncertainty made her nervous. She'd never been so bold as to introduce herself to a stranger.

She needn't have worried. He noticed her and went back to grooming the horse. He kept looking up as she drew closer. Before she could say anything, though, she felt an iron grip on her arm.

"Seems I have business at the fort, too," Thomas said. He pulled Harriet closer to him, keeping hold of her arm, as they passed the man Harriet had been eying. "Stop making eyes at him," Thomas hissed. He squeezed her arm.

Harriet panicked. He was hurting her. She yanked her arm and said, "Keep your hands off me!"

Thomas laughed and held on. A shadow fell over Harriet, and Thomas collapsed with a groan, loosening his grip on her arm. "Are you all right?" asked the stranger.

Harriet looked up into the most caring dark eyes she'd ever seen. His voice caressed her like velvet. "Thank you," she said, "and welcome to Fort Snelling." She'd practiced that casual welcome, but in light of Thomas's actions her words seemed out of place. From the corner of her eye, she could see Thomas getting to his feet, glowering.

"Thank you," her savior said. "You sure you all right?"

She smiled and returned to the agency, knowing he would prevent Thomas from following her.

When she arrived back at the kitchen without the coffee, Ellie made her confess where she'd been. "I'm glad he took care of Thomas for you," she said. "Next time introduce yourself." She laughed when Harriet wrinkled her nose.

On her next trip to the fort, Harriet greeted the new man and said, "You're with the new doc, that right?"

"Yes, ma'am. Etheldred Scott, at your service. You can call me Dred." He bowed toward her and stood up with a sparkling smile that melted Harriet.

"Harriet. My name," she said. "I mean, my name's Harriet Robinson."

"Lovely to meet you, Miss Harriet," he said. "You walk this way often?"

Harriet wanted to tell him she'd walk by every day, but she just smiled. "I live at the agency house. Kitchen door's around back."

He nodded. "I'll be seeing you, Miss Robinson."

"Nice meetin' you, Mr. Scott," she said. His eyes bored into her as he waited. "Oh, I mean Dred." He smiled. As she walked away, she didn't hide her delight. She meant to enjoy getting to know this man.

Later that day, Harriet's euphoria evaporated when a visitor arrived that made Major Taliaferro scowl. His curses filled the house. Harriet brought drinks when her master called for whiskey. A stranger sat in the major's office.

"It's as I'm saying, sir," the strange man said. "You were right that someone is selling whiskey to the Indians, but it's not Colonel Stambaugh at the fort. At least, not him by himself."

"You're sure about Sibley's involvement?"

"Yes, sir. Sibley and Stambaugh are partners, but I believe

the arrangement is outside American Fur. Stambaugh doesn't work for American Fur, I mean."

Major Taliaferro cursed again. It was his job to make sure the whiskey trade with the Indians was controlled. Too much whiskey worsened the volatile relationship between tribes.

"Unrest of another kind is brewing as well."

The man sounded as if he were being forced to continue. Harriet was curious and lingered in the doorway.

"In St. Louis, I saw a horrifying thing. Now, before I say anything, know that I'm aware that people have hung Black men in that city before. This incident, though, was brutal."

Harriet bit her hand to prevent crying out. She didn't want to hear gruesome details, nor could she move away.

"The police arrested a Black boatman, named McIntosh, for helping someone else escape custody. McIntosh was joking with the arresting officers when they suggested a prank like that was a hanging offense. McIntosh panicked and slashed about wildly with his knife. In the process, he stabbed and killed a deputy."

Major Taliaferro cursed.

"Oh, it gets better. A crowd gathered, as crowds do, and turned ugly. They screamed, 'Burn him!' and took McIntosh away. They chained him to a locust tree and piled brush around his feet. Then they set it afire and watched the man burn. I saw the whole thing."

Overcome, the man stopped talking. Harriet heard her master refill their whiskey glasses as she fled to the kitchen with tears filling her eyes.

On another occasion that summer, Harriet lingered by the master's office to hear him talk to a visitor about the court case brought by Rachel, formerly enslaved at Fort Snelling. Just the previous day, Ellie had told Harriet about Courtney, a fur trader's slave who'd lived near the fort. The trader sold Courtney and her son downriver to St. Louis. She'd sued for her freedom, but was waiting for the outcome in Rachel's earlier case. It sounded like that decision had come. Harriet listened.

"Rachel was here at the fort for a year," Major Taliaferro was saying.

"Yes," the visitor said. "She belonged to Lieutenant Stockton. The soldiers get a stipend from the government to pay for servants, you know."

"Rachel was a slave," the major said. "The soldier pocketed the stipend." He snorted. It was a common enough practice. "Go on, though."

"When he left Fort Snelling, Lieutenant Stockton took Rachel to Fort Crawford, where she gave birth to a son. Stockton later sold them in St. Louis."

"Yes, yes, I know," Major Taliaferro said. "She said her enslavement was illegal since Fort Snelling and Fort Crawford are in free territory. What of the decision?"

"I'm getting to that. The Missouri Supreme Court ruled in her favor."

"They set her free?"

Harriet couldn't read her master's tone. He sounded pleased that the law freed Rachel. But he was also a slaveholder in a free territory. Would he now free them? She ran to tell Ellie.

"Good for Rachel," Ellie said.

"What about us, Ellie? Will he free us?"

Ellie shook her head. "Not that easy. Remember that our master owns more slaves than just the half dozen or so who're here at the agency. He rents them to soldiers."

Harriet remembered what she'd heard about stipends. "And the soldiers pay the major their servant stipend. He'll never give that up."

"And Mrs. Taliaferro can't run this household without us."

IT SOON BECAME CUSTOMARY for Harriet to take a stroll with Dred in the late afternoon, in a scant bit of time after she finished her daily chores and before Ellie needed her to help with dinner. They walked together past the stable, where Thomas made himself scarce. As Dred and Harriet headed along the river, the prairie stretched before them in a magnificent floral tapestry. Blazing star, butterfly weed, prairie smoke, bergamont, wild lupine, and thousands of other flowers blended into a colorful carpet.

On this day, Harriet was quiet. Dred let her alone for a bit, then took her hand. "What's troubling you?"

Harriet told him about Rachel. He nodded and said, "They'll set Courtney free, too. It's called precedent. Maybe someday I'll sue for my freedom! And I'll thank Dr. Emerson forever for bringing me into free territory."

Harriet smiled. "What would you do if you were free?"

"Freedom's a state of mind. I'd still care for someone's horse or be a valet. It's what I know how to do. But I'd be free. I could up and go off to New York if I wanted, or to the wilds of Canada." His arms swept wide, indicating the entire world. "I could take a boat to places across the ocean like London."

Harriet laughed and teased him. "So freedom makes you rich?"

He sobered and took both of her hands in his. She felt herself being drawn into the dark pools of his eyes. She'd never felt so comfortable with another human being.

"Harriet, being rich would be unimportant if I couldn't have you by my side. I know we haven't known each other long, but I've learned to act because waiting often has bad results."

Harriet remembered what Dred had told her of his first wife. He'd waited a long time before marrying, only to have her sold away from him after their marriage. Her head began to spin as her heart leaped in hope.

"Harriet Robinson, will you marry me?" He squeezed her hands.

Harriet giggled. He was older than she was, and they were both enslaved, with different owners. Both owners would have to agree. This was a foolish idea. But she did enjoy his company, and she would miss him if they were separated. "If I were free, I'd love to marry you," she said.

"Maybe someday it'll happen." He grasped Harriet around her waist and spun her in a circle. She laughed, dizzy from happiness as well as spinning.

Harriet continued to work in the Taliaferro's kitchen and walk with Dred whenever they both could steal a few moments away.

Harriet hummed with happiness, but Ellie faded. Her son, Jarvis, cried a lot and almost always had a fever. Ellie worried about him and fussed over him. Harriet knew telling her not to worry wouldn't help so, as she had done during Ellie's pregnancy, Harriet took on part of the other woman's duties. She also begged Dred to ask his master, Dr. Emerson, to examine Jarvis. In Jarvis, she saw all her future children, and in Ellie she saw what a mother's anguish could do.

Harriet and Ellie brought Jarvis to Dr. Emerson late in August. The women stood by nervously while the baby cried and the doctor examined him.

"He's not eating right," Ellie said, even though she'd already told the doctor this. "He has a fever, he's so sick. Please, what can I do?"

Dr. Emerson pushed and prodded at the baby's bulging belly. The baby kicked and cried at first, then subsided and allowed the exam. The two women stood nearby, clutching each other for support. Dr. Emerson handed Jarvis to Ellie and said, "He has a hernia. There are surgeons who could correct that in St. Louis, but I can't do it here. I'm sorry."

Harriet knew Ellie could never take her son downriver, even if their master allowed it. Downriver meant slave territory. No enslaved mother would take her son, even mixed-race as Jarvis was, from free territory into slave territory. They continued as they had been.

In September, summer faded from the prairie and Jarvis died. Ellie was inconsolable. Harriet teared up when something reminded her of the baby, but life at the agency went on. Ellie dried her tears and rolled out the biscuits for dinner.

PART THREE
INTO THE FUTURE

CHAPTER 32:

May, 1836
Galena, Illinois

SAMANTHA

Samantha stood on the deck of the Warrior with Emily in her arms. Now that she'd chosen a path, right or wrong, numbness settled over her. She didn't look back at Fort Snelling as the boat pulled away from the dock, preferring to look instead at the future in her daughter's face.

"Can I get you anything?" Dr. Nathan Jarvis asked. He had lost no time coming aboard the boat as soon as he realized it had brought his replacement, Dr. Emerson.

"No, thank you," she said. After returning from Cloud Man's Village, Samantha was determined to be on the next boat that could take her away from Fort Snelling. She allowed Eliza and Lawrence to believe she would wait for someone to travel with her, so it was a happy coincidence that Dr. Jarvis was aboard. She couldn't help but look at him, when he wasn't looking back, of course, and try to see similarities to Ellie's sickly son.

He hesitated, clasping his hands in front of him and rocking on his feet. "So you're visiting your brother in Prairie du Chien? Is that what I heard?"

"I won't be back to Fort Snelling." Samantha didn't want to talk about her brother. She hadn't sent him word they were coming, as if James Henry not knowing might change their destination. But her only other option was New York, and she would never let her father take control of her life again, especially with an I-told-you-so attitude.

"And your husband will join you?"

"My husband is dead." It was true that the man called Alex Miree was dead. Pale Crow had nothing to do with her. It was up to her to help her daughter grow strong and independent, able to make good choices. She knew Dr. Jarvis was only trying to be polite, cognizant of the chaperone role Major Taliaferro had thrust on him. It was much easier to tell people Alex was dead than to explain. If he were dead, though, people might expect her to feel grief rather than the coldness that filled her heart. She'd been angry at first. That had been a hot feeling, wanting to yell and hit things like she never had before. Then the heat faded to a numb despair full of accusation and disappointment. And now she felt nothing, a frozen layer of protection covering her raw heart.

"My condolences." The tight line of his jaw as he walked away from her told Samantha she had succeeded at pushing him away.

Samantha focused on Emily. No man would talk to a new mother if she was staring into her daughter's eyes, smiling and cooing, and there were no other women on board the vessel. In fact, if she kept to her cabin, she wouldn't have to keep up a happy face. She could let sorrow show in her eyes, let her shoulders droop in despair. One thing she would never do was cry for Alexander Miree and his carefree life she once thought was exciting. She'd envied the way he made decisions in the moment and followed his heart. What she hadn't envisioned was the lack of commitment behind those actions. When you loved someone, you worked together to make a marriage work. At least in her world you did.

She'd been wrong to choose Alex, not that those words would ever cross her lips. If her father, or her brother, heard her say that, then she would never have another moment free of their control.

Emily fussed, and Samantha bounced her a bit in her arms. "It's all right, baby. Mama will always be here for you, sweetheart." Unlike Emily's father, who had never even met her. She looked over the deck rail of the boat at the natural beauty of the shoreline. Not for the first time, she wondered if this next move was a good choice. Having made such a colossal mistake in marrying Alex, she questioned herself now. She hadn't sent James Henry a letter about her plan to show up on his doorstep. She imagined greeting his wife, "Pleased to meet you, Catherine. I'm your sister-in-law, Samantha, and this is Emily. We've come to live with you." Nothing about crawling back to James Henry appealed to her, but where else would she go, alone and with an infant? She refused to take charity from the Taliaferros. Going home to Champlain was worse than going to James Henry. Samantha shivered when she pictured her father's face if she arrived home with an infant and no husband. Her failure at choosing a husband, of losing him and crawling home with a fatherless infant, would bring disappointment and disgust to his eyes. For the rest of her life, he would treat her as incompetent. That would be much worse than whatever love and support her mother would offer to counterbalance Papa.

As her mind churned, the river flowed as it always had, oblivious to the boat that floated on it like a child's toy. The river ran vast and omniscient through the ages, capable of taking her to a glowing future or dashing her against its rocks.

By the time the *Warrior* eased into the dock at Prairie du Chien, Samantha had yet to convince herself she was doing the right thing. She forced herself to tie her bonnet under her chin and wrap Emily up tight in her blanket. They were ready. But she couldn't make herself leave the cabin. She watched out the window as normal life happened without her. People shouted greetings to those waiting on the dock, wagons rumbled into position to receive cargo, the boat's steam engine chuffed and groaned as it slowed the boat. Samantha watched, detached.

"Mrs. Miree?" Dr. Jarvis knocked on her door. "Are you ready to disembark?"

"I'll be right there. Please go on without me," she said. She turned to pick up the large cloth bag on her bed, as if she meant to follow him.

"I'll just see to your trunk, then." He tipped his hat to her and left.

She was not a part of Prairie du Chien. This was not her place. Sarah Taylor Davis, her closest friend and supporter, was no longer here. Her brother would be smug. His wife might be smothering in her efforts to soothe, or maybe she would be cold and distant. Prairie du Chien was full of too many half-knowns. It wasn't strange to her, but she didn't know how the people she had lived with so briefly would react to her failed marriage, to her life going backwards into James Henry's sphere of protection. She couldn't keep up the pretense of Alex's death here. Gossip traveled faster than any boat on the river. Everyone would learn soon, if they didn't know already, that her husband was living with his Sioux wife and child.

Samantha stared out the window of her cabin as the sounds of passengers departing decreased. Only the people traveling on to Galena, or even St. Louis, stayed aboard. She hugged Emily tight. Galena might be nice. Anywhere but Prairie du Chien.

In Galena, she could reinvent herself. Someone would hire a widowed mother to work as a housekeeper, or in a store. She could sew for the lead miners in Galena, or cook for them. It was a busy enough town that she could avoid notice as she built a life for her daughter.

What a crazy idea! She was no good at making her own decisions. Her failed marriage proved that. How could she consider taking off on her own to a strange place with a baby? Samantha turned her back to the cabin and stepped into the hallway.

Emily kicked her feet and waved her arms, scrunching up her face in an expression Samantha always interpreted as a smile. More than anything in this world, Samantha wanted this little girl to grow up strong. She wanted Emily to take charge of her own life. She could never teach her daughter to do that if she went crawling back to her brother at the first setback.

Samantha checked the bag she had with her. It held a couple of diapers, a change of clothes for herself and Emily, and half a packet of bread and cheese that Eliza had given her. It was enough to start a new life in Galena. She'd send for her trunk as soon as she arrived. Surely a post office would hold it for her until she found a place to live and work. Samantha went back inside her cabin, heart pounding.

The *Warrior*'s engine growled to life again, and the stack belched smoke as the boat pulled away from the dock. Samantha's heart lurched in panic for a moment. Prairie du Chien was more familiar to her than Galena, which was just a stop on the river. All she knew about Galena was that the townspeople mined lead and James Churchman lived there. Or had lived there. She shook her head at the vague notion that she was fleeing to James.

Emily fussed a bit, and Samantha focused once more on her baby. She stroked Emily's soft brown hair and smooth pink skin. Life would be as perfect for this little angel as it was in her power to make it. That was what every mother vowed. Samantha pictured her own mother, holding her as a baby, promising a life of wonder. Emotion clogged her throat. A tear dropped onto Emily's face, startling the baby. Had Mama cried when Papa banished her? Samantha would never ask.

She would convince Captain Throckmorton to collect her additional fee from James Henry at a later date. Samantha alternated between enjoying the time with Emily and panicking that she once again was making a bad choice. When Galena came into view, Samantha saw a town little changed from her trip upriver. It had grown in four years, with substantial new houses of native limestone perched forty feet or so above the town in terraced ridges, but most of the businesses were nothing more than crude huts of log and sod. Galena was all about the mining, not the comfort of the people.

Samantha wrapped Emily, gathered her bag, and disembarked as if she knew where she was going. She walked among a bustling crowd of miners, gamblers, traders, and rivermen. The main street meandered through the buildings. Samantha walked past log huts that held a leather worker's shop, a church, and a small school. The most prosperous building she saw was the trading post set at the confluence of the Fever River and the Mississippi. She eyed it critically. The building was busier than her brother's store, and more impressive since it was two stories and made of limestone.

Curiosity, or maybe familiarity, propelled Samantha toward the store. She needed to find somewhere to stay, some work she could do to earn her way. Storekeeping she knew. An understated sign identified the store as belonging to John Dowling. With Emily asleep in her arms, Samantha opened the door and walked in.

Although arranged differently than James Henry's store or the sutler's, Dowling's had all the same features: scuffed wooden floors, stacked merchandise, a long counter across one end.

Behind the counter, two men, one a younger duplicate of the other, waited on customers.

Samantha strolled around the store, watching the shop-keepers interact with their customers. The store emptied of customers, and Samantha started forward to talk to the Dowling men about a job.

Before she got too far, the door opened, and a familiar voice called, "Good morning, John!"

Both storekeepers waved and called back, but Samantha turned to examine the shelf of axes in front of her, her heart beating fast. She forced herself to breathe as she perused tomahawks, felling axes and half axes. Of all places, how was it possible James Churchman would arrive in this store at this very moment? She snuck a glance toward the front of the store. A petite, well-dressed woman stood next to James. She laughed up at him and touched his arm.

Samantha, conscious of her travel-wrinkled dress, mussed hair, and untied bonnet, clutched Emily. It had been five days since she'd bathed Emily at the Taliaferro's house at St. Peter's Agency, five days since she'd done more than splash water on her own face. She smelled of nervous sweat and baby. It was not how she wanted to appear to James. It was not how she wanted to meet the strange woman who might be a wife. Samantha hadn't planned to approach him at all even though somewhere deep in her heart she must have known she'd see him here.

The men's conversation wasn't clear, but the sound of James's voice brought tears to her eyes, tears of longing for what might have been, then tears of regret that her father might have been right. When the conversation died, Samantha stayed where she was, uncertain about her course of action.

"I'm not familiar with babies," a male voice said, "but I'll hazard a guess that an axe is a rather desperate ploy."

Samantha's eyes widened. The younger storekeeper had approached while she was lost in thought. His friendly smile revealed a dimple in one cheek. Although his hair was combed, a recalcitrant curl hung across his forehead. She flushed in embarrassment.

"John Dowling, Jr. at your service," he said. "Can I help you with something?"

Samantha's tension evaporated at his kindness. James had left, and she needed a place. She needed food and somewhere to sleep, a way to pay for her life and Emily's. She said, "Sorry, I was thinking. No, I don't want an axe." She gave him a shaky smile. "I'm Samantha Miree."

He gave a deep sigh, feigning great relief. That made her smile wider. He tilted his head and raised his eyebrows, waiting for her to continue.

A woman entered the store and went to the shelf that held fabric. She peered at the bolts, frowning.

Samantha saw an opportunity to show John Dowling how she might help in his store. She approached the woman with a smile. "Can I answer a question for you?"

"Oh thank you," the customer said. "I love this fabric but it seems a little lightweight for Galena. What do you think?" She lifted the end of the fabric bolt and rubbed it between her fingers.

"It is a pretty pattern," Samantha said. She scanned the shelf and selected another bolt. "Maybe you can line that lightweight cotton with this heavier cotton. It would make your dress more practical but still pretty."

The customer's face lit up. "What a wonderful idea! I'm so tired of drab gray flannel. And a bit of pretty will make my husband happy, if you know what I mean." She laughed with Samantha as she took both bolts of fabric to the counter.

"Very impressive," John Dowling said.

He'd come up behind Samantha and stood so close that when she turned to answer him she almost bumped her nose on his chin. "You have a very nice store, Mr. Dowling, but it lacks a woman's touch. Surely you have female customers?"

"More and more as the days go on. You've worked in a store before?"

Samantha nodded. "My husband had the store at Fort Snelling." Her breath caught, waiting for the inevitable questions about why she was traveling alone. To forestall him, she said in a rush, "He's tying up loose ends with our property. He will join us in a few weeks."

Emily fussed and kicked her feet. She needed to be fed, and changed, and bathed, and put down for a nap. Overwhelmed, Samantha trembled.

"Do you know of a place I can stay with my daughter?" Samantha asked. "And I need to support us until my husband arrives. Is it possible I might work for you?" She cringed at the forward nature of her request. "I've shown you how helpful I can be with female customers."

John Dowling's brow furrowed, but he didn't comment on the baby. "Why don't we talk to my father, all right?" He reached out a hand as if to help her walk to the counter. Samantha passed him, and his hand came to rest on her back. As they approached the counter where the elder Mr. Dowling stood, John's hand increased pressure as if it belonged there.

Samantha recoiled, but his hand stayed there, almost possessively, when they reached the counter.

"We have here a mother and child in need of assistance," John told his father.

The elder Dowling peered over the top of his glasses at Samantha. "Husband?" he said.

"He will join us soon. We had to come ahead."

Neither man asked where she left from. The younger man's hand caressed her back and the older one looked more speculative. What was he planning?

Emily began to cry.

"What's wrong with her?" the elder storekeeper said.

"She's just hungry. Usually she's very good." Samantha rocked Emily, praying she would stop crying.

"There's a storeroom in the back," the younger Mr. Dowling said. "You can feed her there." The pressure of John's hand on her back showed her the way to a storeroom with a sink. "Come on out when you've finished," he said, and returned to the store.

Samantha laid Emily's blanket on the table near the sink and put the baby on it. She removed the wet flannel cloth and reached into her cloth bag for her last dry one. She'd have to send for her trunk soon. Emily kicked and waved her arms.

"Hush, little one," she cooed to her daughter. "You'll be dry and fed in no time."

She found a keg to sit on, unhooked the front of her dress, and maneuvered the baby into position to nurse. Calm settled over her. Feeding her baby made her feel like she was the most important person in the world, at least to Emily. The sound of a boot scraping the wooden floor startled her. Something thumped against the door. Samantha rushed to cover herself just as the door latch clicked. She was sure John had latched the door on his way out. Even so, she turned away from the door to finish nursing.

When the baby was full and drowsy, Samantha wrapped her in the blanket and laid her on the table against the wall, securing her in place with the cloth bag. She splashed water on her face and attempted to smooth her hair. The front of her dress was wrinkled from traveling and holding the baby, but she couldn't do much about that. Taking a deep breath, she picked up Emily and straightened her shoulders. Time to get a job to support them.

Both Mr. Dowlings stopped talking when she appeared. They looked at her, waiting for her to speak.

"I am Samantha Miree. I would like to work here," Samantha said, "to pay for a place for my daughter and I to live."

"Until Mr. Miree arrives?" Mr. Dowling, Sr. said.

"Yes. Until my husband arrives."

"What kind of husband allows his wife to travel with such a young baby?"

Samantha didn't know what to say to that. "I have experience. My husband had a store in the north. And I've already shown I can help the female customers."

"She would be an asset, Father," the younger John said.

His father shook his head and waved his hand, in resignation if not approval.

John, Jr. said, "You are welcome to help us in the store in exchange for a place to stay. There's a small room off the store room that I can clear. You can stay there. Can you cook?" Samantha nodded. "You will cook supper for us, too, then."

When he smiled, it was more of a leer. Samantha's gut twisted. But what choice did she have? She could afford to be picky about jobs if she were alone, but Emily changed that. She had to provide for her daughter.

CHAPTER 33:

Moon When Chokecherries Are Ripe, 1836
Mní Sní

$\backsim\!\!\!\curvearrowright\!\!\!\sim$

DAY SETS

Cloud Man's band walked the two miles to Mní Sni. They arrived at the camping place near *Mnigaga Wapke*, or Minnehaha Falls. Day Sets breathed in the dramatic beauty of the tall bluffs dotted with oaks. Legend told that the Seven Fires of the Dakota, including the Mdewakanton, came from the belt of Orion and arrived at the mdote, where the big rivers met. For the first time in months, Day Set's stomach didn't twist at the thought of the future of the Mdewakanton people. Being in this sacred place made Day Sets feel she was in the arms of Maka Ina herself, a child being protected by its mother. Since the dawn of time, Dakota people had suffered and grown. They would continue to do so.

Mní Sni was a sacred place for religious ceremonies and peace councils. Day Sets remembered her first visit. She'd been about eight years old, and her father had brought his family to the peace council. The feasting and dancing had lasted two days. Both tribes had drawn water from the sacred spring that bubbled forth from the limestone all year, and they camped near the falls.

Day Sets and her sisters had enjoyed the dancing. Cloud Man and Blue Medicine joined the chiefs and shamans from the other tribes to meet in the cave under the cliffs. Her father described the walls as covered with ancient drawings of men, birds, animals, fish, and turtles, with large rattlesnakes pointing upward to a common point in the sky above the cave. Cloud Man had spoken of how entering the darkness of the cave symbolized both birth and death. The cave was the womb of Maka Ina, the ever-flowing spring her birth waters, the river her heart's blood. Unktehi, the water spirit, lived in the spring and had an underground route to St. Anthony Falls where he battled Thunderbird. The burial mounds on the cliff above the cave placed ancestors as close to the stars as possible, emphasizing the dichotomy of birth and death. Mní Sni was a place of both destructive and creative power.

Day Sets felt the sacred weight of the place. She didn't even need the drumbeats of the dancers to echo the heartbeat of the Earth Mother in her very bones. Songs and dances were already being performed as Cloud Man's band arrived. Cloud Man and Blue Medicine made their way to the cave to meet with other leaders while the feasting began on the bluff. Day Sets knew the peace treaty was a normal occurrence between the Dakota and Ojibwe, a time of ceremonial singing, dancing, and feasting. This time, though, spirits were already dampened as leaders met to discuss the threat of an outside force, and even the combined efforts of several bands couldn't scrape together a feast worthy of the name.

"Maka Ina holds her children close here," Stands Sacred said to her sisters. She waited outside the tipi while Day Sets and Hushes Still the Night readied themselves for the dancing.

"Wasichu don't understand that," Day Sets said. Iron Cutter hinted more than once that his people wanted the Mdewakanton to leave the land around the fort.

"They built their fort at mdote to break the Dakota spirit," Hushes Still the Night said. "Whoever kills the most people wins."

Day Sets picked up her best beaded shawl. The truth in her sister's words hurt. The wasichu may not understand Mdewakanton ways, but they weren't ignorant either. "They know what they are doing. But enough of that. Let's dance."

The sisters gathered their shawls close around their shoulders and walked to the meeting on the bluff. The Dakota tribes lined up facing the Ojibwe, about 150 yards away, and they all sang the Peace Song. The sisters and the other women folded their scarves and draped them over their arms as they danced behind the line of men. If this had been a time for their Scarf Dance, they would hold the scarves out like a rainbow of butterflies. But this was a somber men's dance. The women's bouncing step, danced in place behind their men, emphasized the beat in the song, the drums, their heartbeats in time with the heartbeat of Maka Ina.

The two lines of braves, with all their weapons, advanced toward each other, singing and dance-stepping. As they drew close, they sang the Braves' Song and shook hands. The men passed peace pipes as a symbol of the treaty renewal. The land of Mni Sota Makoce was once again assured of peace.

Day Sets walked back to the village with her sisters, refreshed in heart and spirit. Ahead of them, Cloud Man and Blue Medicine led the tribe as they walked, not in a formal march, but not a casual stroll, either. Red Cherry Woman walked nearby. Upholding the ancient tradition gave Day Sets a warm glow inside. The ancestors were nearby, and Maka Ina held them close, giving Day Sets hope for the future and a new resolve to bring Mary home so she could be embraced by her heritage. Cloud Man, however, was withdrawn. Day Sets didn't want to take on his fears, but she didn't want him to spread them over the village, either. She hurried over to her mother.

"What's wrong with Father?" she asked. "The tribes have remembered we are all mitakuye oyasin."

Red Cherry Woman said, "Cloud Man knows that spirits will plummet with the first cry of a hungry child or the pleading eyes of a starving newcomer who has left everything he reveres to survive." Red Cherry Woman shook her head. "The bite of hunger will be stronger than vows of solidarity. It's nice to believe we are all beloved by our Earth Mother, but reality disproves that every day."

Day Sets felt the truth of her mother's words deep inside.

Red Cherry Woman walked a few steps in thought. "Cloud Man says not all the Ojibwe chiefs were here. There's a rumor of Ojibwe treaty talks at the fort."

Day Sets wanted to believe Red Cherry Woman was wrong, but Day Set's practical nature felt the truth in her mother's words, and she knew she couldn't further burden her father by bringing Mary back to the village. By doing that, Day Sets would repudiate her father and weaken him further in the eyes of the tribe. She and Red Cherry Woman continued in silence, walking through the tall prairie grass under the towering oak trees. Plovers flew overhead, singing an announcement of their imminent annual migration south.

As they neared the village, swamp forests of tamarack trees leaned over the lake. The wild rice bowed over the water among the bulrushes. Day Sets noted the laden stalks, soon to be harvested by Mdewakanton women in their dugouts, before the loons could eat the precious rice. The corn stalks from the village field hid the lodges, accessible only by a narrow lane between the stalks.

No sooner had they entered the village than a fast-moving horse arrived with a wasichu rider. Day Sets and her sisters paused outside Cloud Man's lodge so they could see and hear the encounter.

"Cloud Man?" the man called from horseback.

Cloud Man stood tall, facing the man, and didn't answer.

Day Sets recognized Henry Sibley, the man who ran a trading post at Mendota, near the site of Oheyawahi, a sacred Dakota burial site. He represented another group of wasichu just taking land that didn't belong to him.

Stands Sacred whispered, "Did you know he plans to marry Red Blanket Woman?"

"Really?" Hushes Still the Night said. "Bad Hail's daughter?"

"One more wasichu taking a Dakota wife." Day Set's prickly tone reflected her irritation with her mother's earlier words. For once, she wanted the peaceful connection to her ancestors, the calm certainty of the Mdewakanton future, to remain in her heart with no interference from forces outside her control.

"Sibley," the man said as he dismounted. "American Fur Company."

Hushes Still the Night snorted. "As if the entire region didn't know him," she muttered.

Cloud Man said nothing.

Henry Sibley said, "Your braves are hungry. They hunt too far north, enter Ojibwe territory, and are attacked. Or they go too far south and have trouble with the Fox and Sauk. You need help from the United States Government."

Day Sets felt sick. This wasichu had Dakota lives all figured out, problems and solutions, as if they were infants. At first, such treatment had irritated her, then amused her. It had long given way to the hopelessness of acknowledgement. Henry Sibley was right about their situation.

Cloud Man said, "The Chief in the East has long ignored our need."

Henry Sibley said, "If you sell some of your land, the government will give you cash now to pay off your credit with American Fur and more in the form of annuities."

"Annuities are monies that never come," Cloud Man said.

Henry Sibley threw up his hands and remounted his horse. "I warn you, Cloud Man. Tougher times are coming and it will be better to be supported by the United States than to oppose them."

He rode off in a cloud of dust, his haste emphasizing his frustration with them.

Cloud Man stood like a stone, staring after the wasichu. Red Cherry Woman approached and led him into the lodge.

IT TOOK A FEW DAYS for the accord at Mní Sní to dissolve. Iron Cutter rode into the village with a plan to take a delegation of chiefs and headmen to Washington, the home of the Chief in the East. The purpose would be to sign a treaty that would keep the Dakota from starving as well as give them financial freedom from traders like American Fur Company.

Iron Cutter rode away, but in the Moon When Geese Shed Feathers, the Ojibwe met with government representatives at Fort Snelling in a major treaty discussion. Henry Sibley was central to the talks. Iron Cutter and his Dakota were excluded.

"This is an insult to me, to my position, and to the Dakota!" he raged to Day Sets.

Day Sets said, "They tell us to sell our land and they'll protect us. They think we are stupid children." She refrained from saying that Iron Cutter believed the same.

In the Moon When Corn is Gathered, Iron Cutter left the territory accompanied by Cloud Man and a delegation of other Dakota leaders. Day Sets watched them go, her husband's back stiff with outrage and her father leaning forward in his eagerness to make everything right for his people.

CHAPTER 34:

July, 1836
Fort Snelling, Wisconsin Territory

HARRIET

There was a spring in Harriet's step as she walked between the fort and the agency that summer, and delight in her eyes when she caught sight of Dred exercising his master's horse or running an errand. She heard talk around the fort of an upcoming treaty between the U.S. government and the Indians in the area. It wasn't the first treaty, and wouldn't be the last, but it was important. The United States needed access to lumber on Indian land. Harriet told Dred that Major Taliaferro said it was an excuse to push the Indians further west so more settlers could build towns, and that the government wanted to buy all of northern Wisconsin. The Indians, jaded from past broken promises, sought only the food and supplies needed to survive. In preparation for the treaty discussions, government commissioners, traders, and Indians began arriving.

One arrival was a familiar face. Harriet was walking to the fort on an errand to the sutler. The meadow was filling with Indian tipis, and the road was busy with arriving dignitaries.

"Jim!" Harriet called, surprised and pleased. Nero, as he sometimes did, had accompanied Harriet on her walk. He barked and wagged his tail when he sensed her pleasure.

Jim Thompson turned at the call and smiled when he saw Harriet. He looked more relaxed and confident than Harriet had ever seen him.

"Aren't you a sight for sore eyes? Won't your Laughing Bird be thrilled to see you?" Harriet peered behind the tall man. "Where's Captain Day? Is he still your master?"

Jim laughed and ruffled Nero's ears. "Harriet, so good to see you." He struck a proud pose. "You're looking at a free man. A group of Methodist missionaries were on their way up here and wanted an interpreter who could speak the Dakota language. They collected $1200 from their congregation to purchase me outright. Then they freed me."

"Oh, Jim, that's wonderful," Harriet said. She marveled at the story. Purchased and freed. What a miracle.

"I'll live with Laughing Bird and the children at the Methodist mission in Kaposia, going to work and coming home each night a free man."

They exchanged another minute of conversation before Harriet continued on her errand. Jim, of course, was in control of his own time.

In control of her own time. Harriet daydreamed about what that would be like. How nice it would be to come home to her own place. She could work as a laundress for pay, and use the money to fix up her place or buy nice things. Fingering the coarse faded cloth of her skirt, she imagined buying pretty calico at the sutler's for a new dress. Harriet was used to working hard. If she were free, she'd still do so, but she'd have a real bed instead of a pallet in the kitchen. She'd prepare simple meals, but they would be more than the cornbread and bacon that was the bulk of her diet at the Taliaferro's. She'd be free to leave the territory and go where? A laundress could find work anywhere. She could go downriver to Prairie du Chien or Galena, but not too far. White men often captured free Blacks and sold them downriver. It would be nice to stay right where she was, where the color of her skin put her outside the major conflict between the soldiers and the Indians. It was nice to dream.

By the end of June, thirteen hundred Ojibwe had set up temporary tipi villages near the agency. The territorial governor had arrived, as well as a New York lawyer. The governor would be the mouthpiece of the talks, the lawyer a scribe. Just ten days before the treaty discussions began, the government transferred troops at the fort to Florida to fight in the Seminole war. Only nineteen soldiers held the peace at Fort Snelling. The replacement troops would not arrive for weeks.

Harriet answered the door for callers at the agency who brought news to the major. There were so many visitors that Nero tired of jumping up to greet them and just wagged his tail. She heard Major Taliaferro rage that he was overlooked when the government selected treaty commissioners. He blamed American Fur Company and Henry Sibley, who seemed to be at the center of treaty manipulations. Sibley bought furs from the Ojibwe for his trading post in Mendota, and the Ojibwe were his best customers. His connections with Stambaugh, the sutler at the fort, gave Sibley influence with the Dakota as well. All the major could do was rant to whoever would listen.

When treaty talks began July 20, seven hundred Dakota had assembled to watch the thirteen hundred Ojibwe negotiate with Governor Dodge under a bower of softwood saplings erected on the prairie near the fort. Since Dr. Emerson outranked the temporary commander of the fort's reduced troops, he sat with the government representatives. Dred stood behind him, as did the other men's servants. Each day, when they went for their walk, Dred regaled Harriet with the posturing and politicking of the talks.

On the first day, he waved his hands in the air as he described the elaborate ritual of the peace pipe, offered to the four points of the compass and smoked by each chief present as well as Governor Dodge. Interpreters with Ojibwe blood mixed with Scot, African, Irish, or French translated English words to Ojibwe. No one translated for the Dakota.

On the second day, Dred could hardly wait to tell Harriet that the Ojibwe hadn't shown up. She'd already spotted the braves around the bark lodges with their women. Dred held her hand as he explained the chiefs wanted more time to talk to each other.

Harriet listened when Dred shared requests made by Ojibwe chiefs on the third day. They sat close together on a log near the path.

"One wanted to sit closer to hear better," he said. "Another wanted more tobacco and more food." Dred imitated the chief. "Have you cut off your breasts so that you cannot suckle your children?"

Harriet leaned toward Dred and laughed. "It sounds like they are delaying," she said. "Why would they do that?"

"The government provides food while they are here. Anything they eat now they don't have to negotiate for. They're smarter than the government gives them credit for."

"That's smart and also sad," Harriet said.

Harriet and Ellie prepared meals for the unending procession of guests to the agency. Dirt rained down on their heads as Major Taliaferro paced above, raging against the American Fur Company. Nero hid in the kitchen, as close to Harriet as he could get, and whined. She talked to him as if he were her child and fed him treats.

"The company is too big," Major Taliaferro insisted to whoever was present. "It openly defies the government on every topic that concerns Indian welfare. They want to eliminate competition in trade and enslave the Indians. They even insist the government replace money they lose in trade. If any official stands in their way, they see him set apart or removed."

Nero's tail thumped. Harriet rolled her eyes at Ellie, who shook her head. Major Taliaferro was certainly more passionate than usual.

That day, she shared the major's tirade with Dred. "He's too passionate," Dred said. "It won't help."

"We'll see," Harriet said. "He's put it all in a letter to the governor."

Dred put his arm around Harriet's waist as they walked. She leaned into him and thought only of this moment, this delightful moment.

One day, as they walked past the stable, Thomas spotted them and walked in their direction. Harriet tensed. Dred moved to her other side, placing himself between Thomas and Harriet. He faced Thomas with his hands on his hips and a determined look on his face. Thomas halted, then turned back to the stable. Without saying a word, Dred resumed walking with Harriet. She smiled and relaxed.

On July 24, a rogue band of Indians arrived. The other tribes expected them, but their arrival surprised and intimidated the white men. A hundred Indians rushed into the negotiations, followed by trader Lyman Warren and the new agent for the Ojibwe, Daniel Bushnell. They demanded that the government give Warren twenty thousand dollars.

"Major Taliaferro shouted something about being terrorized by black devils and drew his gun. A chief urged him to shoot, but the governor stopped him," Dred related to Harriet.

"It stopped everything cold. I've no idea why a trader felt he deserved that money."

"I've no idea. Never heard of him," Harriet said. Her master's uncharacteristic display of violence lost relevance as she lost herself in Dred's dark eyes.

It was several more days before the sound of beating drums drew Harriet and Ellie out of the agency house. Nero raced ahead, barking. Ojibwe warriors in full battle dress carried their war flag as well as the American flag and danced to the drums.

"Are they celebrating or threatening?" Ellie asked.

"Look! The soldiers're closing the gates to the fort!" Harriet pointed.

They watched the elaborate parade proceed to the bower, where negotiations took place. When the lead warrior shook the governor's hand and agreed to terms, a collective sigh of relief went up from the gathered Indians.

Later, Dred shared with Harriet what the Indians had agreed to. "The government will give them $800,000 over twenty years. The Ojibwe will lose almost three million acres of land east of the river."

"Three million acres? I can't even imagine that much land." Harriet thought for a moment, then grinned. "Did that trader get his $20,000?"

Dred grimaced. "Yes. A bonus he didn't deserve." Harriet laughed. Dred took her by the hands and swept her in a dizzy circle. "Imagine having that much money! I'd marry you first thing."

She collapsed against him, laughing. The laughter faded as Dred's intense gaze caught her. He leaned in and kissed her, sending Harriet's heart spiraling.

A few days later, Harriet brought home news. "Major Taliaferro is furious that the treaty left out the Dakota. He plans to go to Washington with a bunch of chiefs to negotiate for their lands east of the Mississippi River. Just like the Ojibwe! He swears the fur company will not have a part in it."

Harriet suspected her master would not return to Fort Snelling after the treaty talks in Washington. He spent a lot of time wrapping up details, including performing marriages. She wondered if she and Dred could convince him to marry them before he left. Her imagination blossomed with a romantic fantasy of what marriage could be. The reality was far less romantic. A union between Dred and Harriet would have to be negotiated by Dr. Emerson and Major Taliaferro. If Major Taliaferro left, Harriet would have to go with him. She wondered if Dr. Emerson would buy her from the major. Or maybe Major Taliaferro would free her. Ellie said that their master spoke of freeing them at an undisclosed point in the future. It wasn't proper for her to discuss marriage with the major, but Dred told her he'd brought it up with the doctor. All they could do now was wait.

Every time the major walked in her direction, Harriet's stomach fluttered in anticipation. Every time he walked past without speaking to her, a rock settled inside her. For several days, she could not see Dred at all due to the flurry surrounding her master's not-so-secret departure.

At last, the major called her into his front room to tell her of the arrangement he'd made with Dr. Emerson to allow her marriage to Dred. Speechless with delight, Harriet stumbled over her words of gratitude. She forgot to ask what that meant for her status.

That afternoon she hurried to meet Dred. As soon as he was within earshot, she called, "It's finally happened! We're getting married!"

Dred caught her around the waist and lifted her in the air. Oblivious to observing eyes, he kissed her on the lips. "I knew

Dr. Emerson had talked with the major. I didn't know when they would make it official, or even if Major Taliaferro would agree. Will you continue to be the major's slave?"

Harriet sobered. "I don't know. Do you think he'll free me?"

Dred shook his head. "It doesn't seem likely. He might insist you continue to live at the agency while I live at the fort near Dr. Emerson."

"Dred, it doesn't matter. We'll be married." Nothing could dampen her spirits.

On her wedding day, for the first time, Harriet entered the front room without having chores to complete. Ellie created a bouquet of summer prairie flowers for Harriet. She even tucked a flower in Nero's collar. Mrs. Taliaferro wouldn't give a big party, of course, but Ellie created a small cake in the kitchen to celebrate with Harriet and Dred. Even Thomas raised a glass of cider to toast the couple's happiness, although he kept his distance.

As a wedding present, Major Taliaferro gave Harriet to Dr. Emerson. She had a new master and a new husband. The doctor in turn gave Harriet and Dred a small private room at the fort. It had a fireplace, a table and chair, a cupboard, and a bed.

"It's all anyone needs," Dred said as he led his bride to the bed.

Harriet's heart was full. She was married to a man she loved, living in a room of their own. The future was bright, even though she was still enslaved. Life would be perfect if she could be free in name as well as spirit.

MAJOR TALIAFERRO LEFT THE agency, collecting Dakota chiefs along the way downriver. The tribes at the agency drifted away. The soldiers disassembled the bower and used it for firewood. By August, even Mrs. Taliaferro had left the agency, taking

Ellie with her. Harriet embraced her friend with teary eyes as they said goodbye over tiny Jarvis's grave. Harriet knew Ellie's tears were more for leaving her son's resting place than for leaving her friend. The hardest leave-taking, though, was of Nero. He didn't understand why Harriet clutched him so hard and cried into his fur. She would miss the big lug, who was always happy, always loving.

After the agency shut down for the winter, Harriet busied herself preparing her own place. The new troop of soldiers arrived at the fort, but Dr. Emerson chafed. Dred told Harriet their master did not want to winter at the fort. Anxious, Harriet asked, "Will he take us south?"

Dred didn't know. "He says a replacement is coming. I don't know where he'll go or what'll become of us."

On October 8, Dr. Wright arrived. A junior officer had paddled upriver for two weeks in an open dugout, bringing the first of two doctors that the government had assigned to the fort.

Harriet knew that Dr. Emerson was impatient to leave. When the doctor called the couple into his parlor, she clasped her hands to avoid showing her anxiety over their future.

Dr. Emerson asked them to sit down. "I can't wait any longer, Dred. I'm expected in St. Louis and I'm leaving tomorrow in the same dugout that brought Dr. Wright." He shook his head. "I'm not looking forward to that long, cold dugout trip through a slushy river, but I have to go before it's completely frozen. There's not enough room for the two of you, or even for my medical books. You'll have to stay here at the fort for the winter."

Harriet stared at Dred in surprise, her mind trying to process what this would mean for them.

Dred said, "I'm not sure I understand, Dr. Emerson. What would you have us do?"

"Keep the hospital clean, I guess." He grinned. "Stay warm. Take care of my horse and dust my books. Dr. Wright will need you, Dred, and Major Plympton's wife has requested your services, Harriet. She has no other servants."

Harriet nodded. In the flurry surrounding the ending of the treaty and departure of the Taliaferros, she'd been called to help the new commandant's wife birth her fifth child. It had been a difficult birth. Harriet would be busy keeping a house with such a large family.

Dr. Emerson left without fanfare, and the Scotts' world changed dramatically for the better. For the first time, Dred and Harriet controlled their own days. Harriet spent much of the day at the commandant's house as a servant in the Plympton household. She had the run of the upstairs and downstairs, but felt most comfortable in the basement kitchen where a stone hearth filled an entire wall. In a hollow in the floor, a little spring kept a small larder cool. As expected, she was busy all day. When her work ended, she had to walk only a short way to her home.

In November, Dr. Erastus Wolcott joined Dr. Wright at Fort Snelling and hired Dred to work for him until March, when he hoped to rejoin his wife and child at Mackinac Island in Lake Michigan. Since neither doctor had a wife or family, they needed little in the way of household maintenance. Dred ran errands for them, but the chores were light.

For the entire winter of 1836, Harriet and Dred worked at keeping warm and learning to be married. Their little room in the hospital basement at the fort was the first household Harriet had kept that she could call her own. She was used to rising early, so she was not bothered by the drummers and fifer who marched the length of the parade ground at daylight each day. She served breakfast at the commandant's house at seven o'clock, then the men went off to their assigned work tasks until noontime dinner. Parades and drilling took up entire Sunday afternoons, and tatoo beat when it was time to extinguish lights. Only the officers stayed up past then.

"It must've been the major's intent to free me," she told Dred in one of their long discussions about their situation. "He married us, even though slave marriages aren't officially recognized. He didn't sell me to Dr. Emerson, just gave me to him. At last, we have this place of our own. What other slave do you know has such a life?"

"We have a good life, Harriet. We are lucky to live in this place, but we've gotta remember we're still slaves."

In her heart, Harriet was free. She ignored her brain, which kept reminding her she had a master, even if he was absent.

In the commandant's household, she heard about Henry Sibley hurrying to Washington to interfere with the treaty Major Taliaferro was attempting to negotiate with the Dakota. The treaty would allow a generous amount of money to the tribe, but Mr. Sibley was angry that Scott Campbell, the metis interpreter Harriet knew from St. Peter's Agency, was to get an annuity and a land grant of five hundred acres on the Mendota side of the river. Mr. Sibley thought everything on that side of the river belonged to him, or rather to the American Fur Company. Harriet brought home all the news of political maneuvering that affected Fort Snelling and its surroundings.

"I could see the steam coming out of Mr. Sibley's ears!" she said to Dred. "Major Plympton told his wife that the government will keep land around the fort."

"If the military reserves the land, they'll evict the settlers at Coldwater Creek. Many of them have been there for ten years," Dred said.

Harriet nodded. "I heard Major Plympton dictate a letter recommending the fort keep the woods where the fort gets firewood."

"Clever," Dred said. "It's a sad day when the government pushes out white men as well as the Indians!"

During their snug evenings in their room at the fort, Dred shared impressions of the two doctors he worked for. "Dr. Wright is distracted. His wife in the East will have her baby any day, and he's been apart from her for a while. Dr. Wolcott has a wife and baby at home, too. They both hate their assignment here."

"At least at home you have happiness and my full support," Harriet said.

"That's what keeps me going," her husband said.

At Christmas, the Plympton household held their annual banquet for officers and wives. Harriet cleaned and decorated the house, prepared the meal, and served it. Mrs. Plympton stood and recited her cousin Henry Livingston's new poem, "A Visit From St. Nicholas."

On Christmas Day, Mrs. Plympton gave birth to a son that she named for his father.

One of Harriet's tasks was to empty the Plympton family's chamber pots. To do so, she climbed the rickety outdoor stairs and dumped the pots into the latrine. From the height of a hundred feet above the shore, Harriet's nose turned red from the cold as she admired the panoramic view of the confluence of the Mississippi and the St. Peter Rivers, bordered by lush green banks and dusted by snow and ice. The interior of the fort, by contrast, was muddy. She clasped her arms around her body as she watched tumbling balls of slushy ice gather along the river shore and freeze together. The surface of the river was lumpy ice below which the current continued downriver to St. Louis and on to New Orleans.

Residents of the fort sank into despair at the loneliness of being cut off from the world for half the year or more. Harriet, though, didn't mind. She was with her husband, snug in a room at the fort, warm in his love. They were their own masters and could live free even if they were still Dr. Emerson's slaves.

CHAPTER 35:

May, 1836
Galena, Illinois

~~~~~~~~

SAMANTHA

By the time Samantha had worked three days at Dowling's store, she regretted her decision. The elder Mr. Dowling spoke very little to her, just looked at her with disapproval. The younger Mr. Dowling was a different story.

Samantha cooked for the three of them in the kitchen next to the storeroom while Emily napped on a pallet in a dark alcove. John found a myriad of excuses to come to the kitchen, and every excuse involved brushing by Samantha, touching her arm or hair, even leaning close enough that she could feel his breath on her neck. On the first day, she'd moved nervously away from him.

"What's the matter?" he asked. "You obviously like a man's touch. There's no husband, is there?"

"Please stop," she said.

He grasped her arm and twisted it. "You'll come around." He laughed and left the kitchen.

She still had bruises on her arm three days later, as well as others. He never hurt her face, or anywhere it would show, but he was getting bolder. Samantha stood at the sink, washing the coffee pot and cups from breakfast, when John came into the room. She tensed and glanced at Emily. The baby slept in a box she'd padded with her cloth bag.

John came too close, as usual, causing her skin to crawl. "Your trunk has arrived. I can put it in the corner there."

His arm reached out to indicate placement, brushing past her breast. Instead of putting the arm down, he used it to pull her closer and turn her to face him. Samantha could feel his chest pressing her amethyst brooch into her skin. She tried to pull away, but backed up against the sink. He stepped forward. Samantha leaned back, but she couldn't get away. He pulled her head toward him and leaned forward at the same time. He pushed his lips against hers hard enough that her teeth drew blood from her inner lip. He kissed her again and pulled her hair as he released her. Shoving her to the side, he laughed and left the room. Samantha leaned against the sink and trembled.

Barely an hour later, James Churchman came into the store again, with the same woman. Samantha peered out at the counter from the back room. The inside of her lip was swollen and tender, and her back ached. Tomorrow it would be bruised.

She longed for the courage to throw herself on James's mercy. The woman was well dressed, about Samantha's age, and fawned over James. She laughed at everything he said, even when he asked John Dowling, Jr. for something he didn't see on the shelf. Her eyes widened and sparkled as she smiled. Samantha heard James call her Henrietta. Samantha hated her.

She went into the kitchen and chopped vegetables harder than necessary. She heard the front door open and close, and she took a deep breath.

John came into the room and leered at her. "I saw you spying on our customers. Your vows to that husband of yours must not mean much. But Miss Henrietta comes from a very wealthy family back East, and she's dug her hooks into James." He laughed as if he were the funniest man in the territory. "You don't need him when you have me." He stepped forward.

Samantha backed against the counter, feeling it hard against her back as John pressed his full length against her. She couldn't even cringe in revulsion as his hand cupped her breast. She closed her eyes and turned her head away. A shout came from the front of the store. John's father needed him. He gave Samantha's breast a hard squeeze and left.

Trembling, Samantha checked on Emily. The small storeroom where they slept did not have a window. John's father had promised to clear it out, but all that meant was that he removed enough boxes to set up a cot. She did have a blanket and pillow, and a blanket for Emily's box. Her trunk barely fit under the cot.

Emily slept, so Samantha stepped out the kitchen door for a breath of fresh air. The store ran the full length of the front, with the kitchen and storeroom sharing the back. The Dowlings lived upstairs. From the kitchen door, Samantha could see part of the main street through Galena. It was muddier than Prairie du Chien.

It had only been three days, but Samantha knew she couldn't keep on working at Dowling's. Her options were limited. She could go back upriver to James Henry, or go home to New York. Maybe she could be someone's housekeeper. She sighed. Or she could get word to James Churchman that she was here. Whatever role Henrietta played in his life, she was sure he would help her.

She went back into the kitchen and baked a batch of her honey cookies. She took one to the elder Mr. Dowling. "I thought you might like these," she said. "I can make them to sell in the store if you like."

He took a bite and his eyes lit up. "That would be wonderful, Mrs. Miree."

Every morning she baked a double batch of the cookies and placed them on a plate under a glass dome near the cash register. Then she waited.

It was another week before James came into the store, this time alone. "New cookies, John?" he asked with interest.

Samantha heard his voice, and her heart cracked. She peered out of the kitchen.

The elder Mr. Dowling lifted the glass dome. "I'll allow you one sample, Mr. Churchman, then I'll have to charge you."

John bit into the cookie and his brow furrowed. He took another bite and looked around the store. "Where did you get these, Dowling? A new baker in town?"

"Let's just say I'm the only one in Galena selling them."

"I'll take the lot." James left the store with every one of her cookies.

Samantha continued to make them every day as she tried to think of ways to let James know she was no longer at Fort Snelling, no longer married, and needed help.

John Dowling strutted into the kitchen. She knew his father had gone to the dock to fetch supplies from a newly arrived boat. They were alone but for Emily, lying on her back and playing happily with her feet in a corner of the kitchen. Samantha was too far from the baby to pinch her and make her cry. She'd resorted to that a couple of times to get rid of John.

He approached her with a leer on his face that announced unwelcome intentions. Bile rose in her throat at the idea. Samantha tried to move around the table, but he grabbed her arm and wrenched it as he pulled her close.

"You're driving me crazy, woman," he said.

He fumbled one-handed with his pants as she tried to get away. Moving forward, he pinned her against the table with his body. His strength dominated Samantha's struggles.

She forced herself to relax, easing tense muscles and taking deep breaths.

John furrowed his brow. He squeezed her arm harder.

Samantha refused to respond.

He cursed and pushed her away, bending her back over the table and pushing up her dress.

Samantha refused to meet his eyes.

Someone called from the store, and John stalked from the kitchen, cursing and straightening his clothes.

Samantha stood upright and rubbed her arm.

The elder Mr. Dowling came in the kitchen door. "Where do you want all this flour, Mrs. Miree?"

She made room for the flour and sugar he'd ordered for her cookies. Then Emily fussed, and she picked her up, hugging the baby to comfort herself as well.

Several days later, Samantha was in her little room sitting on her trunk and nursing Emily. When the baby was full and sleepy, Samantha changed her dress. She froze when she heard James Churchman's voice in the store.

The elder Mr. Dowling came into the kitchen. "Mrs. Miree, could you please wrap up these items for Mr. Churchman?" She came out of the storeroom. He thrust a list into her hand and went back into the store.

Samantha just held the list for a minute. It was a connection to James. Could she write him a note? As she gathered the items on the list, she searched for a pencil without success. After boxing up the order, she impulsively unpinned her amethyst brooch and wrapped it in the list itself. She placed the little bundle on top of the tea in the box. She hoped James wouldn't jostle it into the bottom on the way home, or it might take days before he found it. She heard the door close behind him as he left the store.

The next day, while Emily napped, Samantha stepped outside the kitchen door. It had become her habit to take the air each day. It felt like escape, even though she had no place to escape to. She took a deep breath.

"Samantha?"

Her heart froze at the familiar voice, even as her heart leapt with hope. She turned.

"It *is* you! Whatever are you doing in Galena?" James Churchman stood in front of her, his face full of surprised pleasure. Miss Henrietta was nowhere to be seen.

Samantha's eyes welled. She wanted to throw herself in his familiar arms, but dismay sobered her. He belonged to another woman. She'd lost her chance with him. Samantha swallowed hard to restore her dignity. James knew more about her past than anyone on the Mississippi. She would be foolish to ask him to help her, but there was no other choice. She had nowhere to stay, no money for food. And she had to get away. "James! Such a delight to see you."

"Welcome to Galena," he said. "Where is your husband?" He scanned the area. "I found this." He pulled her brooch out of his pocket. "Are you in danger?"

Samantha felt her throat close with tears. She swallowed again. She would *not* be the sort of woman who cried over her situation. She blinked hard and busied herself fastening the brooch to her dress.

Compassion filled his eyes. "Come with me. We'll have tea and talk."

"I can't." She indicated the kitchen door. "You don't know . . ." She didn't know how to tell him about Emily, about the Dowlings, about her job, her fear, and her helplessness.

John Dowling appeared at the kitchen door. He was holding Emily in his arms. "Mrs. Miree, there you are!" he bounced the baby as if he had a right to touch her.

Samantha panicked, desperate to retrieve her daughter. "Give her to me!"

"Now, now," he said. He handed the baby over to her without a fuss. Samantha couldn't see any sign of tears or red face. Had John woken the baby on purpose?

James Churchman stepped forward. "Who is this?"

Samantha turned to him, her hope for the future. "This is my daughter, Emily." She watched emotions cross James's face, joy for her, questions about Alex, and wonder at the miracle of the tiny person. When he looked at John Dowling, though, his face closed.

"What is your connection to Dowling?" he asked.

John Dowling sauntered into the yard toward James. "She works for us."

Samantha said, "I arrived desperate for a place to stay."

James looked at her. "You didn't think to contact me?"

"I didn't even know if you were still in town." *Or if you were married.* She watched his eyes question her. She had nothing to lose. "If I'd known for sure you were here, I would have found you."

The smile that spread over his face covered her with warmth. "You're coming with me now." He turned to John. "She quits, Dowling." Then he stopped short and faced Samantha. "Is that alright with you?"

Samantha tried so hard to control her emotions that speaking was impossible. She nodded.

"I'll send someone for her things." Without waiting for a response from John, he took Samantha's arm and walked down the street. He was gentle, aware of the baby in her arms, but her body tingled when his arm brushed hers, and she blushed when James looked at her.

She told herself she was making a conscious choice, allowing James to help her and Emily. She told herself she didn't care about Henrietta.

James led her away from Dowling's store and up the street to a pleasantly situated two-story house. It was one of the better houses above the town. James must be doing well. Inside, he saw her seated in the front room, then left to make tea.

Emily had fallen back to sleep. Samantha laid the baby on the sofa alongside her leg. It wouldn't be long before Emily screamed to be fed. She'd have to find a place to nurse. Her shoulders slumped. In the cabin aboard the *Warrior*, it had all seemed easier. She'd used the privacy to care for herself and her baby, to dream of being on her own. Reality was a far cry from the dream. Again. Dare she renew her hope?

She looked around the front room of James's house. The furniture looked new, but a thin layer of dust covered every surface. No fresh flowers filled the vase on the table near the window, no embroidered cushions decorated the couch. Henrietta didn't live here. That made her pleased, then guilty.

James returned with tea in pretty china cups, sweetened just the way she liked it. Samantha felt tears rising again and sipped her tea. She would not cry over her situation. James placed a small plate of her honey cookies on the table next to the couch.

"I knew these were your cookies," he said. "I just couldn't figure out how they got there."

Beneath his words, she heard the inquiry. *Why are you here without your husband? What happened?*

Tired of deception, tired of inventing excuses, the words tumbled from her. She told James about her marriage, about Alex and his new family, about her loneliness, her anger, and her love for baby Emily. She even told him of her days at Dowlings' store and her fear of John. Her tea grew cold as he listened. Her emotion and words ran out, leaving her light-headed and empty. She waited for James's response. If he were her father, he'd point out she'd chosen the wrong husband. If he were her friend, he'd offer support. If he loved her—no, she couldn't imagine that.

James had long since set down his tea cup. Now he rose to kneel before her and take her hand in his. "I am so sorry for all that happened to you, Samantha." He glanced at the baby. "Emily is beautiful like her mother." His eyes returned to Samantha's. "I want to help you. I don't have anyone to help me with this place. You'd be doing me a favor if you, say, cleaned."

"You want me as a housekeeper?" she said in a flat voice. She'd kept house for James Henry, then for Alex, now for James. Only Alex had been her choice, and that had been the worst situation. James would respect her. It galled her to think of preparing meals for James's guests, like Henrietta, but it was a better situation than working at Dowlings' store. What other choice did she really have?

"You and Emily can have the downstairs room off the kitchen. That would be proper, wouldn't it? I'm not here most of the time, anyway. I'm a circuit judge, riding from town to town. It's a miracle you caught me in town at all. Please say you'll help me. And let me help you."

The featherlight wall of her resistance dissolved. "I'd like that, James."

Emily woke and began to fuss.

"She's hungry," Samantha said.

"Let me show you to your room."

James went to the back of the house, where the hallway ended with three doors. One went to the outside, one to the kitchen, and one to the small room Samantha would share with Emily. It was similar in size and furnishing to the room she had at her brother's house in Prairie du Chien. It was clean and bright, better than the dark storeroom at Dowling's.

She followed James into the room, bouncing her fussy baby in her arms. He turned to leave, and she found herself face to face with him and much too close, Emily sandwiched between them. She leaned toward him.

James stepped back. "I'll let you get settled." He nodded to her and left the room, closing the door behind him.

Samantha could hear his brisk step along the length of the hallway. She sighed and turned to Emily. Nursing her daughter was calming for both of them. Emily dozed off on a full tummy. Exhausted by the day's emotion, Samantha curled around her daughter, clutched her purple brooch, and closed her eyes.

IT WAS ODD TO TAKE care of James's house when he wasn't there, but it was odder still when he was home and Samantha played the role of housekeeper. The only thing that kept the situation acceptable for Samantha's reputation was the fact that James was gone a lot. Riding the 7th and 8th circuits through Illinois gave him lots of legal experience and name recognition. He told her it was a good foundation for a political future.

For almost the entire summer of 1837 James rode the 7th circuit, along with another lawyer and a judge. Samantha settled into the rough Galena society and made a place for herself and Emily as Mrs. Miree, housekeeper for Mr. Churchman. She took Emily along to Dowling's store, always timing it for when the *Warrior* tied up at the dock and John, Jr., needed to direct the unloading of supplies. The first time she entered the store, Mr. Dowling, Sr., looked at her with impassive eyes. Samantha wondered if he knew what kind of man his son was.

"Customers miss your honey cookies," Mr. Dowling said as he wrapped up her order. "Might you want to continue making them for the store? I can buy them from you."

Samantha bit her lip, holding Emily tightly in her arms. She rationalized making the cookies for him before as a way of paying for room and board. She had no reason to make them now, and certainly didn't want to spend more time at the store. "I'm sorry, Mr. Dowling, but I'm rather busy in my new position."

"I understand. I'm sorry, too." His eyes drilled hers, as if trying to apologize for more.

Samantha hid her face in Emily's hair, stunned at what appeared to be an acknowledgement of his son's unwelcome attention. Why hadn't he said anything while she was living there?

"Oh, and there's a letter for you." He reached under the counter and handed her an envelope. "Normally I'd have a boy run it up to Churchman's house, but since you're here I'll hand it to you directly."

"Thank you, Mr. Dowling." Samantha took the letter, her heart thudding. Who had written? Alex? James Henry? Eliza Taliaferro? Mama? She put the letter into her bag without looking at the handwriting. "Please deliver my purchases as usual."

On her way out of the store, Samantha almost ran into Henrietta. The two women stared at each other for a long moment.

"Miss Gibson, have you met Mrs. Miree? She's the new housekeeper at Churchman's." Mr. Dowling never came out from behind his counter, but his voice carried well into the doorway.

"I know who she is," Henrietta said, her voice cold enough to cause a shudder.

"Pleased to meet you, Miss Gibbon, is it?" Samantha said. As if on cue, Emily cooed and smiled with her most adorable face.

"Gibson," Henrietta spat at her.

Samantha brushed past her and walked up the street, smiling.

At James's house, she remembered her letter and pulled it out. It was addressed to her, in her brother's handwriting, in care of James Churchman. Samantha wasn't keeping her location a secret, but she was still surprised that her brother had found her so quickly. She placed Emily in her cradle and sat at the kitchen table to open his letter.

Dear Samantha,

I hope this letter finds you. Imagine my surprise when Captain Throckmorton came into the store to be paid for your passage to Galena. I didn't even know you were on your way to Prairie du Chien! I'm guessing you chose Galena because James Churchman is there. I think it's in bad taste to run to him with your baby and your broken heart when your husband is still alive. At least Captain Throckmorton believes that to be true. I've written to Lawrence Taliaferro for information since my own sister can't seem to keep my apprised.

So you're in Galena. What's the plan, Sister? Will you tell James the truth about your husband choosing to live with the Indians? Are you hoping to rekindle his feelings for you? Let me caution you that you are still married and expected to behave like it. In fact, it's probably best if you come to Prairie du Chien after all. It's perfectly acceptable for a brother to protect and provide for a sister suffering from a failed marriage. No need to write ahead. We will expect you.

James Henry Lockwood

Samantha read the letter again. Guilt washed over her as she thought about how she'd avoided her brother. Anger flared at her brother's assumption she'd come to James to make him fall in love with her. Dismay flooded her at James Henry's expectation she'd come right to him. Samantha hadn't succeeded in making her own choices yet, but insisted to herself she was making progress. She'd write to James Henry tomorrow and tell him all about Emily and Galena, but not about John Dowling. She'd not discuss Alex or Miss Henrietta, either.

The next day Samantha took her letter to the post office at Dowlings' store. She planned to go inside, pay for the letter's postage, and leave before John Jr. realized she was there. The plan went well until Miss Gibson entered the store. She sniffed when she saw Samantha and turned her back. The elder Mr. Dowling was at his place behind the counter, but Henrietta waited to speak with John Jr., who came out of the storeroom to help.

Henrietta threw a look toward Samantha then said to John, "Can you believe she shows her face here after you took her in?" She leaned forward and said in a loud whisper, "I think that brat of hers might be James Churchman's. She's come to town to make him marry her."

Samantha's jaw dropped open. She'd never been the victim of such slander before, and Henrietta had never even met her! Before she could think twice, Samantha stepped out from behind the shelf of flour, sugar, and cornmeal. "Why, Miss Gibbon," she said, "I thought I heard you say I intended to marry Mr. Churchman. That would be difficult, you see, because I am already married to Emily's father. When he arrives, our little family will be complete again and you can have Mr. Churchman all to yourself."

Henrietta flushed red. Samantha thought it was more of an angry red than an embarrassed red. She smiled and turned to the elder Mr. Dowling, ignoring John, Jr. completely. "I'd like to mail this letter, please." Without a word, Mr. Dowling took her money and the letter. Samantha thanked the man and left the store.

All summer, even though James wasn't there, Samantha thought of him. She examined everything they'd ever said to each other. It still hurt that he had followed her father's instructions to come west and capture her affections, but a part of her admired his commitment.

In September, James was home but planning to leave for ten weeks on the 8th circuit, which he'd ridden for the first time the previous spring. "I'm looking forward to seeing Judge Davis again, and Abe Lincoln, the lawyer from Springfield."

"You start out in Springfield, don't you?" Samantha said. She set the sleeping Emily into the wooden cradle James had acquired from John Dowling. Returning to the couch by the fire, she picked up a shirt of his she was mending for the trip.

James nodded. "Yes, two weeks in the capital, then fifty-five miles to Pekin. Several days there, maybe a week, then a couple of days in Metamora and a week in Bloomington. All in all, the trip will be four hundred miles." He sat in his great wingback chair, sipping an afternoon whiskey.

"A long ride for a bunch of cases between quarreling neighbors."

"Now Samantha," he said. "The circuit goes through majestic stands of native trees. Sometimes the trail is barely wide enough for Judge Davis's buggy. And the prairie is beautiful in the fall, with its tall grass. In spring, it's about the sunshine. In fall, the wind across the prairie is sharp with impending winter and the tallest grasses turn a rusty red. All year, the familiar smell of damp Illinois earth makes me feel alive. Bringing justice to people in this rustic setting is a satisfying calling."

Samantha grinned. "Now don't go all high and mighty on me. You came home from the summer trip in high spirits and full of tales of adventure with companions."

He smiled back at her, his eyes lighting with the warmth that always made her fidget and want him to come closer. "Davis, Lincoln, and I enjoy what we do. The judge is very heavy set but good-natured. He's always dressed well and neat as a pin. In contrast, Lincoln is tall and thin. He doesn't care much for fancy clothes or even well-combed hair." James laughed. "You'd like Lincoln, though. He's a great storyteller and knows a lot of jokes."

"Maybe I'll meet him someday. Right now, though, I'm looking forward to the return of Eliza Hamilton. I must have just missed her when she went upriver with her son to visit St. Anthony Falls. Imagine if such an illustrious lady had been there when I visited!"

"Eliza Hamilton? Isn't she about a hundred years old now? A little old to come all the way from New York to visit her son in Galena."

"Oh, James. She's eighty, but she's quite spry from what I hear. She's an inspiration to the women of our nation the way she continues to trumpet her late husband's achievements while working on her own. She wanted to see more of our beautiful country and visit Colonel William Hamilton at the same time."

"I know Colonel Hamilton. He's a bit eccentric. Lives in Hamilton's Diggings, a rather crude mining camp not far from here. He mines lead. No place for an elderly mother. I remember when she came through here early in June, though. Spent time out at the diggings before they continued upriver in Captain Throckmorton's new boat, the *Burlington*."

How like a man to pay more attention to the boat than the personage aboard. "She's a national treasure, James. A wife and mother I can only aspire to be."

James leaned forward, his arms on his knees. "You realize the boat stops in Prairie du Chien. The town's most prominent families will meet it."

"Of course."

"Mr. and Mrs. James Henry Lockwood will talk with Mrs. Hamilton. When she arrives here, do you think she'll connect them to Samantha Lockwood?"

Samantha met his gaze and said, "Samantha Miree. My brother knows I'm here. I've received a letter from him and written back." James didn't look surprised. Samantha wondered if he'd also received a letter from James, and if either or both men had written to her father. She sat up straight. "I will be honored to talk with Mrs. Hamilton should the opportunity arise."

James shrugged and sipped his whiskey. His gaze fastened on the fire, and the dancing flames seemed to mesmerize him into thoughts he didn't share. Samantha knitted in silence, lost in her own thoughts.

A knock at the door broke her reverie. She set her sewing down to answer it. It was Henrietta, standing petite and perfect on the doorstep.

"Is Mr. Churchman at home?" she asked. Her eyes brushed past Samantha, dismissing her.

A surge of jealousy spread through Samantha. She didn't want this woman anywhere near James because she wanted James for herself. Like a punch to her stomach, the realization brought her up short. "I'm sorry, he's not here at the moment," she said.

Henrietta's eyes narrowed, erasing her beauty. "Please tell him I'm here."

Samantha pasted what she hoped was a vacuous expression on her face. "I will tell him when he returns, Miss Gibbon."

"Gibson." She ground the name out between clenched teeth.

Samantha closed the door before the other woman had turned to go. She leaned against the door and took a deep breath, trying not to giggle. Would James be angry? She was aware their current situation couldn't last forever. She wanted more for Emily than to be the daughter of a housekeeper. Her mother would want to see her granddaughter. Her father would like to see her married to a judge. Samantha envisioned a happy family coming together over Emily. The vision needed one thing to become reality. She had to let James know she had come to love him at last. She only hoped she wasn't too late.

CHAPTER 36:

Moon When Corn is Gathered, 1838
Cloud Man's Village

DAY SETS

Day Sets seethed as Pale Crow left the village on her father's best horse. Cloud Man was still in Washington with Iron Cutter and the other chiefs, and Pale Crow thought he could make decisions in the chief's absence instead of the council. Day Sets knew her father would never have let her lead, but if he did, she'd make him proud. Not like Pale Crow, who had gone to Mendota to meet with Hercules Dousman, partner in the American Fur Company with Henry Sibley and Joseph Rolette—Five More to the Dakota. Five More ruled Prairie du Chien, and Henry Sibley had gone to Washington to take part in the negotiations. Hercules Dousman ran the Mendota trading post in his partner's absence.

Day Sets knew Iron Cutter hated the treatment of the Mdewakanton by the American Fur Company partners. He'd hate Henry Sibley's intervention in the treaty talks, and he'd hate Pale Crow trading in Mendota.

Pale Crow returned in just a few hours, whooping in delight as he dismounted. Hawk and the other hunters gathered around as Pale Crow handed down jugs of whiskey. "Foolish trader tried to talk me into signing a treaty to get money to pay off the tribe's debts at the store!" Pale Crow said. "Instead, I got more whiskey for us!"

The hunters whooped. Women, who had come out of the tipis when they heard the noise, lowered their heads and returned inside. To make matters worse, Day Sets saw Pale Crow hide a bundle as he unpacked his horse, then take it inside his tipi. Later, Winona appeared in the doorway with a piece of pemmican. Star Dancing pulled her inside in a hurry, but Day Sets saw. Pale Crow had brought food for his family and no one else.

Day Sets' anger erupted. When Pale Crow left his tipi, she stormed over to him. "My father works hard to limit the whiskey that comes to the village," she said. "Your actions today undermine what he is trying to do while he is away."

Pale Crow smirked at her. "Is he everyone's father that he controls what they drink?"

"The traders sell you whiskey then tell stories about the stupid Dakota who run up debts instead of getting money from selling the land." Day Sets narrowed her eyes.

"The Mendota trader knows I was sutler at the fort. He trusts me."

"To him you are just another Sioux," Day Sets spat at him.

Pale Crow shrugged and walked away.

It was hours before Day Set's fury faded.

The whiskey was gone too soon, and the village was still hungry. As fall chilled the air and colored the leaves, Hawk and his hunters became frustrated. Too close to the village, they found no game. Too far north or south, they risked attack. But they had to eat, so hunters went out.

One day Hawk led a small group of hunters who returned empty handed and without Pale Crow. The faces of the remaining hunters were grim.

"Pale Crow ran out in front of the hunters," Hawk said.

Star Dancing sat in front of their tipi. Day Sets saw her eyes drop to the ground in shame. A hunter who ran out ahead risked being shot. Even worse, he could scare off the target. Day Sets looked at the scout for the trip, who sat tall on his horse. It would have been his duty to beat Pale Crow for his transgression. He would have shot Pale Crow's horse and left the man to walk back.

"If he doesn't return on his own, he is no loss to the hunters," Hawk said.

Day Sets stared hard at Hawk, who looked away. Every hunter was important. She wondered when her father would return, and what shape the village would be in by then.

In fact, Cloud Man's village grew as Dakota refugees straggled in, victims of raids and hunger. They sought the protection of the village supported by the Indian agent. They sought the food grown there. Day Sets mentally divided the harvest again and again.

Two days later, a badly beaten Pale Crow stumbled back into the village. He slipped into Star Dancing's tipi without fanfare and, having learned his lesson, was once more included among the hunters.

It was the middle of the Moon When Deer Rut before Day Sets heard that the steamboat *Rolla* was on its way and walked to St. Peter's Agency to wait for Iron Cutter and the chiefs. The boat limped to the dock, struggling through the icy river. The first passengers who disembarked, including a handful of soldiers, climbed the hill to the fort and were visibly shaken. The fort's commander, Major Plympton, hurried to greet them. Day Sets frowned. Something was wrong. She moved closer.

"It was a harrowing journey," a soldier told the major. "An explosion killed a Black boatman and a fine horse."

Other passengers expanded on the details of the accident. Day Sets held her breath until she saw Iron Cutter and her father step off the boat. Iron Cutter headed straight for the agency, where he would be welcomed with a warm fire, tea and food. Cloud Man spotted Day Sets and joined her. He looked older, more beaten, than when he left.

"We signed the treaty." He sounded more tired than happy. "Part of it gives land and money to Mary, Nancy, and Jane."

None of the treaties had ever provided for the children left behind by American soldiers. It seemed a small victory. After a brief rest, Day Sets and Cloud Man returned to Heyate Otunwe. Cloud Man stared at the number of new tipis surrounding the village lodges and at the grim appearance of his people.

"I always thought my people would be happy listening to the advice of Iron Cutter," he said. "But the more we listen, the more people we have to take on from other tribes."

It pained Day Sets to see him so defeated. She led him to his lodge and pushed away everyone but her mother and sisters. Red Cherry Woman set about preparing what food she had.

"Five thousand dollars a year of our treaty money goes to the missionaries. Did anyone know that?" Cloud Man's eyes flashed with anger, but of course none of the women had known anything about that. The anger faded to hopelessness.

During the Severe Moon of 1838, Day Sets watched her tribe members die of starvation and broken hearts. She watched her father grow more disenchanted, and she wondered about the missionary school. She watched Iron Cutter rail at Fort Snelling's Major Plympton with less confidence and more desperation than usual before he left the agency for the winter.

"The wasichu aren't helping us," Day Sets told her sisters. The three of them sat outside Day Set's tipi. Hushes Still the Night held her beadwork out, teaching Stands Sacred a new pattern. Day Sets had already given up on it. She swept her long dark hair over one shoulder and tied it with a beaded thong.

"When have they ever helped us?" Hushes Still the Night asked.

"We had more to eat before we started farming," Stands Sacred said.

Ironic as that was, Day Sets knew it was true.

"The game is gone, scared away or killed for food," Hushes Still the Night said.

"All we can do is plant more corn and hope we have enough to feed everyone," Stands Sacred said. She stabbed her needle into a yellow bead and added it to the pattern she was working.

"Hope isn't enough when planning for the future of the tribe," Day Sets said. Her father led in the way of their ancestors, but the ancestors had never seen times like these. "Maybe it's time to look out for ourselves like the wasichu."

Stands Sacred opened her mouth to respond, but Day Sets held up a hand. "No, I don't want optimism right now," she told her sister. Stands Sacred subsided, her eyes pained.

Day Sets wasn't the only one with doubts. Cloud Man's band greeted the Moon For Planting with an air of futility. Planting corn and squash meant food later in the summer, but it wouldn't be enough. They would do all the work, and refugees from other tribes would come to share it. There would not be enough.

After seeding what corn they could in the Moon for Planting, the women of the tribe went back into their tipis instead of gathering in celebration. Shouting drew them back outside. Day Sets was at her father's side when a fleet messenger stopped in the center of the village. The other villagers gathered far enough away to be respectful but close enough to listen.

The messenger was Dakota, of the Wahpeton band. Day Sets didn't know him, but he drew himself up straight to deliver his message. That meant bad news.

"Hole-in-the-Day broke the treaty of Mní Sni and attacked." The messenger took a breath. "His Ojibwe killed many Wahpetons. I go to Fort Snelling for support."

"I wish you well with that," Day Sets murmured.

Her father glared at her. "We await further news," he said to the messenger.

Red Cherry Woman stepped forward to get the visitor some water and a bit of corn cake. Day Set's sisters went to help. No doubt Stands Sacred would flirt with him. The thought didn't make Day Sets smile as it usually did.

Day Sets followed her father into his tipi. "The wasichu at the fort won't help the Wahpeton against the Ojibwe," she said.

Her father stared into the fire, his shoulders slumped. "To them we are nothing but children squabbling over toys."

Day Sets bit her lip. He didn't need her to harangue him, but she wasn't able to reassure him. She went back to her tipi. If she had even a bit of food, she would bring Mary home at once. Mary's contact with the wasichu now seemed dangerous rather than forward-thinking. She'd agreed with her father's wishes and pushed Mary into school. Now she wished she'd kept Mary home like Stands Sacred had done with her daughter, Nancy. Hushes Still the Night never talked about Jane, who was still at the school with Mary.

Several weeks later, in the Moon When Strawberries Are Red and Corn Is Hoed, the weather warmed as usual, but Day Set's spirits didn't rise with the sun. She'd been right about the wasichu failing to support the Wahpeton, and the Dakota homeland had erupted. Attacks increased as peace treaties lay on the ground in shards. Still no response from the fort.

Pale Crow returned at the head of a hunting party. "Where's Hawk," Cloud Man asked. It wasn't a question. Day Sets knew her father just wanted to hear the words.

Pale Crow indicated the remaining hunters. At least two were wounded. "Wahpeton attack. They killed and scalped Hawk."

Hawk's wife screamed. Stands Sacred went to console her. Day Sets stood by her father, numbed by the news. Cloud Man turned and went inside without saying a word. Day Sets realized his ability to strengthen his people was gone.

If the men at the fort no longer cared to support the Dakota, what did that mean for the school? It wasn't worth a full stomach for her daughter if they taught Mary that the Dakota weren't worthy of support and protection.

When the Moon When Geese Shed Feathers again arrived, Pale Crow led a party that headed north to hunt for the tribe. A small band of Ojibwe attacked, killing several hunters, including Pale Crow.

Star Dancing's grief echoed in the tipis of the other victims. The women began tearing at their hair and taking knives to their flesh. The men rubbed ashes on their faces, put on old clothes, and left their hair rumpled.

The next morning, Blue Medicine announced a medicine dance. Later that day, he sat in council with Cloud Man, several elders, and Reverend Stevens, the missionary in charge of Mary's school.

Day Sets and her mother sat close together, just outside the lodge. Day Sets watched her mother pretend to sew while she listened to the men inside.

Red Cherry Woman leaned against the lodge wall. She shook her head. "Blue Medicine says the entire tribe is sick and he must invoke Taku Wakan to heal us all."

From inside the lodge, Blue Medicine said, "The medicine men of the Christian God are imposters."

Day Sets could hear Reverend Stevens' interpreter repeating the shaman's words in English.

"Some believe the Dakota medicine men are imposters." Reverend Stevens sounded more confrontational than Day Sets had ever heard. She sucked in a breath.

Red Cherry Woman's eyes grew large.

Day Sets said, "Most of the tribe complains about Red Eagle and Grizzly Bear and their Christian God. I don't think any of them believe their lives are better with the help of the wasichu."

"The missionaries say that is because only the women have adopted their religion, and the tribe doesn't respect the women's choice." Red Cherry Woman's voice was hard.

"There's some truth to that. And Blue Medicine thinks the tribe is ill because of the choices of the women. After all, the women who converted gave up the protection of their medicine bags." Day Sets fingered the small leather bag hung around her neck on a cord. It contained private items important to Day Sets, items that protected her, like a lock of Mary's hair and a feather fallen from the Thunderbird. The medicine bag was an important symbol of her faith. It was the first symbol the Christian missionaries took away when someone converted. Men had it worse. The missionaries expected the men to cut their hair short and marry only one woman. "Father won't become a short-hair, will he?"

"I no longer know your father's heart," Red Cherry Woman said. She looked down at the half-finished dress in her hands like she'd never seen it before. "Did you know that Little Bear's father beat him yesterday for going to the Lake Harriet school?"

Day Sets nodded. The boy was almost a man. They wouldn't call him Little Bear much longer. His father wanted him to be a great warrior, and the wasichu school wasn't helping. Little Bear had snuck out of his father's lodge to go to school.

The women looked up as Reverend Stevens stomped out of the tipi. He blanched when he saw Star Dancing, bleeding from a hundred self-inflicted knife slashes, tearing her hair and wailing for Pale Crow on his journey to the spirit world. Day Sets heard him mutter in English.

The interpreter, even though the reverend was leaving the meeting, did his job. "They will never be saved."

As Blue Medicine prepared for the medicine dance, Cloud Man left the village to spend a few days at the Indian agency, meeting with Iron Cutter about a rumor that Iron Cutter was leaving the agency. When he returned, he was even more close-lipped than before.

Day Set's faith in her father's vision had wavered after Mní Sni. Every day since she expected him to rebound, to reassert his commitment to the tribe's future. He never did. She sought him out one day when he was huddled in his blanket, shoulders slumped. Day Sets closed the tipi flap behind her. It would never do for the rest of the band to see him so defeated. "Papa? What troubles you?"

Cloud Man looked up at his daughter, and she saw nothing but despair in his eyes.

"The future is bright," Day Sets told him, repeating the words he'd so often said. "Your granddaughters will make a place for the people in the wasichu world, and your sons will lead them."

"My granddaughters are on a fool's mission." Cloud Man wouldn't look at her.

"How can you say that? Their education has been your dream of the future for as long as I can remember." Day Sets thought of the way Mary's childhood had always been directed toward education. Was it really any different than her own childhood? She'd been taught duty to her people, to the tribe's future. At least she had the daily support of those around her. They could be strong for each other. Who did Mary have? It had been wrong to send her daughter to the school. Anger at the wasted years exploded in her heart. "That's it," she said. "I'm bringing Mary home. The tribe no longer needs its children to live in the wasichu world."

Day Sets went to the school. Mary's favorite teacher, Miss Julia, said, "Day Sets, you're not listening to the traders, are you? That is out of character for you."

"What are the traders saying?" Day Sets asked.

"They are offering the Indians cash for resisting missionaries preaching the Word of God." Julia wrung her hands, looking concerned.

"That just tells me I am right. It is better for Mary to be at home."

Miss Julia's shoulders slumped. "That's what makes the reverend believe he's failed."

Day Sets gathered Mary in her arms. "Let's go home," she said.

"Home?" Ten-year-old Mary furrowed her brow.

Day Sets realized that for half her daughter's life she'd lived at the school or with her father. "I'm taking you to the village," she said. "We'll be together now."

"Good," Mary said. Day Sets smiled for the first time in a long time. "Is Jane coming too?"

Day Set's smile faded. Hushes Still the Night hadn't wanted to come with her to fetch the girls. "Not today, sweetheart."

Jane peeked out the door of the school, and Day Sets waved to her. Jane closed the door.

At Cloud Man's village, Mary was thrilled to see her cousin Nancy. Day Sets enjoyed hearing laughter and squeals of delight coming from inside the tipi. The happiness didn't last long.

The traders didn't want the Dakota converting to the Christian religion. They didn't want the Mdewakanton in school. Iron Cutter would say that proved the missionaries were right. After all, Iron Cutter opposed anything the traders favored. Cloud Man had grown to dislike Red Eagle and Grizzly Bear, ascribing their movement from place to place around the lakes as proof of their lack of commitment, even though he still insisted his people should learn the wasichu ways. All the wasichu were broken. Each one of them seemed to have a different idea of what was best for themselves, and very few cared for their tribe as a whole. That wasn't good for the Mdewakanton, no matter what her father said. She'd keep Mary in the village with her people.

Not even her sisters agreed with her. Hushes Still the Night asked Grizzly Bear to keep eight-year-old Jane with his family. He had married Reverend Stevens' niece Cordelia, and assured Hushes Still the Night that Jane was welcome to live with them. They'd train her to be a teacher. Hushes Still the Night refused to discuss her decision with Day Sets, whose disapproval was clear.

Cloud Man did not participate in that summer's Medicine Dance. He'd returned from the Indian agency with a heavy heart, and his despair led him to a period of private meditation. When he spoke the latest news to the elder council, he had tears in his eyes. "Iron Cutter is giving up his vision. He says our farming village is not working the way he intended. Traders and soldiers who have only their own best interests at heart are being put in charge of the tribes. He says he can't fight them all. He's resigning as Indian agent and leaving the area."

The small group of men sat with backs hunched in despair in front of the chief's lodge. Day Sets sorted beads nearby, pretending they were berries. She stopped when she heard Cloud Man's words. Iron Cutter was leaving? She'd thought the Mdewakanton were in his blood. You couldn't just walk away from blood. It made her glad she'd brought Mary back into the heart of her people. At least the Mdewakanton worked together when the wasichu weren't pulling them in many directions.

She took several beads into her hand and squeezed them until they imprinted on her hand instead of letting her fury erupt. She'd become just another Mdewakanton woman whose wasichu husband had gone away. Iron Cutter had left his only child behind, and he hadn't even said goodbye. In her head, she raged at Iron Cutter for his abandonment.

Over the next few weeks, many of the villagers melted away. Some went back to their original bands, some to the fort, some off on their own. Day Sets watched, her heart numb, as blackbirds ravaged the village's corn. When Laughing Bird and Jim Thompson left for the Pig's Eye settlement, taking their children with them, it was a condemnation of the strongest bond of the Mdewakanton. Day Set's sister felt Taku Wakan had abandoned them, so she left the village, the family, and the traditional spirits. In their wake, they left even more upheaval.

The Indian agent who replaced Iron Cutter did not try to introduce himself to the Mdewakanton. He took office about the same time Major Plympton decided that there were too many hostile Dakota near Fort Snelling and declared Cloud Man's band must move six miles up St. Peter's River to Oak Grove.

Day Sets, Hushes Still the Night, and Stands Sacred took Nancy and Mary with them when they traveled to their new home. The site was a narrow strip of land on the river bank that would flood every winter. There was no timber for building a lodge, and several miles of swamp and lake cut them off from the mainland. A large lump of emotion in Day Set's throat prevented her from speaking. Stands Sacred babbled to Nancy about the beauty of the place, and Hushes Still the Night kicked at the cattails. Mary looked up at her mother. Day Sets swallowed tears and desperately sought something to say to encourage her daughter. That was her true duty, to lead the way for her daughter, to teach her traditions that would serve her well all her life.

But the world was no longer theirs.

Day Sets turned away from her sisters and her daughter, feeling the tears beginning to spill over. Had Mary ever seen her cry?

"Mama?" Mary tugged on Day Set's shirt.

Day Sets took a deep breath and forced a smile as she looked at her daughter. Mary stood before her with shining eyes.

"Mama, look. This place has food." Mary bent over and pulled several mushrooms from the wet ground.

Day Set's heart filled with love. She dried her tears and lifted her head. Mothers guided children forward as best they could. Day Sets and her sisters would teach their children the dances, the songs, the legends of their people. Whatever the future held for the Mdewakanton, it would be different. Their children would lead their people forward, adapting as generations of Mdewakantons before them had.

CHAPTER 37:

March, 1838

St. Louis, Missouri

HARRIET

In March of 1838, Harriet left the Plympton's house early so she could prepare a special dinner for Dred. Over the meal, she took his hand. "Dred, we are going to be parents."

"Parents?" He jumped up in delight, pulled Harriet after him, and spun happy circles in their small room.

Later, nestled in their bed, he said, "You make me so happy, Harriet."

She closed her eyes and basked in happiness of her own. Love multiplied around her.

It wasn't long, though, before Harriet and Dred's idyllic interlude ended. Word arrived from Dr. Emerson that he'd married and needed Dred and Harriet at his new home in Louisiana.

"Louisiana?" Harriet said with dismay. She envisioned the doctor selling her child and shuddered.

"His wife comes from a slaveholding family," Dred said. He couldn't meet her eyes.

Harriet put a hand on her belly. "Of course she does."

They'd been in charge of their own lives for almost a year, but it was an illusion. Doctor Emerson still controlled them.

When the *Burlington* plied its way upriver to the fort through April's slushy water, the Scotts made ready to leave. The *Burlington* brought the Taliaferros, returning for the summer once again, and took Harriet and Dred south on its return trip. The steamboat could accommodate thirty cabin passengers in comfortable staterooms. The enslaved had access to every part of the boat, even sleeping on pallets in their master's room. Traveling alone, though, Dred and Harriet could only camp on the lower deck, barred from all first-class rooms and passageways. Harriet claimed the sound of the engines was comforting, even though it sounded like they were right in the same room.

At least they weren't the only Black people they saw. The cook and steward were Black, as were the deckhands and stokers in the engine room. On shore, Black stevedores moved the heavy cargo on and off the boat, reminding Harriet of the fate of Francis McIntosh, the man they'd burned alive. These people were all enslaved, like Harriet and Dred. She wondered how many of them had experienced the sweet taste of freedom that she and Dred had since their marriage. Was it over, that near-freedom? Sorrow warred with anticipation over the baby.

On their first day aboard boat, Harriet and Dred placed their few belongings in a corner of the lower deck. For security, Dred kept Dr. Emerson's letter in his pocket. It was the only proof they had that they were traveling south at the request of their master. Hopefully, it would convince anyone eager to capture runaways and collect a bounty. As Dred turned to leave the room, Harriet put a hand on his arm. He turned back.

"Dred," she said, "I don' want our child born in slave territory."

She blinked back tears, knowing how little control she had over the birthplace.

"You must take care," he said, clasping her hands, "and pray we're back at Fort Snelling before the birth."

She took no reassurance from his words. There was no guarantee Dr. Emerson would ever return to the fort. If he didn't, why would he send Harriet and Dred there? Her wild imagination conjured wrecked boats, Indian attacks, even capture by savage tribes—anything that could delay their crossing into the slave state of Missouri.

The next morning, as they went to breakfast, Harriet and Dred saw a white boat's officer shove a Black cook out of the kitchen. The cook struggled to free his hands, which were tied behind his back. Dred pulled Harriet back and stepped in front of her. She held her breath, afraid for their safety.

"You got the wrong man!" the cook shouted.

"Of course you'd say that," the white man said, tightening his grip on the cook's arm. "Who would admit to raping a white woman?"

"I didn't do it!"

An outraged roar from the gathering of white male passengers drowned him out. They manhandled the cook to the railing.

"Dred?" Harriet said.

"Hush now," Dred said. "They got the blood lust now and will likely torment any Black faces they see."

The white passengers pushed the cook overboard and watched him fall with satisfaction. Dred and Harriet turned back to seek the safety of the lower deck, where Harriet trembled in Dred's arms. It was a grim reminder that they were no longer in the relative freedom of Fort Snelling.

When the *Burlington* stopped at Galena, Dred helped Harriet onto the dock. She needed fresh air and to walk a bit to ease her aching back. Outside the trading post, Harriet spotted a familiar face. "Mrs. Miree!" she called.

Samantha Miree had a big bag of supplies in one hand, and the other hand grasped her little girl's hand. "Harriet, what a surprise!"

Harriet examined the white woman critically. Her brown hair looked less lustrous than it had at Fort Snelling, but her brown eyes sparkled. Mrs. Miree was barely five feet tall, but built solidly. Harriet's mother would say Mrs. Miree was built for work, not pleasure.

"This is my husband, Dred," Harriet said, pulling him forward. "Emily has grown so big!"

The toddler recognized her name and gave Harriet a wide smile. The two women exchanged news, including Harriet's pregnancy and Samantha's job with James Churchman, until Dred shifted from foot to foot.

"He's impatient to go," Harriet said, smiling. "We need to get back on the boat. Nice to see you, ma'am."

"Likewise, Harriet. Have a safe journey." Samantha walked up the street with little steps that matched her toddler's.

Harriet watched Samantha go. Tears pricked her eyes when she considered how the other woman never had to worry about her daughter being sold away from her. Dred tugged at her arm, and they re-boarded the boat. As it continued downriver, Harriet thought about Samantha, who had left the fort intending to go to her brother in Prairie du Chien. She hadn't shared with Harriet why she'd ended up in Galena, and Harriet hadn't asked. She assumed it had been Samantha's choice. Harriet would choose to stay in Galena herself, to have her baby born in the free state of Illinois. She could open her laundering business for the lead miners. They'd be a free family. The point was, though, that she wasn't free. She didn't have a choice. The *Burlington* steamed downriver accompanied by Harriet's fervent prayers that she could return upriver before the birth of her baby.

The boat continued south. Harriet paced as the river broadened and the weather warmed. Fourteen days later, the *Burlington* arrived in St. Louis. All steamboats stopped there, whether going upriver or down. Dred and Harriet disembarked with the small leather trunk containing all their belongings. Dred double-checked that his letter from Dr. Emerson was still in his pocket. Harriet's trepidation at stepping once more into slave territory created nausea that was not related to the growing baby. She knew Dred intended for them to board a boat heading further south as soon as possible. He left Harriet standing on the dock as he went to see about passage. Harriet kept the suitcase between her and the wall she leaned against. Porters pushed past her, looking through her since she had no trunks and therefore no need to hire them. Vendors hawked milk and fresh food, and Harriet's stomach growled. The baby inside must have been hungry, too.

Dred returned, but before he could say anything, Harriet said, "We can't go south, Dred. I don' want our child born into slavery."

Her husband frowned. "Harriet, Missouri is a slave state. We can't return to Fort Snelling without Dr. Emerson's approval." He took her hand. "We are his slaves."

"Major Taliaferro wanted to free me," Harriet said, "and we lived free all winter. Dr. Emerson'll understand." Her words sounded brave, but she glanced over her shoulder. Slave catchers were everywhere, waiting for some indication a Black person was an escaped slave.

Dred shook his head, disagreeing but not willing to discuss it further on the dock. "The southbound boat leaves in the morning. Dr. Emerson paid for the passage, and we've a meal and a room paid for. Let's eat somethin' before we make a hasty decision."

Dred asked a Black boatman for directions to Leah Charleville's boarding house. She was a free Black laundress who rented rooms to Black boatmen and travelers. Following the directions to the boarding house on Third Street, Dred steered Harriet past temporary slaveholding pens. She averted her eyes, unable to witness such misery, but tears still threatened.

Harriet followed Dred into the boarding house. A trim Black woman in a nice dress and frilly white day cap turned to greet them. Harriet stood straighter and patted her headscarf.

Leah Charleville showed Dred and Harriet to a mattress in a room with several makeshift beds and looked at Harriet. "Are you going to have a baby?" she asked.

Harriet said, "Sometime this fall." Her hand went to her stomach. She couldn't tell if the squirm she felt was the baby or anxiety.

"Let's get that meal into you," Leah said. She led them to the kitchen and put a simple meal of cornbread and bacon in front of them. She poured a glass of milk for Harriet. "For the babe," she said.

Harriet nodded her thanks.

"You folks from upriver?" Leah asked.

"Fort Snelling," Dred said. "About as far upriver as you can go."

"And headed south?"

"Louisiana," Harriet said. "Our master is there."

"Ah, that explains why a pregnant Black woman is going south. I would've done anything in my power to birth my children in a free state."

"You've got children?" Harriet asked. There was no sign of children in the boarding house.

Leah pursed her lips. "My children are slaves of Reverend Meacham at First African Baptist Church. My husband is bringing a freedom lawsuit against the reverend on behalf of the children."

Harriet remembered the Black preacher from her previous time in St. Louis. He'd been enslaved, but bought his own freedom and opened St. Louis's first Baptist church. How could he be a slaveholder himself? "Freedom lawsuit?" Harriet thought of Rachel and Courtney, the two Black women who had sued for their freedom.

"I won my own lawsuit for freedom only by allowing transfer of my children's ownership to the reverend. He's a good man, Reverend Meacham. He's helped many slaves buy their freedom, or he's gotten them on the Underground Railroad to freedom in the north." She rubbed her neck. "Reverend Meacham takes too long sometimes, though. He's bought slaves and freed many of them who, in turn, pay him back. With the money, he frees other slaves. He owns twenty or more slaves, though, and can't afford to just free them all. Now that I've married Peter Charleville, though, I want my children with me now. I don't want to wait for the reverend to free them."

"Understandable," Dred said. He eyed the piece of bacon still on Harriet's plate. "You goin' to eat that?"

"Hush now," Leah told him. "She's eating for two!"

Leah and Dred laughed, but Harriet couldn't muster a smile. At one time she had a fleeting notion of suing for her own freedom, but it was more complicated now. Dr. Emerson didn't even know she was pregnant. How would he react? How would his new wife react? This unknown wife's influence over the doctor could be terrible for them.

Later, Harriet sat on the mattress where she and her husband would spend the night. Two other Black men huddled on mattresses in the room, trying to ignore everyone to pretend they had privacy. Harriet turned to Dred. "We don' have money for a lawyer, I know. But what if I sent word to Dr. Emerson that I want to sue for my freedom? I lived in a free territory for several years."

Dred hesitated.

"Dred, if I'm free, our baby will be born free, no matter where we are when it's born. Please. Reverend Meacham'll help us." She grabbed his arms, intense and earnest.

"Maybe we can talk to the reverend."

He loved her. She loved him. They would try.

In the morning, Leah walked with them to the First African Baptist Church. They had to duck down a side street to avoid a city patrol. "They'll put unfamiliar Black people in jail for vagrancy if not for running away."

Harriet shuddered. It would be impossible for them to refute such serious charges. The day was hot and dry, turning the unpaved streets to dust.

At Seventh and Chestnut Streets, a charred locust tree stood wrapped in yellow ribbons. Leah saw Harriet looking at it. "Where McIntosh was burned. You heard?"

Harriet nodded. She remembered the Black boatmen who'd been burned alive. She forced herself to look away.

A block away from the church, a dog barked at them and lunged, its mouth foaming.

Leah stamped her feet and shouted, scaring it away. "I'm sorry," she said. "They shot five rabid dogs this month. The mayor ordered all loose dogs to be rounded up. That one has escaped so far."

Harriet missed Nero.

When they reached the church, it truly felt like a haven. The reverend welcomed them, and Harriet relaxed. Leah excused herself to visit her children.

Reverend Meacham assured the couple they could stay at the church as long as needed. "Going further south could be disastrous," he said. "I don't know of any slaves that have gone south from here and returned as free persons. Or returned at all."

On Dred and Harriet's behalf, Dr. Meacham wrote to Dr. Emerson, stating that they were staying in St. Louis and contemplating a freedom lawsuit. While they awaited a response, the Scotts stayed at Leah's. Harriet let out the seams in her dresses to accommodate her growing belly, and she helped Leah with her laundry business to pay for their room and board. Dred helped the reverend around the grounds of the church. Once again, time stretched as she put her life on hold, awaiting someone else's decision.

In early July, the reply arrived. Harriet waited anxiously for Dr. Meacham to read it to them. Dred squeezed her hand. Dr. Meacham scanned it before Harriet tugged at his arm and begged to know what it said. "He's coming north himself," Dr. Meacham said, "concerned about land he bought in Iowa. Land sales to settlers are about to begin there, and he doesn't trust the lawyers he left in charge. He says nothing about your lawsuit, or about the two of you joining him there. I say you wait here."

Harriet exhaled a breath she'd been holding. What a relief.

As the summer dragged on, the dry weather created drought conditions that lowered the water level in the rivers. Travel was difficult on the smaller rivers to the east, and steamboat mishaps were even reported on the Mississippi. In August, word came from Dr. Emerson telling Dred and Harriet to stay where they were. He and his new wife planned to come north and take charge of his Iowa holdings on the way back to Fort Snelling.

"Oh, good news," Harriet said, her eyes shining. "Our baby'll be born at Fort Snelling, born free, Dred!" Euphoria gave her energy to dance around the room.

With effort, Dred lifted her and swung her around. "Oh happy day, Harriet!" He tucked Dr. Emerson's letter into his pocket, always prepared to prove his master's intentions.

September slid by so slowly it felt like years. On the 18th, a solar eclipse dimmed the sky and Harriet's emotions darkened, too. The Emersons wouldn't arrive in time. Her baby would be born to a slave woman in a slave state. She cried herself to sleep, Dred helpless to console her.

The Emersons arrived on September 21. The hugely pregnant Harriet was overjoyed. She chafed at the delays while Dr. Emerson's new wife took her time shopping for clothes and items she thought she would need in the north. Five days later, they boarded the steamboat *Gypsy*, which was much smaller than the *Burlington*, so more able to navigate the drought-depleted river. Passengers crowded the boat and the small barge towed behind it. Only two group cabins were on the boat, one for ladies and the other for gentlemen. The accommodations were hot and noisy, but it didn't matter because they were heading north.

At night, Harriet slept on a floor pallet near her mistress's bed. The discomfort of her enormous belly made sleep impossible. During the day, Mrs. Emerson didn't often need Harriet's services since they were aboard the boat. Harriet spent most of the day pacing back and forth below deck with Dred, worried that the searing heat of the wood furnaces and noise of the steam engines would cause the baby harm. Her anxiety over the birth added to her anxiety about where the birth would take place. Harriet was determined to wait until the boat crossed the Missouri line into free territory before having her baby, but it would be a near thing. She searched for somewhere private on the boat to have her baby.

When Harriet's labor pains began, Dred led her to a spot between the cargo barrels on the lower deck where he'd spread a blanket. Then he ran for Dr. Emerson. Harriet screamed with the pains, and asked for the position of the boat. She had to know if they'd crossed the Missouri line into free Iowa territory.

As the hours wore on, though, a successful birth became more important as Harriet focused on her body. At last, a baby's cry rose above the pounding of steam engines. Harriet turned her sweat-soaked face toward Dred. "Where are we, Dred, please. Where are we?"

"We have a beautiful baby girl who was born in Iowa Territory," Dred told her with delighted pride.

Harriet cried tears of joy and exhaustion, barely able to see the free baby girl he laid on her chest.

"A perfect healthy baby," Dr. Emerson told her.

"Ellie," Harriet said. She imagined arriving at St. Peter's Agency and introducing her friend Ellie to her namesake. Nothing could dampen Harriet's joy. "Her name is Ellie."

After resting for the afternoon, Dred and Dr. Emerson helped Harriet to a cot in the ladies' cabin. "Named for me?" Mrs. Emerson said. "I didn't even realize you knew my given name, Harriet!"

"Her name's not Irene?" Harriet whispered to Dred.

"I think I heard Doc say Elizabeth Irene," he whispered back.

Harriet just smiled at her mistress and let the other ladies coddle her like an infant. Enslaved women gave birth and went right back to work. She'd seen Ellie do so in Taliaferro's kitchen. But Harriet wouldn't complain. Let the white women wait on her for a change. She looked into the innocent face of her daughter, who would grow to be a strong, free Black woman. To make that happen, Harriet vowed to sue for her freedom, and she would encourage Dred to do the same.

CHAPTER 38:

November 1839
Dubuque, Iowa Territory

SAMANTHA

In November 1839, James Churchman was elected to the second territorial House of Representatives in the territory of Iowa. In celebration, Samantha cooked a beef dish with onions and tomatoes. It simmered over the fire all afternoon and filled the house with mouthwatering scents. When James was due home, she made gravy from the drippings and sliced bread to accompany it.

James entered the house and sniffed. "Oh, something smells delicious," he said.

"It certainly does!" a feminine voice said.

Samantha froze with the platter of meat in her hands. Why would James bring Henrietta here tonight? Scolding herself, she muttered, "I am just his housekeeper. It doesn't matter that he once wanted to marry me. I chose another who left me with a child. I have no claim to James's time or affections." She pasted what she hoped was a smile, not a grimace, on her face and took a deep breath. Wishing she had put something in the seasoning to make the other woman sick, she carried the platter into the parlor and placed it on the table.

"Congratulations on your victory," she said to James. His eyebrows furrowed at her formal tone. Samantha ignored Henrietta.

Returning to the kitchen, Samantha fed Emily her dinner. The three-year-old would play quietly while Samantha ate. She turned to the gingerbread cake she'd made earlier. It seemed a shame to waste it on Henrietta Gibson. It was a shame to waste the entire dinner on her. After all, she'd set the table for two and not planned on Henrietta.

Samantha took Emily by the hand and entered the parlor. Emily sat on the floor and picked up a doll that had been hiding under a chair. Taking another place setting from the hutch, Samantha joined James and Henrietta at the table as if it was normal even though she trembled inside. James grinned at her. Henrietta had a storm on her face. "So nice you could join in James's celebration, Miss Gibbon," Samantha said, mustering the sweetest smile possible.

"James, please tell your housekeeper to refrain from using my name at all if she cannot get it right." Henrietta's back stiffened as if a wooden plank had been placed inside her bodice.

Samantha smiled at James. "Did the others at the courthouse congratulate you properly, James?"

He smiled at her with real warmth. "Yes, they did. In order to represent Iowa, though, I will have to move across the Mississippi to Dubuque. It's no good having a representative that doesn't live in the place he represents."

"I shall miss you so, James," Henrietta said. She batted her eyelashes and pouted, which made Samantha laugh.

"Oh, I almost forgot." James got up from the table and retrieved a package he'd left on the table by the door. "I picked this up for Emily. To celebrate my victory." He looked proud of himself but a little nervous as he returned to the table.

"For me?" Emily heard her name and came to investigate the package.

Samantha helped her open the package to find a doll with a porcelain head and fancy dress. "Oh, what a beautiful doll! It's much too fine for Emily to play with."

"Nonsense," James said. "She should have nice things if she's to live in the household of a territorial representative!"

"Thank you, Papa James," Emily said. She took the doll back to her place on the floor.

"Papa James?" Henrietta said with a raised eyebrow. "What a waste of money."

Samantha ignored her. James wanted them to come with him to Iowa. That was all that mattered in this moment.

"At first, I'll get a suite at a hotel. Abe Lincoln recommends Waples House, so we'll start there. It will be a suitable residence until I can find a house."

It took a week for Samantha to arrange the household move. Some things would be stored until James found a house, and some they would need in the meantime. Henrietta didn't visit again, and James said nothing about her. Clearly she held no special place in James's heart. Samantha could only dream that she and Emily might have a place there.

As they followed James off the boat into Iowa, Samantha took Emily's hand. The little girl had insisted on carrying her new doll herself, and she clutched it tightly. The Waples House, on the corner of Second Street and Main Street, was the first building they saw. It was four stories high and quite elegant Samantha used the name Mrs. Miree for propriety, but she thought that she and James were growing closer. He bought Emily dresses and a doll. Who would do that for another man's child unless he loved the mother? Samantha had fixed his favorite meals and they ate together. Now that they lived at the hotel, they ate as a family in the dining room. She wished she'd just told James that her husband was dead. Surely no one in Galena would bother to prove her wrong.

ONE SUMMER DAY LATE in 1840, Samantha walked back to the Waples House with Emily, now four years old. Emily walked beside her mother, having refused to hold her hand. "I am a *big* girl," she said as she snatched her hand away. Samantha smiled, watchful, and let her be. She could refuse her daughter nothing. Emily loved the noise and scents at the leather shop. Craftsmen hammered designs into the leather, and Emily watched with rapt attention. One man gave her a scrap of leather with a flower design carved and stamped into it. Emily loved to feel it and smell it, and she kept it in her reticule always.

Francis Mangold's bakery was Samantha's favorite shop. The German immigrant's baked goods filled the air with the scent of fresh cookies and cakes. Samantha had bought a cake to celebrate moving out of the hotel into a brick house that would belong to James in reality, to both she and James in her flights of fancy. Emily, of course, received a cookie for being a good girl in the shop.

That night, the three of them dined as usual in the hotel dining room. James enjoyed spending his money on good food, and the meal left them all replete. Samantha had left the cake with the kitchen staff, and the waitress brought it out with three plates and forks.

"Surprise!" Samantha said. "To celebrate our new house." She sounded like a wife to her own ears, and that role appealed to her. Unfortunately, she was still married to Alexander Miree, even if she never heard from him. It had been four years. Everyone in Fort Snelling and Prairie du Chien knew where she was and who she was with, even if she rarely heard from them.

"Chocolate, my favorite," James said. His eyes were warm with love, and she couldn't even remember the way Alex's green eyes had made her tremble.

Emily insisted on eating her cake by herself and got more on her face than in her tummy. Samantha was too happy to care. "I'll bathe her and put her to bed," she said.

"I'll help tuck her in," James said.

They went upstairs for the last night in their suite. James was true to his word. Samantha tucked Emily into her bed and James gave her the requisite ten nighttime nose kisses.

In the parlor, the fire crackled merrily. The flames danced as if echoing the contentment of the family. James said, "Aren't we a happy family?"

Her heart twisted. "Yes, we are. And no, we aren't." Sometimes in these moments, she had touched his arm or brushed against him. Sometimes that led to a shared kiss, but James always broke away and stammered an apology. She was, after all, a married woman.

"The election is heating up," James said. He was running to represent the Iowa Territory to the United States Senate. The election was three months away.

"Do you have the votes?"

James hesitated. "A rumor is circulating that I have an improper relationship with my housekeeper."

Samantha blanched. "Did Dodge say that?" She didn't have any respect for James's Democratic opponent, Augustus Dodge.

James shrugged. "Someone said it. Samantha, you know I would marry you."

Her heart sang. She'd felt that he loved her, but doubted herself over and over when he never said the words. "You mean if I weren't already married?" Her tone was bitter. Her absent husband was a continual reminder of her poor decision making. "Marrying Alex was a mistake, I know. Could it be that staying with you is a mistake for your career? If so, James, I'll go."

"I don't want a career without you beside me." He crossed the room and took her hands. "Samantha, I love you. I have always loved you."

"Oh James." Her heart raced. "I love you, too." She remembered this was the result her father had worked for, but it no longer mattered. This was what she wanted.

He took her in his arms and kissed her, for the first time both secure in the other's love. Then James pulled away, shaking his head. "I'll make inquiries. It's possible your husband may divorce you. If he can be found."

Samantha sighed in exasperation.

He reached inside his jacket pocket. "These came for you today. So many letters! Are you sure you're not the one running for office?"

His teasing fell flat, but she appreciated the attempt as she took the three letters with shaking hands and went to her chair by the fire. One letter was from her sister Mary Ann. Of all her siblings, five sisters and three brothers, Mary Ann was the only one who wrote back after Samantha had written to her family when she settled in Galena four years ago. Samantha set the letter aside for now.

The second letter was from her mother, who didn't write often but kept in touch. Mama provided quiet support, but Samantha could feel Papa's cold disapproval seeping through her words. He must know his wife and daughter corresponded. He never did. Samantha opened the letter.

Dear Samantha,

However is sweet Emily doing? Did you receive my gift for her fourth birthday? I don't know what use a little girl may have for such an elegant doll in the wild frontier, but when I saw it, I couldn't resist. Someday you will have to bring her east for a visit, please. I'm of an age where such a trip is impossible for me, so you must come. It's sobering to acknowledge that age is preventing me from doing things I want to do.

But enough about me. Are you still working for James Churchman? Working seems such a harsh word. I know you receive no wages. What an untenable situation you have created for yourself traipsing off with that Mr. Miree and crawling back to James! I comfort myself that you must love him after all to choose that situation over coming home or at least returning to James Henry. I'm sure you know James Henry and Catherine have no children. They would love to have Emily in their home. With you, of course. I still think James is a fine man. But truly, dear, aren't you jeopardizing his career?

Samantha stopped reading. She scanned to the bottom of the page for news of her other siblings. Mama never changed. She loved Emily, sight unseen, the one grandchild she'd never met. The doll she'd sent wore a dress covered in fine lavender lace and seed pearls. Samantha had given it to Emily instead of putting it on a shelf because she believed dolls should be played with. Emily preferred the doll James had given her a year earlier, though, and slept with it every night. She smiled at James, who sat in the chair facing hers near the fire.

She'd love nothing more than to introduce Emily to her New York family. But why couldn't Mama come west? Eliza

Hamilton had done it at eighty and Mama was only seventy. Samantha sighed. Mama was seventy. It seemed old. She missed Mama and her sisters. It was one thing, though, to write about James and quite another to travel east with him. She imagined introductions, "This is my daughter, Samantha, and her ... um ... this is James." It would be impossible for her mother and cause her father's dormant rage to erupt.

The facade of Samantha being nothing more than his housekeeper had fallen away in Galena, but at least she had her own room. In Dubuque, they'd shared a hotel suite, if not a bed. People could see they cared for each other, but could they see how she tried to keep her distance? Whenever James was near, her entire body yearned for him. Her heart beat faster, and her very soul cried out. It was a miracle they'd restricted themselves to half a dozen passionate kisses over the last year. Emily's presence had helped.

She set Mama's letter aside. A small lavender envelope slid out from between two of her letters and fell to the floor. Samantha picked it up. It was heavy stationery, addressed to James in a feminine hand. He must have included it with Samantha's letters by mistake. She peered at the postmark. Galena. It must be from Henrietta Gibson. Samantha was sure now that she loved James Henry with a forever love, but she didn't trust that he felt the same about her. She was afraid to test it. She threw Henrietta's letter into the fire. Watching it burn gave her great satisfaction.

James looked up at her with eyebrows raised, no doubt wondering about the burning letter. She said nothing and reached for her last letter. It was from James Henry. Over the last year, her brother had written to her once to say he knew she was in Galena, and to James at least once to congratulate him on election to the territorial House of Representatives. She opened the letter with trepidation as well as eagerness.

Dear Samantha,

Catherine and I hope this letter finds you and James well, and little Emily happy. I am writing because word has come from the northern tribes of a white man killed in a Dakota raid. I know your husband is not the only white man living with the Dakota, but I took the liberty of investigating, with the help of Day Sets. She confirms that Miree's Dakota wife is mourning the loss of her husband. You are free, Samantha.

Wishing James good luck on election to the Senate,

James Henry Lockwood

The letter fluttered to the floor as Samantha's breath caught in her throat.

"Samantha, are you all right?" At her nod, James retrieved the letter and scanned it. He set it on the table, got on one knee in front of Samantha, and took her hands in his. "My darling, will you marry me?"

She let the tears fall as she cried for her past and her future. "Yes, my dear, I will."

James stood and pulled her toward him. They kissed for the first time with no overtones of regret or shame. "We'd better sit," he said. "We've waited this long, we can wait for the wedding." He led her to the couch, where she snuggled against him.

"I'm so happy, James," she said. "I have to admit my father was right. Why did I have to make so many mistakes before I learned that?"

"Hush," he said, kissing the top of her head. "You chose your way, and you've grown into a wonderful woman, a wonderful mother. You're not the spoiled brat I met in New York."

"Spoiled brat? Stuff and nonsense!"

He laughed. "Your father could have forced you to marry the first doddering old man who came asking for your hand. Instead, he allowed you to choose. It's not his fault he was frustrated by your inability to decide."

Samantha considered his words, which put a new light on her father. "You're right. He gave me a choice all along. How foolish was I not to allow myself to realize that? To allow myself to love you?"

"Did you love me then?" James sounded surprised.

"Oh, no! I thought you were boring and practical. I wanted adventure!" She laughed and shook her head. "That didn't turn out well."

"I'm sorry it took such an adventure for you to learn my value." He teased her with love, and her heart sang.

The next day, they moved into their new home in Dubuque. It was a two-story brick house, suitable for a government official. Emily was delighted with her room, and Samantha delighted with the house. She would be the mistress here, not just the housekeeper.

Her euphoria didn't last long. In November, Augustus Dodge narrowly defeated James for a seat in the Senate. Worse than a Democrat going to Washington was the new Whig president, William Henry Harrison. Samantha tried to tell James he wouldn't want to be there with a Whig in the White House, but it didn't console him.

"Illinois reelected Abe Lincoln to the Legislature," James said. "At least he will be there to see to things."

James's term as representative ended with the election. He threw himself into establishing a law practice in Dubuque while Samantha concentrated on wedding plans.

In December, James and Samantha threw a lavish Christmas party, their first as host and hostess. Emily was adorable in a red velvet dress Samantha sewed. In February, Emily turned five. The child's entire focus was on starting school that fall, but Samantha's was on the wedding, set for May 15, 1841.

James came from a Quaker family in Pennsylvania. Samantha teased him that he had come west so he could enjoy his whiskey. With the dancing and drinking planned for their celebration, James didn't feel his family would be comfortable. Samantha wanted her eight siblings there, as well as their spouses and children. James would invite her large extended family, but didn't know how they'd accommodate them all. Samantha had to accept that James Henry and Catherine would be there, but the rest of her family would not.

James Henry and his wife, Catherine, arrived on May 12 and took a room at Waples House before visiting James and Samantha's home. James greeted James Henry with a firm handshake. Both men respected each other and had kept in touch since James had arrived in Prairie du Chien eight years earlier.

Samantha's correspondence with her brother had been infrequent. She greeted him with a hug. "Welcome, James Henry, it's so good to see you." She tried to imbue her words with her thoughts. Water under the bridge should move on downstream and not try to come back.

"Sister, congratulations." He drew his wife forward. "Catherine has been eager to meet you."

Catherine Lockwood was as pretty as her brother had always claimed. Her smile for Samantha was warm. "So pleased to meet you at last."

"Likewise," Samantha said, giving her sister-in-law a hug.

The two couples settled in the front room. Emily played with her doll near the fireplace. She'd waited to be introduced, as instructed. She stood now and walked to her mother. "This is Emily," Samantha said. "Say hello to your Uncle James Henry and Aunt Catherine, sweetheart."

"Hello." The child's eyes were wide and curious. She'd never been face to face with an aunt and uncle before.

"Your mother tells me you will start school in a few months. How wonderful!" Catherine's voice was at once enthused and bereft. Samantha felt a pang in her heart for her childless sister-in-law.

"So tell me about your town," Samantha said. "How are the Taylors?"

"Colonel Taylor left Prairie du Chien several years ago. He went to Florida for the Seminole War, but is on his way this month to Arkansas. Our new president has made him commander of the Second Department of the Army's Western Division."

"Impressive," Samantha said. Her mind, though, pictured the sadness that must follow Colonel Taylor and his wife after their daughter Sarah's death. She wondered if Colonel Taylor ever regretted trying to keep Sarah and Jefferson Davis apart. Maybe if he'd been supportive, she'd still be alive. She didn't want to bring up past events, though, especially sad ones.

James Henry had turned to James. "Do you remember General Street?"

"The Indian agent, right? In Prairie du Chien?" James asked.

James Henry nodded. "Agent for the Fox and Sauk. He went to Washington, D.C. with them in 1837. They brokered a land deal with the government that formed an agency here in Iowa, on the lower Des Moines River. He brought his family here the following year, but he passed away last year."

"Oh, dear," Samantha said. "I remember Mrs. Street. They had a very large family. That poor woman."

Conversation turned to the present, with James Henry and James discussing the political climate, Indian treaties, and mining. Samantha went to the kitchen to fix tea and arrange a plate of honey cookies she had baked the day before. James Henry came to find her.

"I've missed you," he said.

Samantha took in his graying hair and the lines around his eyes that even the familiar gold-rimmed spectacles couldn't hide. He'd mellowed since his marriage, turned back into the brother she remembered from her childhood. She reached out her arms for a hug. "I've missed you, too, James Henry."

He hugged her and drew back, eyes on the amethyst brooch at her throat. "You still have it and still wear it." He touched it, and a tear appeared in his eye.

Samantha frowned. "This was Mama's." Did her brother know she'd taken it from their mother's dresser?

James Henry frowned. "No, Mama gave it to you. I remember the day it happened. You were a little thing, much too young for such a fancy piece of jewelry. You'd already shown a preference for everything purple, just like Mama." He laughed.

"Mama likes purple?" Samantha said. Why didn't she remember this about her mother?

"Oh yes. You couldn't keep your fingers off the brooch. Mama unpinned it and fastened it to your tiny dress and told you to wear it until you could give it to your daughter." He smiled. "You must have been too young to understand."

Samantha's eyes teared up. How could she have forgotten? "I do remember Mama letting me wear it sometimes." In a rush, she understood why the brooch had always been a source of comfort to her. It was like carrying a bit of her mother with her. Her unconscious mind had known how important this piece of jewelry was. That was why she'd taken it. Her hand closed over the brooch.

The next morning, Catherine helped Samantha into her wedding dress. Samantha turned to Emily, looking beautiful in her lavender lace dress. "Emily, come here, baby." Emily frowned at being called a baby, but came to her mother. Samantha picked up the amethyst brooch. Instead of pinning it to her dress, she showed it to Emily. "My mother gave me this brooch when I was about your age. See how pretty it is?"

"Pretty flower, Mama," Emily said.

"It's very special to me. Now I'd like to give it to you. Wear it until you have a daughter of your own." Samantha's eyes filled with tears. She hoped her own mother would know that the brooch had reached her granddaughter. Samantha pinned it to Emily's dress. "How very grown up you look! You must take very good care of it."

"I will, Mama." Emily touched the brooch and turned to Catherine. "See, Aunt Catherine? Mama gave me a pretty flower."

Catherine's eyes were already filled with tears.

A judge friend of James's performed their marriage at home. There were only a dozen guests, mostly friends of James. All the white flowers Samantha and Catherine could find decorated the room.

"White is the color Queen Victoria wore in February at her wedding," Samantha said, "but I'm wearing blue because my love is true!" She laughed at her allusion to the old rhyme, having chosen to ignore the parts about Saturdays and May being bad days to wed. She'd waited long enough for James.

James spared no expense for the wedding brunch. White frosting swirls adorned the rich, dark fruit cake. Traditional charms were hidden inside according to the verse:

> The ring for marriage within a year;
> The penny for wealth, my dear;
> The thimble for an old maid or bachelor born;
> The button for sweethearts all forlorn.

Guests packed slices of fruit cake in boxes to take home. Two more traditional cakes sat in a prominent place on the table. The dark groom's cake was cut into the right number of pieces for the small wedding party. The luscious white bride's cake was set aside, to be packed away and eaten on their twenty-fifth anniversary.

Wine, punch, and hot chocolate flowed freely as guests partook of cold sliced meat, venison pie, ham and eggs, and fresh bread with an assortment of jams and marmalades. The sparkle and glamor of laughing, well-dressed friends, good food, and sumptuous decorations made the occasion special.

At one point, Samantha found herself alone. No one was congratulating her, or drawing her into conversation, or trying to feed her something. She could take a reflective breath and enjoy the moment. It had been a winding path that brought her to this day, to a place she ought to have been years ago. If she had chosen this path when it first showed itself, it would not have been as true. The twists and turns she'd followed had shaped her into a woman who could appreciate a shared road forward. She and James would work together to further his career and to raise Emily to be a strong young woman. Maybe there would be more children to spread their joy. The future lay ahead. No doubt the path would twist, but together they would weather it.

EPILOGUE

Brown men, black men, white men, and yellow men cross the river and travel upon it. They tell stories of the river and sing songs about it. Dugouts give way to steam-powered boats, then to diesel. Men fight wars over ownership of the riverbank. They build towns, then cities. Population grows until ten states flank the river. The river basin collects water from thirty-one states and supplies drinking water to millions of people.

Man's spiritual link to the river weakens. He dams the river to transfer power from the water to the people, and builds locks to ease the boats' way upriver and down. The river floods, and he wrestles it into submission. Lumber mills pour sawdust into the river. Settlements dump sewage and garbage. Pollution in the river affects the homes of carp, catfish, sturgeon, pike, and gar—260 species of fish. Wildlife deteriorates as people destroy their habitat. Chemicals taint the runoff from farmland, and the river poisons the people. Man builds a water treatment plant, but urban waste and agricultural chemicals still find their way to the river.

Still, the headwaters of the river remain pure. The water that begins at Lake Itasca flows downriver for three months gathering silt, sand, and clay particles until it deposits 500 million tons of sediment into the Gulf of Mexico as it always has. The current churns in the spring and the surface freezes in the winter as it always has. The life force of the river survives as it has for millions of years. It nurtures those who respect it and destroys those who presume to control it. The tears of nations run in the river, and the river remembers.

Acknowledgments

O nce again writing this novel has been a labor of love for my family. One of the stories my grandmother told me was about a female baby born at Fort Snelling in Minnesota in 1835. I was curious about that, since it seemed early to have families with soldiers. For two years I pored over stories about the fort and its surroundings during this very important pre-Civil War era before condensing it all into *The River Remembers*. Many thanks to Thomas Shaw, past assistant site manager at Historic Fort Snelling, for fact-checking and providing invaluable historical tips. Any remaining errors are my own.

I'd like to thank my team at She Writes Press—Brooke Warner, Lauren Wise, and the incomparable cover designer Julie Metz—for once again creating a beautiful package for my story.

The unwavering support of Paper Lantern Writers, my group of historical fiction authors, has made it possible to build a network of fans on social media who are anticipating the release of this book. I hope new readers will follow us, too.

Thanks also go to my critique group—Jill Caugherty, Jen Olson, and Laura Beeby—for your honest feedback and willingness to read and reread large parts of this story at a time.

My family—my husband, sons, and daughter-in-law especially—are my best cheerleaders. Thank you especially to my husband, who drives me to book events and carries boxes of books. Since my last book, my first grandson was born. Frankie, you are the future of the family and will be the caretaker of all these stories. I look forward to telling them to you like my grandmother told them to me.

HISTORICAL NOTES

In researching this book, I was struck by the confluence of cultures at Fort Snelling in the 1830s. Many important people, or people who became important later, spent time there. I only wish I could include them all! I have tried to portray the Dakota and the enslaved Blacks truly but fairly. I have tried to show the white missionaries, traders, and government people as well-meaning in theory but devastating in action.

In a few cases, I had to play with the timeline a bit for the sake of story flow. For example, Eliza Taliaferro only spent one winter at Fort Snelling. Jefferson Davis served at both Fort Snelling and Fort Crawford during this time, and was transferred to Fort Gibson sooner than I have depicted here.

All three of my main characters are real women. I've included here the rest of their story, after *The River Remembers* ends.

HARRIET ROBINSON

In 1843, Dr. Emerson died and willed Harriet and Dred to his wife, Irene. They lived in St. Louis. In 1846, Harriet and Dred filed separate petitions for freedom from Irene Emerson. Both cases were dismissed on a technicality in 1847. The Scotts' lawyer filed for a retrial, but it wasn't until 1850 that the case was heard and the jury ruled in favor of the Scotts. They were free! Irene Emerson was not pleased, and appealed. At this point, Harriet and Dred's cases were combined into one. In 1852, the Missouri Supreme Court ruled against the Scotts. Harriet and Dred took the case all the way to the U.S. Supreme Court. In the famous Dred Scott decision in 1857, the U.S. Supreme Court ruled the Scotts and their children should remain enslaved. Later that same year, the Scotts' master died and their ownership transferred to a man who finally freed them. Dred Scott died of tuberculosis one year after gaining freedom. Harriet lived as a free woman until her death in 1876.

Eliza Scott, born on the river in 1844, was a slave according to the law because of her mother's status as a slave. Another daughter, Lizzie, was born five years later. They were 19 and 14 when their parents finally achieved freedom. Eliza married and had two sons, but she and her husband died young. Lizzie never married and raised her sister's children.

DAY SETS

Not very much is known about Day Set's life. Lawrence Taliaferro did not speak the Dakota language, and Day Sets spoke no English. Day Sets died when their daughter, Mary Taliaferro, was in her late teens. Mary lived alternately with the Dakota and the Pond family until her marriage in 1848 to soldier Warren Woodbury. Woodbury had lived on the frontier since 1835. Mary and Warren lived in St. Paul until the Dakota War, when Mary and the children returned to Dakota territory. Warren was killed in the battle of Vicksburg during the Civil War in 1863. Mary went to live with the Dakota on the Santee Reservation with her children. She died in 1916 at the age of 88.

Hushes Still the Night died in 1847. Her daughter, Jane Lamont, lived with the Ponds for 13 years. Jane became a teacher at Oak Grove and married Samuel Pond's nephew, Starr Titus, in 1850. She was trained to be a missionary teacher, but rejected that life when she refused to move to the reservation.

Stands Sacred's daughter, Mary Eastman, married a Santee Sioux and had five children with him, dying at the birth of the youngest, later known as Charles. After adopting Christianity following the Dakota Wars, her husband and two of their surviving sons took the Eastman surname. Her father, Seth Eastman, did return to Fort Snelling, with his white wife, Mary, in 1841. Between 1841 and 1848, he served as commander of the fort four times. He also produced a large number of oil paintings, drawings, and watercolors of his surroundings and the Native people of the area. Both Seth and Mary built strong relationships with their Dakota and Ojibwe neighbors and learned their languages.

Day Set's other sister, called Laughing Bird in this novel, was named Mary. I was unable to find her Dakota name.

In addition to the three sisters, Day Sets had at least three brothers. In 1863, the Mdewakanton were removed to Crow Creek in South Dakota, then to the Santee Reservation at Niobara, Nebraska.

SAMANTHA LOCKWOOD

Samantha was married to a Mr. Brown from Prairie du Chien for a couple of months before she wed Alexander Miree. I chose not to include this brief marriage in this novel. I don't know if Alex Miree actually had a Dakota name and family. He did die or disappear from Samantha's life before her next marriage.

Zachary Taylor commanded Fort Snelling until 1837, when he was reassigned to Florida in the Seminole Wars. He became president of the United States in 1849. His daughter, Sarah, was indeed the first wife of Jefferson Davis, who later became president of the Confederacy.

Samantha and James Churchman attended President Lincoln's inauguration. The president appointed James ambassador to Valparaiso, Chile. When they returned, the Churchmans went to California Gold Country. They had another daughter, Nina, and a son, Ney, in addition to Emily. Nina Churchman was one of the Innocents Abroad featured in Mark Twain's book. She became an actress and lived in Portland, Oregon, until her death in 1921. Nina is the subject of my next book, working title *Innocents At Home*.

Emily Miree married Edward Williams, who would become the first president of the San Jose Water Works. Their daughter, also Nina, was my great grandmother. Emily died in 1870.

Samantha's Honey Cookies

⅓ C butter
¾ C flour
2 eggs
½ C honey
1 grated lemon rind
¾ C flour
4 tsps baking powder
¼ tsp salt

Cream butter. Beat in flour. Add one egg yolk and one whole egg. Beat until light and fluffy. Add honey and rind. Sift dry ingredients. Knead until smooth and chill. Roll very thin. Brush with egg white. Decorate if desired. Bake on a greased cookie sheet 350°F until lightly browned.

GLOSSARY

PLACES

Dakota	English	French	Meaning
Bde Unma	Lake Harriet		The Other Lake
Heyate Otunwe	Eatonville		Village at the Side, Cloud Man's Village
Mde Make Ska	Lake Calhoun		White Earth Lake
Mnigaga Wapke	Minnehaha Falls		
Mní Sní	Coldwater Spring		
Mni Sota Makoce	Minnesota		Land where water reflects the clouds
Mni Sota Wakpa	St. Peter's River		Minnesota River
Owamni Yomni	St. Anthony Falls		whirlpool
	Pig's Eye		St. Paul
		Prairie du Chien	Dog's Meadow
Wakpa Tanka	Mississippi River		Big River
Wita Waste	Nicollet Island		Beautiful island

WORDS

Dakota	English	French	Meaning
ate	father		
Ate Makpiya			Father Sky
hirharha nampetchiyuza	I give you my hand with pleasure		Begging for food
Inyan			stone spirit
Iya			storm spirit
iyeska	Half breed	métis	Mixed European and native blood
		bois-brûlés	French and native blood
Maka Ina			Earth Mother
mdote			Baby's first cry; the place where rivers come together
mini	water		
mitakuye oyasin			Part of the family of living beings
Taku Wakan	Great Spirit		Life force
teya			second wife
Unktehi	god of streams and rivers		malevolent god
wasichu	white man		Any non-native
Wakinyan	Thunderbird		powerful sky spirit
wasna			an energy food
wiyaka	sand		

MONTHS

Dakota	English	Meaning
Witehi wi	January	Severe Moon
Wicata Wi	February	Raccoon Moon
Istawicayazan wi	March	Moon of the Sore Eyes
Magaokata wi	April	Moon When the Geese Lay Eggs
Wozupi wi	May	Moon For Planting
Wazustecasa Wi	June	Moon When Strawberries Are Red and Corn is Hoed
Canpasa wi	July	Moon When Chokecherries Are Ripe
Wasuton Wi	August	Moon When Corn is Gathered
Psinhnaketu	September	Moon When the Rice is Laid Up to Dry
Wazupi Wi	October	Moon for Drying Rice
Takiyuha wi	November	Moon When the Deer Rut
Tahecapsun win	December	Moon When the Deer Shed Their Horns

ABOUT THE AUTHOR

L inda Ulleseit, from Saratoga, California, has an MFA in writing from Lindenwood University and is a member of the Hawaii Writers Guild, Women Writing the West, and Paper Lantern Writers.

She is also the award-winning author of two novels, *Under the Almond Trees* and *The Aloha Spirit*.

She recently retired from teaching elementary school and now enjoys writing full time as well as cooking, leatherworking, reading, gardening, walking her dog, and playing with her new grandson.

Author photo © William F. Ulleseit

SELECTED TITLES FROM SHE WRITES PRESS

She Writes Press is an independent publishing company founded to serve women writers everywhere. Visit us at www.shewritespress.com.

Answer Creek by Ashley E. Sweeney. $16.95, 978-1-63152-844-6. Starvation. Desperation. Madness. As the Donner Party treks west on the Oregon–California Trail, one young woman risks everything—values, faith, reputation, and every last coin sewn into the hem of her skirt—for the mirage of a better life in California.

Eliza Waite by Ashley Sweeney. $16.95, 978-1-63152-058-7. When Eliza Waite chooses to leave a stagnant life in rural Washington State and join the masses traveling north to Alaska in 1898 during the tumultuous Klondike Gold Rush, she encounters challenges and successes in both business and love.

The Green Lace Corset by Jill G. Hall. $16.95, 978-1-63152-769-2. An artist buys a corset in a Flagstaff resale boutique and is forced to make the biggest decision of her life. A young midwestern woman is kidnapped on a train in 1885 and taken to the Wild West. Both women find the strength to overcome their fears and discover the true meaning of family—with a little push from a green lace corset.

The House on the Forgotten Coast by Ruth Coe Chambers. $16.95, 978-1-63152-300-7. The spirit of Annelise Lovett Morgan, who suffered a tragic death on her wedding day in 1897, returns in 1987 and asks seventeen-year-old Elise Foster to help her clear the name of her true love, Seth.

The Vintner's Daughter by Kristen Harnisch. $16.95, 978-1-63152-929-0. Set against the sweeping canvas of French and California vineyard life in the late 1890s, this is the compelling tale of one woman's struggle to reclaim her family's Loire Valley vineyard—and her life.

The Same River by Lisa Reddick. $16.95, 978-1-63152-483-7. Two women living on the Nesika River in central Oregon—Jess, a feisty, sexy, biologist who fights fiercely to save the river she loves, and Piah, a young Native American woman battling the invisible intrusion of disease and invasive danger in the same place 200 years earlier—learn that wisdom comes from the recovery of wildness.